P9-CFN-484

A Heart to Heart Talk

Karish rose to his feet. "Let's take a walk, Lee."

Now he wanted privacy. Excellent timing. And quite the perfect example of the magnanimous lord escorting the servant out for a well-bred chastisement.

He strode down the sidewalk. I glared at him, for I needed two steps to his one. I probably looked like some little rat-dog scampering along beside him.

He pushed a hand through his hair. "What the hell did I do, anyway?"

"Sorry?"

"What did I do? Tell me. My hair isn't blond? I'm not tall enough?"

Prat. Did he really think I cared about such trivial things? "I am a simple girl, Karish," I said. He snorted in disbelief, which surprised me. "And I never anticipated being bonded to the Stallion of the Triple S."

"You may stop referring to me in that manner any time now," he instructed me coolly.

"I didn't want to work with a legend. I wanted a quiet life, do my job without anyone much noticing." I let myself sigh. "No chance of that, now. Certainly, you'll be the focus of all the attention but some of it is bound to splash onto me. Lord Shintaro Karish's Shield, easiest road to his favor." Oh, he didn't like that at all, and he scowled to prove it. Well, too bad. He'd asked for it. "You've got no right to complain about my behavior. I've been polite."

"Barely."

"Right back at you . . ."

Resenting the Hero

Moira J. Moore

ACE BOOKS, NEW YORK

THE BERKLEY PUBLISHING GROUP
Published by the Penguin Group
Penguin Group (USA) Inc.
375 Hudson Street, New York, New York 10014, USA
Penguin Group (Canada), 90 Eglinton Avenue East, Suite 700, Toronto, Ontario M4P 2Y3, Canada
(a division of Pearson Penguin Canada Inc.)
Penguin Books Ltd., 80 Strand, London WC2R 0RL, England
Penguin Group Ireland, 25 St. Stephen's Green, Dublin 2, Ireland (a division of Penguin Books Ltd.)
Penguin Group (Australia), 250 Camberwell Road, Camberwell, Victoria 3124, Australia
(a division of Pearson Australia Group Pty. Ltd.)
Penguin Books India Pvt. Ltd., 11 Community Centre, Panchsheel Park, New Delhi—110 017, India
Penguin Group (NZ), Cnr. Airborne and Rosedale Roads, Albany, Auckland 1310, New Zealand
(a division of Pearson New Zealand Ltd.)
Penguin Books (South Africa) (Pty.) Ltd., 24 Sturdee Avenue, Rosebank, Johannesburg 2196,
South Africa

Penguin Books Ltd., Registered Offices: 80 Strand, London WC2R 0RL, England

This is a work of fiction. Names, characters, places, and incidents either are the product of the author's imagination or are used fictitiously, and any resemblance to actual persons, living or dead, business establishments, events, or locales is entirely coincidental. The publisher does not have any control over and does not assume any responsibility for author or third-party websites or their content.

RESENTING THE HERO

An Ace Book / published by arrangement with the author

PRINTING HISTORY
Ace edition / March 2006

Copyright © 2006 by Moira J. Moore.
Excerpt from *The Hero Strikes Back* copyright © 2006 by Moira J. Moore.
Cover art by Matt Stawicki.
Cover design by Rita Frangie.
Interior text design by Stacy Irwin.

All rights reserved.
No part of this book may be reproduced, scanned, or distributed in any printed or electronic form without permission. Please do not participate in or encourage piracy of copyrighted materials in violation of the author's rights. Purchase only authorized editions.
For information address: The Berkley Publishing Group,
a division of Penguin Group (USA) Inc.,
375 Hudson Street, New York, New York 10014.

ISBN: 0-441-01388-0

ACE
Ace Books are published by The Berkley Publishing Group,
a division of Penguin Group (USA) Inc.,
375 Hudson Street, New York, New York 10014.
ACE and the "A" design are trademarks belonging to Penguin Group (USA) Inc.

PRINTED IN THE UNITED STATES OF AMERICA

10 9 8 7 6 5 4 3 2 1

If you purchased this book without a cover, you should be aware that this book is stolen property. It was reported as "unsold and destroyed" to the publisher, and neither the author nor the publisher has received any payment for this "stripped book."

*For my parents, Charlie and Kathy,
and my sisters, Deirdre and Eileen*

Acknowledgments

There have been so many people who have provided an ear, advice, and support, and I know I won't be able to list them all here. Melissa Stone is my best friend, first reader, and gentle critic. Joe and Alisa Spinelle read an early draft and trusted me enough to give me excellent constructive criticism. People who have listened to me talk plot lines and character development for hours include Elizabeth DiSabato, Deirdre Flynn, and Erin Kinnally. Finally, I have to thank my agent, Jack Byrne, and my editor, Anne Sowards, for taking a chance on me.

Chapter One

"Not feeling any uncontrollable urges, are you?" the low voice in my ear teased.

I looked up at the speaker and said, "Huh?"

Lamer put a hand on my shoulder and pulled me into her taller, leaner frame. "Picture it," she said. "The dark night sky, the torches, the drums. Brought here from our academy in carriages with the windows covered, we stand in the Matching Circle, finally Shields, dressed in our best whites and our brand-new braids." She plucked at the tightly sewn knots in the left shoulder of my robe. "Knowing you have to compete with fourteen of your peers to be Chosen by one of—is it six, this Match?—Sources. Who are out there somewhere, waiting in their best blacks, for the chance to look us over like a herd of cattle."

I snickered.

"The excitement. The anticipation. The fear. Doesn't it make you feel like . . . dancing?"

"Dancing? Are you crazy?"

"Don't try to kid me, Mallorough. I heard about that night after the First Landers' play."

"Ah." That explained everything. "So have I. Don't I wish

it had been that interesting." Alas, never had I ever, under the influence of either alcohol or music, danced on a table.

How did these rumors start?

Lamer suddenly sighed with impatience. "What's taking so long?"

McAllistair, standing on my other side, snorted in amusement. "Karish, I'll wager," he said. "Maybe there's a mirror back there."

"Hm." That seemed to pacify Lamer somewhat. "Can't rush perfection, I guess."

I didn't roll my eyes. I was proud of myself.

Karish was one of the Sources. We would be meeting six that night, and six of us might end up bonded to one of them as a result.

Lord Shintaro Karish was a name I'd heard most of my life, and he was the Source all the Shields wanted. He was, according to rumor and his records, talented, gorgeous, and charming. He was called the Darling of the Triple S because he could feel natural events—earthquakes, cyclones, anything—long before they happened, and he could channel enormous amounts of power, eliminating the events before most people even realized there was any danger. He was called the Stallion of the Triple S for talents that had nothing to do with being a Source.

Katherine Devereaux was also an excellent Source who had proven herself while training in the field, but she had avoided the need to make an icon of herself. Reputed to be a steady, sedate woman, she was more my style than any of the other Sources I would be meeting that day. I had high hopes for her. She and I would work well together.

Thomas Black was a solid, reliable Source, no dramatic rescues in his history but no major screwups, either. A little too proud for some, but no one could expect humility in a Source. If his portrait were any indication, he wasn't bad looking, either. Not that such things mattered, but I had no objection to looking at a pretty face.

Then there were the twins, one man, one woman. Therefore not identical but looking so much alike they might as well have been. They were, to all reports, extremely weak and would probably never be sent anywhere dangerous. Viola and

Sebastian Bradford were said to recognize their limitations cheerfully and were rumored to be two of the kindest, friendliest people a person could ever hope to meet.

The fear of not being Chosen was the first reason the Shields were so tense. A Shield who was never Chosen might end up a professor in the academy, or part of its maintenance staff, or sent out hunting for new young Shields and Sources, all occupations far inferior to that of being a properly bonded Shield.

Stevan Creol was the second reason. He was an adequate Source but was said to be odd, even cruel. Reputed to have tormented younger years as a student, he carried rumors of assault and rape as an adult. Nothing that anyone was prepared to submit to the law, but I'd yet to hear from a person who'd worked with him who had anything good to say about him. Some said he was crazy. Others claimed he was just evil. All anyone could say for sure was that he seemed unable to Choose a Shield. He was forty and still hadn't managed it.

My first choice was Devereaux, then Black, then either of the twins. If I didn't get Chosen by one of them, I didn't want to get Chosen that Match at all. I wanted someone calm, steady, and reliable. As calm, steady, and reliable as a Source could be, anyway.

But I didn't get to choose. Neither did the Sources, not in the true sense of the word. When Source met Shield for the first time, if they were meant to work together they knew it the moment they looked at each other. Kind of like love at first sight only permanent, and it had nothing to do with physical attraction or emotional compatibility.

The bond, everyone thought, matched skill to skill and created a stronger partnership than what could be found in an unbonded Pair. It enabled a Shield to feel when his or her Source's mental protections were lowered or raised. Sources needed mental Shields to protect their minds from the various forces swirling about the world, the forces that made the sun rise and set and the winds blow and the tides flow and ebb. Otherwise the minds of the Sources would be overrun and destroyed by those forces, a vulnerability unique to their kind.

Those mental barriers needed to be lowered when the Sources channeled, leaving their minds vulnerable. It was the unique talent of the Shields to shape secondary barriers for the Sources, protecting them while still allowing them the freedom necessary to work.

Any Shield could protect any Source, but bonded Shields and Sources worked better together. And only a bonded Shield could feel the Source's protections lowering without being told, which was a necessary ability when the partners were not in physical proximity.

Poetry, songs, and plays written by regulars added all sorts of other attributes to the bond. Things like the partners being able to read each other's mind, or see through each other's eyes and hear through each other's ears. They made entertaining reading, and none of them were true. All the bond did was facilitate Shielding.

There were, however, other effects of the bond. Some Pairs experienced a sort of physical harmony. It had been described to me as an added comfort level when the two partners were in close contact, and even some relief of pain when they touched. It was a rare phenomenon, thank Zaire. It seemed rather intrusive to me.

Other effects were even less positive. The bond seemed to search out inherent emotional characteristics of the partners, drawing them out and amplifying them, and the wrong combination of such characteristics could be disastrous. Some partners hated each other, and this could be a serious problem, for once the bond was formed it was permanent. There was no separating, no working with anyone else. And the death of one meant the death of the other, the bond was that powerful.

Without training and emotional preparation the bond could be destructive, resulting in obsessive love or hatred between the partners, drawing them into each other and rendering them incapable of dealing with the rest of the world in a rational manner. So young unPaired Sources and Shields were segregated from the rest of society and each other until they were Chosen, the best that could be done to prevent spontaneous pairings. It was impossible to eliminate all instantaneous pairings, for some Sources and Shields remained undiscovered for years, and not all such Pairs were afflicted with emotional instability, but everyone felt the separate academies were the best way to keep such unfortunate Choices to a minimum.

I had been sent away to one of the Shield academies when I was four years old, and had remained there for the following seventeen years of my life. It was the only home I could remember.

And so I stood in the Matching Circle with most of the members of my class and a handful of older Shields who had not yet been Chosen. We stood in a single long line, side by side, waiting. We were watched by friends, family, and former instructors. We had been placed in alphabetical order according to our family names.

I was Dunleavy Mallorough. I was somewhere near the middle.

A door creaked as it opened. Heads whipped around. I felt the Shields around me stiffening, standing straighter, standing prouder. The Sources had arrived.

They filed into the Matching Circle silently, and I had to admit they looked a little eerie, black figures floating over the white floor. Most of them didn't look at all nervous, which I found irritating. This night was as important to them as it was to us, and they had no more control over the results than we did. They should have been as apprehensive as we were. More so. They were Sources, after all. They were supposed to overreact to everything.

I was not nervous. To be nervous was to waste one's strength on a fruitless emotional reaction. I was calm. I was always calm.

Really.

I would not wipe my palms against my trousers. I would not shift my feet. I would not flick my hair off my shoulder. I would be calm, I would be serene, in success or failure.

But I wouldn't fail. I would be Chosen. This was a certainty. That I was standing with fourteen others who were just as firmly convinced of their success was irrelevant, because I was right. I was always right.

Damn it, I couldn't feel the floor against my bare feet. That wasn't good.

All Shields were rather insensitive to physical sensation—to better enable us to concentrate solely on our Sources, it was said—but I'd always been particularly insensitive. Which was an endless source of humor for my classmates. I had been taught to feel things, of course, as all Shields were. It was just that sometimes I sort of forgot.

The floor was wood. Sanded so smooth it felt like cloth. Cool and almost soft against the skin, as incongruous a thought as that seemed.

The door was closed behind the last Source. I looked them over discreetly, noting the differences between the portraits we'd been shown and the people standing before me. We waited.

Another, smaller door opened in a dark corner of the room. An elderly man, wearing the black braid of a Source, stepped in, followed by an elderly woman wearing the white braid of a Shield. Source Ivan McCrae and Shield Emil Cloudminder, the Presiding Pair of the Match. They walked between the row of the Shields and the row of the Sources, ascending onto the low dais at the other end of the room.

Cloudminder cleared her throat. "We would like to welcome you all to this, the third Match of the 573rd year of recording." Her voice was clear and surprisingly strong for a woman of her age and stature.

Silence greeted her words.

"It is perhaps best, at this time, to acknowledge our origins," the Shield continued. "To remember that nearly seven centuries past, our ancestors arrived here from another world, brought here in huge ships that flew between the stars. And in this world they saw beauty and wealth, and they thought to settle here."

I had been warned to expect this, the recital of our history. As though we didn't already know it. Waste of time.

"We are told that they brought with them great tools. Tools for speaking to each other over great distances. Tools for traveling with rapidity and without effort. Tools for raising buildings and tilling soil. Even, it was written, tools that controlled the sun and the sky."

This was where the story always lost me. I believed in the tools, in their existence. A professor at the academy had shown me articles made of strange, light metals, the use for which no one could guess. But controlling the sun and the sky? That couldn't be possible.

"Yet for all the wonder and power of these tools, this world was stronger still. The tools lost their power here. This world resisted their use, with earthquakes of such ferocity, with cyclones of such destructive force, with volcanoes of such frequency and reach, that these tools were largely destroyed and swept away from all hands.

"The destruction did not end there. The great cities of the ancestors were leveled. Their crops, stretching wide, were laid waste. Their high dams were swallowed whole.

"Our ancestors decided they could not shape this world as they wished. Those who were weak left our world, returning to their own." And the Shield made a dismissive gesture with one trembling hand. "The strong remained to build a new life, one more suited to this world. But that life was hard. One might almost feel that the world was angry, that our ancestors dared to use such tools against it. Cities built with nothing more than human hands were quickly torn down again. Our modest crops were destroyed by droughts and floods. Many, many died. People fell into despair and became certain that the planet would kill them all. Yet they strove to survive. They rebuilt. They sowed new crops. They had children.

"One of these children was a boy named Bora Zaire. A very odd young man, who spoke nonsense, and was prone to tears and fits of rage. An idiot, many thought. And one day, a cyclone approached his settlement. While others fled in fear, this young man stood in the strengthening winds, staring as though in challenge. And the cyclone faded in strength and size until it disappeared.

"And Bora Zaire died.

"He was only the first to die in this way. The same happened in other settlements. An event would threaten, and some young man or woman—always one who was considered strange and odd—would stare the event down. The event would disappear, and the young person would die. No one could understand why.

"We know now that these young people were Sources. We now know that these were people with a special talent, an ability to feel the approach of an event, to reach into that event with their minds. They could draw the forces of the events into their very bodies, draining the events of all their power until they simply disappeared. The forces of these events could be directed away, harmlessly.

"This we call channeling, and we now know channeling the forces is fatally hard on the body. The heart beats too fast. The mind tears itself apart. The forces are displaced in a manner most unnatural, and they curve back on the Source to crush that fragile human shell.

"We know this now, because this is what Shields tell us.

"Nirah Kadaf is the first Shield we have in the history books. A quiet, serious young woman who couldn't like another young woman in her settlement, a strange girl named Mandir Olsworth. When their settlement was threatened by a tidal wave, and Mandir felt compelled to stand out in it, Nirah stood beside her. The tidal wave sank harmlessly into the soil. And neither woman died.

"For while Sources can reach into the heart of an event, Shields can reach into the minds of Sources. They can slow the heartbeat of a channeling Source, calm the mind, and erect their own barriers around a Source to protect that Source from the curling forces.

"Stories of this pair of women spread wide and reached the ear of Sylva Westphal, a holder of the north. She sent men out to collect these two women, and others to search for more of their kind, to bring them to her hold. And once they were there, she hired healers and people of learning to study these young people and determine what they were.

"Years of study revealed little. There was no one physical or mental characteristic shared by all. The talent did not appear to be inherited. Nor could it be learned by others. It was something inborn and completely unpredictable.

"What was learned, however, was that Sources and Shields, when they were brought together, bonded. And bonded Sources and Shields worked better together than those who were not bonded. And the bonding was as unpredictable as the talent itself.

"Holder Westphal continued to search for people of these talents. She housed them, fed them, and then charged for their services. Those with the money to pay the fee could have their homes and settlements protected from the natural events of this world. Those who could not were destroyed.

"Many protested of this to the Empress, for all perceived the talents of the Sources and Shields to be vital to the survival and prosperity of the whole world. So the Empress demanded that all Sources and Shields be turned over to her.

"Holder Westphal refused.

"The Empress called on her Imperial Guard.

"Holder Westphal assembled an army of mercenaries.

"The Sources and Shields, foreseeing a lifetime of servitude to either the Holder or the Empress, declared they would hide themselves in some deserted place and let the world shake itself to pieces.

"And so a compromise was reached.

"The Holder would be pardoned from all charges of treason and be permitted to keep her lands and tenants in exchange for releasing her claim on the Sources and Shields in perpetuity.

"The Empress would fund the education of all Sources in Shields, in perpetuity, with the vow that no monarch would attempt to control them.

"The Sources and Shields would be self-regulating, with the understanding that they were obligated to protect all who needed it, with no payment.

"All others were obligated to house, feed, and clothe all Sources and Shields as it was demanded of them, without payment.

"And thus was born the Source and Shield Service.

"Those before us are embarking on the most honorable of tasks, high in privilege and equally high in responsibility. Many can claim to hold the future prosperity of this world in their hands. Only we can say so with literal intent. Without us, cities fall, oceans will swallow the fields, and this world will be laid waste.

"And because of this, we are held high in the esteem of others, and we are freed from the day-to-day burdens others carry. Some feel that our higher responsibilities also free us from the laws others must follow, from the notions of duty and honor that bind others." I could have sworn she looked right at Creol then. "This is a fallacy. On the contrary, we have higher expectations placed upon us, not less. The honor of the Source and Shield Service rests on all of you as you take your places in the world beyond the academies. Remember this."

There was a moment of silence. I wondered if I would feel

irked, were I a regular, to be so thoroughly chided when I hadn't even done anything wrong.

"Sources," said Cloudminder, "Choose your Shields."

Finally.

Source Black stood in front of the first Shield, Patrick Addington. They looked at each other. One exchange of glances was all it took. If nothing happened then, nothing was going to happen, ever.

Nothing happened. Though Addington was no doubt disappointed, no one would know it by looking at him. Good man. Black took one step down to face the next Shield. Source Bradford, Sebastian, stood before Addington.

I hoped, desperately, that Creol would not Choose me. For some reason a part of me was certain that he would. The fear had been lurking under my skull for months, ever since I learned that he hadn't Chosen anyone at the last Match. I repressed a shiver. Refusing a bond was not only physically impossible, it simply wasn't allowed. Sources and Shields were pretty much owned by the Triple S, and once a Pair had bonded, they worked together, no exceptions.

Unless they were titled. An aristocrat with a title was considered even more valuable than a Source or a Shield, though not nearly as useful. Unfortunately, I was strictly merchant class, and Creol, he was too crazy to be granted a title. If he Chose me, I was stuck.

There was a cry of delight from the beginning of the line. Bradford, Sebastian, had found his match in Liam Everette, an excellent Shield. Almost as good as me. A bit of a ponce for a Shield, too, so I had thought he would be the most obvious Choice for Karish, but these things couldn't be predicted. Everette and Bradford left the line and moved to one side of the Matching Circle, out of everyone's way, talking animatedly. And the Match went on.

Black stood in front of me and looked me in the eye. A nice strong, solid look. I was surprised to find myself holding my breath. One moment slid by, and then another. How long was it supposed to take, anyway? Surely it took more than a fleeting glance. Maybe we were supposed to wait a little bit, make sure nothing was going to take hold. It couldn't be exactly the same for every Pair.

But Black seemed fairly confident nothing was going to happen. He moved to the Shield on my right, and I smothered my disappointment. Two of my preferences were down.

Another exclamation of delight. Damn it. I glanced down to the beginning of the line. Source Devereaux had made her match. And it wasn't me.

I took a deep breath. And then another. *Stay calm, damn it.*

There had been no guarantee that Devereaux would Choose me. Absolutely none at all. To become upset that the results had not been what I hoped would be childish and unproductive.

Bradford, Viola, stood before me. We looked at each other. Nothing happened. Big surprise.

Sources Creol and Karish were left. Wonderful selection. I carefully clenched my teeth.

I watched the two remaining Sources work their way down the line. I watched the Shields react to them, despite their best efforts to appear stoic. When Creol approached, one could perceive the slightest stiffening of neck and shoulders as the Shields did their best not to lower their gaze and avoid the Choice. When Creol left, one could detect the relaxing of the posture as the Shields breathed deeply in relief.

Karish, on the other hand, brought quickened breath and brightened eyes. There was a subtle shifting of balance to the ball of the foot, as though each Shield were ready to leap into a run at the Source's word. And when Karish moved on, the slight drooping of the shoulders screamed disappointment.

And then he was before me. Creol. Staring down at me with horribly piercing, yellowish brown eyes. I steeled my spine and glared right back, daring him to Choose me. He was not going to know I was a quivering coward.

And nothing happened. For an endless moment I waited, not even breathing. I still wasn't sure how long it could take, and with the luck I had already experienced that night it seemed certain that Creol must Choose me. But time drained by, and there was no pull or shock or anything else I'd been told to expect, and Creol was already looking beyond me to his next victim. I figured he had to know what he was doing, he had done this so many times before.

The sharp relief I felt at not being Chosen by that man was a nice, cool shock. It almost made up for the earlier disappointments. So Devereaux and Black and neither of the Bradfords had Chosen me. Neither had Creol. Life was wonderful.

My brothers would never let me forget it, that I was left all alone and pathetic in the Circle. There were worse things.

Karish stood before me. He had gone through half the line without Choosing. I wondered if he was getting worried. I wondered why I was even there. I looked up at him.

Light slapped into my eyes, blinding me and setting my ears to ringing. It almost hurt. Lightning raced through my veins and burst through my skin, I could feel it. My lungs threatened to collapse in my chest. I couldn't breathe, and I thought about panicking.

Just as abruptly, the light vanished. I could see, I could hear, I could breathe, and I was standing on my own two feet. I looked up into gleaming dark eyes, and I thought about panicking.

Karish. The Stallion of the Triple S. My Source. I was chained to a legend. An infamous legend. Stories of drunkenness, whoring, and general recklessness filled my head. Oh. My. God. I must have been *evil* in a former life.

This was it. The person I would work with the rest of my life. Moving with him as we were transferred from post to post. Learning how he moved and felt and thought. Most importantly, learning how he channeled. Because from that instant on, my most important task was protecting this man while he worked, making sure the forces he manipulated while calming tsunami and cyclones and other natural events didn't end up killing him.

I would die with this man. He'd catch some sexual disease, or some enraged spouse would kill him, and the bond would drag me down with him. He was that sort, the sort that shone too bright and burned out fast.

Hell.

He grinned, and of course my brain immediately froze solid. He took my hand and kissed the back of it, which was odd enough behavior to keep me silent. I let him pull me out of the line because I really couldn't believe what had just happened. "I'm Shintaro Karish," he said, as if there were any chance I didn't already know who he was. "My friends call me Taro. I am very pleased to finally meet you."

Finally. Like he had been aware of my existence for more than half a moment and had been desperately anticipating our introduction. Very good. And he had a tenor born for the stage. I'd always been soft for a good male voice. But what was that accent? Sources and Shields were raised in different academies, but we all ended up with the same bland accent. His drawl, with its rolling *r*'s, was definitely aristocratic, and the pretension disgusted me.

He was beautiful. I usually preferred blonds, but even I had to admit that he was visually stunning. The slightly longish black hair, the black eyes with just a touch of an enticing slant, the finely drawn nose, cheekbones, and jaw. Good teeth, well-shaped mouth, warmly bronzed skin. A gold ring glinted in his left lobe in defiance of the rules and tradition of the Match. He wasn't too tall, but he was lean, with elegant hands and an excellent stance.

Was that my mouth watering? Of course not.

But he slept with a different partner every night. Or so they said. And I'd never been one to follow a crowd.

On the other hand, we were Paired. For life. No matter how impossible that seemed at the moment. I couldn't ignore him as I would like, and being rude to him would only make things difficult for me. So I smiled politely. "Dunleavy Mallorough." I remembered to withdraw my hand. "It will be an honor to serve."

He raised an ebony brow in obvious amusement. "I see," he murmured.

I was immediately suspicious. Just what did he think he saw?

Another shout distracted me. Black had found his match in Jamin Tan.

"Are your family here?" Karish asked.

Oh, Zaire. My family. Wouldn't they just be thrilled? Especially my father, his little girl bonded to the Stallion. For of course they had heard of the Stallion, even though they weren't part of the Triple S. Everyone had heard of the Stallion.

Aye, they were there. "Are yours?" I asked him, because I had to say something.

He smiled again, but this time it was a rather twisted effort. "Of course not."

Oh. Well. Now what? I had no questions to ask him. I already knew all about his life. I looked back at the line.

The Match was over. Sources Creol and Viola Bradford hadn't Chosen. I wondered if they were as disappointed as all the Shields who had suffered the same fate. I doubted it.

No one was directing at Karish the poisonous glares I was receiving from some of my former classmates.

You want him? Please, take him. I would be forever in your debt.

Idiot. For all his flaws, Karish was reputed to be an excellent Source. I could have done far worse. Just because he wasn't the one I wanted didn't mean we couldn't work well together. And being Chosen by him was better than not being Chosen at all. Really, it was.

Really.

The spectators had left their seats and were making their way into the Circle. I could see my family heading toward me. My parents, my older sister, my two younger brothers. They looked happy and proud. That helped me relax a little.

Mother hugged me first, a tight squeeze and a kiss on the cheek. "We're so proud of you, honey," she whispered fiercely. Though, really, there was nothing to be proud of. It wasn't as though I had actually accomplished anything, or won something through merit. Getting Chosen was merely the luck of the draw.

Father cupped my face with a long hand and kissed me lightly. "Good work, little one," he said gruffly.

Big sister Kaaren and little brothers Dias and Mika, both of whom towered over me, crushed me in a series of embraces. Mika was the only one who had something to say about my Source. "Lucky girl," he muttered, running an admiring gaze over Karish's form.

I ruffled his hair because I knew he hated it.

There were introductions to make. "Lord Shintaro Karish, I would like to present my parents, Trader William Mallorough and Holder Teshia Mallorough, my sister Holder Kaaren Mallorough, my brothers Dias and Mika Mallorough."

With each name, he bowed slightly, and then looked the

person right in the eye, a heavy, intense gaze accompanied by
a melting smile. If I didn't know better, I would say he was
silently flirting with each and every member of my family. Including my father.

My father cleared his throat uncomfortably. "You're the
Duke of Westsea's brother, aren't you?"

"Aye," Lord Karish said smoothly enough, but his smile
suddenly seemed fixed.

My father glanced about the crowd. "Where is he?"

"Taking the tip off the blade, I imagine."

I almost sighed. Sources were known for expressing themselves oddly; it was something to do with the way their minds
worked. I'd harbored the secret hope that my Source would be
an exception.

Karish gave me a smile that put me on immediate alert.
"Shall we head on over to the Horse's Head?" he asked.

Oh, lord. That was right. Tradition declared the newly
bonded Pairs were to celebrate at that ancient drinking establishment and trade life stories. It was something everyone
looked forward to practically from the moment they understood what drinking themselves senseless meant. *I* had been
looking forward to it. It not only meant that one had been
Chosen, it was also the first time Shields and Sources were
allowed to be out of their academies without official supervision. It was the big send-off before leaving the only home
most of us really remembered and heading out into the real
world. It was the one time we could act like idiots without
anyone thinking less of us. It was a thousand little signals and
symbols rolled into one major event, and I had fully planned
on enjoying it.

But not with Karish.

I'd been hearing about Karish for years. I'd gossiped about
him just as much as everyone else, admiring the stunts that obviously required a lot of skill and snickering at the high jinks
that just as obviously required as much moxie and no discretion at all. Like everyone else, I'd known where he'd come
from and who his family was. But I'd never felt anything
about him, any more than I felt anything about a character in a
story. He was just a piece of local color that had nothing to do
with my life. Even once I understood he'd be one of the

Sources at my Match, I'd only felt pity for the person who would be bonded to him. He could have nothing to do with me. And so I'd felt nothing about him.

Only now he had everything to do with me. I had to work with him every single day of my life. I had to go where he was sent, explain his behavior to offended regulars, try to convey important information to him. His reputation would shape mine. His conduct would determine where I lived and for how long. And every time he channeled I would have to listen to his blood and calm his heart and crawl inside his brain.

I pulled in a deep breath. I was a Shield. This was my task. That it was so incredibly disappointing—well, there was no point in whining about it. Might as well begin as I meant to go on and get used to him as soon as possible.

I cocked my head to one side and said in assent, "Of course." I turned back to my family.

Mother sighed. "I'd hoped we'd have a bit more time," she murmured, embracing me. "Be careful out there. The real world is different from the academy."

I imagined so. I hoped so. I'd enjoyed the academy, of course, but the number of rules had been stifling. "Aye, Mother." I exchanged quick hugs with the others, wishing, too, that we would have had time for a proper conversation. It had been expected, however.

When I turned back to Karish, he held out an arm to me, obviously expecting me to take it.

Chivalry. No doubt another remnant of his aristocratic background. I was a Shield with a serious task to perform, not a sickly maiden. What need had I for chivalry?

I'd deal with it. I had to. He was my Source, and I was stuck with him and his quirks for the rest of my life. If he took his work seriously—and according to his reputation he did—then I could ignore the rest.

I took his arm.

And felt the muscles along the back of my neck and shoulders ease and loosen.

Ah, hell.

Chapter Two

It was only as we were leaving the Matching Circle that I was able to see what the building itself looked like, as upon our arrival we had been driven up in covered carriages and bundled directly into the entrance.

Small. Just large enough, I guessed, for the Circle itself and the antechambers we had been waiting in. Made of black wood and only the one story high, with no windows, and the Triple S emblem over the entrance. Rather a grim looking place.

The carriages that had brought us to the Matching Circle were needed to take the unbonded participants back to the academies. The rest of us were walking, and that, in itself, was a new experience for me. It was the first time I had put foot to ground outside of the academy in nearly seventeen years.

I was ashamed to discover my difficulty in resisting the distraction of all the people—all the regulars—swarming about on the evening streets. The rattling carriages. Dogs and cats darting about. Sights I had read about but had never seen. It felt noisy and crowded. I slipped my hand from Karish's arm, trying to stay focused in all the confusion.

I didn't know where the Horse's Head was, but the Sources

seemed to. Sources were kept in their academy for far fewer years than Shields and spent the remainder of their training out in the world under the strict supervision of training Pairs. Karish would have never been permitted to walk through streets in this way, for fear of a spontaneous bonding, but he may have seen streets from a distance, and thus had been able to understand better any directions that were given to him.

I'd been shown a map, but I was finding it difficult to change mental pictures from a flat drawing to the reality.

Karish didn't seem to be experiencing any difficulties at all, if the way he was rattling on were any indication. He appeared to be one of that sort who was uncomfortable with silence and needed to fill it with words regardless of their lack of necessity.

"You do have the stoic Shield act down pat, don't you?" he was saying. "Patience on a pedestal indeed. Solid proof you're fresh out of the academy. You'll be relieved to know that no one really expects you to act that way in the real world. All the Shields I've met were far more relaxed."

Was he aware that he was insulting me?

Then he threw me a smile that I supposed was meant to be charming.

"Indeed," I said.

"Yes, indeed," he mocked. "You're too young to be so reserved."

Reserved by nature, reserved by training. He was out of luck. "I'm a Shield," I said, for it did appear that he needed to be reminded.

"Don't worry. I won't hold it against you."

He slung an arm around my shoulders. I instinctively tensed at the unexpected contact while at the same time feeling that damned relaxing effect. My body didn't know how to react.

Wrenching away would probably look undignified.

The Horse's Head tavern and inn was an old establishment, like all buildings in the city of Shidonee's Gap. All three Triple S academies were held in that city, which meant the effects of natural events were kept to such a minimum as to be practically nonexistent. So the Horse's Head was constructed without a thought for possible earthquakes or floods. It was several stories high with huge windows.

Our arrival had been anticipated by the proprietor, who rushed up to greet us as soon as we passed through the entrance. "Welcome!" she crowed, shaking each of our hands. "Let me be among the first to congratulate you on this special occasion. My name is Mala Nadare, and I am here to make sure your every wish is catered to tonight. Come, come."

I barely had a chance to glance at all the regulars sprinkled throughout the room before we were swept through a door into another room. An appealing room, with a peaked ceiling, solid long tables, and dozens upon dozens of thick candles. No windows at all, though, and no second entrance. If a fire ever started in there, I thought, we were cooked.

Food was being placed on one of the tables, dishes piled with sliced meats, cheeses, and juicy fresh fruits. Decanters of various sizes, some of glass and others of metal, were standing in trays of ice. Wines and ales, I assumed. I had no reason to complain of the food I'd been given at the academy, but never had I seen such an array, and I had to admit that, despite my disappointment of the evening, my appetite was tempted.

After all, I did have my priorities.

So did his lordship, apparently. "My dear woman," he drawled. "No chocolate? I'm devastated." And his expression, I thought, was a shade away from a pout.

I would not roll my eyes I would not roll my eyes I would not roll my eyes . . .

"Oh aye," said the landlady, smirking. "Which one are you, then?"

I opened my mouth to introduce him, chagrined by my lapse so early in my new profession.

He beat me to it. "Source Shintaro Karish." He caught one of her free hands, bowing over it briefly. "And it is my very great honor to meet you." The smile that curved his lips invited her to think them the warmest of acquaintances.

Nadare's smirk softened into a smile of her own. "Ah, it is an honor. I've heard a great deal of you." And she looked at me with more interest than she'd demonstrated before, then asked Karish, "Solid or beverage, my lord?"

"Solid, if you have it. But if not, I'll take anything. It's been a day of much import."

"Right away, my lord."

Pampered prat.

There were three musicians getting settled in the corner of the room. A pipe, a lyre, and a drum. The sight was exciting and intimidating at the same time. Music was carefully regulated at the academy, except for tests and lessons when we were deliberately exposed to arousing music, to gauge our vulnerability. I'd been taught that all musicians were warned, as part of their training, to have a care when playing before Shields. But musicians were like all other professionals. Some were better than others, some were more conscientious than others.

This was the Horse's Head. They had newly minted Shields in there after every Match. They knew what they were dealing with.

Good thing, too. Karish, as my Source, was supposed to guard me through music, make sure I didn't start a fight or start a fire or sleep with someone I shouldn't. And while I had heard nothing to indicate he wasn't a brilliant channeler, there were no rumors floating around out there about him being particularly good at taking care of other people.

And I was embarrassingly sensitive to music. Some of my professors claimed they'd never seen anyone worse in their however many decades of experience in the academy. With my excessive vulnerability, and the unlikelihood of Karish being solicitous to the needs of anyone else, I had to wonder what quirk of nature could think the two of us were well-matched.

At least the others were there. Jandi Bacall, who had been Chosen by Devereaux, and Everette had been in all my classes, and knew how sensitive I was. Of course, they were affected by music as well, but not so badly as I, and they would probably warn their own Sources. I could be confident that I wouldn't cause any damage, no matter how lax Karish may be in that area of responsibility.

Though, of course, primary responsibility for making sure I did no harm was mine, and I was pretty good at that, if I did say so myself. While music did have the most powerful effect on me, I was very good at resisting it. And I would only get better, I was sure, as I was exposed to more and more music as a professional Shield. I looked forward to the day when I needed no help at all.

"Good evening, Sources and Shields," the player of the lyre called out. "I am Lauren, this is Cas and Denner. We'd like to congratulate you on your successful night and to assure you that we have played for members of the Triple S many times before. We know what to expect, so don't worry."

"Are we to spend the whole night in here?" Tan asked, voicing a question I had had. A party of eight wasn't all that exciting.

"Not if you don't wish to," Lauren told him. "After most Matches, Pairs take this opportunity to enjoy their food and music in private, while getting acquainted. But many wander out after a while. It's up to you. For now, are there any requests?"

I let someone else ask for a song. I headed to the table, looking over the decanters. We had been given the odd glass of wine or ale at school, but nothing to exult over. I'd heard there was much better out in the real world and wondered whether we'd be getting any of it that night. I poured out some of the white. I sniffed it. Smelled good. I tasted it. *Mmmm.*

"One of those, are you?" Karish asked, and I nearly jumped, startled. Apparently he'd slithered right up behind me without making a sound.

"One of what?" I responded, because manners demanded I must.

"Those self-conscious types that head straight to the food in the middle of a party."

I took another long, soothing sip of wine. I was not self-conscious. Just not interested in my current company. "Many understand that sharing in drink and food facilitates conversation." Though not him, obviously. "No doubt that is why it's here."

"Don't try to get the better of Mallorough, my friend," Everette chuckled, reaching between us for a jug of ale. "You're wasting your time."

Karish raised an eyebrow. "She is so witty, is she?"

"Not so much. But she always takes time with what she says. Won't be rushed into saying anything stupid. Kind of irritating, really."

"Love you, too, Everette," I murmured.

He flashed me a grin. Really, he had the demeanor of a Source.

I looked over at Devereaux, who was already in quiet conversation with Bacall. They both looked serious but comfortable. I didn't usually waste my time with envy, but I couldn't help wishing things had turned out different. I'd rather be over there having a quiet, calm conversation instead of gulping down wine because I just wished the evening was over already.

I noticed when Karish turned to follow my gaze, and then looked back at me with a bit of a frown.

My, how indiscreet of me. "Perhaps you could tell me of one of your adventures, my lord," I said. "We hear you were permitted to travel much more widely than most Sources, before they are bonded."

He was still frowning. "That's an honorific."

"It is still the appropriate means of addressing you, is it not?" Damn straight, it was.

"Well, if you want to be strict about it, you should be calling me Source Karish." Then he assumed another smile. "But you're not going to be all stiff and formal for the rest of our lives, are you? My friends call me Taro."

Do they? I nodded, and let him make of that what he would.

"So, those adventures of yours?" I'd let him do the talking. I had the feeling he liked to talk about himself, and he needed only a little nudge before going on for hours. I could pretend to be fascinated for a while, then claim fatigue and beg off.

He was looking at me oddly. I wasn't sure why I felt it was odd. There was nothing mocking in it, or angry, or in any way inappropriate. More like, there was a certain weight to his gaze that I hadn't been expecting, that caught me off guard and made me wonder if I was being too transparent.

"Let us partake of this meal," he suggested, his tone even but his eyes still . . . close. "Then we can settle down and tell each other our life stories."

I hoped to avoid the life stories, but I was willing enough to dive into the food. My answer to him was to hand him a plate.

The music started then, and I froze at the first notes, bracing myself. The music played, however, was a nice light air, pretty dining music, and I relaxed. I sat down at another part of the table, and Karish sat across from me.

"So, Lee . . ."

I halted halfway through biting into a slice of bread. Lee? Only members of my family called me Lee. But my mouth was too full of food to make an immediate protest.

"Who was the last person you slept with?"

My mouth still full, I glared at him.

He grinned back.

It was a hard meal to get through. I couldn't get a serious word out of him. He flirted or teased the whole time, and it was irritating. I always enjoyed the occasional droll comment, but joke after joke spilling out of someone's mouth was tiring. It made me feel I had to either laugh or shoot back something equally urbane on a regular basis, and that was a game I'd never enjoyed. All I could do was respond as though the comments were serious, and hope to slow him down a little.

And then there was a knock on the door, and the landlady walked in, holding up an envelope. "Which one of you is Shield Mallorough?"

The thrill of hearing my title for the first time was shot through with apprehension. Why was I receiving correspondence, delivered right to me at the Horse's Head? That bespoke an emergency. "Here," I said.

She looked my way and handed me the envelope. She was smiling, though, so the news couldn't be bad. "Congratulations," she said.

Frowning, I cracked the wax Triple S seal and pulled out a single sheet of paper. It was a short message, quickly read.

"What is it?" Karish asked.

"Our post," I said in an absent tone. We weren't supposed to receive our posts until the next day. How had they even made the selection so quickly? They hadn't even known who was going to be bonded, never mind to whom. "We're to start off for High Scape as soon as possible tomorrow morning."

"High Scape?" Devereaux demanded, reaching out to snatch the missive from my hand.

I let her. I was thrown into shock.

High Scape. The biggest city on the continent. Said to be exciting and dangerous and full of crazy people. Also said to be increasingly unstable, threatened with natural disasters on a daily basis, a frequency unheard of anywhere else. It had more Pairs posted there than anywhere else, six, who were put on a schedule so that one Pair was always doing nothing but waiting for the events.

We were to be the seventh. An increase on the roster, to accommodate the sudden increase in natural disasters.

Only highly experienced Pairs were posted there. I wouldn't have even considered it a possibility so early after bonding. Why in the world would they . . . ?

I looked at Karish.

Ah.

It had started already.

Chapter Three

The ride from Shidonee's Gap to High Scape was three weeks, and that was all the time I had to learn everything about one Lord Shintaro Karish—how he moved, how he slept, how he ate, how thoughts traveled across his brain and blood through his veins, his every physical quirk and habit—before I might be required to put all that information to use and Shield him. The bond enabled me to feel when he was about to lower his protections, but I needed observation to know just how to craft my Shields to his specific requirements. So I watched him. It was my job, I expected to have to do it, and I did it as thoroughly as possible.

It didn't hurt that it drove him crazy. Which, enjoyment factor aside, surprised me. Surely such a popular fellow was used to being under scrutiny of one kind or another. But no, after only a couple of hours he was twitching in his saddle, shifting his shoulders, glancing back at me with his eyes narrowed. Didn't like it at all.

Granted, I wouldn't want anyone staring at me for hours on end, either, but then I wasn't a Source, and my life didn't depend on it. So he could just get over it.

After hours of shooting annoyed little glances at me, he

turned in his saddle to stare at me. "Are you going to be this sociable the whole way there?" he asked. He spoke with an air of amusement, but his irritation leaked through.

I assumed the question was rhetorical.

He made a gesture with his head that one could only call imperial. "Come up here where I can see you. I'm not going to throw out my spine twisting around to talk to you."

So don't. "This is the best vantage." Behind and to the right, the traditional place of the Shield.

"I'm not channeling now, Lee."

Once more the use of my nickname shocked me. I wanted to tell him not to use it but didn't know how. No one had ever imposed on me in quite that way before. "This is where I belong, Karish."

He frowned. "I don't like being called by my family name," he said tightly.

"It's tradition."

"It's rude," he retorted. "I am not my family. My name is Taro. You will call me that."

Well, yes, sir.

"Are you going to move up here or not?" he demanded.

"I'm working right now, Karish." No doubt he was used to people putting aside duty in order to show him the attention he craved. I would have to break him of that. "Please leave me to it."

He turned to the front again, good boy.

We rode all day. When the air began to darken into dusk Karish led the way into a travel village. He didn't bother to consult me about it, but I had no desire to protest. Hours in the saddle had left me longing for a bath and a bed. I had no problem with letting him play lord of the manor when his wishes coincided with mine.

Nothing more than a beaten path showed the way from the highway to Over Leap. From studying our map I knew the tiny village was really just a stopover for travelers. One small tavern with accommodations, a mercantile, and a whorehouse. All the essentials for the road.

We trotted into the tavern yard and stabled our own horses. We carried our own saddlebags through the door to the front bar. The interest in the landlord's eyes faded as they lit on our braids. "Ah, another one," he said with some disgust. "You might as well join your mates in there." He nodded toward the taproom. "Just try not to drain my barrels dry, all right?"

This was my first encounter with a merchant who was not a member of my own family. So far I wasn't impressed. No doubt it was irksome to have to hand over goods to Triple S Pairs without receiving anything in compensation, but it wasn't as though this were a new law. Shouldn't they be used to it?

"And," he told me, "I've no music for tonight."

I nodded, grateful for the reprieve. I didn't really want to test Karish's ability to guard me just yet.

"One room or two?" the landlord asked me.

"Two."

"I've got two adjoining—"

"That's not necessary," I interrupted him.

"Aye, it is, 'cause that's all I've got right now."

Ah well. It didn't really matter. "That's fine, then. Thank you."

"How long'll you be staying?"

"Just the night."

"That's something, at least," he muttered, not quite under his breath. "Upstairs, second and third doors on the right."

Food or bath? Which came first? Well, my stomach was screaming with hunger, and if I stank I couldn't smell it, so that answered the question for me. I went up to my minuscule room only to dump my gear and come right back down. So did Karish, unfortunately. I'd hoped for a chance to get rid of him for a bit. We headed to the taproom.

Which was crowded. I should have anticipated that, after the landlord's comment about all the other rooms being taken. Every table was filled, and people stood at the bar three rows deep. The chattering was deafening, and I hesitated at the door, suddenly less hungry. But I was aware that Karish was standing right behind me. I didn't want to appear nervous in front of him.

"Little Mallorough!" was shouted out, the words piercing the din. "When did they let you out?"

I grinned. I couldn't help it. I hadn't expected to meet up with anyone from school for, well, a year or so at least. The familiar voice was soothing in that strange place.

The big blond man seated at one of the tiny tables waved a long arm. "Over here, Mallorough!"

I squeezed through the crowd, uncaring as to whether Karish followed or not. "Good evening, Caspian." Ian Caspian, a Shield three years my senior who also happened to be my cousin. I had no memory of him before going to the academy, but once there he had at first tormented me and then, as we got older, induced me into some fairly scandalous behavior.

"Ooh, so formal," Caspian hooted. "You can tell you're newly minted."

"Why are you here?"

"Heading back to Shidonee's Gap for reassignment. You?"

Pairs didn't go back to Shidonee's Gap for reassignment. They got a message at their post, telling them where and when to go. If Caspian and his Source were going back to Shidonee's Gap, it was because there was a problem, the kind of problem that might require discipline.

But it wasn't any of my business. "We're going to High Scape," I told him and let it stand at that. Bragging was beneath me.

Bragging was unnecessary. Everyone had heard of High Scape. Caspian was impressed. Sort of. "Not bad for a fledgling."

I noticed the woman only when she linked her arm through Caspian's with that unmistakable air of possession. The black braid on her left shoulder said she was a Source. The hard glare she sent me said she was Caspian's lover. Which screamed that Caspian was being stupid. "My Shield has no manners," she said, sounding amused unless one listened carefully. "Here I sit with no introduction." She squeezed Caspian's arm.

I supposed I was just as ill-mannered, for there stood Karish, just as introductionless.

"Sorry," Caspian said easily, not too concerned. "Helen Garrette, this is Mallorough."

I nodded at her, and she nodded back, not too stiffly. I stepped aside to show off Karish. "Garrette, Caspian, this is Lord Shintaro Karish."

"My honor," the lord said cheerfully, and he smiled, the same sort of smile he'd inflicted on my family.

I could have predicted the results. Garrette nearly melted.

So did Caspian, but it was less obvious. He looked at me, brows raised in inquiry. I kept the negative shake of my head almost imperceptible.

"Have you eaten?" he asked.

"Is the food any good here?" I'd heard some gruesome stories about food in public places.

"It's all dead," he told me. "Which gives it points over the academy."

The other patrons at the table left with a willingness I found a little uncomfortable. A waitress rushed over to clear the table off and had four mugs in front of us before I even knew what kind of food there was to eat.

"So, Karish," Caspian said once we were all served. "We've heard a lot about you." Karish responded with a rather coy shrug. "They say that at Jo Bat's Arm you charged in before anyone else even knew there was a disturbance. Saved the day."

"And stole the glory," Karish added lightly. It was, of course, what Caspian had really meant.

Caspian smiled, unabashed. "Aye."

"It worked."

"Aye, and there's no point in waiting for others to catch up once you know what wants doing."

I buried a groan in my mug. I'd forgotten how painful it was to watch Caspian trying to be suble.

"So, High Scape," he continued. "Lots happening there right now."

"So they say," Karish murmured, pushing the turnip in his stew to one side of his plate.

"It takes six Pairs to keep it stable. Works Pairs harder than any other site on the map."

Karish held a spoonful of stew aloft, not spilling a drop. The utensil was elegantly balanced between thumb and two long fingers. "I didn't train all my life to sit on my hands somewhere safe."

"Ah." Caspian put his hands over his heart in a revolting melodramatic gesture. "How like a Source you are. How very brave."

Caspian was either flattering him or taunting him. Either way, there was a good chance Garrette would be spending the night alone. The way she was glowering at her shameless Shield, she knew it.

"Have you any idea why High Scape is becoming so unstable?" I asked Caspian. He could flirt with Karish on his own time. I needed some warning about what to expect in High Scape.

Caspian shrugged. "I haven't been there. I'm sure you know as much about it as I."

How helpful.

My cousin wasted little more time on me, or on his partner. The campaign was on to win Karish's heart, or at least his company for the night. Caspian at his most flirtatious was, well, overwhelming. Karish rebuffed his advances with cool humor. And Garrette fumed.

No one, except perhaps Caspian himself, could have been more surprised than I when Karish courteously but firmly refused the invitations being sent his way. On the other hand, I had noticed him noticing the gorgeous young woman who had just showed up to work at the tables.

Making a bit of a show about how tired he was, Karish bade Caspian and Garrette a charming good night. When he turned to me, however, his eyes narrowed. "Good evening," he said coolly.

I nodded back at him.

He strode out of the taproom.

Caspian was looking at me with an expression that told me he thought I was an idiot.

"What?" I demanded waspishly.

"Have you lost your mind?"

"What?"

"Look at him!"

"So?"

"You could have him in an instant."

"So could anyone."

"He turned me down."

The look of pure loathing Garrette shot at him should have carved out his heart. Without a word she charged to her feet, scraping chair and bumping table. She left the taproom, too.

Caspian grinned. "The Sources are offended. Are we good or what?"

"Aye, we're excellent," I said dryly. I swallowed the last of my ale and set my mug aside. "Think back, Caspian," I suggested. "Search back into the misty reaches of your narrow little mind. Remember Ahmad's class? Remember rule number one?" I deepened my voice so it sounded something like that of our ethics professor. "Never sleep with your Source."

"Rule number two was never sleep with your students." He bobbed his eyebrows suggestively.

I wasn't exactly shocked. "You're such a whore, Caspian. Why aren't you called the Stallion of the Triple S?"

"Because I've got shoulders the width of the proverbial barn door while Karish is lean and sleek and dark, more like the ultimate stallion. What have you got against him, anyway?"

"I've got nothing against him."

"Give over, Mallorough. I've never seen you so stiff with anyone you could stand."

I shrugged. "He's slept with everyone on the continent. Or he will."

"So?"

No, Caspian wouldn't see the flaw in that. Which came as no surprise to me but made me pause and think. Why would I find the same trait harmless in one man but reprehensible in another? Why should I find it reprehensible at all? Why should I care who anyone else slept with? "He's too . . ." What? Reckless? There were worse crimes. Confident? There was nothing wrong with that. "Full of flair," I finished lamely.

Caspian's expression told me what he thought of that.

"He's not Devereaux," I admitted. And I had expected to get Devereaux.

"And you've decided to punish him for that." He nodded, as though he could have predicted such behavior from me.

I scowled at him. I was not predictable. And I wasn't trying to punish Karish. "My disappointment doesn't change the fact that he is a prat," I snapped.

"You're alienating your Source, Mallorough."

"Worry about your own Source, Caspian," I suggested acidly. "You're fouling things up royally."

He shrugged.

Irritated by his cavalier attitude, I prepared to launch a shot concerning the gross stupidity of endangering an important lifelong partnership just for the sake of a little sex, which he could pick up anywhere. The next moment I exhaled and let it all out. None of my business, and I didn't like arguments. And I was tired. I rose to my feet, ready to call it a night. "I've got to get some sleep," I said. "Will I see you tomorrow?"

He smiled, and as easily as that all was forgiven. "I doubt it. Garrette and I'll have to be up with the birds to make it to Shidonee's Gap in time for our meeting, and you've never been an early riser."

"Then I'll wish you well now." I held out my hand, and he clasped it firmly. "It was good seeing you, Ian. I hope we have a little longer next time."

He didn't release me. "Take care of yourself, Lee," he said, suddenly solemn. "I know you're good and Karish is some kind of wonder, but High Scape is dangerous. Don't be too anxious to show your colors. Let the veterans do their jobs."

Touched, not to mention disconcerted, by the concern, I leaned down to kiss his cheek. "You worry too much about the wrong things, Caspian," I said. "Take care."

"You, too, love."

Feeling depressed, I left the taproom. Climbing the stairs I remembered I'd planned to take a bath. The hell with it. Too much trouble right then. I went to my room and stretched out on the lumpy mattress and was out in an instant.

Waking was disorienting. I was in a strange, small room, awkwardly curled up on a tiny cot. My body was stiff, my muscles screaming. There were strange noises coming from the walls and from beneath the floor.

Oh, right. All day riding. Over Leap.

It was the first time I could remember waking up somewhere that wasn't the academy.

I dragged myself out of bed and pulled on my clothes. I slipped into the hall, heading for the taproom.

The Stallion was there. I joined him because to do otherwise would be too much of a snub.

Karish's greeting was not what one would call warm. "Your friend has already left," he said.

Too bad. It would have been nice to see him off.

There'd be other times. I gestured at the waiter, and the brilliant man brought me a cup of coffee almost immediately.

"You look lovely this morning," Karish drawled sarcastically. "I especially like the hair."

I glanced at him through the locks falling over my eyes, then raked them back to have unobstructed access to my coffee. I knew I looked awful. When red hair was uncombed it looked a thousand times messier than any other color. Fortunately, I didn't care what Karish thought of my looks.

Karish wasn't in the mood to be ignored. "So you know the slings and arrows, do you?" he asked.

It's too early in the morning to be indecipherable, Karish my love. "Sorry?"

"It's just that I noticed that after we got here last night, you relaxed your vigilance somewhat. So I'm just complimenting you, that you learned absolutely everything about how I work in only one day."

He was miffed because he hadn't been the center of all my attention the night before. Pathetic. It would be enough to make me laugh, except he was also accusing me of dereliction of duty. I couldn't let my own Source believe I wouldn't do my duty. It would be difficult for him to do his job if he thought I wouldn't be doing mine. Plus it was irritating.

I drained the last of my coffee.

Karish looked horrified. "Zaire, woman, how can you gulp it down like that when it's still hot?"

Because I was a Shield. I gestured at the waiter. "You're left-handed," I said as my mug was filled. "But you use your right when you eat. You drank three mugs of ale and ate two bowls of the stew. You enjoyed it very much, even though you don't like turnip."

"Actually," he interrupted me curtly, "I'm allergic to turnip."

I almost smiled. Was he trying to shake my confidence? Amateur. "If you were allergic to turnip you wouldn't have touched the stew at all." *Wouldn't want hives defiling that perfect skin.* "You eat your bread like a woman—"

"What the hell does that mean?"

"You tear it off in chunks instead of biting into the whole slice. And you slather all sides with butter. That's disgusting, by the way." Butter was not icing and shouldn't be treated as such. "You sat straight in your chair, as you are now, without touching the back, despite certain fatigue. I would guess you spent some of your formative years with a wooden rod up your spine." He leaned back in his chair, then, crossing his arms. "But for much of the evening you had your right foot wrapped around one leg of your chair. Your mother wouldn't approve." Another slow sip of glorious coffee.

He looked at me, frowning. And then the frown turned into a smile that I didn't trust at all.

"You're staring," I pointed out tartly.

His response to that was to sweep up my free hand and kiss the back of it. In an instant every ache I'd been feeling was gone, so swift and so complete that the lack itself was almost painful.

I jerked my hand away, and the discomfort flooded back.

I was starving. I opened my mouth to call for the waiter. Before I could speak, however, I noticed a curious stillness about Karish, a stillness I had been taught to recognize. Then I felt the slight adjustments within him, the shifts, the little releases.

"Cyclone," he whispered.

No. It was too soon. I'd had only a day with him. That wasn't enough time. And Over Leap was supposed to be a cold site. That was why it didn't have any Pairs of its own.

Karish drew in one long, deep breath. Walls within him fell away completely, and as his inner shields tumbled down I snapped mine into place.

Power roared through him. I didn't know exactly where it came from, I never would, but I could feel it rushing through him like water gushing from a ruptured pipe. As it pulsed through him it pressed against the fragile walls of his flesh, testing, pushing, wearing down until he was nothing more than a thin shell separating the internal forces he was channeling from the external forces tearing about freely, a shell that threatened to explode into a million pieces at any moment.

I couldn't touch the forces myself. I could only feel them through Karish. I wondered what it was like, to have all that power rushing through one's body. A part of me mourned that I would never know.

I had Shielded before, during my training with veteran Pairs. I had never felt such a massive flow of power through one person. Maybe, just maybe, Karish actually deserved some of the praise cast at his feet.

I measured Karish's breathing, breathed in time to him, then made us both slow down. I listened to his blood and eased its pressure. The activity in his mind was giving me a headache, so I soothed it into a more natural pace.

My eyes began to burn with the strain, my head pulsing as I weighed every particle of man and force and made constant minute adjustments. I had no idea how long it all lasted. It felt like forever. It could have been no more than a couple of moments.

And then it was over. The cyclone was gone. The air felt cold enough to sting. The sudden painful silence was broken only by Karish and me, panting like a couple of horses after a hard run. Then people were crying out in relief and disbelief. I could hear their feet slapping the ground as they ran toward us.

I was exhausted, every muscle a useless puddle. Sweat lined my skin. My heart was pounding in my throat, my ears were buzzing, and I couldn't quite see straight.

I felt really good.

I grinned at Karish. I couldn't help it.

He looked puzzled for a moment, eyebrows dipping together. Then he grinned back.

Chapter Four

High Scape. Once a tiny little village no one knew the name of, a series of massive earthquakes had brought three waterways through it, changing it forever. Eight major trade routes lured merchants, travelers, and criminals from all over the world. There was every kind of person and every kind of product, and the variety of entertainments was the stuff of legend. It was a huge, dangerous, intoxicating place, and all the people who lived there were lunatics. After all, High Scape was one of the hottest sites on the planet, a target for every imaginable disaster. Pairs prevented the disasters, but the citizens felt a certain pride over the potential for total destruction. Strange.

Karish nudged his horse into a walk down the road to High Scape. I waited a few moments and then followed. Karish no longer objected when I chose to ride or walk behind him. He knew, though he had never admitted it to me, that my close observation of him that first day was probably the only reason I was able to Shield him so well during our little trial by fire in Over Leap. So he left me alone about it. In return, I was no longer quite so vigilant about maintaining those few paces behind. After the first little while it wasn't so essential, and I had always found such a placement just a little too servile. But upon the arrival at our first assignment it was only prudent to follow protocol, and in a place as potentially dangerous as High Scape it would be stupid not to keep my eyes on my Source.

Meanwhile, I had a new life to start, a life that was going to be incredibly free compared to what I'd known before. No one to tell me what to eat or when to sleep or when to study. I could walk anywhere, eat anywhere, casually meet people of every stripe without worrying about instantaneously bonding with them and ruining my future. When I wasn't on duty, my time was mine, and I got to spend it in the most exciting city in the world.

And the ugliest. I had to say that. The buildings in High Scape were hideous. Possibly because none of them matched. So much of the city had been torn down and rebuilt over the centuries, and it appeared that every time they needed a new building they hired the most demented apprentice architect they could find to design it.

A pathetic effort had been made to brighten things up. There were banners hung from windows, arches, and every likely anchor that could be found. Streets were obstructed with gaily decorated platforms and stalls boasting goods of the frivolous variety. And the people seemed to be moving around a lot, full of excitement.

I frowned as I remembered the date. *Ah, hell. Damn, damn, damn. The Star Festival.* It was around that time. I'd forgotten all about it. There'd been no preparations going on at the last village we had ridden through, but different places celebrated at different times.

The Star Festival, when we celebrated the First Landing, when the first people came from who knew where and started living on our world. For most people it was just a time to get together and eat and dance and get drunk for a few days, with no other significance. Which was fair enough, as no one knew the exact date of the First Landing anyway.

I'd never celebrated the Star Festival outside of the confines of my academy. Unbonded Shields did not go to public festivals. The combination of the general excitement, the activity, the drinking, and the music could be extremely dangerous, driving a Shield to unimaginable acts of violence or sex, sometimes sending them cowering in fear. Some Shields even suffered hallucinations. At the academy the activities, beverages, and music had been carefully chosen to keep the Shields calm. In public festivals, no such care was taken. Only bonded Shields could attend, because their Sources were there to keep them under control.

I studied Karish's back. He had done nothing—yet—to suggest he was irresponsible, but he was a Source and an aristocrat, and he lived to satisfy his passions. How could such a creature be expected to forgo his own pleasure just to make sure someone else didn't behave inappropriately?

I'd beg off that night, claiming fatigue, which was true enough. He would be relieved, free to chase pretty young things. I would worry about the next day tomorrow.

That settled, I kept my eye out for the Triple S residence, where Pairs posted in High Scape lived. Again, High Scape was different than other posts, in that it required all of the Pairs to live together. Most sites had only one Pair, and each in a Pair was permitted to find his or her own accommodations. I supposed there would have been complaints, however, if fourteen forms of accommodation had been demanded without payment in one city.

I had to ask for directions to the large, sprawling building with the Triple S emblem over the door. We left our horses at the hitching post, and I pounded on the entrance.

The door was opened a few moments later. A plump woman with graying brown hair and the white braid of a Shield looked at us, and then at our own braids. "Yes?"

I noticed no sense of recognition in her. "We are Lord Shintaro Karish and Shield Mallorough," I said. "We're the new Pair for High Scape." I dug my hand into my belt purse and pulled at the letter I'd received at the Horse's Head.

"Oh," she said, sounding surprised. The next words she spoke were delivered in a more moderate tone. "Forgive me, but we weren't told when the new Pair was arriving, and you're . . . well, you're rather younger than we'd been expecting. Please, come in." She held the door wider, closing it behind us once we'd entered. "I'm McKenna."

Karish took her hand. "My friends call me Taro," he said, smiling. "It's a great honor to meet you."

She smiled back, admiration tinged with amusement. "I hear you have a lot of friends, Karish."

He cocked his head to one side. "I like people," he said.

"I bet you do." McKenna retrieved her hand, her expression one of tolerance. "All the bedrooms are upstairs. I'm afraid you've been stuck in the smallest, number thirteen and seven. We've been using them for storage. But we did know a Pair was coming eventually, so they've been emptied and furnished. Ben will take up your bags, and I'll start some tea for you."

"Thank you," I said, and she nodded and strolled away.

An older man appeared from a side door, holding out his hands for our bags. "Claim a room before we've seen them," Karish said as we followed Ben up the stairs.

I shrugged. "Thirteen." I was sure whatever they provided us would be adequate.

From McKenna's description, I'd been expecting the room to be a closet. It was more of a suite. A sitting room with a small collection of chairs and settees, a bedroom with a large quilted bed and two dressers, and an antechamber with a huge, deep bathtub. I looked at the bathtub longingly but felt McKenna had as good as ordered me to go back downstairs immediately.

I took the stairs down and found myself a little lost. I was back in the foyer where we had entered, and followed the corridor past a larger version of the sitting area I had in my suite, a large dining room, and then into the kitchen. I realized I couldn't remember ever seeing a kitchen before. I'd never entered the one at school. There was a long wooden table, with a few high stools scattered about, and rows of cupboards, and a multitude of implements of which I didn't know the names or uses.

"First post, eh?" McKenna asked. She was pulling mugs from one of the cupboards.

"It's that obvious?"

"Aye. That look of panic at the sight of a kitchen." She grinned at me. "Feel lucky you weren't sent to one of the other posts, where you're stuck in your own place with nary a lesson in a kitchen to tell you how the stove works. Have a seat."

"I was told we could rely on public fare," I said, hiking myself up onto a stool.

"You can, but you get tired of it. And taverns aren't always open when you're wanting food."

"And there are no staff here for that sort of thing?"

"Just Ben. He cooks well enough. But I'm not comfortable asking him to fix something for me whenever I've got the whim. Besides, it's good for you to learn for your next post."

"Shame on you, Lee, for expecting servitude." Karish appeared to come out of nowhere, slipping onto a stool beside me.

I chose not to answer. I didn't expect servitude. I also didn't expect to cook. No one had ever taught me nor encouraged me to learn, so obviously it wasn't considered one of my responsibilities.

We heard the outer door open, followed by masculine laughter.

"Afternoon, Van Staal," McKenna called. "The new Pair's here."

Looking back, I could never be sure whether my mouth actually dropped open or not. Surely I had a little more polish than that? But the man standing in the doorway was truly divine. His hair was golden, his eyes were golden, his skin was practically golden. He was long of leg and broad of shoulder and quite thoroughly delicious.

He was followed in by a slightly older man, a little less golden and a lot less dazzling but somehow still looking like his partner. Did that happen after a while? The dazzler thrust out a hand. "Van Staal," he said, then gestured at his companion. "Stephan Rundle."

"Mallorough," I answered. "This is Lord Shintaro Karish."

"Dunleavy is so impressed with my title," Karish added smoothly. "I'm sure everyone would forget all about it if it weren't for her."

I didn't glare at him as he shook hands with the others. I refused to feel embarrassed about introducing him by his proper legal name. If he didn't like it, he should have mentioned it earlier.

"We've heard a lot about you, Shintaro," said Rundle.

"Taro, please."

"And all of it good," Van Staal said, settling onto another stool.

"You're lucky you're here in time for the Star Festival," McKenna said to me. "I take it you can dance the benches?"

Of course. "I'm a Shield, aren't I?"

"Are you any good?"

I was excellent. "I've never broken anything." Which should tell them enough about my skill without my having to brag.

The outer door opened again, and three more people entered the kitchen. Shield Ogawa, a tall, skeletal woman with her blond hair cropped close to her scalp. Source Bet Farin, a small woman with dark hair and eyes and a lot of curves. She was McKenna's partner, and from the way the older woman tensed, it was obvious that the two did not get along. And Source Val Tenneson, Ogawa's partner, a plain, thin man with merry eyes.

"Febray and Heiner are on duty in the observation post right now," McKenna told us. "The others are helping set up for the festival. You'll meet them tonight." She said to Ogawa, "Mallorough's going to dance."

"Excellent." Ogawa smiled. "I like a challenge."

"Uh." Time to nip that in the bud. "I actually won't be dancing tonight. I'm exhausted. I'll just get some sleep."

"You can't do that," Ogawa objected. "It's the Star Festival. You can't miss that because of a few aches and pains. You're too young to let one day of riding wipe you out."

"I'm really very tired."

"So take a nap. A couple hours' sleep, a bath, and a good meal will put you back in fine form and give me the chance to beat you on the benches."

"Really, I wouldn't be a challenge."

"Really," Karish interrupted sharply, "she's very sensitive to music, and she doesn't trust me to guide her through it."

Well. That stopped everything.

Van Staal took a quick sip from his mug for something to do and hit his teeth against the rim so hard we could all hear it in the sudden silence.

No one had anything to say. I could have smacked Karish for making everyone so uncomfortable. I wondered how he knew about my unusual sensitivity to music. I didn't remember talking about it.

"I never said that." Ugh. It was the first thing out of my mouth, and it was weak. But I let it stand. Adding anything would only make it worse.

He was watching me, his face blank. Perhaps he thought to intimidate me. I looked right back at him. I had nothing else to say. He had made his accusation, and I had denied it. Sort of. His turn.

He rose to his feet. "Let's take a walk, Lee."

Now he wanted privacy. Excellent timing. And quite the perfect example of the magnanimous lord escorting the errant servant out for a well-bred chastisement.

I could refuse to go with him. Then he would ask me again, and again, becoming ever more patient as I appeared increasingly childish. Or he could just say whatever he had to say in front of everyone else. That wouldn't look terribly professional, either. So against my better judgment I tilted my head in acquiescence and set my mug on the table. "If you will excuse us," I said to our audience, then I followed my irritating Source.

He strode down the sidewalk. I glared at him, for I needed two steps to his one. I probably looked like some little rat-dog scampering along beside him.

"Have I ever insinuated you couldn't do your job?" he asked sharply.

"You insinuated I wasn't doing it."

He stopped so suddenly my own momentum carried me a couple of steps beyond him. "When?" he demanded.

Back at the first tavern in Over Leap. "What difference does it make?"

"I certainly never did it in front of other people."

"Neither did I. You're the one who felt like dragging the true reason out back there. They were believing the exhaustion excuse."

He couldn't reasonably deny that. He pushed a hand through his hair. "What the hell did I do, anyway?"

"Sorry?"

"You were friendly with the blond fellow back in Over Leap, and the innkeepers and shopkeepers and strangers on the street, and everyone back at the residence, but with me you have this chilly, polite facade going."

So? Why couldn't he just leave it? We were getting along well enough. So what if I didn't adore him? By tomorrow morning he would have a hundred admirers tagging his heels.

"So what did I do?" he asked impatiently. "Tell me. My hair isn't blond? I'm not tall enough?"

Prat. Did he really think I cared about such trivial things? "I am a simple girl, Karish," I said. He snorted in disbelief, which surprised me. "And I never anticipated being bonded to the Stallion of the Triple S."

"You may stop referring to me in that manner any time now," he instructed me coolly. "I asked you to call me Taro."

"Hey, if the horseshoe fits." And he ordered me to call him Taro. Big difference. "I wanted to be Paired with someone discreet."

"And of course I'm not."

"You're too"—I gestured vaguely as I tried to think of a suitable word—"legendary. You have all this dash and flair, running hither and yon saving the world. Everyone knows who you are, and everyone loves you."

He smiled crookedly. It wasn't a happy expression. "Do they?"

"Well, look around." At all the people who turned heads to take another look at him. He was honestly that beautiful. He didn't look, so he didn't see, but he probably didn't need to. No doubt he had seen it all before. "I didn't want to work with a legend. I wanted a quiet life, do my job without anyone much noticing." I let myself sigh. "No chance of that, now. Certainly, you'll be the focus of all the attention, but some of it is bound to splash onto me. Lord Shintaro Karish's Shield, easiest road to his favor." Oh, he didn't like that at all, and he scowled to prove it. Well, too bad. He'd asked for it. "You've got no right to complain about my behavior. I've been polite."

"Barely."

Completely. "Right back at you."

He stiffened his jaw before saying, "I have guarded Shields before."

It shot out of the mouth before the brain had time to kick in. "When?"

"During my training," he gritted out through his teeth. "When do you think?"

Oh.

"We *are* trained."

"I know that." Not as much as we were, but they got some smattering of discipline, I knew.

"We are not these uncontrollable forces of nature unleashed on the unsuspecting world with nothing more than one frail Shield standing between us and chaos."

"I know." I supposed.

"And believe me, we're made well aware of our obligations to the regulars and to our Shields."

I knew that. Still, this was a social event. Why would he want to be saddled with any responsibility at a festival? Any normal person would resent that, never mind someone of Karish's ilk.

Karish swore. Under his breath. Very prettily. The refined accent gave the oaths a certain venom I had never heard before.

"Listen, I just think it's a little early in the schedule to be asking you to guard me for something like this."

"It wasn't too early for you to Shield me in Over Leap," he pointed out, as though he honestly thought the two situations were comparable. "But that's different, isn't it? You're a Shield. Sober and responsible and disciplined. Unshakable in your duty. Whereas Sources are nothing more than a horde of irresponsible perpetual adolescents. We'd be dangerous if we didn't have you Shields to keep us under control, wouldn't we?"

That was an exaggeration, and I knew it. Yes, Sources were a tad overemotional, but so were lots of regulars. So were some Shields. I didn't think it made them dangerous, just harder to work with.

But all right. Perhaps it was time to do a little bending. I was no longer the free and independent entity who could be as stubborn as necessary. Whether I liked it or not I was bound to this man, and I had to give his feelings some consideration, especially when I hadn't yet proven they weren't valid. I didn't trust him to watch me well when I needed it, but I couldn't afford to force that point until he actually failed.

Theoretically, music could move me to kill someone. In reality, there was almost no chance of that actually happening.

The braid identified me as a Shield. People, complete strangers, would be keeping their eye on me, and the minstrels would be careful with their selections. There would be plenty of people to stop me in the unlikely event that I went berserk.

I would let Karish guard me that night. He would be distracted by some fine young thing and lured away. I might have a crying fit or sleep with something that had slithered out from under a rock, but I could live with that. And the next time we had this sort of discussion I would have the evidence to back up my argument, and Karish would just have to stew. "All right."

He wasn't appeased. "Pulling teeth takes less time."

"I said yes, didn't I?"

"With images of humiliation dancing through your head. Or maybe you're just worried about being proved wrong. What, has that never happened to you?"

I was regretting my answer already.

He studied me a moment longer than I liked, then he smiled. My stomach clenched. He surprised me by tapping my cheek, and I pulled away. "Poor little Lee," he taunted. "The philosophy's undreamed of, isn't it?" He punctuated that bit of nonsense with a wink before he wheeled away and deserted me. I could hear him whistling as he walked.

Chapter Five

Karish was no fop, and that night he wore only two colors. Black and red, far more subdued than customary festival wear. The trousers were not too tight, the soft black shoes were really rather unremarkable. The black vest did show off the hard chest and flat stomach, though. The shirt under the vest was dark, dark red, the sleeves flaring, the collar unlaced and revealing a strong, masculine throat. Unruly black hair had been temporarily tamed by a red ribbon at his nape. A red stone twinkled in his left earlobe.

Every eye lingered, which was, I was sure, the point. He was certainly setting himself up to fail our little challenge. He would get a thousand invitations that night. There was no way he was going to be able to resist every single one of them.

But I was engaging in countermeasures. No beauty to begin with, it took artful dressing and plenty of paint for me to attract much sexual interest. Not short enough to be pleasantly petite, neither lean nor voluptuous, it was too easy for me to escape notice. Especially when I was dressed as I was that night, in a loose-fitting shirt and trousers of a pale green. Not my usual garb for a party, but under Karish's uncertain care I wanted as little attention as possible.

Well, I would be dancing the benches, and that would get me a lot of attention, but that was different.

Everyone was out for the festival. The streets were packed, and the noise was deafening. Dogs and cats and children skirted through the legs of people dressed in their best. Bright colors, high hats, flowers weaved into hair and shirt lacings. Merchant stalls competed for space with magicians and miracle healers.

"Zaire, Lee, the moon's not going to be envious tonight," was Karish's sweet comment. "Could you look any more drab?"

"You'd be surprised."

"Aye, I would."

So I had more important things to do than gaze at myself in the mirror and make sure my hair was just so. Sorry.

It took us a while to find the bench dancing circle in the mess of stalls and tables and people. If it weren't for the flag, dark red with four black horizontal lines, we probably wouldn't have found it at all. There were a dozen or so dancing sets, each consisting of two benches, roughly eight feet long and barely the width of the average male foot, with two black bars lying between them and one on either side. Boring things to look at, really.

Timpani were being tuned on the side, four in all. I loved the sound of the kettledrums, it made me shiver, but I hadn't been allowed to listen to them very often. Only while dancing under the supervision of my instructors. The stalkers, the people who would be manipulating the bars while we danced, were placing pans of chalk throughout the dancing circle and wiping down the bars. The dancers were stretching or testing their balance on the benches.

"Hey, you're the new Pair," a voice said from nowhere. A hand was thrust out at us. It was followed by the rest of the body and a warm smile. "I'm Elias Arter," she said, grabbing Karish's hand for a quick shake, then mine. "This is my Shield, Kennis Mao. Sorry we didn't meet you when you first rode in, but everyone who can lends a hand with the Star Festival." Her gaze scanned over me, and she looked like she didn't know what to say. Wasn't impressed with my outfit, I supposed. "Are you going to dance?" she asked.

With her other hand, Arter was keeping a good grip on her Shield, a solid-looking fellow who was staring off into space. I didn't know if he was even more sensitive to the noise than I, or just bored. "I'm Mallorough," I said, though I figured she already knew. "This is Shintaro Karish. And yes, I've been ordered to dance."

She grinned. "Poor girl," she said mockingly. "But you Shields get so few opportunities to shine, you've got to grab your chance when you can."

Mao woke up then, staring at his Source with obvious astonishment. I heard Karish making a swiftly repressed choking sound behind me. I kept my expression blank. I hoped. "Aye, there is that," I agreed mildly.

Mao got his own expression under control and looked at me. I could see the traces of apology in his eyes. I shrugged imperceptibly. She was a Source. "Do you dance?" I asked him.

"Only when it's absolutely necessary," he said wryly. "I'm stricken with a case of two left feet. But I shall enjoy watching you and sighing with envy."

"My, how optimistic you are. When does it start?"

"After sunset. It'll be a bit yet. Grab something to eat."

There was plenty of typical festival food, too spicy and too heavy. I didn't want any of it right then. It would weigh me down. Nothing to drink yet, either. But I promised myself I would indulge freely after the dancing.

Karish had already lasted longer than I'd anticipated. He was aware of the long, admiring glances sent his way, and he responded to them with nods and smiles. I saw him send a few admiring looks of his own. But he kept a hand on me at all times. I didn't much care for that, it made me feel like a child, but it was an accepted method of keeping track of a Shield, an easy way to sense and stop a dangerous act before it started. It would be better if he learned me the way I had to learn him, so he wouldn't have to hang on to me all the time, but that would never happen with his eyes everywhere but on me.

I shifted my feet uneasily. Someone was playing music somewhere near. It was the gorgeous, languid call of an oboe. It chilled me, but in a good way. I shifted my shoulders in the attempt to relax them. Then I clenched my teeth and dug my nails into my palms. Karish's grip tightened. "Shall I tell them to stop?" he asked, his voice so low and smooth it sent shivers down my spine.

I shook my head. I didn't want it to stop. It felt good.

"Are you sure?"

"I'm all right."

The words were barely out of my mouth before a pair of cymbals crashed together inside my left ear. At least, that was how it sounded. I'm sure my feet cleared the ground by a good arm span, but I didn't scream. Good for me.

Karish pulled me to him, close to his side. I could see a passerby giving us a strange look. I felt suffocated. I struggled free. "Let me go." He was far too ready to touch me, and I wasn't used to it.

"You're more sensitive than I thought."

"I'm not so bad you have to hang all over me."

"I won't have you accusing me of neglecting you."

"So don't neglect me. Watch me. But don't be touching me all the time."

He didn't like that at all. "I'm sorry I'm so offensive," he said coolly.

Someone snickered and said, "I'll watch her for you."

I looked at the man with surprise, ready to be offended again. I wasn't a child who needed to be supervised. But then he smiled at me, and it was a cute smile, so I smiled back.

"No, thank you," Karish refused him with chilly disdain.

The man didn't appear to be impressed by the note of hostility. "No, I'm serious. I know about Shields."

"I'll bet you do," Karish sneered.

The man's face darkened. Didn't like the insinuation that he would take advantage of a woman made susceptible by music. Always a good sign in a man. "I will keep her out of harm's way for you," he said with a controlled voice. "Since you seem to find the task so troublesome."

Nice shot.

Karish deliberately stepped in between the stranger and me. "You may leave, now," he said loftily.

The regular shrugged. "Let me know if you change your mind," he suggested. "I know how overburdened you Sources tend to feel. Have fun." And he wandered off.

"Prat," Karish muttered.

I watched the stranger walk away. He'd been appealing in a nondescript kind of way. Wiry build, nice brown eyes, good smile.

Then I forgot about him.

The sun finally disappeared, and I took off my shoes and stockings and started stretching, rotating my ankles and wrists. It had been nearly a month since I last danced the benches, and I was finding it hard to get loose. The drummers did a few warm-up rolls on the timpani, and I let the music work my muscles over.

Bench dancing was a dangerous pastime. People who were bad at it didn't do it. Two opponents stood on the benches, facing each other, a foot on each bench. Four stalkers, two on each end of the benches, worked the bars. The bars were lifted to just over bench height and were clattered together. The dancers had to jump and hop from bench to bench to keep their feet from getting caught between the bars. There were three rules. The opponents couldn't touch each other. A dancer couldn't have two feet on the same bench at the same time. And no touching the ground. Getting caught between the bars didn't mean an automatic loss according to the rules, but it hurt, a lot, so in such cases the dancer usually forfeited.

All Shields had to learn bench dancing at the academies. It was a wonderful way to force us to pay attention to what was going on around us. Some regulars danced just for fun. There were amateur competitions for those who took it a bit more seriously. Then there were the professional bench dancers who traveled from city to city, collecting purses. And where you have professional sports you must also have gambling, with stakes rising to ludicrous heights. Dancers could get rich, some honestly, some by taking dives. Shields couldn't make money from bench dancing, though. We were supposed to donate any winnings to charities.

The list of competitors was called out. I nodded to my first opponent, a young girl who was an idiot to be dancing at all. She had the look of someone in the middle of a growth spurt, gaining inches every day and having to relearn her own proportions every time she walked through a room. She should have waited until she finished growing before dancing again, especially in a competition.

I allowed myself a few more stretches, then dipped my feet in a nearby chalk pan. I stepped up onto my assigned benches, rubbing my soles into them. I watched the girl climb up at the other end of the benches and settle into a half crouch. She stared at me intently.

Don't look at me, girl. This isn't a sparring match. How I move isn't going to affect how you move.

There was a warning roll from the drums. I felt the pounding in my stomach, and my whole body shivered. I shook it off. Bent knees, hands loose at my sides. Silence descended on the circle.

One moment, all was still. The next, an explosion of sound and movement. I was never sure exactly how or when it started. All of a sudden I was dancing, pulling one foot off the bench and feeling the faintest breeze as the bars crashed together under my sole. That foot went down, the other came up.

Just as suddenly, it stopped. I looked up in surprise. That had to be one of the shortest dances of my life. The girl had fallen off.

She started crying.

I rolled my eyes as a woman I assumed was the girl's mother ran out to soothe her disappointment, shooting nasty glances at me for defeating her precious daughter.

I looked over the other dancers. Some had been defeated as quickly as my opponent. I saw the appealing fellow, the one who had offered to keep an eye on me. He had won his dance.

He noticed me watching him. He winked. I smiled.

The first round was over. Some bench sets were dragged aside. New chalk for the stalkers, and a new drumroll. The bars would be lifted half an inch higher for this round.

New opponent. I beat him, too. My third opponent was more of a challenge. All the dancers were in fine form, but he was in particularly hardened shape. He spent a lot of time practicing, I could tell. He was possibly a professional. And he looked like he meant to be troublesome.

But I beat him, too.

I'd never danced against regulars before. At first I thought I was defeating them so easily because they were regulars. No doubt they didn't enjoy the high levels of rigorous training all Shields endured.

But then I faced Ogawa. She was good and had a height
advantage, but she was tired before we even started, and I
could feel her thinking about her feet too much. Every step
she took, she shifted her balance just a little too far. Shortly
after we started, her movements became less fluid, less sure,
her breath coming too hard. Her stamina deteriorated rapidly,
and I knew she would fall the instant before she did. She hit
the sand, unhurt, and I jumped down after her.

"You're very good," she said as I helped her to her feet.

"Because I beat you?" I teased her.

"Aye," she answered somberly. "And you don't even feel it."

"I will tomorrow," I promised her. "Believe me."

She smiled wearily and limped out of the circle. Tenneson gave her a comforting clap on the shoulder and a goblet of wine.

I suddenly realized my throat was dry. Swallowing was a
difficulty.

Don't think about it.

My name was called again. I approached the benches, and
I found myself facing my would-be protector, the one who
"knew about Shields." So he was that good, was he?

I looked him over. Very good build. Quite a bit taller than
me. Elegant feet, for a man. He was soaked with sweat and
breathing hard, as I was. He was also trembling, as I was not.
Apparently the music didn't fortify him as it did me. That was
my advantage.

I could take him.

We mounted the benches. The drums rolled. The bars rose
to slightly above knee level—for me—and crashed together. I
had to leap higher than he did to avoid them. One foot went
down on the off beat, the other came up. I grit my teeth and
forced exhausted muscles to move.

I refused to lose. I concentrated on the music, willing it to
take me over. I reminded myself what the timpani did to me,
and I felt a roll shiver through me. I felt it coat the pain a little.
Good enough.

I sneaked a look at my opponent. He wasn't landing on the
benches well, wasn't quite centered. His trembling was even
more pronounced. I could practically feel it. Or maybe that
was me I was feeling. I had started to wobble, too.

My opponent got caught. He shifted his weight too heavily to his down foot and he couldn't shift it back again. Two bars tried to meet and found their course obstructed by his knee. I was jarred back to the benches, and he screamed as wood crushed bone and cartilage.

He collapsed to the ground and rolled onto his back, digging his hands into the ground to keep them from clutching his shattered knee. There were calls for the healer, who was mysteriously absent. No one went near him. No one knew what to do for him, and no worried companion came out of the crowd to comfort him.

I dropped onto the ground, barely on my feet, watching it all through a haze. Sweat was running into my eyes, my heart was pounding in my ears, and my chest heaved in a desperate attempt to suck air into my lungs. The music had stopped, and I was shaking so hard I thought something might fall off.

I saw Karish force his way through the crowd, a goblet in one hand. Wine, I supposed. He knelt beside my victim, insinuating an arm under the man's back and raising him enough to sip at the wine.

Then I felt it, even through my own raging senses. Those tiny releases, those subtle adjustments that meant only one thing. He was channeling. He was channeling? Right then? What the hell was he thinking? We weren't on duty, and I was exhausted.

He was channeling. That meant I had to Shield. I cleared my head of my heartbeat and forced myself to pay attention to his.

Only there was no real rush of power through him, not like before. Just an odd rambling trickle that curled in on itself and barely made it past the Shields I'd erected. His blood wasn't racing, his mind was calm, it was almost like he wasn't really channeling at all. But he was doing something. I could feel it. I could see the tension flowing from the body of my opponent, the breath easing.

The healer arrived. Finally. She was rummaging through her sack as she ran, pulling out a small bag as she knelt beside my opponent. I watched her take out a small leaf, which she stuck into her patient's mouth. He chewed on it and waited for the sedative to take hold.

The small flow moving through Karish grew weaker, and weaker still, and trickled off into nothing. Karish's own internal protections snapped back into place. I let my Shields drop.

I nearly dropped with them, but Van Staal, who had snuck up behind me, caught me when I would have collapsed. "You'll ruin your clothes," I warned him. I was glad I could speak at all. Shielding hadn't been much of a challenge that time, but it had eliminated what reserves the dancing had left me.

"Too late," Van Staal said, hooking an arm around my waist and helping me across the sands. I stumbled with every step. "I'll say this for you, Mallorough, your introduction to High Scape will certainly be remembered. I wouldn't have taken you for the dramatic type."

He lowered me to a bench at one of the tables, and Mao handed me a mug of ice-cold wine. "Bless you," I gasped before drinking deeply. A nice light wine that flooded my parched throat. It flooded my brain, too. Wonderful stuff, wine.

My Source came back with a jaunty stride, looking so fresh I wanted to hit him. When I could move. Of course he hadn't been dancing, but it was the principle of the thing. Mao rose to his feet. "Congratulations," he said because, incidentally, I had won the competition. "It must be wonderful to be able to move so swiftly." He looked a little wistful as he turned and left.

Karish took Mao's place beside me, elbows propped on the table behind us, legs sprawled out in front. I drank my wine and contemplated what had just happened.

My last opponent was carried away. The dancing competition continued, but I had lost all desire to watch it. I watched Karish, instead.

"Now I know you're not admiring my profile," he said.

"You channeled his pain." It was obvious. There had been no disturbance, the channeling had felt strange, the man had been rigid in agony one moment and relaxed the next. It was the only explanation, and it was ridiculous.

He tossed me a quick glance, then pointed at a woman walking by in a truly hideous gown. "What color would you say that is?"

He didn't stare at me and ask if I had lost my mind. He didn't laugh and tell me I was an idiot. Pretty much settled the issue for me. "Are they teaching that sort of thing at the Source academy? How come I've never heard about it?"

"It doesn't really go with her hair, does it?"

"Are you a healer? How does it work?"

"Does she not have a mirror at home or what?"

I was losing patience. "I really can ask questions all night."

His sigh ended with a bit of a growl. "What?" he demanded testily.

"Did you channel his pain?"

"Don't be ridiculous."

Too late. "I know what I saw, and I trust what I see."

"If nothing else," he muttered.

"*Did* you—"

"Will you please keep it down?" he hissed.

"Why?"

"I just got out."

Talk about pulling teeth. "From where? Prison?"

Finally, he looked at me, and he didn't appear at all pleased. "I don't want to be shipped back to Shidonee's Gap just to answer a thousand questions and go through a hundred tests while the council does everything short of splitting my head open trying to discover why I can do this." With one impatient tug he pulled the ribbon out of his hair, then ran his hand through it, making an appealing mess of it. "And I don't imagine you want to be sitting around in a tavern doing nothing while they pick me over, so leave it alone."

"So no one knows you can do this."

"Brilliant deduction."

"So how did you learn to do it?"

He sighed again. "My favorite professor is an elderly man with joints that give him a lot of pain when it rains," he explained irritably. "I was helping him rub a lotion into one of his hands and I sort of"—he gestured vaguely—"did it by accident."

Tending to the elderly didn't really fit Karish's image, but I had more important things to think about. "And he didn't realize it."

"He'd been taking some wine, too, for the pain. Laced with a sedative. He thought the combination kicked in a little faster than normal."

"But if you weren't being Shielded, how come you're not dead?"

He shrugged. "I'm not sure. Except, it's such a low level of power, and it's very different from channeling in the usual way, maybe I just didn't need it."

"Or maybe," I said slowly, "you don't really need a Shield at all." Maybe the Stallion was really that good. And maybe I was really that useless. Gods. Wouldn't that just be perfect? Bonded for life to a Source who didn't need me. Training my whole life for nothing.

It was my turn to look away. I blew out a quick breath.

"It's not a theory I'm willing to test, Lee."

He was trying to reassure me. How sweet. How annoying. "No, of course not." Maybe I could take up a productive hobby. Gardening was said to be very calming.

"Your dancing is amazing," was his next comment, straight out of nowhere.

Of course it was. I'd practiced it every day of my life in the seventeen years I'd been in the academy. Just another useless pastime at which I excelled.

"And you were very quick with your Shields when I started channeling. With no warning and exhausted as you had to be, you were right in there. That was really good."

Oh, lord, he was back with the flattery again. That the motivation was entirely different this time didn't make it any less inappropriate. Did he really think I needed my esteem stroked in that way? It wasn't that I'd found out I was incompetent, just superfluous. An entirely different arena of uselessness.

But it was kind of funny. Here I was thinking up ways to deflate his pride while he was trying to pump up mine. I bit back a smile. If I let him see it he'd think his moonshine was working, and that would never do.

"Endurance. Strong will. Quick thinking. Very good."

Well, aye.

"Are you going to say anything any time soon?"

"What, you expect me to deny any of that?" Just because it was flattery didn't mean it wasn't true.

He grinned. Oh, gods. I held on to my mug very, very hard.

"You know, I think I'm going to like you after all."

I didn't want him to like me. It was way too dangerous.

"Go dance or something." The ordinary kind, not bench dancing. Sources didn't tend to bench dance very much for some reason.

He shook his head. "Can't leave you."

"I'm too tired to do anything stupid. I'll stay with Mao and Arter. She'll keep an eye on me."

"Aye, and next time you'll throw my leaving you in my face. Forget it."

He'd proven himself well enough. I was suddenly quite anxious to have him gone. And really, it wasn't fair to make him sit with me for the rest of the night. "Please, Karish, all this temptation before you." I nodded at all the pretty people around us. "Something's going to burst."

He smiled. No, leered. "You offering to do something about it?"

I reached back for one of the dishes on the table and found a wicked-looking knife. I raised it and cocked a suggestive brow.

He paled. "You're a sick, sick woman."

"Still think you're going to like me?"

He leaned forward and kissed me before I could dodge him. Just a quick brush of lips on lips, nothing to get excited about. I was too tired to get excited, anyway. "All that's gold doesn't glitter," he said with satisfaction, as though it actually made any sense.

I pulled in another deep breath through my nose and looked out unseeing at the crowds swirling by. Definitely too dangerous.

Chapter Six

I had expected to sleep like the dead that night, after my day of riding and my evening of bench dancing. I didn't. I kept seeing my final opponent arching in pain in the sand. I kept imagining I could hear the crunch of his knee shattering. Over and over again, I saw it, I heard it, and when I did manage to doze off, I dreamed about it.

People were injured while bench dancing. It happened all the time. I'd even witnessed some pretty brutal injuries. But I'd never caused any of them, never been dancing against the person when they suffered them.

It was not my fault. I'd done nothing but dance as the sport was meant to be danced, and he had gotten tired and hurt himself. I knew all that.

But I couldn't help thinking I'd been responsible.

I couldn't help wishing he hadn't suffered that injury while dancing against me. If it had to happen, why couldn't it have happened to the dancer before me or the one after?

That was a selfish thought. But I was a selfish person. I knew this about myself.

The festival was still continuing. The thought of attending any of the events while this person was suffering seemed obscene to me. I told Karish I didn't want to attend the festival that day—he gave some impression of being disappointed—and then I went looking for the injured bench dancer.

That, all by itself, was an extremely intimidating task. I had grown up within the confines of the academy and its grounds. The villages and towns Karish and I had stopped at on the way to High Scape had been small, the people easy to talk to. High Scape was another matter altogether.

For one thing, it was something of a mess. The three waterways divided it into six parts, called quads. Each quad really comprised its own little city, with its own moneylenders' row, bakers' street, and glassblowers' avenue. The night before, Ogawa had told me that the North Quad, the largest part of the city, was the poorest section, and the South Quad held the wealthiest residents, and the quads in between held everyone else.

Finding a nameless stranger in all of that was a daunting task for someone like me, someone unused to tall buildings and hordes of regulars jostling me in the street. It meant going to the festival after all, to hunt down the moderator of the bench dancing from the day before. She had the list of all the competitors and where they lived. The address she gave me meant nothing to me. She told me it was located in the Lower West Quad. The second-poorest region of the city.

To me, wealthy versus poor were vague concepts. The wealthy would have, I imagined, larger homes. Nicer clothes. More space, perhaps. Those were the only differences I could imagine.

Finding my way to the Lower West Quad, I realized it meant something more than that. It meant cobbles missing from the streets, or the streets not cobbled at all. Narrower streets, missing the wooden side paths. No apparent lantern posts. Buildings going unpainted and falling into some disrepair.

People staring at me and obviously wondering what I was doing there.

A good question, I thought.

Punishments for crimes against Pairs were particularly high, but so were punishments for murder. Didn't stop people killing each other. Perhaps it had been just the tiniest bit stupid to wander into this quad alone. But then, who was I going to ask to accompany me? And I would be damned if I would feel the need for an escort every time I stepped out my door.

I stood a little straighter, glared at the environment in general, and dared anyone to molest me.

I could be a real idiot sometimes.

Especially as I had to ask these people for directions.

The braid on my shoulder didn't convince some people that I wasn't some kind of prostitute, apparently the only kind of woman who would willingly talk to strangers in this area. I had to endure a few offers of employment—which I declined most politely, really—before I found the house I was looking for. It was as rickety as all the others. I was disappointed.

I stared at the door for a few long moments. I could hear no sounds from within. Perhaps there was no one in there.

I almost hoped there wasn't. I really, really didn't want to face this person. He was going to be angry. In pain and resentful and afraid and furious. He was going to yell at me.

It was stupid to be intimidated by the thought of a stranger yelling at me. It was only noise, after all, and could do no harm. But people had rarely yelled at the academy. It was unbecoming in a Shield, though some of my Source professors had indulged in it at times. It had always shocked me and had made me more certain that I would never lapse into such behavior.

I wouldn't find out by standing out there.

I pounded on the door. Got no answer. Pounded again.

"So come in, already!" a voice shouted from within.

I paused for a moment, realizing it was kind of careless to walk into a strange house in a strange place alone. When no one knew where I was. But then, it was kind of careless for him to call someone in when he had no idea who they were. We could be careless together. I went in.

The place screamed bachelor. Clothes tossed everywhere, along with the odd food-encrusted dish. My lip curled in disgust, and I wondered why I was there.

I found him in his bedroom, which was also a mess. He was staring out the window, apparently disinterested in the person invading his home. His leg was encased in a splint, he had a day's worth of stubble on his face, and his hair was sticking up in a thousand different directions. The lines about his eyes told me he was in pain, and there was a small bottle on the table beside the bed he was lying on. The bed was small. Its twin on the other side of the room was hidden under a pile of clothes. "Do you switch from night to night?" I asked him.

He looked at me then, his eyes slightly bloodshot. He seemed surprised to see me, but not, curiously enough, angry. "My brother's out," he said. His voice was a little slurred, perhaps from the medication.

I didn't know what to say. I said the first thing to pop into my head, rarely a good idea. "This place is a sty."

He didn't appear offended. "Are you going to nag?" Not a warning. It sounded more like idle curiosity.

"Just making an observation."

"What did he do to me?"

Following sudden changes in conversation was not my forte. "Who?"

"Your Source."

Ah. "He gave you some wine."

"He did more than that." His head fell back on the pillow. "I hope I don't have to thank him."

My eyebrows rose at that. "Why not?"

"I hate Sources."

My eyebrows couldn't go any higher, so there was no way I could express the increase in my surprise. "You hate Sources?" I'd never heard of such a thing. Why would anyone hate Sources?

"My brother's Source is an ass."

"Your brother's Source." His brother was a Shield? And lived with him?

"Not this brother." The dancer waved a languid hand about the room. "The other one."

"Ah." I didn't think this conversation could get any less intelligent and still contain words.

"Are you lovers?"

"What?"

"You and your Source."

Huh. Blunt. Really, how could anyone look at Karish and then look at me and think we could possibly be lovers? "Of course not." I settled down on the other bed. "That sort of thing is disapproved of in the Triple S." It threw a highly unstable emotional ingredient into an already potentially dangerous mix.

"You'd never know it."

"Your brother sleeps with his Source?"

The dancer looked appalled. "Of course not!"

Interesting. Very. There was a story there, but it clearly wasn't my place to ask. "How's your knee?" There, that didn't sound nearly as apprehensive as I actually felt.

"Shattered," he answered grimly. "The healers say I may walk in time, but I'll always have a limp, and I'll never dance again."

I wanted to look down at my hands, to hide in some way. Instead I stared at him and waited for his anger to come, as it had to. It didn't matter that such was the way of the sport. Everyone knew the risks, but they never expected to suffer from them. If they did, no one would ever dance.

But no words of recrimination came from him. The silence stretched out, and I had to say something to fill it. "How badly will this affect your livelihood?"

"Pretty thoroughly. I'm—I *was*—professional."

I had to look down then. Hell. I knew it. I'd just destroyed this man's life for the sake of a damned hobby. My stomach churned with disgust. What a pathetic waste. What was I going to do? How could I ever compensate him for something like this? "Healers don't know everything," I said feebly.

"They know a hell of a lot more than I do."

"They get things wrong all the time. The stupidest mistakes. My cousin was pregnant, but the local quack thought she just had indigestion until she actually gave birth." So my mother had written to me once.

"I will not dance again," he said firmly. "And I don't blame you."

That was just not natural. "I rather wish you would."

"I'm afraid I can't help you there."

"I can handle being yelled at. Especially when it's for a legitimate reason."

"There is no legitimate reason," he said. "I'm angry, but at myself. It was my foul, not yours." He shrugged. "It's the way of the dance."

He wasn't supposed to make me feel better. I was supposed to grovel before him and take his verbal abuse. Though

I really wasn't very good at either. "You are being freakishly reasonable," I told him.

IIe smiled then, the same charming smile he'd used on me the first day of the Star Festival, and I felt *really* awful then. "I like being unpredictable," he admitted. "It keeps the ladies guessing."

"That's a motive I can appreciate."

"Are you sure that Source isn't your lover?"

What was his obsession with Karish? "Uh, I think I would have noticed."

He held out his hand. "Aiden Kelly."

I shook it. "Dunleavy Mallorough."

Chapter Seven

Because of the increasing frequency of the natural events assaulting High Scape, the Triple S had deemed it necessary to build a small one-room structure on the outskirts of the Upper Eastern Quad, where the Pair standing watch were to . . . well, concentrate on High Scape, I supposed. A bizarre requirement of the position, but its purpose was to prevent the Pair from being so distracted by the wonders of the city that they failed to notice an approaching disaster.

I didn't know how any Source could fail to notice an oncoming event. Certainly, some were quicker at it than others, but no Source let an event become apparent to a regular without channeling it. And I couldn't imagine any kind of distraction that would prevent a Source from feeling the event coming.

The official name for the building was the observation post. McKenna had dubbed it the paranoia stall, which was then shortened to the Stall. It had been designed to keep the Pair suitably bored. A stove, a table with two chairs, no windows. I had the feeling all the books, games, and decks of cards were contraband.

And so, three out of every four days, for seven hours a day, Karish and I sat in the Stall and warded off events. Every shift there were at least two, possibly three events to channel, and while at first I found myself exhausted by the end of a shift, I quickly built up my stamina. It soon got to the point where we could carry on a conversation while we channeled. If we wanted to.

We usually didn't. Not out of any ill feeling. We simply had little to discuss. Karish and I had nothing in common. Really. He liked to play cards and considered drinking alcohol a form of recreation. He loved to watch the races, both horse and dog, and the results were the only part of the news circulars he cared to read. I, on the other hand, read history and poetry, preferred bench dancing over any sport, and couldn't think of anything to say that might be of interest to an aristocrat.

I started bringing Triple S records, stored at the residence, to read while waiting for Karish to channel. I had hoped to find some explanation for the increase in the frequency of events. I was bound for disappointment. The reports were full of speculation, some accusations, some counterarguments, but nothing that could explain anything about what was happening in High Scape, because no one really knew.

All of the Sources had made recent reports claiming the disturbances had been unusual in their execution, but they couldn't really say how. It was just a feeling. One Source claimed to feel some kind of intent in the forces, as though there were a mind directing them. That perception was firmly denied by every other Source. With good reason, I thought. The idea was ridiculous.

During my free time, I explored the city. A task, I thought, that could take the rest of my life. Every new street was another little adventure. Though getting lost, as I frequently did, was frightening, I never suffered for it.

I visited Aiden. A lot. At first, yes, it was primarily an issue of guilt, a sense of duty and responsibility. It quickly became something more. I liked him. It took a big man not to resent the person who did him such an injury, with such far-reaching and permanent results. He had a quick wit I enjoyed. He had traveled a great deal, in his pursuit of dancing purses, and he told excellent stories.

He was not a member of the Triple S. The first regular I had ever known who wasn't family.

And he was my excuse whenever Karish asked me out for a drink after our watch. I spent enough time with Karish. We worked together and lived in the same building. I didn't think it was healthy for partners to spend too much time together. They might start to lose sight of their professional relationship and become overly irritated with each other.

Besides, I heard what Karish got up to in his free time. Drunken debaucheries, for the most part. That wasn't my idea of fun, and I was rather disappointed that he indulged in that sort of thing. However, as he never once appeared for a watch at anything less than his best, it was none of my business, and I didn't speak of it.

Karish didn't like Aiden. I wasn't sure why. True, Aiden had been snarky to him during their brief meeting at the Star Festival, but then Karish hadn't hesitated to help Aiden when he was hurt. I had thought the tension had been forgotten. Yet Karish sneered every time I mentioned Aiden's name.

So I think I could be forgiven when, after declining to join Karish for a drink so I could instead visit with Aiden, I suspected some childish motivation when I felt Karish's inner shields drop in the middle of said visit.

He was channeling. Halfway through a comment to Aiden, I closed my eyes, picturing Karish in my head. This was why I had spent all that time staring at him.

Really.

There was a Pair on duty. There was no reason for him to be doing this.

He was channeling. For the moment it didn't matter why. I would Shield. I would yell at him about it later.

It was more difficult than I'd expected, though. We had slid easily into a pattern of channeling and Shielding during our time in High Scape, and I had felt confident that I knew what to expect. But there was something strange about the power Karish was channeling.

For one thing, I seemed to feel it myself. I didn't simply observe it through him. I could feel it. Me.

For another, it felt . . . sharp. Like it was scraping over me, the teeth of a bread knife not quite weighted enough to hurt. That wasn't normal.

I gasped as a small, sharp pain pierced the back of my left eye. It lodged itself in firmly, grew roots, and expanded. Jagged agony crawling across my brain, cutting in, pushing out, until it threatened to crack my skull open from the inside.

I opened my eyes and found myself staring at my own Shields. Never before had they appeared to me as an image. Thick walls made of solid black bricks. The bricks wanted to slip apart, I could see them shivering in their places, but I held them up with my hands and my mind. That was causing the pain. If I released the bricks, the pain would stop.

Where had the wind come from? Ragged, slicing wind that filled my ears and tore at my throat. I winced.

The bricks were growing heavier, the mortar flaking away. The bricks loosened. I saw one sliding away from its fellows. Through the red haze of pain I glared at it and willed it back into place.

And a part of my mind went black.

More bricks shook and slid, scraping apart piercingly. I grabbed at them and pushed them back. But it was hard to move my hands. They were sluggish and slow, it was like pushing them through water, only there was no water there. My hands were numb; I could not feel. I pushed my hands against the bricks, and they disappeared within them. My throat was raw, my ears shrieked, and I could not see.

What the *hell* was going on?

Another part of my mind darkened, and then another. Panic welled up and was forced back down. More and more bricks trembled, started to fall. I pushed myself to catch them all. I felt my skull cracking under the pressure.

And then it all disappeared.

When I woke, the first thing I became aware of was a headache so intense my nose stung and my stomach heaved. Knowing my head wouldn't survive an action so violent as vomiting, I took careful shallow breaths and kept my stomach under control. My skin crawled. My clothes felt cold and grimy, soaked with sweat. My throat felt like it was stuffed with cotton, cotton filled with broken, rusted razors. And every single muscle I possessed was tied into a thousand little knots.

I opened my eyes. Big mistake. I shut them again.

"She's coming up," said a voice I didn't know.

"I can see that," was the tense response. That was Aiden.

Water hit my forehead. It did not feel good. I let my breath hiss through my teeth.

"What happened?" Aiden demanded.

I presumed he was addressing me. I had no intention of answering, not right then. I was in no shape to be answering questions. I was pretty sure I was supposed to be dead. Though no one ever died while they were channeling anymore. Except when they were really old, or drunk, and didn't have the focus for it.

"Talk to me, Dunleavy!"

Shut up, *Aiden. Can't you see my brain is in danger of exploding?*

"*Talk* to me!"

"Zaire, mate, back off," said the voice I didn't know. A wonderfully sensible woman. "She's not settled back, yet." She wiped more water on my forehead.

I raised a feeble hand. "Please, no," I muttered in a terrible, rasping voice.

"Aye, girl, no worries. Rest for a bit. I'll look out for you."

She had an interesting voice. Oddly clipped consonants and flattened vowels. I wagered she could insult people impressively.

I woke again when someone started poking at me. I could open my eyes without feeling pain, and glare at the man who insisted on pressing my temples. That didn't feel wonderful.

"What are you doing?" I asked in a pathetically weak voice. I sounded like I had a vicious cold. My throat felt that way, too, only worse.

"You collapsed for no reason," he said.

"Who are you?" I asked bluntly.

"Healer Dickens."

"Healer Dickens, there is nothing wrong with me that lemon tea won't fix. Sorry for the wasted trip." Especially since he wasn't going to get paid for it.

"I'm not finished my examination," he said, trying for my temples again.

I blocked his hands and glared at him as hard as I could. "It's a Shield thing." Here's to hoping he didn't really know anything about Shields. It sounded like he didn't. "I need sleep. Please go."

He was offended. Too bad. Whatever had happened, it was nothing he could do anything about. He was willing enough to leave, though. I got the feeling he didn't care for the neighborhood. He lingered a little too long, hoping to be paid and offended all over again when he realized that wasn't going to happen. Then he left, finally.

I really didn't like healers.

"Told you there was no point," a woman—the same one as earlier—said to Aiden. "Right quack, he was."

"Something was wrong with her," Aiden said sullenly.

"Nothing a healer can fix." I sat up slowly. I'd been stretched out on the bed, and though I didn't really want to be going anywhere, I thought I'd better find out what had happened.

"So what was it?" Aiden asked.

"Strange channeling."

"It has to be more than that. You were screaming."

"Aye," the woman said dryly. "I heard you from one street over."

So that's what happened to my throat. Lovely. I must have looked like a lunatic. I had to find Karish and ask him what he'd done. Maybe I'd smack him around a bit, too. I rose to my feet, and my head didn't swim too much.

"Where are you going?" Aiden said sharply.

"Home." And if he wasn't there, to the taverns until I found him.

"Sit back down! You're not going anywhere."

Oh, lord, I was in no condition to be patient. "Sorry to scare you, Aiden. I will come back soon."

He struggled up to his feet. "Lie down, Dunleavy," he tried to order me.

I looked at the woman, who was watching Aiden with amusement. "Dunleavy Mallorough." I offered my hand.

She shook it. "Clair Donner."

"Thank you."

"No worries. Take care."

"I mean it, Dunleavy."

I looked back at him. "Aiden," I said, and that was all I said. It was enough, for he was silent as I left. It appeared he was a smart lad. I liked that in a man.

The streets looked normal. No sign of imminent disaster hastily averted. That, I supposed, was only how it should be, but I felt that a few of the buildings should have fallen down, or that there should be a wild eye or two. Well, a wild eye caused by something other than a stimulant.

Maybe it hadn't been a near disaster at all. Maybe it had been something totally unrelated to what Karish and I were supposed to be doing. Some other secret talent Karish hadn't bothered to tell me about.

I didn't find Karish at the residence. I didn't find anyone else there, either. I did find Karish in a tavern, surrounded by people. The atmosphere was subdued, though. Karish and about four others sat around a table, talking quietly. Only Karish wasn't talking, but staring off into space. He looked a little pale, his eyes a little wild, and his hair was particularly disordered. He saw me as soon as I entered and rose from the table, rushing over to me.

He hugged me, and I was so shocked by it I could neither fend him off nor hug him back. "Are you all right?" he asked when he pulled back, his voice a rusty mess. He put a hand to the side of my face, careful of the temple. He knew where the pain had been. "I went to the residence but you weren't there."

I suddenly felt wonderful. Warm and relaxed, and my throat didn't hurt at all. "What happened?" I asked in a whisper, for the regulars were watching us.

He shrugged, standing back a pace. "It wasn't normal," he said in a low voice. "I didn't know what disaster it was going to be."

He was saving his words, but he'd said enough to alarm me, for of course Sources always knew what kind of disaster was coming. They could just tell.

Karish seemed uncomfortable. He wasn't looking straight at me. He was rubbing the palm of my hand with his thumb. "Are you in pain?" I asked him.

He smiled a little. "Not now." He tugged on my hand. "Come. Sit."

There was no need for that. As he was all right, I would go back to Aiden and reassure him that I wasn't about to keel over. "No, thanks. I'll go home."

He let my hand drop. Every ache and pain came screaming back.

A group of men crowded into the tavern. One glanced our way, eyes lighting on our braids. "You two'd best head over to the Upper Eastern hospital," he said bluntly. I wondered how he knew we had suffered some pain. Did we look that bad? "There's word some of your crew are dead."

We gaped at him, then at each other, and then we ran. Not fun, with the way my head was feeling.

We got to the hospital, where we were instantly recognized for what we were, and we were shown to a cool room in the basement where the bodies of Van Staal, Rundle, South, and Ali were laid out. There wasn't a single mark on any of them, and they were dead. Over the next few hours, the pale and silent bodies of McKenna, Farin, Mao, Arter, Febray, and Heiner were brought in. Ogawa and Tenneson had been brought to the hospital, too, but they weren't dead. They were in a deep sleep and couldn't be roused.

The healers asked us what had happened. All Karish could say was that there had been a strange sort of disaster, which didn't help the healers any. Or us. Because for the moment what had happened didn't really matter. All that was important right then was that the only thing standing between High Scape and its next disaster was us. One novice Pair.

I couldn't help glaring at Karish. I would have never landed in this situation if he weren't my Source. It was starting already. The trials and tribulations of being Paired to a hero. It was a childish thought. And selfish. But it was true.

Chapter Eight

Karish was watching me. It annoyed me. Not that he was watching me, but that I was aware of it. My attention should have been wholly absorbed by the letter in front of me, the letter I hadn't even started writing yet and had to finish as soon as possible. I rubbed the back of my neck, which was aching nicely, and dipped the quill in the ink.

"My lord and lady Mao, it is with deepest regret that I beg leave to inform you . . ."

The event we had helped channel was not a normal occurrence in High Scape. Obviously, as the Pairs in High Scape didn't have a habit of dying due to channeling. Karish said he'd had to channel it, even though we weren't on duty, for it had felt as though the forces were aimed right at him, and he'd had to react almost in self-defense. He had then refused to elaborate on what he meant in making that claim. Natural disasters didn't have minds of their own; they didn't attack people. They just happened.

As the only functioning Pair left in High Scape, Karish and I were on duty constantly until other Pairs arrived in High Scape to relieve us. So we had to stay together all the time. We didn't go to the Stall, which was too small to actually live in for any length of time, but we also never left the Triple S residence.

". . . while in the line of duty . . ."

It had been a hellish two days. "Seeing to the others," and all that entailed. Mostly contacting everyone in High Scape who knew them, arranging to have their belongings collected, arranging interment procedures. I'd sent messages to the nearest sites begging any Pairs who could be spared to come to High Scape. Karish and I had written reports describing what had happened, to be sent to Shidonee's Gap.

"I did not know your son well but . . ."

I was writing letters of condolence to all the next of kin. Each letter took forever, as I struggled to put something personal into missives about people I barely knew, to people I had never met. I had been taught how to write such letters at the academy, formal phrases that were probably offensive to read, phrases that I'd always sworn never to use. That was why it took so long.

". . . kind to me from our first meeting, always ready with a warm smile and sensible advice . . ."

This was the job of the veteran Shield of the site. That was what I was, until Ogawa and Tenneson woke up. Less than two months out of the academy, and I was a veteran. What a horrible joke.

I jumped at the touch of hands on my shoulders. I smudged some of the ink on the paper. I glared up at Karish, even as a wave of warmth flooded through me, easing out the pains I still carried from that horrible channeling.

He ignored the look. "Take a break, Lee." His voice was still a little rough. "You haven't stopped since the Rush."

That was what he'd called it. That was what it had felt like to him, an overwhelming rush of power that, he'd said, almost drowned him. "I have to finish these," I said, and my voice wouldn't have won any prizes, either.

"Not tonight."

"As soon as possible. They have the right to know as soon as possible." It was the very least I could do, after all that had happened. "Before they start hearing rumors."

He released my shoulders and knelt beside my chair. The aches and pains came rushing back. "Granted," he said, and it took me a moment to remember in response to what. "But it's not a priority right now. We're the only Pair left, Lee. We need our minds to be clear and alert. How well could you Shield right now?"

I sighed and rubbed my tired eyes. The truth was that I really didn't want to think about Shielding again. It hadn't been much fun the last time.

"You know I'm right."

Of course I knew he was right. My brain was numb, and a headache was humming at the base of my skull. But I was afraid of stopping. I knew once I stopped it would be very hard to start up again. Unpleasant jobs were best done quickly, with no pauses.

He rubbed my arm, a light and soothing touch. I was tired, and the returning flood of warmth was pleasant, so I didn't snap at him. Because I was tired and it had nothing to do with what I was supposed to be doing, my mind wandered as it had an evil tendency to do, and the realization came to me that Karish had dropped the flirtatious manner—with me, at least—ages ago, yet he still had a tendency to touch me when I stood too close, or when he wanted my attention. As he did with everyone. That had been my second realization. He seemed to touch all people a lot, and not even Lord Shintaro Karish could want to sleep with *everyone*.

Besides, it felt good.

"I have to finish these," I repeated firmly, only to have my stomach growl. Loudly.

Karish didn't laugh, but I could feel he was amused. "Dinner's ready," he said. "Eat and sleep. I'll help you with the letters after."

"You will not," I said with asperity. "It's my duty."

"I know how to write," he answered sharply.

"What has that to do with anything?" His response was to rise to his feet and pull me to mine by the shoulders. "Karish!"

"I'm aware you'll be breaking some rule of yours by eating with me," he said coolly. "But for the horseshoe nail, and all, eh?"

Ben was too busy packing up the belongings of the slain Pairs to see to Karish and me right then. Karish and I were doing for ourselves, which meant little in the way of cooking.

We ate a quick meal of bread, fruit, cheese, and cold meat. I didn't think I could manage more, anyway.

Inevitably, upon eating I became exhausted, my eyes and head filling with sand. I was suddenly so tired I could easily be persuaded to just put my head down on the table and go to sleep.

Karish narrowed his eyes at me. "Are you all right?"

"Certainly."

"Would you tell me if you weren't?"

"Certainly."

"Well, you look awful. Go to bed."

I sighed. I really didn't think I could face those letters and do them justice. And if there were another disaster I would be useless and kill us both. So yes, it was time to get some sleep.

"I will clean," said Karish, taking my plate before I could pick it up.

"You're being too nice, and I don't like it," I said bluntly.

"That's not the reason I'm doing it," he said, deadpan. "Though it is an added benefit."

I couldn't hold back my smile. The sentiment was one I'd had so often it was almost frightening to hear it coming from Karish. But it didn't show either of us in a mature light, that we did things simply to annoy the other partner. That was something I would have to think about. Later.

I didn't sleep as deeply as my exhaustion had led me to expect. I ended up tossing quite a bit, my head filled with strange dreams. Karish played a role, which was annoying but understandable. The strange thing was that Stevan Creol made an appearance, too, and I hadn't even thought of him since I was Chosen. When I woke, any coherence or plot the dreams might have had crumbled away. I hated it when that happened. It made me feel like I'd left something unfinished.

I got out of bed, changed my clothes, and left the room, making some effort to be quiet. It was morning, but early. No reason to wake Karish.

Who was at the table I'd been occupying the night before, writing letters. My mouth tightened, but I decided not to say anything. It was my duty, not his, but if he was so damned determined to write letters, there was no reason not to let him. Maybe it was part of his way of dealing with what had happened. If so, it would be petty of me to snipe at him for it, though I really didn't like him interfering with my work. "Have you been up long?" I asked him, and my voice was calm.

He looked up from his letter, rubbing the back of his neck. "A couple of hours."

Did the man never sleep? "Would you like something to drink?"

"Tea would be good," he said. "Then you can look these over."

"You said you could write." And this was apparently an issue with him. "I believe you." I went to the kitchen.

I found the water kettle. I had so far learned to boil water and to brew tea and coffee. I could make toast, too. I was very proud of myself.

"No," said Karish, from the doorway. What was the point of me offering to fetch him a drink if he was going to get up anyway? "I looked at your letters, to see what you were doing. You're really good at it."

"It's my job," I said, trying not to sound irritated.

He laughed softly. "Just because someone has a job to do, it doesn't mean they do it well."

No, but the way he complimented me on what I could do, it was like he didn't expect me to be able to do it as well as I could. It was as though he expected me to be incompetent. So I pumped water into the kettle and put it on the stove and said nothing.

I reviewed the letters. The phrasing was a little disjointed, but he gave the awful news gently, with no hint that it was only duty that had killed these people and so nothing to fret over, and not a trace of aristocratic hauteur. He didn't use his title in his signature, but the families probably knew exactly who Source Shintaro Karish was and would find some small—minuscule—comfort in knowing he had taken the trouble to write. "They're good," I told him.

"Are you sure?"

I had the feeling he was interested less in being stroked and more in making sure the families would receive appropriate letters, and that impressed me. "Aye, they're well done."

He nodded. "That's all of them, then."

That was one unpleasant job finished. I was happy enough

not to have to write any more of those letters. "Thank you."
He shouldn't have done it, but I was grateful for his contribution. This one time.

Karish made breakfast. For himself, for when I didn't sleep well I usually lost my appetite. Besides, the very idea of eating hot rice, especially in the morning, made me nauseous.

All the chores were done. There were no more reports or letters to write. I had nothing to do, and I wasn't the right kind of tired for sleeping. I went to one of the sofas in the living room and hugged an extra cushion as I stared up at the ceiling.

Karish brought his food to the living room. More sociable and more polite, I supposed, but I'd have rather he stayed in the kitchen or the dining room. My mind felt numb, and I really wasn't in the mood for conversation.

"Sure you don't want any?" he asked, holding up a spoonful of rice.

My stomach twisted a little. "Rice is a dessert," I announced. "It is not a breakfast dish."

"Peasant."

Freak. I waved a hand at the ceiling. "We've got cracks."

"Hm?"

I pointed, and he looked up. "Maybe I can plaster it."

I looked at him. "I am not buying that one, Karish," I declared. "No way can Lord Shintaro Karish do handy work."

He had been sipping at his tea. He set the mug on the table beside him with a sharp smack of pottery hitting wood. "My name," he said, with sudden irritation, "is Taro. Why the hell is that so hard for you to say?"

My eyebrows rose before I could prevent it. "And why does that bother you so much?" I asked him. "Shields call people by their family names. It's what we do."

"You call Aiden by his first name," he reminded me irritably.

That was not an appropriate comparison. "He's not Triple S."

"How is that relevant?"

It just was. I'd been addressed by my family name from my first day at the academy. I called all my friends, lovers, and professors by their family names, with few exceptions. Regulars, however, followed different codes of behavior that we were encouraged to adopt when we interacted with them, so I was more likely to address a regular by his or her personal

name when their manners demanded it. But everyone within the
Triple S expected a Shield to use family names. "It's tradition."

"It's rude."

"No one else thinks so. You're the first Source I've ever
met who's had a problem with it."

He stirred the rice with his spoon. "People address servants
by their family names," he said in a tight voice.

I cocked a brow at him. "Surely you're not accusing me of
treating you like a servant?" Because that was ridiculous.

He ignored that. "No one likes servants, you know," he
said. "Those who can afford them consider them a necessary
evil. Because they feel it's almost impossible to get good help,
and when you offer these people a good position the ungrateful little wretches only take off on a whim. So you can't afford
to feel anything for them, not respect and certainly not anything like affection, because they come and go so quickly."

My family had servants, and they addressed them all by
their family names. That was tradition. "As far as I know," I
said carefully, as I didn't really know where he was going
with this, "the servants prefer being addressed by their family
names. It maintains a distance they're comfortable with."

"Aye, distance," he said. "And Zaire knows, Shields must
maintain their distance. Always hide behind the family name.
Always walk a couple of steps behind. Never talk any more
than you absolutely have to."

Here we were. Back to the fact that I didn't worship Karish. Though I was aware that he no longer wanted me to lust
after him, if that was what he'd ever wanted, I did understand
that I didn't treat him as he would like, and as he thought he
deserved to be treated. "What did you expect from your Shield
before we were bonded, Kar—Shintaro?"

He made a derisive sound. "I knew exactly what to expect," he said bitterly. "Pairs would come to the academy, to
tell us what real life was like."

I nodded. We'd had the same at the Shield academy.

"The Shields always had this blank expression on their
faces, and used these flat tones when they spoke. At first, I
thought it was because they didn't feel anything, but later I
realized it was merely that they didn't want to express what
they were thinking, and that was worse. Sometimes a Source

would say or do something the Shield didn't approve of, and I could tell the Shield thought the Source was an idiot. One Shield thought no one was looking at him, and he rolled his eyes, something you do, too. But whenever the Source looked at him, there was that blank face and that flat tone again, and the Source probably had no idea what his Shield really thought of him."

"Of course he did," I objected, but without undue force, as Karish clearly thought he had a genuine grievance. "Not even a Shield can control all of her expressions and all of her feelings all the time."

"Maybe you're right," Karish agreed sourly. "You certainly made no secret of what you thought about me."

I let that go, because he was right, and I was ashamed of it. I'd thought Karish nothing more than dandelion fluff, and even if it were true, I shouldn't have let him see it.

"The Sources always spoke first, but they never had much to say that wasn't directly related to channeling. After they made their little speech they stood back while the Shields told us all about the various sites, and what kind of record-keeping needed to be done, and how to deal with other Pairs. Not that we had to worry about that much." His eyes glittered. "Because, of course, our Shields would deal with that. And we would have to requisition our own supplies and arrange for our accommodations, and sometimes merchants and landlords weren't all that happy to deal with us because we didn't have to pay them, but we weren't to worry about it, because our Shields would deal with that. And sometimes we expressed ourselves in a manner that confused and even offended regulars, but we didn't need to worry about it. Our Shields would handle any problem we caused."

It was true we were supposed to smooth any ruffled feathers, but the Sources weren't really supposed to be aware that that was what we were doing. Or so I'd always been taught.

"We were expected to guard our Shields if there was music playing, at parties and festivals and such, but we were assured we probably wouldn't be stuck with that duty very often. Our Shields would do their best to get their friends or lovers to take over that responsibility." He picked up the spoon and tapped it against his lips.

"All any of that means is that your time is considered too valuable to waste on such trivial chores. How can you possibly complain about that?"

He looked disgusted. "We're not too valuable. We're too incompetent. To ask for directions or write a letter. Run along and play, Karish, I have work to do."

"I have never said that."

"You don't have to. Your whole attitude reeks of it."

All right. This was getting us nowhere. He was just venting. There was nothing I could say in response, nothing that would appease him. So I supposed I would just let him rant on and hope he calmed down sometime soon.

His eyes narrowed. Not at me. He wasn't focused on me anymore. I felt the internal shifts within him, and I knew it was happening again. I barely had time to raise my Shields before it hit.

The pain was different this time. It didn't penetrate the back of my eye and expand. It splashed against my face, against my arms, chest, back, and arms. All over. It sank through my skin like hot acid and seeped into my blood, yellow poison running through my veins and pumping through my heart.

It was water, rushing, driving, crushing. I pushed at it with my hands, and it gushed through my fingers, eating at my flesh. I collected my thoughts and threw them at the water, leaning against it, pressing against it, holding it in place.

I had no idea how I did that. I had no time to wonder about it.

I could feel the forces slashing at Karish's mind. They weren't supposed to do that. His heart was beating too fast. I couldn't slow it down enough.

The yellow poison gurgled up into my throat, scalding me. I couldn't breathe.

It wanted to crush Karish. I could feel it. It wanted to wrap around him, swirling poison, to strip his skin and burn his blood and melt his bones with its corrosive touch. I held the water back from him, though the effort made my mind scream.

I couldn't breathe.

I couldn't hold it. The water kept shifting, rolling toward Karish. I reached out with my bleeding mind and pushed it back.

I couldn't breathe.

But I could feel, and this was ticking me off. It wasn't supposed to be like this. We were just novices, and we weren't supposed to have to deal with this sort of thing yet. Ever.

There was anger radiating from elsewhere, too. From Karish, I could feel it. And from somewhere else not immediately obvious, and I was in no condition to think it through. I gathered up the anger and threw it against the water.

I wasn't supposed to be able to do that.

The water moved back. I shoved at it again, and it gave again.

I felt surprise. It was not my own. It wasn't Karish's. But I dragged it in with the anger and threw that against the water, too.

Perhaps I was simply going mad.

The water sank away. Disappeared. I collapsed. It was over.

I could feel the floor against my cheek. It was hard and too hot. My head rang with such sharp agony it brought tears to my eyes. Retching was a serious risk. Breathe lightly.

I felt like my skull was going to splinter into a million pieces.

I heard a groan. "I feel terrible." Karish's voice was gone again. And he'd had such a lovely tenor. "What did you do?"

What did *I* do? I hadn't done anything. Except my job. Someone else was responsible for that nightmare of an experience. But answering was completely beyond my abilities right then. Instead I willed the room to stop spinning. The room was being stubborn.

"Lee?"

Shut up, Karish. I mean, I'm not dead. If I were, you would be, too. So leave me alone.

"Lee!"

Weak but insistent. *Bastard.* "Here," I croaked, and that was all he was getting out of me.

He didn't say anything after that. I supposed he'd just wanted to make sure my brains were still functioning. It wasn't enough that I was alive. I had to be in my right mind, too. And who said aristocrats weren't demanding?

If there was another disturbance, we were dead. I could not Shield again, not soon. Maybe not ever. I wasn't sure I could keep my brains together through another such episode. I still wasn't sure all my brains had survived the last one.

In time I could move, though my body wasn't thrilled about it. I moved from the floor to the sofa I had fallen off of, which was all the progress I was going to demand from myself right then. Karish was much more ambitious, moving from the floor by the table to the sofa. He sat beside me and without the slightest hesitation or diffidence wrapped his arms around me and pulled me close, and I bonelessly complied. Pain eased, muscles loosened, and the beating of his heart helped to drive disturbing images from my mind. For the moment not giving a damn about how it looked or whether it was a bad idea, I curled around him and flattened my palm against his chest so I could feel the blood pulsing through him.

I fell asleep with Karish's arms wrapped tight around me and his face buried in my hair. It was the deepest sleep I'd ever had. Later I learned Karish had slept, too, just as dreamlessly. The residents of High Scape never knew how precarious their position was during those hours. Ignorance is bliss.

Chapter Nine

One week later, and we had a nearly full roster once more. Four Pairs had been pulled in from other sites and off the circuit, a temporary measure until the Triple S could make more permanent arrangements. Another Pair was on the way.

If Ogawa and Tenneson didn't wake soon, a final Pair would be summoned to replace them. I visited them in the hospital every day and felt guilty for having come through the Rushes unharmed.

In the week since the second Rush, High Scape had been calm, and our minds and throats had been given time to heal. But the memories weren't fading at all. I was even suffering nightmares. I never had nightmares.

But at least life was back to some kind of order. Watches in the Stall were longer and more frequent, but at least they were defined watches. The events that Karish channeled were more natural, and I stopped wanting to wince every time I felt his protections go down.

I visited Aiden almost daily. He made me laugh. He told marvelous stories. He was a wonderful distraction from my work.

It was only a little more than a week after the second Rush that I knocked on Aiden's door and was not called to come in, and was not greeted by Aiden's brother, Piers. I knocked on the door again, and a long time later, it was opened by Aiden himself.

I stared at him. He was pale and sweating and trembling. He was leaning heavily on a crutch. His left leg hung crookedly and obviously uncomfortably. "Are you insane?" I demanded.

"I'm tired of being in bed," he panted.

"Keep up this idiocy and you'll consign yourself to it for life."

"Don't nag."

I shrugged. "Hey, it's your leg. Are you going to let me in or what?"

He shuffled back with some difficulty, and I eased into the house, closing the door behind me. I watched him anxiously, restraining myself from offering to help him to a chair, but only just. It infuriated me that Aiden would risk crippling himself for the sake of—what? Pride? Men were so stupid.

I sat in one chair and watched him settle into another. It looked like a painful process, but I didn't make a single sound of sympathy. When he was finally seated, the crutch leaning against the wall behind him, I said, "Aren't you going to offer to get me something to drink?"

He glowered at me.

Sometimes I was so funny I couldn't stand myself.

I left my chair and headed for the kitchen to make some tea. "When did this particular brand of insanity start?" I asked, hunting for tea leaves.

"Yesterday," Aiden called from the living room.

"Are you sure it's a good idea?"

"I'll find out."

Aye, I supposed he would. I guessed I wouldn't feel guilty if he couldn't dance again, after all. He had to be doing at least as much damage to his leg as I had.

"Tell me something," he said.

"Perhaps."

"Do you like being a Shield?"

I was surprised by the unexpected question. No one had ever asked it of me before. I had certainly never thought of it myself. "Of course," I answered.

I heard him laugh. "Like there could be no doubt about it."

I felt my eyebrows draw together and intentionally smoothed them out. "Why should there be?"

"I just can't see you being content to be Karish's servant."

Ah. That. "I'm not Karish's servant."

"Aye, you are."

How irritating. "I thought Ryan had told you all about being a Shield." Ryan was the brother who was a Shield.

A snort from Aiden. "He's been complaining about it for years. I never really believed any of it, though, until I met you and Karish. I can't believe all the refuse you take from him."

I had to leave the kitchen then, so I could look at his face as he spewed all this nonsense. I leaned against the doorframe, arms crossed. "You met him once," I reminded him.

"Aye, and a proper lord of the manor he was, too. If he's like that in public, I can just imagine what he's like when you're alone. Always giving you orders."

"Karish doesn't give me orders."

"I don't expect you to admit it," Aiden said, generously relieving me of the responsibility of confessing. "I know he'd punish you if you told us what he's really like."

I stared at him. "What has your brother been telling you?"

"Nothing but the truth, it seems to me."

"Somehow I doubt it. Karish never tells me what to do."

"He doesn't have to, does he? You're trained to anticipate his needs. You're trained to do what he wants before he even has to ask you. You think you're acting independently, from your own initiative, but it's all training."

This conversation was getting boring. It always irritated me when people rambled on about subjects they knew nothing about.

"Sometimes I wonder how thorough the training is," Aiden muttered.

I was speechless. He was jealous. I couldn't believe it. It was ludicrous on so many different levels. Karish had the whole city to choose from. There was no reason for him to risk his partnership by sleeping with me. That had to be obvious to anyone of even the meanest intelligence. But nothing else could explain Aiden's bizarre behavior.

"I remember Karish from the night we danced, Dunleavy.

He was a little too possessive of you for someone who is just a disinterested Source."

"He felt he had something to prove that night. I'd accused him of being irresponsible." I didn't know why I was bothering to answer, though. My words weren't having the least impact on him. I could tell.

"I know what he looks like, Dunleavy. And I've heard what he is. Are you seriously trying to tell me you don't feel the slightest bit attracted to him?"

Not the slightest bit attracted? What was I, dead? And if he tried to tell me he wasn't attracted to almost every good-looking woman he saw I'd call him a liar. But right then wasn't the time to mention reality. It was a moment when I had to pick my truths carefully. "I've never considered Karish a possible sexual partner," I said. "We're taught having sexual relations within a Pair is a bad idea, and I've always believed in that. To me, the Source is out of bounds. It would be like suggesting I sleep with one of my brothers." Well, maybe that was pushing it a little. "I mean, I can look at him and admire the scenery, but it doesn't mean anything. I don't feel anything."

"Aye, I buy that," he said sarcastically.

One . . . two . . . three . . . I shrugged. "I can only tell you what is. I can't help what you believe."

He didn't look convinced, and right then I didn't care. It was none of his business, anyway.

"Tell me something, Dunleavy."

Must I?

"If you'd had the power to Choose freely, would you have Chosen Karish?"

"No," I answered promptly, no careful honesty required. "I had my eye on Katherine Devereaux." It was the first time I had thought of her in what felt like a long time. I wondered what she and her lucky Shield were up to. "My life would be so much easier if she were my Source."

"Is Karish so difficult, then?" Aiden asked eagerly.

"No," I said slowly. "It's just that who he is creates circumstances I would rather not have to deal with."

"Do you like him?"

I had to think about that. Did I like him? Would I spend time with him if I weren't bonded to him?

Yes. I would. If I didn't have to work with him, I had no doubt I would be thrilled to be one of his adoring fanatics. I liked looking at him. He could be witty when he chose to be. And I would probably fall in love with him from a nice safe distance. But Aiden really didn't need to know that. "He is a better man than I had thought he would be, when we first met."

It appeared Aiden was struggling with whether he should be satisfied with that or not. He settled with saying, "Ryan despises his Source."

I went back to the kitchen and poured the tea. "That happens sometimes."

"And you think that's all right, forcing someone to work with someone they despise?"

I mixed milk and sugar into the tea. "We have a rare ability that's more important than personal differences."

"Ah," he said mockingly. "How noble."

I carried the two mugs of tea into the living room. "Why are you trying to pick a fight with me?" I asked plaintively, giving him his tea before settling into my chair.

"I'm not picking a fight. I'm pointing something out."

"This must be my day to be stupid. What are you trying to point out?"

"That you're packed up and sent away from your family at a very tender age—"

"Boarding children at school is a common practice among the merchant and High Landed classes," I told him. "My sister and brothers boarded, too."

He wasn't in the mood to be enlightened. He glared at me for interrupting him. "Away from your family's eye you're trained in the beliefs of the Triple S and trained to live up to them. You're isolated from normal society for years—"

Isolated? *Normal?* That was open to debate.

"And then you're matched up with some high-and-mighty Source who has complete power over you."

Zaire give me patience. "You're being ridiculous. You make it sound like some nefarious conspiracy to enslave us or something."

"Isn't it?" he demanded. "I mean, you go to the academies to be trained, right? But why do you need to be trained? Everything you do is by instinct. You just do what comes naturally, what you'd do if you had no training at all."

"Listen to two singers, equally talented but one with training and the other without. The difference is obvious."

"For that difference you have to suffer through years of isolation?"

The problem with Aiden's skills as a storyteller was that he sometimes spoke too melodramatically in ordinary conversation. "Leave it alone, Aiden."

"I can't. That's what this is all about. Your minds are warped for the benefit of the Triple S, and most of you don't even know it."

"But Ryan does."

"Him and a few others."

"Where is he posted, by the way?" I asked to change the subject. "You've never said."

"Middle Reach."

Ah. Light strikes. Middle Reach was a miserable little town out in the middle of nowhere, economically and politically and artistically if not geographically. It was once a thriving community, but the same upheavals that had given High Scape its waterways had deprived Middle Reach of its own. A nearly cold site requiring little talent to keep stable. So it was one of the dumping grounds for criminal or incompetent Pairs. Either Ryan or his partner had done something to earn that exile. From the sounds of things, the Source was responsible, which would certainly explain Ryan's bitterness.

Aiden was looking at me, a dangerous glint in his eyes, daring me to say something disparaging about his brother. Well, I generally didn't take dares. I sipped at my tea and gazed back at him. No accusations here. I was not going to help him start a fight, no matter how much he was itching for one.

"I just don't like seeing you being taken advantage of," he said.

"Why don't you let me worry about that?"

"But you're not worrying about it. You're just taking it, accepting it as natural." His face assumed an expression of pity.

"But it's not your fault. Your mind has been forced to think that way."

All right. That was enough. I'd come for some amusement and light conversation, and instead I was enduring an interrogation. And I was being pitied for being feebleminded. I set my mug on the table. "I'm going now." I rose to my feet.

"Dunleavy, no." He tried to rise as well but couldn't manage it so quickly. "Don't take it like this."

Like what? I wasn't storming off in a huff. I was perfectly calm. But there was no reason for me to sit there and listen to him attack everything I believed in, then have him finish off the tirade with the reassurance that I wasn't to be held responsible for my faith as I was a naive, ignorant child. "I only came in to say hello. I have to be somewhere."

"With Karish?" Aiden asked coolly.

Men. Bah. "Have a good day, Aiden." I bowed to him, and wondered where I'd picked that habit up. I never bowed. Then I left.

Chapter Ten

Upon leaving Aiden I went to the hospital to visit Ogawa and Tenneson, as I was in the perfect mood to be around vulnerable people. I didn't know how the healers were keeping them alive, but I had the feeling it wasn't going to be working for much longer. They were both getting so thin.

I sat beside Ogawa's bed. I looked at her slack face, and I felt furious.

Ogawa was dying, and I was just letting it happen. She'd seemed a sensible, steady person. I'd liked her. It was ridiculous that she was dying because of some strange natural disaster that hadn't been natural at all.

"Wake up, Ogawa," I ordered crisply. "You've had your little vacation. It's time to go back to work." Nothing. Not so much as a flicker of the eyelids. Well, no kidding. I leaned forward in the chair, taking up one of her hands. "Come on, Ogawa," I said in a softer voice. "It's time to come back. I need you. I haven't got many friends here." I hadn't really had a chance to get to know any of the new Pairs yet. Some of them sort of intimidated me. And Karish and Aiden didn't count, though for different reasons. "I'm starting to get bored."

I thought it was rather too Shield of her to refuse to respond to that heartfelt plea.

I sat back on my seat, defeated. Well, what had I been expecting? That she would open her eyes and jump out of bed simply because I'd told her to?

I wasn't a healer. I hadn't a clue about how the body worked. I didn't even know what was wrong with Ogawa, not really. The healers seemed to feel they couldn't lower the explanation to a level I could understand. Maybe they were right, but it was frustrating.

Sometimes an idea hit you so hard it almost hurt.

Pain plus unnatural things equaled Karish.

I dashed out of there, collecting protests from the medical staff. What did that matter? I was on a mission. So inspired, I ran all the way to the Triple S residence.

I ran through the entrance. At the foot of the stairs I came to an abrupt halt. Someone was having a party, a loud one. The music was being played expertly and at high volume. Fiddle, flute, and two drums. Immediately the little shocks began to skitter over my skin and through my muscles.

Of course someone was having a party. I bet I knew who, too. It was just that kind of day. I grit my teeth and mounted the stairs.

The music grew louder as I climbed. My heartbeat quickened to match the pounding drums. I gripped the handrail. Hold on to something and don't let go. But I had to let go to keep climbing, and despite myself my pace increased until I was practically running up the stairs.

The noise was coming from Karish's suite. Of course it was. A dozen different impulses converged on me at once. I needed to talk to Karish about Ogawa and Tenneson. I wanted to run back down the stairs to safety. And I wanted to dance. The music was of a particularly driving nature, and I felt deliciously uncomfortable.

Think about Ogawa and Tenneson. They are wasting away in hospital beds. Hold on to that thought and don't let go. One deep breath. Good girl. Now knock.

The door was opened, music blared out, and I was pulled into a whirlwind.

I didn't know the laughing man who had me by the waist,

spinning me around the room. He was a good dancer, and he had nice broad shoulders. Big hands. I liked him immediately.

Colors and laughter and music flashed around me, filling me and freeing me. I laughed, too, I couldn't help it, and I danced. It felt so good, working my muscles, listening to real music, enjoying a hard, masculine body against my own.

Then that hard masculine body was pressing into me a little more forcefully than dancing normally required, and there was something solid and ungiving at my back. It still felt good—it felt wonderful, in fact—but something in my brain woke up again. When the man kissed me I was an enthusiastic partner, but then the image of Ogawa flashed behind my eyes.

I jerked my head free. "No!" I gasped. "I have to talk to Karish."

"Taro's occupied right now, darlin'," the man drawled. "But don't you worry. I'll take care of you." He leaned down to kiss me again.

But I once more had a thought to hold on to. I twisted my head away. "No," I said, much more firmly. "I need to speak to Karish." I raised my voice. "Stop the music, please!"

The music stopped. So did the dancing. The sudden stillness was almost as dizzying as the chaos had been. Not so dizzying that I wasn't aware that everyone was staring at us. Lovely.

And then Karish was charging in, and in my current condition the way his shirt hugged his chest and stomach was just too distracting. "What the hell is going on?" Karish demanded, very much the lord of the manor ordering an accounting. He raised his eyebrows at the sight of me. "Lee? What are you doing here?"

So now I had to apologize. This day just kept getting better and better. I found myself licking my lips and wanted to cringe with embarrassment. "I'm really sorry about this disturbance, Shintaro." Hell, was that breathy voice mine? "I felt I had to talk to you, and I didn't think it could wait until tomorrow." I rubbed my arms once, then stopped myself.

"Well, all right, but what's with this?" He gestured at my dance partner.

"Linc assaulted her," a bystander said.

Two of us objected to that. "It was the music, Shintaro."

"She jumped right into it!"

Karish looked at me with too much concern. "Are you all right, Lee?" he asked, reaching out to touch me.

I flipped my hair off my shoulder, making the evasion of his hand look accidental. I hoped. I was a little off balance and I needed a bath, but aside from that I was, "Quite all right, thank you."

He studied me for a moment longer, for of course I didn't know my own mind about such things. Then he nodded and looked at Linc. His expression wasn't friendly.

"Really, Shintaro, it wasn't his fault. Can we go somewhere to talk?"

"You're wearing your braid," he said, without removing his gaze from Linc.

"Aye." Of course. I always did.

"Everyone knows what the braid means."

Linc was looking down at Karish, obviously annoyed with the melodrama. "She's at a party. One of yours. Why did she come here if she doesn't want to cut loose?"

There was a certain logic to that. And really, I had gone along with it. It was my fault for insisting on climbing up the stairs once I heard what was going on. I should have stayed away. And now I had disrupted Karish's evening, and everyone was staring at us, and I just wanted to sink through the floor. "He stopped as soon as I told him to," I said to Karish, which was only a little bit of a lie. No harm done, and there were more important things to worry about. "Please, Shintaro. It's Triple S business."

One more long look at Linc, and then at me, and Karish shed the aristocratic hauteur like a cloak that had gone out of style. "Michael, my love," he said, all cheer. "If you could freshen everyone's drinks"—he was momentarily interrupted by loud sounds of appreciation from his guests—"I will be your slave forever. And my lord and lady musicians, it might be a good idea if you played a few of the milder selections from your repertoire. I think everyone's a little overheated right now." That brought good-natured shouts of denial from his guests, but not one protested. They settled into conversation, two or three people shifting about the room pouring liquid into goblets. The music started up again, light and soothing.

I wanted to crawl into a hole, to disappear. I had ruined Karish's evening, and that of his guests. The reason was valid, but I really wished it had happened differently.

Karish touched my arm. The brief contact sent an almost painful jolt through my whole body. Still a tad sensitive from the earlier music. "Come to my room," said Karish. "We can talk there."

I felt a little alarmed as I followed him. He hadn't been "occupied" in his bedroom, had he? He wasn't going to kick someone out of bed, was he? That would just be too much. But he was fully—and neatly—dressed, and he didn't seem frustrated or annoyed. When we entered his room I saw that the bed was made, and I relaxed. At least something was going right.

I sat on the end of the bed, as there was nowhere else in the room to sit. Karish sat beside me, just a little closer than I found comfortable. He started to rub my arm. I knew the touch was meant to reassure me, but I had to jerk away. "Please don't touch me!" I said, much more sharply than I'd intended. He frowned, and I hastened to explain. "I'm sorry, it's not you. I'm just a little . . ." What? Heated from the music and the dancing? I wasn't going to say that to him.

He drew back a little. "I thought you had plans with Kelly, or I would have invited you here."

I almost laughed at that, though I didn't find it at all funny. He thought I was upset because he hadn't invited me to his party? Did he really think I was that petty? Of course he wouldn't invite me to such an affair. He'd have had to spend the whole of it watching me. A guaranteed method of sucking all the fun out of it for him. "I was at the hospital."

"How are they?" he asked promptly, meaning Ogawa and Tenneson.

"That's what I want to talk to you about." Time to shake off the effects of everything distressing that had happened that day and get down to what really mattered. "Do you remember what you did for Aiden after that bench dancing competition?"

He shrugged. He never liked talking about it.

"Do you think you could do the same thing for Ogawa and Tenneson?"

"I don't understand."

"You know. Heal them."

"I can't heal people, Lee."

"You healed Aiden."

He took one of my hands, and I had no natural way to avoid it and look like I wasn't trying to avoid it. If he noticed the slight resistance I put up, he ignored it. He stroked the side of my hand. "I took away some of his pain for a moment, that's all. I didn't heal him. He didn't walk away from that dance."

Normally guilt would have made me tense up a little, but Karish's attention to my hand was making me relax whether I liked it or not. "Maybe not," I said in an even voice, "But he's walking now."

He looked up swiftly. "Surely it's too soon for that."

"That's what I thought, but today he met me at the door. He was using a crutch, and he wasn't too graceful, but he was upright."

He thought about that for a moment, then dismissed the idea with a shrug. "So maybe it's not too soon. What do I know? I'm not a healer."

"So maybe you can't understand the full impact of what you do," I pointed out. "Maybe you did heal him, at least a little, and you just didn't realize it."

"And maybe you're letting your concern for Miho and Val cloud your judgment, though the gods may strike me down for such blasphemy."

I felt no need to make my resistance subtle then, and I pulled on my hand. Unfortunately, he felt no need to ignore my resistance then, and he held on. "What are you doing?" I demanded.

"Your evening has been something less than fine," he said. "You went from visiting Miho and Val in hospital to coming here and being assaulted by one of my guests, and I am truly sorry."

"None of it is your responsibility."

"All that happens in my home is my responsibility," he announced grandly. "And I can make you feel better. And there is no one here to see you being less than stoic, so relax."

No, no one to see, but everyone knew where we were, and

I could just imagine what they were thinking. But I'd known that was how it would be, so there was no point in getting upset about it even if I were so inclined. Which I wasn't. "Will you come to the hospital?"

"There's nothing I can do for them, Lee."

"How do you know unless you try?"

"Why don't you go and heal them?" he challenged me.

That was just stupid. "I can't heal them."

"Exactly what *I* said."

How irritating. "I didn't help Aiden, either." No, I'd crippled him. "You obviously can do something that other Sources can't."

"A minor thing. I don't heal damage."

"As far as you know," I reminded him. "Maybe you can do something more if you put your mind to it. And even if you can't, well, it can't hurt to try."

He sighed. "I'll take a look at them," he said reluctantly, "But I really have no idea what I can do. I'm not promising anything."

Relief. "Good. Great. That's all I'm asking." I rose to my feet, eager to be off. To be honest, I wasn't really all that confident that Karish could do anything, either. The idea that he could use his skills as a Source to heal was really rather ridiculous. But I couldn't just stand back and do nothing while Ogawa and Tenneson waited to die.

"I suppose you want me to go right now," he said dryly.

"I know you have guests," I began in the most apologetic tone I could dig up. But really, his colleagues should be more important than a party, even to him.

He waved a hand. "All right. Might as well show you you're wrong immediately."

Karish made charming apologies to his guests, claiming he was off on Triple S business and promising to return as soon as he could. There were some protests, and I garnered a few foul looks, but Karish didn't let himself be dissuaded from going. Once more I was impressed. I didn't think I would have been able to withstand such heartfelt pleading.

We went to the hospital. One of the nurses pointed out that it was a little late for visitors, but Karish smiled at him, and that was the end of that. We settled at Ogawa's bedside and looked at her for a while.

Then Karish took one of Ogawa's hands in his. "I don't know what to do," he confessed.

"What did you do with Aiden?" I asked.

He had to think about it for a moment. "Pain is like a force," he said finally. He made a long, fluid gesture with his hand. "I let it flow through me as though it were part of a natural event."

"Why can't you do the same with Ogawa?"

He studied her again for a few moments. I felt little adjustments within him, and I readied myself, but he didn't need my Shields. Not yet. "There is no pain there. I don't think she's feeling anything." He cocked his head to one side, considering. "I really don't know what I'm talking about, but maybe a lack of the proper forces is the reason she's like this."

I looked at him with surprise. "People have forces? Just like natural events?"

"Of course," he said, as though it were obvious, as though everyone knew it. "Everything that exists has forces. Even rocks. But Miho doesn't have enough, or she doesn't have enough of the right sort, and that's why she's dying."

So I rearranged my thinking. "Could you channel forces into her instead of out?"

I would have sworn his voice squeaked up at least two octaves when he demanded, "What?"

"She's lacking forces. Give her some." It seemed easy enough to me.

Karish looked like he was wondering where the lunatic ward was and how quickly he could get me there. "That's never been done before."

That struck me as entirely irrelevant. "So?"

"I might kill her," he objected. "I'll probably kill her."

"She's already dying."

His voice dropped to a hoarse whisper. "You're not the one who'll have to live with it if this doesn't work and it kills her. And Val."

"Aye, and I'm also not the one who'll have to live with it if I sit back and do nothing and let her die," I said tartly.

He flinched. "You are such a bitch," he muttered.

I couldn't believe he required even a second thought about it, never mind the third and fourth and fifth he seemed to be indulging in. How could he have the potential to heal Ogawa and hesitate to use it? Yes, it was a risk, and I would be devastated if it went wrong, but Ogawa and Tenneson were dying. How could Karish even consider not making the attempt? "Tell me what I have to do to convince you, and I'll do it."

He laughed bitterly.

Anger flared. "What the hell is so funny?" I demanded.

"Nothing," he said. "Absolutely nothing." The laughter disappeared as abruptly as it had arrived. His inner Shields dropped.

I erected Shields around him.

For a long time, nothing happened. He was open to the forces, I could feel that, but he didn't seem to be doing anything. Perhaps he was just feeling things out. I didn't bother him with stupid questions, but it was kind of boring, sitting there doing nothing, ready for action.

It was strange when it finally started, different from anything I'd felt before. I could feel him sort of reaching out, gently touching the forces that moved around him. I could practically feel it on my skin, a not unpleasant sensation. I suppressed a shiver.

And then he began to pull the forces in. I did shiver then, it felt so odd. I could feel the forces sliding from around us, into him. He was pulling in something even from me. It was just a slight thing at first, like he was pulling out a string from deep within me, but it quickly grew stronger and faster, until it felt like the very air was rushing right out of my lungs. I couldn't tell whether it felt good or not. Maybe good.

I Shielded him. There was nothing else I could do. I couldn't help him directly. I had to let him do whatever he was going to do and hope he didn't screw up. I hated that.

I spared some attention for Ogawa. There was no reaction from her. I had no way of knowing whether Karish's efforts were having any effect on her.

There was nothing to do but wait.

So I waited.

Did Ogawa's eyelids flicker?

I looked at her. Her face was slack and as pale as I imagined marble would be, just as it had been when we first came in. But I thought I'd felt something from her.

My imagination.

Ogawa took a deep breath.

Ogawa's eyes opened.

Ogawa blinked, her eyes glancing about.

Karish's internal defenses snapped back into place, and the forces stopped.

I dropped my Shields. I looked at Ogawa. She didn't look quite aware, but there was something in her eyes that told me part of her brain was functioning. The relief that swamped me was so powerful that I was completely unbalanced. That was why I crowed so loudly, threw my arms around my Source, and gave him an exuberant kiss on the cheek. "You did it! You're magnificent!"

"Hush!" he said sharply.

"What's going on here?" an authoritative voice demanded from somewhere in the insignificant background. Healer Singer glowered down at us, her eyes narrowing. I felt like kissing her, too.

"Miho's come around, ma'am," Karish said respectfully.

Singer looked at him suspiciously but had more important matters to attend to. She leaned over the bed and gently touched Ogawa's brow. "Shield Ogawa?" she said softly. "You're in hospital. You've been injured, but it looks like you're going to be fine. Can you understand me?"

Ogawa didn't respond at all. She was looking at Karish. I wondered if she was actually seeing him.

"Please excuse us," the healer said, her hands beginning to roam over Ogawa. "I have to examine her now."

That was fine, because our work wasn't finished yet. "Yes, ma'am," I said, rising to my feet and pulling Karish to his. "Thank you, ma'am." I practically dragged Karish from the side of the bed.

"We'll be back tomorrow, Miho," he promised.

"Aye, Ogawa, tomorrow," I echoed. Moving faster, once more annoying the medical staff.

Once we were back out in the corridor Karish shook out of my grasp. "What the hell is your hurry?"

What did he think? "Tenneson's next."

"If they both recover while we're visiting them, especially one after the other like this, someone's going to figure it out."

"No one's going to figure it out. It's impossible, remember? All that's happened is that Ogawa has recovered, and she will soon drag Tenneson up with her. No one will suspect anything else." And because it was all so simple and was working so well, I grinned up at him.

"You're glowing," he muttered.

"You should be, too. You should be proud." I wondered why he wasn't. He had just saved a life, after all, and was about to save another. But maybe he was tired. "Come on. It's time to bring Tenneson back to the land of the living."

We did precisely that. I would have never been able to do that with Devereaux.

Chapter Eleven

"Karish never struck me as the modest type," said Ogawa, licking cream off her bottom lip. "I didn't think he was a braggart, exactly, but I didn't think he would have any trouble talking about it when he does something amazing." She reached for another cream roll.

I savored the sugary confection melting on my tongue and said nothing.

We were in Ogawa's suite, lounging on sofas and enjoying the unhealthy pastries I had picked up. After a week of constant eating and sleeping, Ogawa was on her way to full recovery, but her memory had suffered a blow. She remembered the strange forces that had driven her into her deep sleep, and she remembered Karish pulling her back to consciousness, but she couldn't recall anything in between.

She had been devastated by the loss of her colleagues, and then had swiftly hidden anything she felt about it. For the first time I heard in another Shield the flat tone Karish had mentioned.

"I tried to talk to him about it," she continued as she settled back into the sofa. "I tried to thank him. He was perfectly charming as he brushed me off. He claimed he didn't know what I was talking about, that he just happened to be there when I woke up, but I know he had more to do with it than that."

With my finger I scooped up some cream from my roll and stuck it into my mouth. Sometimes I really resented the way Karish had come to dominate so much of my life. It wasn't enough that I worked with him. People always had to talk about him. Sometimes it seemed that the only reason anyone spoke to me at all was to talk about Karish. It was starting to bore me. I searched for a subject to switch to.

"You don't like him much, do you?" said Ogawa.

I didn't want to get into it. "I like him fine."

"Then why don't you ever go to the taverns with him?" Ogawa asked. "Every time I saw him out, he was always alone."

I raised a brow at her.

"All right," she conceded. "I mean, he wasn't with you."

"Too much togetherness is a bad thing."

"You're missing quite a show," she told me.

"Really," I said flatly, hoping I sounded like I couldn't care less.

"Oh, aye. Just picture it. An ordinary night at the tavern. Quiet, slow, a few desultory conversations leaking through the silence. The whores seeking customers, the thugs seeking fights, the brokenhearted seeking oblivion—"

"My, Ogawa. How poetic."

She grinned. "Then *he* walks in"—I didn't have to ask who *he* was—"and the whole place seems to light up. Everyone looks at him, admires him, and he starts greeting everyone as though each were his particular friend. Suddenly everyone is talking louder and laughing harder and straining their brains for the wittiest lines. A dull evening in the local tavern turns into a party, and there's Karish in the middle of it, smiling that lethal smile that makes your stomach muscles clench." She sighed.

I had to smile. *Wipe your chin, dear, you're drooling.* "I'm not a tavern sort of person," I said, which was true enough in its way. "Were you happy when Tenneson Chose you?"

She grinned again, obviously understanding the sentiment behind the question. "I was thrilled to be Chosen," she said.

"I didn't much care by who. At that Match there were no Sources who were particularly glorious or particularly vile. I had no opinion of Tenneson when he Chose me. But I got to liking him quickly enough. It wasn't a snapping together of like minds or anything like that, but I found him comfortable. We've had our rough patches and we still have our fights, but for the most part we've worked well together. I know I'm fortunate to have someone like him as my Source."

Aye, and I envied her. Tenneson did seem to be the perfect Source. Talented, steady, and easy to understand.

But not nearly so nice to look at.

I heard a quick knock on the front door, and the guest walked in without waiting for permission to enter. "Hello, hon," a delightfully throaty alto called. "It's me." A woman I had met only a couple of times before, at Ogawa's bedside, walked in.

She hesitated at the sight of me, as she always did, then strode over to Ogawa and gave her a smacking kiss on the mouth. "How are you feeling?" she asked, sitting down close beside Ogawa and picking up her free hand.

That was my cue to leave. I rose to my feet. "I must go."

"No, you don't," Ogawa objected, but not too strenuously.

"Aye, I do. I want to drop in on Aiden before I start my watch."

"Ah." Ogawa smiled knowingly. "I see."

"I'm sure you do. So take care of yourself, Ogawa. We're missing you on the roster."

A shadow flickered in her eyes before she smiled and thanked me. It made me pause and consider asking her if something were wrong. I let it go. If there were something wrong, and she wanted to talk about it, she would without my prying it out of her. I left.

Aiden answered his door himself. I was sure that under normal circumstances he would just shout at whoever knocked, telling them to let themselves in, but right then he was personally answering the door out of principle. He surprised me by greeting me with a quick kiss.

I pulled back and noticed a light in his eye and a feeling of excitement in his air. "You're in a good mood."

He grinned widely. "Aye."

I stepped inside and closed the door behind me. "Any particular reason?"

"I made forty-seven imperials."

I frowned. "What?"

"I earned forty-seven imperials." He sprawled onto a settee, and I settled into the nearest chair.

I assumed, from his expression of pride, that that was a goodly amount. "Doing what?" I asked suspiciously.

"Telling stories."

"To who?"

"People in the park. That pathetic little one by the bakery."

"You just started telling stories and people paid you?"

"Well, I wanted to stretch my legs, so I got as far as the park. And," he admitted reluctantly, "coming straight back was more than I wanted to think about. So I sat on one of the benches, and this pert little miss came up to me and asked what I'd done to myself. And after I told her, she demanded I tell her a story. So I did."

That alarmed me. "Not one of—"

He laughed. "Not the kind of stories I tell you, love. I just took a princess and a wizard and some dragons and"—he made a spinning gesture with his finger—"mixed them together."

I raised my eyebrows. "You made up a story right then and there?" I said. "I'm impressed."

"I'm sure I stole the plotline from somewhere. A story doesn't have to be original as long as it's delivered well."

"And yours was well-delivered?" I asked in amusement.

This time his smile was smug. "If I do say so myself," he answered. "She liked it, anyway."

"She gave you forty-seven imperials for it?" *How old was this pert little miss, anyway?*

"Of course not. She stayed for another story though. And other children drifted over to listen, dragging their caretakers over, until everyone in the park was sitting or standing around me." He wrapped a lock of my hair around his finger and gently pulled the lazy curl out. "It was so strange, Dunleavy. They had been jumping on each other like little maniacs before, trying to kill each other it seemed, but then they were sitting there so quietly, listening to me. It was almost eerie, the way they listened so closely. I didn't know children could stay focused on one thing for so long."

I didn't know anything about children, having spent very little time with them, but I wouldn't be surprised if they found Aiden's storytelling entrancing. He really was good, throwing himself into the characters with enthusiasm, and convincing. A couple of times I'd forgotten where I was, listening to him. That was a pretty powerful effect to have on a Shield.

"People noticed us from the street and came in to investigate, then stayed to listen. After a couple of hours most of the children had left, but their caretakers all left money by my feet. I tried to refuse it, but they looked at my crutch and said keeping the children quiet for so long was well worth the money. So all the children left, but the adults continued to come in from the street, and before anyone left they always gave me some money." He grinned. "One fellow tried to sneak away without paying anything, and everyone else hissed at him until he tossed me a few coins. After a couple more hours I had a nice little pile of coins at my feet. I didn't know how much I had, though, until I came home."

"I am really impressed," I said again. "You have an astonishing range of talents." And I couldn't help but envy him a little. I had no such range. I couldn't do anything but Shield. I couldn't imagine what I would do for money if I were somehow severed from the Triple S and had to make my own way.

"Just as well," he said, the light in his eyes dimming a little. "Because I'm never going to dance again."

No, no guilt. "You don't know that."

"I do, Dunleavy. I can feel it when I walk. There's some new kind of movement in my knee, some strange kind of clicking and snapping. Like there are two pieces in there that no longer fit together the way they should. It doesn't hurt, exactly, but it certainly slows me down." He picked up my hand, kissed the back of it. "The healers are amazed I've come so far so quickly, but they still think I'll never dance. They've always thought it. And I've always believed them."

I wondered if Karish would take another look at him. The first time he'd helped Aiden, he didn't know all he could do. He'd thought all he could do was channel pain. Maybe if he tried, he could fix Aiden's knee. I didn't know if it would work at all, the damage being physical, and Karish would probably be very reluctant to work on a person who was alert enough to know what he was doing. I doubted Aiden would even allow it; he seemed to despise Karish without even knowing him. But I would ask Karish, just to see if it might be possible.

Aiden was in such a high mood, it was hard to leave him. By the time I arrived at the Stall, I found Karish waiting for me alone. Which was unusual and a breach of procedure. Firth and Stone, the Pair with the watch before ours, should have waited with him until I arrived, even if I were late. Which I wasn't, though it was a near thing.

Karish was seated at the table, shuffling a deck of cards. He didn't greet me when I walked in.

"Good evening," I said.

He grunted in response.

I looked him over. Shoulders slumped. Spine curved. Foot wrapped around the leg of his chair. His fingers lax, almost clumsy, as he shuffled the cards.

"What's happened?"

He continued to shuffle. "The Duke of Westsea is dead," he answered in a listless tone.

It took me a moment to remember that the Duke of Westsea was his brother. "Oh."

"I found out this afternoon."

I remained standing. I hadn't the vaguest idea what to do or say. Karish just sat there silently, no help at all. If he had been a friend I would have known what he wanted, but I didn't have a clue. "Do you want me to leave?" I asked diffidently.

"You can't," he said flatly.

"I can go out and . . . stand just outside the door." My, what a stupid suggestion.

He thought so, too. "Don't be ridiculous."

I stood there silently for another couple of moments. It was a horrible silence, so to break it I said, "How did he die?" Then I wished I could snatch back the words. Were you supposed to ask that sort of thing?

Karish laughed harshly. "Too much bad company."

"What?"

"A ridiculously polite way of saying he died of a sexual disease. Her Grace has a gift for evasive understatement."

Her Grace? Oh, yes, his mother.

"Sit down, Lee," he ordered, and I sat. "How old were you when you were sent to the academy?"

He wanted the subject changed. I could understand that. "About four."

"How perceptive of your parents," he commented. "I was eleven."

I stared at him. "Are you serious?"

"Quite."

Eleven? I couldn't believe it. True, Sources were usually discovered a little later than Shields, as how they spoke was a big clue and no one expected rational sentences from anyone under the age of six or seven, but to go unnoticed until the age of eleven was unheard of in recent times, and incredibly negligent on the part of his family. If he had lived at a more active site and went undiscovered a couple more years, his instincts to channel would have killed him.

"My grandsire went insane in his middle years," he told me, his tone mild. "Said the most nonsensical things. So when I came along and said things they couldn't understand, they thought I was insane, too, or heading that way. They were horrified, of course. How embarrassing, to have one's child afflicted with such a disability. Apparently, there were quite a few arguments about whose fault it was. Her Grace won, though, because the source of the problem was obviously my grandsire, His Grace's father."

People argued over such things? What for?

"They consoled themselves with the knowledge that at least I was only the second-born, not the first, but even as a spare I was useless. So they went to work on producing another. That didn't work out. Apparently Her Grace did quicken a few times but never carried to term. His Grace was happy to cast that failure in her face."

What a lovely family. Glad I didn't have to know them. I searched for a polite way to shut Karish up, for I knew he would regret telling me all of this sometime soon.

"It was a servant who realized what I was." Karish started

dealing the cards, not in any pattern I recognized. "She was a bright woman. Brave, too, to mention me to the Graces, daring to insinuate she might know me better than they. They dismissed her, of course, and they shipped me off to the academy." He picked out a card and flipped it over on the table. It was the fool. "I was excited about going somewhere, but I was frightened, too."

"You weren't excited about being a Source?" I could understand feeling nervous about going to the academy, about leaving home, but being a Source was akin to being a hero. Surely it would seem a dream come true to a young boy, especially one who was unable to please his family.

"I'd never heard of the Triple S. I didn't know what it was." He picked the card back up and added it to the others, shuffling them again.

I kept my face blank as I tried to make sense of what he was saying. How could he have never heard of the Triple S? Everyone knew what it was. His friends would have told him, if no one else. And if not, surely his parents would have explained the whole thing to him before they sent him to the academy.

"Did your family visit you, Lee, while you were in the academy?"

"Of—" I swallowed the rest of that then said, "Yes." I didn't return the question. I knew the answer. And really, it wasn't that unusual for families not to visit their academy-bound children. Some couldn't afford the expense. Some simply didn't care. It happened.

He smiled. "Of course," he said. He fanned the deck expertly, then flipped it closed and kept shuffling. "His Grace died without producing any more children, and her Grace had become too old to have them. So it all rested on the new duke, who dutifully became betrothed but whose fiancée wanted a huge wedding, which takes a great deal of time to plan, so they never actually married. For which I'm sure she is now screaming at herself, because without that legal tie, she has no right to the title. Which means," and he pulled in a deep breath, the first crack in his composure, "it falls to me."

Hell. Aristocratic titles were, of course, passed around a family. Karish was the only sibling of the previous titleholder. The law said it could go to anyone in the family who'd been

properly chosen and prepared, but custom, and the fact that
it was unlikely a duke as young as Lord Westsea had been
would have chosen an heir, said it would go to Karish. Shintaro
Karish. Lord Shintaro Karish. The next Duke of Westsea.

I bit my tongue to make sure I stayed quiet. What a mess.
He'd have to go to Flown Raven. He didn't have to live there,
but if he had any sense of responsibility at all, and he did, he
would spend most of his time in Flown Raven because it was,
I believed, the principal seat of the estate. Flown Raven was
completely cold. Not so much as a shiver for centuries. It had
never been assigned a Pair, it didn't need a Pair, so what was
I supposed to do while he was off playing duke?

All right, I was a selfish cow. I should have been thinking
about Karish losing his brother. But all I could think about
was that this ruined my life. My Source was going to a place
where Pairs were useless, and he had something important he
had to do there. I could go with him and be a parasite. Or I
could go somewhere else and be a parasite. I couldn't be a
Shield for anyone else; I was bonded to Karish. I couldn't do
any other kind of work, not only because I had never been
trained for anything else but because I belonged to the Triple
S. The only thing I could be was Karish's Shield, and he
didn't need me.

Which left me precisely nowhere. Except in a panic. Which
would accomplish nothing. I had to think.

"Her Grace will write," Karish continued. "She will demand my immediate attendance. She will give me the heir's
code so I can recite it to our solicitor, and he will then give me
the title. I will be expected to forget all about this Source nonsense and assume my proper place as the head of the Karish
family. Despite the fact that I know nothing about tenancies or
bookkeeping or farming or politics or anything else connected
to being a real lord." He arched the deck of cards between his
thumb and middle finger and fired all the cards off into the air.
They descended on the floor in a fine mess.

Karish steepled his hands and looked at me. It was a hard,
angry look, and I wondered what I'd done to deserve that. Be
present, I supposed. "What a piece of work am I, yes?" he
said coolly. "Quite a monster you've gotten yourself bonded
to. Here my brother dies, and all I can think about is how

inconvenient it is. Though I'm sure you're not surprised by my lack of family feeling. Selfish, self-absorbed Karish. But the fact that I'm not leaping for joy over the title, that must throw you a circle."

Actually, I was merely thinking how spooky it was that our thoughts seemed to be following a similar pattern. Never let it be said that Karish and I were similar in any way. As to what he felt about his family, none of my business.

"Isn't that right, Lee?" Karish prodded, and this time he was definitely testy. "Quite the selfish bastard, aren't I? Not dissolving into tears at the death of my brother. Overemotional Source that I am, I should have been devastated to hear he had a cold."

Not if he hadn't seen him since he was eleven.

"Say something, damn it!" he snapped.

"I'm sorry."

He snorted. "Surely you have more to say than that."

"No." What did he expect? Did he really think I would lecture him on the proper way to mourn family? What did I know about it? No one of my family had ever died.

No one I knew had ever had family who died, either. I had no experience in comforting people. It wasn't part of my Shield training.

The rest of our watch passed in silence.

Chapter Twelve

The following weeks were . . . unpleasant. Karish spent most of them in a vicious mood, swinging from simmering silence to snippy sarcasm. Completely gone was the slightly vacuous charmer, and I was beginning to wonder just what was his true nature.

He was impossible to deal with. Nothing I said was appropriate. If I spoke about work, he sneered at me for playing the part of the duty-bound Shield, with no regard for natural feelings. If I asked him how he was feeling, I received more lectures about how shocked and appalled I was at his apparent lack of family feeling.

I had to admit, though only to myself, that I was surprised that he didn't even want to go to his brother's funeral. At least, he didn't ask to have us removed from the roster to enable him to go to Flown Raven. No matter what ill feeling there had been between the two of them, surely he would have wanted to participate in the funeral rites? The man had been his only sibling, after all.

Not that I spoke a word about it. None of my business.

Karish also refused to discuss his taking the title. Of this,

I had less sympathy. I could understand that it was an unexpected shock to him, and apparently not one he was embracing with any enthusiasm. But this was my life, too. It uprooted every single plan I had. I had a right to know when he was planning to assume the title and move to Flown Raven.

I didn't dare bring it up, however. I could only wait. I discovered that sometimes I had less patience than I would like.

And we had another Rush. No one died that time, but it hurt like hell and put everyone on the roster in a foul mood.

For distraction I visited Ogawa. She was improving rapidly and was up and about and chatting amiably, trying to appear her normal self. She wasn't quite managing the normal part, though. I noticed the tension about her eyes and mouth, and a slight rigidity in her movements that hadn't been there before. I didn't think the problem was physical, but I didn't ask about it. If she wanted to talk about it, she would.

Finally, during one visit, she decided she did. After complaining about convalescence in general and the fact that Tenneson hadn't visited her often enough, then mining for details about Aiden, Ogawa poured us some tea and splashed some of it over the rim. As though that were some kind of signal, she sat abruptly and stared at me. "I'm scared," she declared.

"Of what?"

She looked at me as though she thought that was a stupid question. "Shielding."

Sorry, I'm still a moron. "Why?"

She paled as though my ignorance had somehow made her fear worse. "Didn't you feel it when it happened? Didn't it hurt?"

Oh, that. The Rushes. A shudder tried to fight its way from my core to my skin, but I wouldn't let it. "Aye, it hurt." But perhaps not so much as it had evidently hurt her.

"Aren't you afraid to Shield again?"

"I have Shielded again." I'd had no choice. The second Rush had come so hard on the heels of the first, there'd been no one else to channel or Shield. Then we'd had to continue working, while waiting for the other Pairs to arrive. The third

Rush had been easier to manage. So I supposed, painful as they were, I was getting used to them.

And I hadn't almost died. Sure, it had hurt, but after a few days of rest I had been back to normal. Ogawa had lost her senses for a good while, and once she roused she was told she'd been on the shores of death. Then she'd had to endure weeks of recuperation. Perhaps if I had suffered what she had, I'd be scared, too.

Still, there was nothing to be done about it, until we discovered why the Rushes were happening and figured out a way to stop them. "Is Tenneson nervous about channeling again?"

Ogawa looked down at her hands clasped in her lap and shrugged. "He doesn't remember anything."

"Have you told Tenneson how you feel?" I asked.

"Not really," she said. "I tried to hint around it. I asked him when he thought he would be ready to channel again. He said any time, no hesitation. I couldn't tell him I wasn't sure if I was up for it."

It was worse than I thought. "You're not sure you're up for it?" That was different from simply being afraid. It was much, much worse.

Tears filmed her eyes. That was alarming. She couldn't look at me. She shrugged.

"Ogawa!"

"All the other Shields are dead, Mallorough!" she snapped angrily.

"You're not, and neither am I," I reminded her. "And everyone survived the last one."

"Survived the last one! Listen to yourself. We're not supposed to be worrying about surviving channeling!"

I wasn't supposed to be worrying about my Source being turned into a duke and rendering me useless. "What are you saying? You don't want to Shield anymore? You can't do that."

"I can. What can anyone do if I just refuse to Shield?"

"They can die."

Ogawa bit her lip. "I really don't think I can Shield again, Mallorough. I mean it."

"You have to do it again," I told her, wishing I knew how to use rhetoric, or was better at comforting people. Or something. "You're a Shield." Made it all pretty obvious to me.

"It's not that simple, Mallorough," she claimed with a sad smile.

"Aye, it is. You've promised to Shield your Source for as long as you're able."

"That's just it. I don't think I'm able anymore."

"You're only scared," I said, feeling like an idiot as I said it. As reassurances went, it was weak. "You'll be fine. Once you're needed again, you'll fall into habit. You'll naturally Shield Tenneson as you always have in the past."

Ogawa settled back in her seat and said nothing. I felt foolish. And then I felt angry for feeling foolish. I wasn't the one who was letting fear frighten me from doing my duty.

My, how pompous.

I took a deep breath and pushed it out slowly. Really, what was wrong with me? Swinging from annoyance and apprehension to anger and back again. I was supposed to be calm. That was my role. And I'd been good at remaining calm regardless of the levels of stress I faced, while I was at the academy. Why did I have so much difficulty with it now?

Ogawa recognized in another Shield the tricks for remaining serene. "Are you all right?"

"Of course," I said. "And you are, too. Or you will be; you'll see. It's only that you've been off the roster so long, and you had such a difficult time with the first Rush without getting back into things and realizing they're not so bad. The first one was the worst for me, too, but the later ones are better. Once you're working, you'll find the same thing, and you'll feel better."

She shrugged. "Perhaps," she said, not sounding at all convinced.

No one had ever taught me how to reassure people. And it was clear I lacked any natural talent for it.

This feeling of unsettlement was undermining my training, that was it. Because I had no idea when Karish would come up to me and tell me he'd decided he was heading out, and it was a great pleasure knowing me and thank Zaire he'd never have to deal with me again.

It would be hard to be rendered useless like that, but at least I'd know it was done, and then I could start figuring out what to do next. But until Karish made his move, I was left groundless. And I was realizing that was a state I really, really hated.

Chapter Thirteen

Very early one morning, in response to a message I received on my free day, I went back to the hospital. On my previous visits, I had been worried and upset, but this time I was ashamed to notice that my heart was pounding, up somewhere near my throat, and I seemed to be sweating.

The tersely worded message said Karish had been attacked on the street by some lone assailant. He was expected to live, but in case he didn't, I should be at the hospital, too.

That's all the note said. The bastards.

I could guess at their thinking. Mustn't have me collapsing dead, all of a sudden, out in public. It might disturb the regulars. Besides, the morgue was under the hospital. It was far easier for me to walk in than for them to send someone out to carry me in.

And then, when I got there, they wouldn't even let me see him. A nurse told me he had been stabbed several times by the assailant, who apparently had expected the job to be much easier than it had been, for he had run away before it was finished. First priority on everyone's list, after making sure Karish didn't die, was finding out who had attacked him and why. And to that purpose, now that Karish was awake, there were two Runners in his room interviewing him.

So all I could do was sit outside his room and wait.

I wasn't at all sure how this worked, this procedure of dying when your partner did. Would I feel anything in advance, get any kind of warning? Or did everything just stop between one breath and the next?

I shivered and told myself not to think about it.

Sitting in that hospital, hearing moans from other rooms, and someone crying because someone had died, not thinking about it was impossible.

I jumped to my feet when the door to Karish's room opened. Two Runners and a healer stepped out.

"He's asleep," the healer told me, giving me a hard look and closing the door.

"Is he all right?" I asked.

"He should be."

And I had to be satisfied with that vague response, because the healer took off. I sat down. I thought I was relieved, but I wasn't sure.

"Shield Mallorough?"

I looked up at the Runners.

I'd never spoken to Runners before, though I'd seen them about the city, running in response to headache-inducing whistles that told them the nature and location of the most recent crime. They were menacing-looking people, dressed all in black with black cloaks falling from their shoulders and tools jangling from their belts.

This pair was comprised of a tall, lean woman with beautiful warm brown skin and incongruously red hair, and a short, skinny man who was eyeing me with overt hostility.

I hadn't even spoken yet. How could I have possibly annoyed him?

"I'm Runner Demaris," the woman said, "this is Runner Wilson. We're sorry about your partner."

Her words sounded perfunctory to me. "Thank you."

"He looks like he might be real pretty when he isn't so pale and drugged up."

My eyebrows flew up to my hairline. Maybe not so perfunctory after all.

Wilson looked at his partner with disgust. "We're trying to find out who might have attacked him," he said.

"I have no idea," I admitted.

"Did he have any enemies?"

"No."

"Universally adored, was he?" Wilson drawled.

Yes. As far as I knew.

"What about this new title of his?" Demaris asked. "We heard he's going to be a duke."

"Aye."

"Is there anyone in his family who might be really unhappy about that?"

"I have no idea," I repeated. I hadn't considered that possibility. But why would anyone object to Karish being the next duke? He was his brother's natural heir. It couldn't have been a surprise to anyone.

"What are your impressions of his family?"

He didn't seem to like them, but that didn't seem much to go on. "I've never met any of them."

Wilson's eyes narrowed. "How long have you been his Shield?" he demanded.

"A few months."

"Pah!" He glared up at Demaris. "She's useless."

Demaris rolled her eyes. "Then she's in good company. Why don't you run off and find a thief to arrest with unnecessary brutality and leave the civilized stuff to me?"

"My pleasure," he muttered before stalking off.

I raised an eyebrow at Demaris.

"Little man issues," she explained.

"Ah."

"But seriously, have you got any idea who might be behind this?"

"I don't know anyone who doesn't like Karish." Except Aiden. But even he didn't hate Karish that much. And he was nearly a cripple, so he wouldn't be capable of it anyway.

Demaris smirked. "He is something, isn't he?"

"You're kidding. He's half-dead and he's flirting?"

"He's got a killer smile."

What was it like, I wondered, to have people really like you, crave you, want to be around you, moments after meeting you? People of all ages, all types. It had to be wonderful. It had to make a person feel bright and light and high.

"Let me know, though, if anything comes to mind. Risa Demaris, at the Lower Western Runner Headquarters. And take care."

"Aye. Thank you."

And then I was alone again.

A healer went into Karish's room. After only a few moments he came back out, disappeared, then returned with two more healers. That couldn't be good, but no one would tell me what was going on.

People began arriving, sitting down to wait for word of Karish. I vaguely recognized a few of them, but not to name, and the rest were complete strangers. The sheer number astounded me. How had he even been able to meet so many people in the time we'd been in High Scape?

I was surprised to see Source Chris LaMonte in attendance. He was one of the new Sources who had been sent after the Rushes, and grateful as I was to have him in High Scape, he was not one of my favorite people. He was a condescending sort, and he was too proud of being a Source. He wasn't the most social of people, either. I'd heard he didn't even talk to his Shield unless it was absolutely necessary, and what he did on his own time was a mystery because he refused to tell anyone about it.

But apparently Karish had charmed him, as he charmed everyone else.

"Good afternoon, sir." He was an older man, so it was wise to address him with respect, even though he wasn't my superior in any hierarchical sense.

His response was a cool nod. The condescending prat.

Hard heels hitting the floor made all of us turn our heads to look. A woman on a mission came striding up the hall. Instinct told me she belonged to Karish. She wasn't a stunner, which didn't surprise me so much as the fact that she didn't even look interesting or unique, not in her features, not in how she moved. She was small and slight and terribly efficient looking, her brown hair cropped short, her clothing of simple lines and good quality. Pretty drab, though. But I really couldn't claim to know Karish's tastes.

I bet she worked in the government.

"You here for Karish?" I drawled in the most peasant accent I could find. A compulsive reaction to her appearance.

She looked at me with annoyance. "I am," she said. *And what possible business could it be of yours?* her expression asked.

"Take a seat." I gestured at the free chairs. "They're not letting us in right now."

"They'll let me in," she announced coolly, sweeping into the room.

LaMonte and I exchanged a glance.

The bureaucrat was swept back out again, protesting loudly. Don't you know who I am? The door was firmly closed behind her. I kind of wanted to smile, but I didn't.

"Well, really," she huffed, pulling on her sleeves to smooth out nonexistent wrinkles. She sat down a few chairs away from us, crossing her legs primly. She didn't bother to introduce herself.

I studied her. I wondered if she really was one of Karish's lovers or if she only wished she were.

And then, finally, staff began leaving Karish's room instead of always entering it. The healers looked tired but not particularly depressed. But then they were healers, so who knew?

They did look annoyed, though, at seeing so many people lingering in the hall. "He'll live," one barked. "Go home."

There were, naturally, objections to that. They were ignored with expert ease, the staff elbowing their way through.

The bureaucrat stood, eyeing the door.

LaMonte looked at her. "Don't be ridiculous," he said crisply.

She huffed and went back to her chair.

So maybe I liked LaMonte after all.

A young man sitting next to me touched my arm. "Are you all right?" he asked me. "You've gone gray."

I frowned at him. Of course I was all right. I was fine. Karish was the one who had been assaulted. Nothing had happened to me. There was no reason for me to be anything but all right. There was no reason for me to be reacting to anything at all. I was great. I was wonderful. My hands were strangely cold, but that was probably nothing.

It wasn't long before the last healer came out. Like his colleagues, he was surprised and obviously irritated by the number of people waiting in the hall. He glanced over us, then asked, "Which of you is Lord Shintaro's Shield?"

I quietly cleared my throat. "That would be me."

He leaned his head toward the door. "His Lordship's asking for you."

There were a few pouts at that. I was rather surprised myself. I rose to my feet, a little unsteadily. Because I'd been sitting still too long.

"The rest of you might as well go home," the healer announced to the others. "He's barely awake, and one visitor's going to be enough to put him back under."

"I don't want to overtax him," I said.

A look of exasperation crossed his face. "He's demanding to see you."

Ah.

There were some grumbles from the others. The bureaucrat crossed her arms, looking mulish. "I'll wait," she declared.

I didn't really blame her. If I'd waited so long, for the reasons she did, I would have been offended at my true love's colleague being given precedence. But hey, Karish was quirky. She might as well learn that from the beginning.

I entered the room quietly. The light coming through the window was dim. I was surprised, though I wasn't sure why, to see it was night. A low lantern had been lit. In the faint light I couldn't see how pale Karish was, but he did look awfully young for some reason, not much older than a boy. Strange what lighting and bedding and boneless exhaustion, his and mine, could do for a person's looks.

He was awake, his tired eyes clear. He was all right. I could breathe. I smiled at him as I pulled a chair close to his bed. "I'm going to ask you a stupid question," I warned him.

"You want to know how I feel." His voice was a little weak but perfectly audible.

"You *can* read minds."

"I'm told I'll live."

"They're spreading the same lies outside." I leaned forward in my chair. "Did you babble anything embarrassing while you were delirious?"

"I spilled my guts, and you missed it all."

"Damn it. All those financial opportunities wasted." He smiled, but I could tell it took more effort than it should have. I was tiring him already. "I was told not to stay too long. I'll let you sleep." I started to rise from my chair.

"No, wait," he said softly.

I froze. "If you have any deathbed confessions to make, you're decades too early."

"Sit down."

I sat. "Yes, sir."

He ignored the sarcasm. "How are you?"

"Me? Fine. No one's tried to stab me. Do you know there are about a thousand people waiting in the hall for you?"

"A thousand?"

"All right. A couple dozen. That's still a lot."

Another weak smile that quickly faded. "Someone tried to kill me."

I stomped down on another strong emotion. This one rage. Because how dare they. "Aye."

"I didn't think anyone hated me that much," he said softly.

"I think it's a little early to be thinking along those lines. It might be a bungled robbery."

"No one would bother trying to rob a Source. I don't have anything."

Oh. Right. Stupid suggestion. But really, who would want to kill him? The idea was ludicrous. Everyone adored Shintaro Karish.

"Are you taking care?" he asked.

"Nothing's happened to me."

He seemed pained by my stupidity. "Whoever is doing this obviously doesn't care that you'll die with me. It won't take them long to remember that they can turn that around and do the job through you. I'll be harder to kill while I'm in here. You'll make an easier target."

I felt my eyes widen as his words sank in. Holy hell. He was right. While perhaps not providing the same perverse satisfaction as a direct assault, if this person was determined to kill Karish and couldn't get to him, he would come after me. That aspect of the bond was not a secret. "Zaire."

"Aye."

"And you have no idea who might be behind this?"

"Did they catch the fellow who did this?"

"I don't know. Did you know him?"

"No." He carefully smoothed away a wrinkle in the blanket. "The Runners think it might be a relative. I'm sure there are many who'll object to having a Source as their head of family, and they might have found out about the duke's death long before I did. But I can't pinpoint one person. I haven't even met most of my cousins, don't even know all of their names."

Thank you, Karish, for dragging me into your family politics. Just what I needed to spice up my boring life.

"I'm going to Flown Raven as soon as I'm able. I have to check this out. We can't spend the rest of our lives dodging knives."

I nodded. It made sense.

"And you'll be coming with me."

That woke me up. "Excuse me?" I demanded.

"We're a Pair," he explained patiently. Like that had anything to do with anything.

"So? I don't know anything about that aristocratic world of yours. I'd be no use at all."

"It'll be too dangerous for you here, Lee."

And who was the one in the hospital bed?

Of course I was going. I'd be a wreck waiting in High Scape while he was flitting about Flown Raven, doing all sorts of stupid masculine and dangerous things. More I might drop dead-any-moment tension. No thank you. "I'll think about it," I told him with expertly feigned reluctance. "Go to sleep. You look awful." I stood.

"Leaving so soon?"

"I was told not to tire you out." I looked at him. I would have wagered he couldn't lift his head if he had to.

He could have died.

"I'm glad you're going to be all right." Weak words, insufficient for the relief I felt, but I'd never claimed to be any kind of poet.

He smirked. "Glad enough to get me some chocolate?"

I raised an eyebrow at him. No, not glad enough to fetch and carry for him. "I bet the bureaucrat out there would do that for you."

Was that panic that flared in his eyes? "Amanda is out there?"

It amused me that he knew exactly who I'd been referring to. Assuming that was her name. "Want me to send her in?"

"Not if you hold the slightest affection for me in that cold, hard heart of yours."

"Now that'll take some serious self-examination," I said, opening the door.

"What, no good-bye kiss?" he protested.

"Don't tempt me, Stallion." And because I was tired and light-headed with relief, I blew one at him before I left.

Chapter Fourteen

When I told Aiden that Karish had been attacked, the goal of said attack likely to be murder, he started swearing. Most creatively. Most furiously. I hadn't been expecting anger. That would imply he actually liked Karish, wouldn't it? That he actually cared that something dangerous was happening to him? "What's the problem?"

"It's—Don't they—Doesn't the person who did this know that if he kills Karish, he kills you, too?"

Oh. "I guess he didn't care."

"What happened to him, the attacker?"

"The Runners are looking for him." And I really didn't want to talk about it anymore.

"Maybe you should leave."

"Leave?" The house? He was that upset?

"Leave High Scape. Go somewhere safe."

There was no place safe. As long as Karish was in danger, I was, too. "I can't leave."

"Why not? You can't work until Karish is back on his feet, anyway."

I couldn't leave Karish. For someone to be struck down as Karish was and have his partner desert just to save her own skin was a little too cold even for me. And I couldn't shake the absurd notion that Karish would be safer if I were around to watch over him. Besides, we were going to Flown Raven as soon as Karish was able.

"I'll be able to travel soon," he promised rashly. "We could go to Middle Reach."

"Middle Reach? Why would we go there?" Why would anyone go there, if they had the choice? There was nothing in Middle Reach.

He offered up an awkward half shrug. "I've been thinking about how you feel about being a Shield, and how different it is from everything Ryan says. He's so bitter. I think it would be good for him to talk to you. Besides," he smiled crookedly, "I'd kind of like you to meet him."

Well, all right, that was all very flattering, but what was the rush? Why couldn't Ryan come to High Scape rather than me going to Middle Reach? Middle Reach could spare a Pair more easily than High Scape, especially right then.

"I'm sorry, Aiden," I said, "but I can't go to Middle Reach right now." Or ever, if I had anything to say about it. "I can't leave Karish hanging here while there's some lunatic after him." Aiden frowned. It irked me. It was bad enough I had to consider one person—Karish—whenever I made a decision of any significance. I wasn't going to add another. "And we have to figure out who it is. So once he can travel, he and I are going to Flown Raven."

His face stiffened. "Are you?"

What was his problem? "It may be a member of his family. Someone resenting that he's going to be the next duke. We need to find out if that's true, and what can be done about it."

He didn't like that at all. I could see it. And for a moment I feared we were going to have a genuine argument. But then he pulled in a deep breath, and he visibly calmed himself down. "That makes sense," he conceded. "So when do you think he'll get out of hospital?"

I was relieved. I hated arguments. And as he had no right to argue with me over something like this, it would have made me angry. That would have ruined my whole day.

We spoke a while longer, about Karish, and it was the most civil conversation I'd had with Aiden, about Karish, since we met. It pleased me, because the instantaneous dislike between the two of them had definitely been mutual. Perhaps this attack would have the beneficial consequence of enabling Aiden to see Karish in a more sympathetic light.

My next visit—I had nothing to do but visit people until Karish and I were back on the roster—was to the Stall. Ogawa and Tenneson were on duty, their first shift since their full recovery. It was nice to know they were working again. It meant they were now the veteran Pair of High Scape, and I was happy to pass that responsibility on to them. I had enough to worry about.

They made me tea and grilled me about Karish. I was delighted to tell them it looked like he was going to be fine. I didn't tell them about the suspicions concerning who had attacked him, although they asked. It was just speculation. And I was really hoping it was just some kind of fluke. The man had attacked Karish by mistake, or had been smoked, or some other explanation that meant Karish wasn't facing some kind of long-term threat.

Ogawa tapped my foot with her toe. "So why are you here?"

"Bored."

Tenneson chuckled. "You're in High Scape," he said. "This is the most exciting city in the world. How could you possibly be bored here?"

I shrugged, a little embarrassed. I had never had a chance to be bored while I was in the academy, with all the training I'd had to do. As a bonded Shield I was suddenly left with hours of free time on my hands, and I didn't know what to do with it.

Ogawa took pity on me. "Have you come up with an act for the Hallin Festival?"

It was said that Octavia Hallin was the founder of High Scape. Otherwise the name meant nothing to me. "What's that?"

They made such emphatic sounds of astonishment that I wondered if I should duck.

"I know you haven't been here long, Mallorough, but that you've managed to avoid hearing about one of the most important festivals in High Scape is inconceivable."

"My talents are many and varied."

"You haven't been spending enough time with regulars," Tenneson chided me. "You spend all your time with Triple S company, and you'll become isolated."

Sure, whatever. "So now that you've whet my appetite, do you want to tell me what this all-important festival is about?"

"To mark the end of summer, everyone takes the week off and performs onstage for the benefit of their fellow citizens. By law, everyone must perform."

"Hm, by law, right."

"I'm serious."

I refused to accept that. "There's no way every single person in High Scape performs. It would take forever."

"It doesn't happen at the same place. Dozens of stages are erected all over the city."

"So you take out a copy of the census and round up every single person in the city? That's impossible."

Tenneson conceded that with a slight nod. "I'm sure some slip through, but most people have friends and family who will force them onto the stage. And anyone who's at all known hasn't a chance of escaping."

They had to be joking. Me, get on a stage and perform? "Can I dance the benches?"

"Only if you want to get booed off the stage," Ogawa warned me.

"They frown on athletic displays," Tenneson told me.

"You could sing something," Ogawa suggested.

"No, I certainly could not." Actually, my voice wasn't too bad, I could carry a tune within a limited range, but it certainly wasn't of the quality to be trotting out in front of others.

"It doesn't have to be good," Ogawa assured me. "In fact, spectators often prefer that it isn't."

"I'll bet." Dodging fruit wasn't my idea of a good time, either.

"You could arrange some kind of group performance."

"No." *No way, no how.*

"You have to do something, Mallorough. I'm serious."

So was I. A law, was it? I would see about that. Someone would have to show me the act in the law book that said I was required to make a fool of myself in public. And even if there were a law so ridiculous, there had to be a way out of it. I

mean, I could hardly perform if I wasn't in the city, could I?
That trip to Flown Raven was sounding better all the time.

I opened my mouth to ask when exactly this Hallin Festival
was held, then snapped it shut as something drew my attention
to Tenneson. There was that stiffness of posture and the glazed
look, screaming warning signs. He was about to channel.

And Ogawa panicked.

Not noticeably, or at least not to the eye of a regular, but to
another Shield she might as well have broken into tears of
hysteria. I saw her face go pale. I saw her bite her lip. I saw
her eyes stay clear and outwardly focused.

If Tenneson was aware he was unprotected, he gave no sign
of it. I wondered if Sources could feel their Shields' protections.
Karish claimed he could feel mine. Not that there was much
Tenneson could do, even if he could feel Ogawa's hesitancy. He
was the only Source on duty. Responsibility and instinct—and
trust—forced him to act.

"Shield him!" I snapped at Ogawa.

"I can't!" she admitted in a broken voice.

"What?"

"I can't!"

I'd understood her the first time. Her words, not her behavior. "If he dies, you die, and so do the rest of us."

"I can't think! I can't do it!"

"What do you mean you can't?"

"You don't understand, Mallorough! It hurt too much last
time!" She squeezed her eyes shut, pressing her hands to her
temples as though she were in pain right then. "I can't do it!"

"So you're going to leave him unprotected?" What the hell
was the matter with her?

"It hurt!"

"I don't care!" Zaire! I couldn't believe she was going to
let her Source kill himself and anyone else who got in the way
of whatever event was brewing. But there was no time to argue with her or smack her around. I looked at Tenneson.

I hadn't studied him, nothing beyond the casual obser-
vations presence and conversation unearthed. I had never
mapped his blood flow, his brain ways, his interior shields.
And I hadn't Shielded anyone other than Karish since being
Chosen.

I was the only other Shield there.

So I Shielded him. It was hard. It was clumsy. But it was, evidently, good enough.

It wasn't another Rush. I didn't know if I could have Shielded him through something like that. Still, the disturbance was strong enough and lasted long enough that by the time it passed, I had developed a shattering headache from Shielding someone else's Source.

Tenneson was staring at me with astonishment.

Ogawa was staring at me with undisguised bitterness.

"What?" I asked.

"You do like making a spectacle of yourself, don't you?" Ogawa demanded angrily.

"Excuse me?"

"And you accuse Karish of being a glory hound!"

I'd never said any such thing to another person. "Your Source was endangering his life, and you were doing nothing," I said coolly.

"So you stepped in and saved the day," Ogawa spat. "The Great Shield Mallorough and her legendary Source, saving High Scape from the incompetence of its own veterans. Do you think I don't know how proud of that you are?" She laughed, and there was more than an edge of hysteria to the sound. Tenneson, looking as shocked as I felt, touched her shoulder. She slapped his hand away. "You hold your head so high and smile so smugly and look so pleased with yourself. You make me sick."

Well, that had come out of nowhere.

Tenneson offered me his hand. "I think you'd better go now," he said quietly. "Miho and I need to talk."

"Aye, Mallorough, perhaps you'd better go monitor the streets," Ogawa added with heavy sarcasm. "You know no one is safe without you to take care of them."

And Tenneson had better hope there would be no other events during his watch. I ignored his hand as I stood.

Tenneson followed me to the door, and once I was outside he touched my shoulder sympathetically. "Miho doesn't like to fail," he said.

Who does?

But I was a Shield. One who was properly trained, and who

would never let a stupid thing like fear prevent me from doing my job, or anger and hurt prevent me from being civil. So I nodded at Tenneson. "Have a good shift," I said, and let him close the door behind me.

What the hell was wrong with everyone, anyway?

Chapter Fifteen

Karish was going home. He was still weak, but his wounds were healing nicely, and if he was careful, he was safe from infection. So I'd been told. Also he'd threatened to walk out whether they authorized it or not, so really they'd had no choice. I thought it was too early, but no one ever listened to me. In only a few weeks, the healers said, if all went well, he'd be fit to work.

Thank the gods. Not to be selfish, but I had been going out of my mind with boredom. I had never been so inactive for so long in my entire life. No duties, no classes, my Source in the hospital, my only friend still largely confined to his house, and a potential friend refusing to speak to me. Oh, and then there was the constant fear of getting killed, with nothing to distract me from my thoughts. It had not been a fun couple of weeks.

There had been no attacks on me or on Karish. Still, I was a wreck waiting for the assault that never came, and I was quite prepared to seek out this enemy of Karish's and dismember him, slowly, to thank him for the way he had disrupted my life.

Only I wouldn't be back on the roster any time soon, if ever. Once Karish was able we would be off to Flown

Raven, where we could clear up the business with the whole assassination/jealous heir situation. We had no choice. The Runners still didn't know who was responsible, and if they had any theories, they were refusing to tell me.

Once we were there, Karish would accept his title. I had no idea what I would do when that happened, and I didn't want to think about it.

Karish had written to the Triple S council from the hospital, explaining about his prospective title, and they had given him permission to go to Flown Raven and be duke. Not that permission was required. The title was a higher duty. I hadn't been mentioned in the correspondence. I figured I could pretty much do as I liked because I was useless and, as a Paired Shield with no chance of spontaneously bonding, harmless.

Maybe I could work on figuring out what those strange Rushes had been. There had been no more after the first three, and perhaps they had been only an aberration of some kind, but I felt there had to be a better explanation than that, and it was important that we know it. I didn't know if it was something I could explore on my own, though, without a Source.

But Tenneson no longer had a functioning Shield. He and Ogawa had been taken off the roster, too. So maybe he and I could work together. That sort of thing had never been done before, but when had that ever mattered?

I had come to the hospital to escort Karish home. It was a move to head off the horde who would bicker for the privilege and probably show up en masse. I could see Karish limping home with his dozens of fans scampering after him like rats, none of them noticing how exhausted he was and how little he wanted their company. I could accompany him alone, without offending anyone, and I didn't expect him to entertain me.

At the moment, we were waiting for final permission from Healer McLean to leave. Sick of being in bed, Karish was sitting in a chair while I sprawled on his cot. He was opening a paper package that I had brought him the day before, offering it to me. I shook my head. "You're a most unnatural creature, Lee," he declared. "You don't seem to have the proper understanding of the importance of chocolate." He snapped off a sliver and popped it into his mouth, sucking on it instead of chewing it like a normal person.

I liked chocolate well enough. I just didn't love it. I could go a day or a week without eating it. Karish was addicted. I'd had to bring him a package every few days to keep him supplied, and I knew I wasn't the only one bringing it to him.

I looked at the table, cleared of the flowers and letters visitors had been bringing to him. "Where are your tributes?"

"Sent ahead." He snapped off another piece, then rewrapped the package almost reverently. "How's life?"

He asked me that every day. "Same as yesterday."

"Miho speaking to you yet?"

I shrugged. I hadn't told Karish about my Shielding Tenneson, and I didn't know who had. A couple of days after it had happened, he had greeted me with a smug smile when I came in to visit him. He'd asked me why I hadn't told him I was brilliant. I'd said I'd assumed it was obvious. "Apparently not."

"You can't blame her."

I most certainly could, but I didn't bother saying so.

"You've proved to her that she's useless."

And Zaire knew I understood how that felt. "So you've said before."

"You did her job. You Shielded her Source."

I was drawn into the argument despite myself. "I should have let him die?"

"Of course not. I'm not saying you made the wrong decision. You did the only thing you could, and Tenneson should be forever grateful. But surely you can understand how she feels."

"I'd understand if she feels ashamed for falling apart, but she has no right to be angry with me for having to do the job she refused to do." Especially not for so long. She should have forgiven me before then. Not that she had anything to forgive me for.

Change the subject. "What's the first thing you'll do when you get home?"

"Take a bath," he muttered. "It'll be a nice change not to have an audience." I cocked a brow at that, thinking of all the people who would be desperate to attend him. He mimicked my expression. "Unless, of course, you'd like to scrub my back."

"I dream about it nightly."

He grinned.

"How are you?"

"One of the healers could give you a total rundown of all my bodily functions."

"No, I mean about your"—I paused, gesturing vaguely, wondering what idiocy had caused me to even bring it up—"family."

"What aspect of it?" he asked coolly. "That one of them apparently wants me dead? Or do you want to know whether natural grief has struck me yet?"

Definitely a bad idea. "Whatever."

"I got a lovely little missive from Her Grace. Care to hear about it?"

"Probably not," I said uncomfortably.

"Oh, but you should. It is the essence of elegance and style as she informs me of my duty to attend her. She wants me in Flown Raven. She wants me there immediately. Yesterday would be even better."

"She doesn't know you're in hospital?"

"I wrote to her about it. Not in explicit detail, of course. Far too likely to upset a lady of her delicate sensibilities." He snickered, and I didn't ask. "But I let her know some ruffian had thought to use me as a whetting stone and that as a result I was spending some time in hospital." He smiled that bitter little smile he seemed to use whenever he thought of his family. "She chided me for allowing it to happen."

"For *allowing* something to attack you?"

"Shows an unseemly lack of control, don't you know. I am a duke, after all. Or almost. I owe a lot to our revered name. I can't allow such distasteful disruptions to occur in my vicinity." His accent grew stronger in the last phrase, and I knew he was quoting her.

I studied him for a moment, trying to interpret his expression. "No," I decided finally. He was pulling my leg. He had to be. No one would say something like that. Not to her own son. Not to anyone, really. Not only was it heartless, it was just plain stupid.

He patted his clothes. Apparently he had the letter on him somewhere. "Want to see it?"

He was serious. I shook my head and thought of how I had

misspent the night we had bonded. We should have spent
the night with my family. Father would have grilled him on
gambling, Mother on politics, Kaaren and Dias would have
teased him to tears, and Miko would have drooled all over
him. I knew now that he would have gotten on with them
beautifully. I wondered if he had any idea what a normal family was like. His mother sounded like a horror, and the thought
that he would have to live in close proximity with her was depressing.

The door opened without anyone knocking. I quickly sat
up on the cot.

I'd seen Healer McLean before, on my visits to Karish. He
was a tall, dark, stern-looking middle-aged man who always
made me feel I had no right to be there. I couldn't help being
what Karish called my most Shield-like whenever I was
around the healer.

McLean nodded a greeting to me, then said to Karish,
"You can go now. Can't say I'm sorry. You've brought a lot of
confusion with you."

He also didn't have the greatest bedside manner.

Karish grinned. He smiled too much, I decided. "You'll
miss me," he promised the healer. "You know you will. I've
brightened your days and put a spring in your step. That's why
you want me gone. You're holding on to your professional
ethics by the fingernails, and you're afraid that if I stay just
one more day it'll all break loose."

For an instant the healer's professional demeanor slipped,
and he shot Karish a look of unalloyed disgust. A moment
later it was gone. "Any questions?" he asked in a flat voice.

Karish shook his head.

"Good." Another nod and he was out the door. I had the
feeling he would have hurried more if he hadn't thought it beneath his dignity.

"What was that about?" I asked.

Karish shrugged and rose from his chair with less grace
than was usually at his disposal. "He wants me so badly it
scares him," he said matter-of-factly, offering a hand to help
me up.

I ignored it. He still looked a little fragile, and I was afraid I
might break him. "Everyone wants you, eh?" I said, hoping the

sarcasm came out clearly enough. While I didn't doubt for a moment that he was right, for him to speak of his appeal so blatantly was too immodest for my liking.

"He does. But he doesn't like my character. Thinks I'm quite a flighty, useless creature. And it disgusts him. How could he possibly lust after someone he doesn't respect? He isn't an animal, after all, but a highly trained professional. So he's angry and confused."

If Karish felt the sting of McLean's dislike, he hid it well. "So you decided to play with his mind."

"Not really. I just spoke the truth. It's not my fault his mind and body are in conflict with each other, so he shouldn't take it out on me. If he were a true professional he would handle it better." Another one of those annoying grins. "Like you do."

I just looked at him. So he thought I shared the healer's predicament, did he? He couldn't have been more wrong. I didn't despise his character. Not much. And I didn't lust after him.

Not much.

"Going to deny it?" he prodded.

"Wouldn't dream of it," I said mildly. What would it accomplish? He would believe what he wanted to believe. "Ready to go?"

His smile dimmed just a little.

When we got back to the residence, there was a small, folded piece of parchment with his name on it, left on the shelf in the foyer on which all of our mail was deposited. He opened it and read it quickly. I knew it was none of my business, but I asked anyway. "It's not bad news?" Because I didn't think either of us could take any more bad news.

He handed it to me. It was a note:

Dear Taro,

We knew you'd be too tired for company so we decided not to mob you on your first day back—though a few heads had to be cracked together before they saw the wisdom of this. But we wanted you to know that we know you're coming home today and that we're thinking of you. We'll be there as soon as you want us.

Love,

It was signed. A quick count showed about thirty names. Karish didn't seem moved by the tribute. Used to it, I supposed.

There was a second letter for him, a proper letter in a proper envelope. It was sealed with wax, and I remembered seeing that seal before. He slit the letter open, and I wondered if I should leave him to it.

A part of me thought I should accompany him to his suite, make sure he got settled in and had everything he needed. But I wasn't his mother, and it would probably just make us both uncomfortable.

He started swearing. "What's wrong?"

"Another letter from *her.*"

His mother. "Oh." Yes, I should definitely leave him to it. I thought about escaping up the stairs.

"Can't even fake some interest, is that it?" he snapped.

"Just trying to mind my own business."

"It is your business."

All right, so I supposed I should stay. He obviously needed someone to rant in front of, and I appeared to be the only one available. "Only indirectly." I went to the living room to settle into a chair. He could follow me if he chose.

He chose. "Believe me, she won't let it be indirectly. Not once we're living there. She'll be showing unprecedented interest in my life. And yours."

I froze. "Once *we're* living there?"

"Aye." He refolded the letter and crammed it back into its envelope.

"I'm going with you. To find out about this fellow who attacked you. But once he's found and you're the duke, I'm not staying there. I'm not going to live there."

That seemed to surprise him, which I found odd. Why would he assume I'd stay in Flown Raven? "Where would you go?" he demanded.

"I don't know. Back to Shidonee's Gap. Maybe I will teach at one of the academies." Horrible thought. "Maybe the council will let me work with my family." Though I didn't have the slightest interest in doing tradelike things. "Maybe I could be a professional bench dancer." But again, only if the council allowed it. So none of those were likely.

"Lucky you." His eyes narrowed. "You can pretty much do as you damn well please, while I have to be hauled out to Flown Raven and live in that mausoleum and deal with " He cut himself off abruptly. He rubbed his forehead, a gesture of fatigue. "I don't want to take the title," he said. "Why the hell should I have to? It was never meant for me. That was made perfectly clear through my entire life. They got rid of me as soon as they could find an acceptable reason for it."

I was the wrong person to be hearing all this.

"They never had the slightest use for me, and now they want me to drop everything and rush over there to be their duke and listen to them verbally slice each other for fun. Taking me away from everything I've worked for. I've earned." He started pacing, his agitation giving him vigor. I watched him, and I didn't know what to say. He needed someone he trusted to confide in, someone who could give him adequate advice. "She barely knows what a Source is, what I do. She doesn't know what it means that I was posted here. But she doesn't hesitate to order me to leave it all behind."

The idea of a grown man's mother ordering him to do anything struck me as too bizarre.

"I wish I didn't have to take the title," he muttered. He stopped midstep. He seemed to think for a moment, and he frowned. "I *don't* have to take the title." He looked at me. The truest smile I'd seen from him in a good while spread over his face. "Lee, there's no law that says I have to take the title. I can abjure it!"

I said nothing. Yes, he could refuse the title. In theory. That sort of thing had been done a couple of times. But no one liked it when that happened, and there were repercussions Karish had possibly not considered. He would lose his name, part of the legal severance from his family. He would lose his status. And if he even so much as hinted that he wanted the title back, he'd be committing a crime with sanctions like incarceration and execution.

He couldn't really want to give up being the Duke of Westsea. Going to Flown Raven, being a duke, it would be a change, and maybe he didn't like that, but once he got used to the idea, he'd love it. Who wouldn't, all that money and power and prestige?

Karish was watching me. I hated it when he did that. "Lee, I will refuse the title," he said.

"I heard you the first time."

"But you didn't believe me."

"Of course I did," I lied smoothly.

Karish knew it was a lie. "You will believe me."

I nodded. I was too depressed to say anything.

Karish, on the other hand, was thrilled. He was glowing. He really thought he was going to refuse the title and be happy about it. He really thought he could stop being Karish and not care.

It wasn't that simple. A family was more than a collection of annoying relatives. It was part of a person's identity and their only real connection to the rest of the world. No one could cut that connection without doing great damage to themselves.

As for him not wanting the title, that was ridiculous. For the first eleven years of his life he had no doubt been taught that the duchy was the only prize worth having, a prize he would never possess. Some part of him had to want it, and once he was back in Flown Raven, surrounded by his own kind of people, the coronet held before him, he would step into place.

And I couldn't think any less of him for it. It would be only human of him, and it would be, in a way, his duty. The impact it would have on my life, that I would find it devastating, was irrelevant.

Chapter Sixteen

A Runner tracked me down to Aiden's house, where she gave me the news that Karish had been abducted. People had seen four men assault him and toss him into a carriage that was driven away at a neck-threatening speed. Neither the men nor the carriage had been recognized by anyone, and there had been no further word of their whereabouts. That was all the Runner said, before suggesting that I make an appearance at the Lower Western Runner Headquarters and running off on other business.

I could claim with all honesty that I never fainted. I had always been healthy, my clothing had always been loose, and I had never been one to indulge in hysterical fits. But standing there in Aiden's doorway, staring at the space in which the Runner had stood, my vision went black, my mind shut down, and for a moment I wasn't quite sure where I was.

"Dunleavy?" I heard a voice say. "What's happened?"

The voice seemed very far away, yet it grounded me a little, helped my mind return to the then and there. "Karish is missing."

"What?"

"Karish is missing." *Want me to go for three?*

He'd just gotten home. He'd had no chance to get better. Why did these things keep happening to him?

Aiden, now able to walk without relying on a crutch, put a hand on my shoulder. "You'd better sit down," he told me. "You look like you're about to drop."

I was not. I was in perfect control of myself. Shields were trained to be calm in difficult situations, not fall apart. However, it was very early, and I hadn't had much sleep the night before, with one thing and the other, so my legs were a little weak. So I sat down.

My hands were shaking. I stared at them, alarmed. They weren't supposed to do that.

I snarled, suddenly irritated. "Idiots!" I spat. "Why would they deliver news like this with so few details? Heartless bastards!"

"I'm sure they had their reasons."

"I'm his Shield!" I snapped. "You don't palm off this kind of message to a man's Shield. Irresponsible, insensible, incompetent, clueless little *bureaucrats*!"

He sat down beside me, a little too close. "I'm sure you'll learn more when you get to Headquarters."

His mild tone was getting on my nerves. "Aye, I'll learn more, if I have to carve the information out from their tiny little brains." I jumped to my feet and strode to the door.

Aiden followed me. "I want to go with you," he said.

I froze for a moment. I kind of wanted him there, for the company, but I was afraid that if he were there being all supportive I might fall apart. I would hate that.

"I know you don't need me there," he said in a flat voice. "And I know this is Triple S business. But I'd like to come. Will you let me?"

That tore it. If he had gone all demanding and strong and insisted on coming, it would have been easy to refuse him. But he had asked, so I had to let him go. I nodded.

I hadn't been told how long ago Karish had been taken. Still, I was expecting Karish's horde to be at the Headquarters before me and was surprised to see no familiar faces. So while the message I'd received had been far from satisfactory, it appeared that I had been the first to get it. That made me feel a little better.

I could be petty sometimes.

As soon as we arrived, one of the Runners offered to escort me to the captain's office and asked Aiden to take a seat somewhere. "I don't know how long this will take," I said to him. "You don't have to stay."

He shrugged. "I've got nothing better to do, and I need to rest a little, from the walk." Ah, that was right. We had moved a little fast. I hadn't given a thought to his leg. "Don't worry about me. I'll try out some of my repertoire on the rogues. That'll be fun."

I was reluctant to leave him, but I couldn't admit that. I followed the Runner to the office. After a swift knock he opened the door and let me in, closing the door behind me.

Upon my entrance an elderly man rose from behind the desk, holding out a hand. "Captain Mulroney," was his introduction. "Are you Shield Mallorough?"

"Aye, sir." I shook his hand.

"Please take a seat, Mallorough." Mulroney took his own advice and settled back behind his desk. "And let me assure you than I am aware of the danger you're in right now. I promise you we will find Lord Shintaro, and we will find him soon. No one's going to lose their life over this."

Sure. I'd believe that once we had Karish safely back, thanks. "Please, sir, can you tell me exactly what happened? The message didn't give me many details."

"We haven't got many details, yet," Mulroney admitted, "Obviously," he gestured at me, "he's not dead. He would be, if murder were the goal. But it's too early to say what the goal might be. For now, we just want to talk to as many of Lord Shintaro's acquaintances as we can. You and the other Pairs and his friends. Would you be able to give us any names?"

"If you give me a bit of time," I said, thinking of the list that had been waiting for Karish at the residence when he'd returned from the hospital. "And they can probably give you others."

"Excellent. We appreciate it. Now," Mulroney leaned forward, clasping his hands on the desk, "can you think of any reason why anyone would want to abduct Lord Shintaro?"

And so it began. First we discussed Karish's sudden elevation in rank and its possible connection to recent events. Then we talked about Karish's skill and post. Could professional jealousy be behind it all? And then came the questions, endless repetitive questions. All asked politely enough but, I thought, there were more than were strictly necessary. And a few times I thought, from the wording and the tone, that there was some suspicion regarding my own character, but I dismissed those fancies as soon as they flittered into my head. Ridiculous.

I was happy when I was given permission to leave so I could pick up the list of names. That had been important information to get to the Runners, and the captain had wasted all that time questioning me.

Aiden was still sitting there waiting when I left the captain's office. I was relieved but surprised. Surely I had been answering questions for at least a million years? He had to be bored out of his head.

LaMonte was there with his Shield Hammad. There were a couple of other familiar people lingering about. It appeared that the parade of acquaintances had already begun. Wait until I brought the note in. The trickle would roar into a flood, I had no doubt. And I thought this place had been chaotic before.

Aiden stood when he saw me. "You look shattered," he said, and he hugged me.

I appreciated the gesture, but I couldn't relax into him as he no doubt wished I would. "Let's get out of here," I suggested, easing away from his embrace. "I've got to pick something up at the residence and send it back here."

He nodded, and we threaded our way to the exit. "So what's happening?"

Mental exhaustion sank into my overworked little brain. I did not want to talk about it. But I owed it to him for waiting so long, and we had to talk about something as we walked back to the residence. There was little enough to tell, and perhaps Aiden would have some ideas. So I told him all that the captain had told me, and of course he had nothing to say about it. How could he? No one knew anything.

Karish's suite was a mess. It shocked me just looking at it. Papers scattered all over, furniture moved around, decorations removed from the cabinets. "What the hell—?"

"Looks like the Runners have already been here."

"The Runners did all this? Why?"

He shrugged. "Guess they don't have time to be careful."

Damn.

"Well, we might as well start," I said. "I'm looking for a single sheet of paper that's folded in quarters. It has a short note and a long list of names."

"Likes to keep track of his stable, does he?" was Aiden's snide comment.

"You don't have to be here." I went to the tasteful little writing desk snuggled in a corner and opened the first drawer.

"What's your Source going to think about me pawing through his things?"

"Under the circumstances I really don't think he'll care." The first drawer had nothing in it but blank stationery, wax, and pens. The next had the racing section of the newspaper. I picked it up and read some of the notations Karish had made in the margins, all about the horses' lineage, riders, owners, and racing history.

Aiden had looked through the emptied shelves in the room without success. "Try the bedroom," I said, going to the third drawer.

"Must I?" he muttered, and I snapped a look at his back as he disappeared into a location that was surely a legend in some circles.

I hoped Karish had kept the list. I would have tossed it, myself, but something told me Karish was the type to keep such things. Not that it would be such a disaster if it didn't show up. I knew the names of some of Karish's friends—Michael Whiteknife, for example—and the Runners could work from there. But the better the start, the faster they'd find him. I hoped.

The last drawer was completely empty, the contents no doubt the pile of correspondence dumped onto the floor beside the desk. I looked carefully among and within the envelopes but found nothing. I rifled through the rest of the room and was equally unsuccessful. I joined Aiden in the bedroom.

The bedroom was a wreck, too. Aiden was taking what little was still in place and pulling it out. The jumbled mess was having an irritating effect on my mind. "How about we detract from, rather than add to, the chaos?" I suggested.

"Under the circumstances I really don't think he'll care," Aiden quoted. "Will you look at those?" He gestured at the wardrobe.

I obliged him, and couldn't figure out what "those" he was referring to. There were no whips, no restraints, nothing unusual. "What?"

"There are more clothes there than I'll ever wear in my life."

I rolled my eyes but said nothing. "What is all this?" I nodded at the mess on the floor.

"Bills and gambling IOUs. Why does he bother holding on to either?"

"I don't know." I poked through them. There were many more IOUs than bills. I started to add up the money owed to Karish and came to a staggering amount. I knew it was staggering because Aiden whistled when I told it to him. Apparently Karish was a good gambler.

I fanned the notes in my hand. Maybe Karish was too good. "Do you think Karish would have been taken by one of the people who owed him money?"

"Of course not," was Aiden's immediate response. "Karish can't force them to pay. The law won't support a Source's claims."

"Does everyone know that?"

He shrugged. "Everyone should. A real gambler would."

But what if these IOUs belonged to idiots? Lots of stupid people gambled. Or what if the assault on Karish had started out of anger, out of revenge for a humiliating defeat, and had gone further than planned, requiring his removal? It was surely a possibility. I made a note of the names on the biggest IOUs. Perhaps the Runners didn't think anything of the gambling debts, but I was going to see if I could find anything out about them.

Aiden handed me a paper that had been folded into a small, neat square. "Is this it?"

I opened it and scanned the note. "Aye, this is it." Job done.

We took the list to the nearest messenger station and had it sent to Mulroney. And then, that was it. It was kind of anticlimactic. We went back to the residence, because I wanted to be easy to find in the case of any news. "There's got to be something else I can do."

"Have you read his mail?" Aiden asked.

"Read it? Of course not."

"Aye. In case he's gotten any threatening letters."

"Wouldn't the Runners have found anything like that?"

"I don't know. What do you think?"

The Runners were the experts. Surely they would know better than I what constituted a significant piece of information. On the other hand, the Runners didn't know Karish at all. Neither did I, really, but there was no harm in using another pair of eyes. Only I didn't like the idea of reading his mail. That was really too personal. "All right, then."

"I'll go downstairs and fix us something to eat," Aiden said. "I'm starving."

I wasn't. "Tell them I said you could, if any of the others question you." I hadn't seen any of the other Pairs about the residence in the time I had been there. I wondered if they all knew what had happened.

Back in Karish's living room, I scooped up all the letters and sat with them on the nearest settee. I couldn't believe how many letters Karish had received in the short time we had been in High Scape. I'd gotten no more than a handful. I wondered how nauseous I'd feel after slogging through them. I was imagining line after line of fulsome compliments, and my stomach was a little delicate when it came to bad poetry.

The first letter was a surprise. Instead of being from a forlorn lover, it was penned by one of Karish's professors. An elderly man from the handwriting, but one who had held on to his wit and humor. The epistle informed Karish of all that had been going on at the academy in his absence, in such a manner that had me cackling, even though I knew none of the people involved. I hoped to someday meet the brutally funny Professor Saint-Gerard.

The next letter was more along the line of what I had been expecting. Endearments all over the place, worshipful praise of his beauty, and a thorough description of his sexual prowess. Yes, I read it. I was curious. It wasn't nearly as nauseating as I'd anticipated.

I had never gotten a letter like that.

The next letter was something different yet again. The

salutation set off a warning all on its own. The other letters had begun with varying degrees of formality, but this correspondent had made an effort to drag out every title he could find.

Lord Shintaro Ivor Cear Karish, Duke of Westsea, Magistrate of Flown Raven, Source Principal of Site High Scape

Sir:

With humble respect we hope this missive finds you in health and peace. We must admit, however, that news of the recent insults inflicted upon your noble person has reached our ears. We offer our respectful condolences. We find ourselves appalled and enraged on your behalf. These indignities cannot be allowed to continue. Surely they are the result of ignorance and arrogance, for if the truth of your talent and nobility were known as they should, none would dare such assaults.

We do most humbly beg you, again, to come to the safety of our association. You would bring honor and glory to our number, and we would serve you well. Together we would learn the identity of the foul miscreants who would sully your person with their degenerate ambitions, and see them punished. Together we would ensure you are shown the respect your eminence demands.

It is honorable of you to wish to serve the academy to which you gave your oath, but have they not already broken their oath to you? They have bonded you to an insolent Shield. They have sent you to an inferior site filled with the refuse of all societies. They have prevented you from assuming the responsibilities and privileges to be bestowed upon you by your noble family. They have in all ways failed to show the honor and respect due to a person of your birth and talent.

With the greatest of deference we exhort you to carefully reconsider our invitation. We are eager to accommodate you in the manner to which you were born and bred.

Your servant,
Stevan Creol
Middle Reach

The crazy Source was on the loose. In Middle Reach, of all places. What was he doing out there? They weren't supposed to let him out of the academy unsupervised until he was bonded. And if he was so old he was no longer considered dangerous, he should have been sent somewhere to work. One of the staff at the academy or at the very least out looking for undiscovered Shields and Sources.

Of course, he could be doing that in Middle Reach, but Middle Reach already had Pairs who would, in their spare time—and I imagined they had a lot of it—perform that task.

And why was he writing to Karish? In such a sickeningly submissive manner. Your talent, your breeding, with the word "noble" used at least half a dozen times. They couldn't have been friends, could they? It was impossible that Karish, with his enormous circle of acquaintances, could feel any sort of attraction to someone as twisted as Creol.

Hold on, there. Remember to think a little before you make a judgment. You relied on reputation with Karish, and look where it got you. You have never even spoken to Creol; you can't possibly know what he's really like.

Still, it was odd that he was, apparently, urging Karish to leave his post, and me, which would be an illegal act on Karish's part. And not just for a vacation, but permanently. Very strange. And to Middle Reach.

Why was he in Middle Reach? No one chose to go there. Everyone who lived there had been forced there by one unfortunate act of circumstances or another. Or had been born there and couldn't get out. The only reason I could think of for Creol to be there was if the Triple S was punishing him for something, but that was an unusual punishment for someone who wasn't even Paired yet, and nothing had come through the rumor mill.

I set the letter aside with plans to look at it again later.

I suffered through a long series of love letters. Some embarrassed me, they were so blunt in their expressions of desire. Some made me laugh, because surely no one really believed Karish was an actual son of a genuine god. One disturbed me, for the author was piteously pleading for forgiveness for some unnamed crime, his words filled with such self-loathing that I almost squirmed in discomfort.

I went through a series of letters from relatives asking

Karish to use his influence over his brother to encourage him to give them money, positions, introductions, and other forms of assistance. The tone of these letters ranged from embarrassed and apologetic to petulant, demanding, and even a little threatening.

There was a letter from a Reanist, asking Karish if he would like to be the religious group's next sacrifice and earn his place in the garden of the gods.

More love letters. Ho-hum. Another letter from Saint-Gerard, which made me laugh except for one line: "I'm happy for you, that things are going better with your Shield." So, Karish had been complaining about me, had he? I wondered how many people thought I was an impossible bitch. Prat.

More demands for assistance. More love letters. Another letter from Creol, asking Karish if he had reconsidered his offer. Then another letter from Saint-Gerard. It was the first Karish had received from him after we had arrived in High Scape, and it spoke of me at great length. Naturally I read it.

> As to your problems with your Shield, I don't know what I can offer in the way of advice. Each Pair must find their own way. Also, I have never met young Mallorough, and know her only according to reputation. Please remember that my speculation is nothing more than that.
>
> I doubt she is afflicted with class jealousy. She has worked with members of all classes with little trouble beyond the natural belief in her own class's inherent superiority. There is no evidence that she seeks attention, so it seems unlikely that she resents you for the attention you receive.
>
> You might remind her of someone she despises. She may just honestly dislike you. Or perhaps there is some element only remotely connected to you, or something going on you're not aware of. It is possible that she is going through some difficulty that has nothing to do with you at all.
>
> You have complained that she judges you by your reputation and nothing else. I say a man who has allowed a certain kind of reputation to develop around him and has made no effort to dispel it shouldn't resent it when people start using that reputation as a standard with which to judge him. And make certain that this is not a case of

wounded vanity. You've always been a popular lad, and it must have been a bit of a shock to come across someone who wasn't awestruck by you.

All I can suggest is that you keep yourself above it. Show her you are more than your reputation. Be patient, though of course you shouldn't put up with any abuse. Never give her the right to accuse you of shirking your responsibilities. If she is as sensible as she is supposed to be, she'll eventually learn your character and come to appreciate it. If not, at least you will not have made things any worse. It is the lot of the tolerant partner to shoulder the majority of the emotional burdens. I know your shoulders are broad enough.

Is she cute?

Reading half a correspondence was just as unsatisfying as eavesdropping on half a conversation. You ended up with less than half a message. It was an interesting letter and one I would have to think about, but no one else needed to see it.

More love letters.

Another letter from Creol, according to the date the first Karish had received in High Scape, and it was by far the longest. In it, Creol reminded Karish that they had met several times while in their academy and had even done some of their training together. I thought that a little odd considering the disparity in their ages. He commiserated with Karish on his miserable assigment—High Scape, a miserable assignment? Was the man crazy?—and warned him that the Triple S would never treat him well. Some details on his own failed career were offered as proof of the incompetence of the Triple S. Then an invitation to join an association of Sources and Shields in Middle Reach, who were seeking independence and power for the "talented." That was how he referred to anyone with the potential to become a Source or Shield. His association, he claimed, would show the world what the talented truly were.

A very disturbing letter. An association of Sources and Shields. Not Pairs. Something about that tickled my brain. And I'd never heard of any Pair associations outside of the Triple S. There was no need for it, there were so few of us. And whatever this club was, Karish's Shield was not invited. Odd.

Aiden returned from the kitchen. "Find anything?" he asked.

My first impulse was to brush the question aside. Triple S business. But my second thought reminded me of the previously unappreciated wisdom of getting an opinion from outside my own head. "A few letters from this Creol fellow, asking Karish to come out to Middle Reach and join his association."

"Association? What kind of association?"

"An association seeking independence and power for Sources and Shields," I paraphrased.

Aiden's eyebrows rose. "Sounds a bit odd."

"Aye."

"So what do you think?"

I shrugged. "That's what I was going to ask you."

"I don't think I know enough about it." He set a platter of sliced meat and cheese on a nearby table. "Do you think Lord Shintaro is interested in joining this group?"

"From the sound of these letters, I don't think he's said yes." Karish didn't need to join an association to get power and independence. The ducal title would do that for him.

"There are also some mildly threatening letters from estranged relatives, and one from a Reanist. Any one of them could mean something, and maybe none of them do. Too many choices." And I really didn't know what to make of any of it.

"Well, leave it for a bit and eat something. You'll be better for a break."

"Aye." I still wasn't hungry, not at all, but I felt obliged to eat after Aiden had gone to the trouble to get the food. "How's the leg?" I asked him.

"Not too bad."

"You were moving really well today. Sometimes you don't even limp."

He smiled. "Aye."

"So do you think you'll try dancing again?" I didn't mean in competition. Just a little practice run, with some friends manipulating the bars very slowly.

Aiden looked me in the eye. "I won't dance again, Dunleavy," he said. "I can walk, and the night this happened I was afraid I'd never get even that much back. I certainly thought

I'd be bedridden much longer than I have been. I'm grateful for what I've gotten." He reached across the table to take my hand in his. "The clicking in my knee is still there, Dunleavy. I don't expect it to go away."

I rubbed my temple with my free hand. I was developing a headache.

"I didn't tell you that to make you feel guilty," he said gently. "I told you because you asked. Can I not talk about this?"

"Of course you can," I answered.

"Without you getting that guilty look on your face?"

"Guilt is a waste of an emotion."

He looked amused. "One of your tenets?"

"Simple truth."

Unfortunately, the fact that it was true didn't seem to make it particularly effective. I did feel guilty. Even though I hadn't done anything, either deliberately or accidentally, to cause Aiden's injury. Even though injuries were a risk every dancer faced, including me. I couldn't help feeling responsible for it, and badly about it. My professors would be disappointed.

Chapter Seventeen

Karish was missing.

That was the first clear thought in my head as I woke at an uncharacteristically early hour. The letters I had taken from Karish's desk were on my table. I'd wanted to run them over to the Headquarters as soon as I'd gotten through the lot, but Aiden had persuaded me it would be too difficult to convince the Runners of the letters' significance when it was the middle of the night and everyone was tired and irritable and stubborn. Wait until morning, he'd said, when everyone was rested and thinking clearly and in a better mood. After all, they'd either seen the letters and dismissed them, or had missed them altogether. Either way, they weren't going to like my going in and telling them how to do their job. No point in going out of my way to make the task more difficult than it would naturally be. So he'd gone home and I'd gone to bed, where I barely slept, certain that I would die in my sleep.

I did eventually doze off, and when I woke, before taking note of the time and place, I noticed anew that Karish was gone. It was almost something I could feel, deep in my mind. It was disturbing.

I got up. I dressed. I made myself some coffee. Aiden

arrived as early as he had promised to, and we went back to the Runners' Headquarters.

A lot had happened since the day before. There were more familiar faces at Headquarters; I remembered them from the hospital. From them I learned that everyone on the list had been ruthlessly rounded up and questioned. The hospital where Karish had convalesced had been searched, and all the staff had been questioned. Every route out of the city was being posted with Runners, and a house-by-house search had been started. Overnight.

"He's Lord Shintaro," Aiden said when I commented on this. "What, you think all the Runners in High Scape are in love with him, too?"

He chuckled, and smiled, and kissed my cheek. "I forget how . . . innocent you are, sometimes."

I looked at him for a long moment. "I'm going to hit you now," I announced.

"It's not your fault. You've been holed up in an academy for most of your life, so you don't know how the world works for the rest of us." His mouth crooked up with sympathetic amusement. "Lord Shintaro isn't human, you know."

I didn't think so, either, but I suspected the reason for Aiden's belief was different from mine. "Isn't he?"

"He's a duke," Aiden told me gently, with all the condescension of a tutor with a particularly dense student. "Or he will be soon. He's practically royalty. To the rest of the world he might as well be, for he's just as remote in his way, just as privileged and blessed and untouchable. People will deny it to their last breath, but buried in the back of our minds is the knowledge that Karish and his kind are, in many ways, different from us. Better than us. No, I'm serious." For I had smiled at that. And how could anyone think Karish untouchable?

"The aristocracy is worshipped," Aiden continued. "When something like this happens"—he nodded at a Runner rushing by him—"people do everything they can to fix it."

I couldn't deny that was how it appeared. The Runners had accomplished in one night what I would have thought would take days. I did doubt that so much effort would be made for an ordinary person.

"Aside from his godliness, Karish is an extremely important

person. I don't know much about Westsea, but I know it's huge. He'll have enormous political power. He'll be a magistrate director. He'll be extremely wealthy. If he dies now with no clear immediate heir to step in, it'll be a mess. The political and economic repercussions could be staggering. Every potential heir he's got will be up in arms, grabbing for the seat. Hell, an estate that size, it could start a war."

I stared at him. I'd had no idea. Well, I had, in a vague sort of way, but I hadn't really thought about it. It had never had anything to do with me.

"Don't be embarrassed," he said. "I'll wager Lord Shintaro doesn't understand, either. But he'll find out once he's able to get to Flown Raven and look into his affairs."

And any faint hope I'd had that he really would refuse the title evaporated. He couldn't refuse. If Westsea was that important, if his refusal could do that much damage, he would have to take the title. I really had to start looking into what I was going to do as a bonded but Sourceless Shield.

Later. After I found him. I had Karish's letters, and I had to point out their significance to someone in authority. The Runners in the common area tried to tell me the captain was too busy to see me. Risa Demaris was there, and she remembered me from the hospital. She easily brushed off the Runner holding me back and led me to the door to the captain's office. After a brisk knock I entered, Aiden at my heels.

Mulroney was too busy? Hah. He was alone, staring sightlessly at the one paper he held in his hand. He looked up at me with the worn face and reddened eyes of a man who'd had too little sleep or too much alcohol. Possibly both. Irritation at the interruption gave way to resignation as he rolled his eyes. "Zaire," he swore. Then he spied Aiden. "Who the hell are you?" he demanded.

"I belong to her," Aiden answered, and I suppressed my surprise at his choice of words.

"This has nothing to do with you. Unless you're intimately familiar with Lord Shintaro's activities of the past couple days."

"Not at all, sir."

"Then get out."

That seemed unnecessarily brusque.

Looking almost humble, Aiden bowed and left the office.

"I've got some letters that might be of use to you," I said quickly, before the captain could start yelling. "And I want to know what's going on."

"I told you yesterday I would contact you if anything came up."

Had he really expected me to sit at home and wait until he decided to send word to me? "The letters were sent to Karish. I think they might have some useful information."

"We looked through Lord Karish's correspondence."

"I know," I said, to be polite, "but none of you are his intimates." And I felt like a bit of a fraud as I said that, for I could hardly be called one of Karish's intimates, either. I held out the letters to him. "I think these might give you some ideas about who might have taken Karish."

He accepted them gracefully enough. "I'll have another look at them," he promised me, "but it's pretty clear he's been taken to Flown Raven."

"Why is it clear?" And why had no one told me that? What was that he had just said about informing me when anything new came to light?

"Dosh's livery got an order for a small carriage with sprung wheels from some out-of-towners who claimed to be from Shina Lake. One of them had a tattoo of a black sun over his left temple. Have you heard of the Reanists?"

"Of course," I said, a little too sharply, for he gave me a look.

"They're on the rise again. Guess they've gotten sick of the flash floods Shina Lake's been getting and decided to soothe their gods' nerves with a little aristocratic blood."

"That's what they do." And why every last one of them hadn't been rounded up, I couldn't fathom. They all insisted on wearing those ridiculous tattoos on their faces. And they were fanatics. Pretty easy to spot. The fact that a handful of them had managed to get hold of a prince about eightieth in line to the throne and stake him before the Imperial Guards caught them should have been all the excuse anyone needed. Instead, they'd executed the ringleaders and let the others free to wander about and be abused by the general population. It had been claimed that only the ringleaders had been actually involved in the murder, and therefore only they could be executed, but I found that hard to believe. "One of those letters is from a Reanist, inviting Karish to be their next sacrifice."

Mulroney snorted. "Aye, I've heard of that," he said. "A lot of aristocrats get them, but of course it doesn't usually come to anything. But I don't think a religious sacrifice is what this is all about, though no doubt we're supposed to think it is. More likely the ringleader is using some of these old fanatics to do his dirty work. I don't imagine it would be difficult to turn that sort of person on to another 'mission.'" Mulroney picked up another paper from the collection on his desk. "Someone saw the same carriage leaving High Scape by the west gate the night Lord Shintaro disappeared. We've tracked the wagon some distance, and we know it's going west and south." The general direction of Flown Raven and Shina Lake and a dozen other major sites. "We've also started asking questions about the person most likely to be designated Lord Shintaro's heir, a cousin of his by the name of Alcina Mass. Infamous for her gambling, as well as her lack of skill in it. We haven't gotten far with her yet, but I wouldn't be surprised if she had a few heavy debts hanging around her neck." He dropped the paper on the desk. "Flown Raven and Shina Lake are the obvious places to start."

He was the expert. I had to assume he knew what he was doing. "What's the next step?"

"Send some Runners to Shina Lake and Flown Raven."

"I'm going with them," I announced.

Oddly enough, Mulroney didn't seem at all surprised. "Don't be ridiculous."

I raised a brow at him. "I beg your pardon?"

"What do you know about investigating a kidnapping?"

Like that had anything to do with anything. "He's my Source."

"I don't care what he is to you." He shoved all the papers on his desk into a pile. "I'm not letting you anywhere near this."

"I won't get in your way," I promised him. "I'll only look around and ask a few questions. There's no harm in that."

Mulroney muttered something. Highly complimentary, I was sure. "There's a hell of a lot of harm in it," he snapped, "if you start asking the wrong sort of people the wrong sort of questions. Lord Shintaro is the one they'll want to keep in one piece. They won't care about *your* health."

"If I die, so does Karish," I reminded him. "Everyone knows that."

That slowed him down not a jot. "They don't have to kill you to incapacitate you, do they? If you're lucky they'll only leave you bound and gagged in a cellar somewhere. But if you irritate them they might gouge out your eyes or chop off a few body parts. That'll do the trick and won't do a lick of harm to Lord Shintaro."

I tried to keep the expression of disgust off my face, ignoring the lovely little images of torture and mutilation that were dancing through my head. "I can be of use to you," I said. "I can feel where Karish is. When we're within a certain distance, I mean. If he's in Shina Lake or Flown Raven, I'll lead you straight to him."

He looked at me with hard eyes. "You're a good liar," he commented flatly.

Hell. I hated lying, so when I did it I should at least be good at it. Good enough to fool a stranger, at least.

"If I didn't know for a fact that wasn't true, I might have bought it."

What did he mean, know it for a fact? It was a very popular myth.

"I've lived in High Scape all my life. Known a lot of Pairs."

Oh. "If you don't let me go with them, I'll just follow them," I threatened him.

"Try it, and I'll toss you into a cell until this is finished."

That shocked me. "You can't imprison me without just cause," I objected.

"All right. I'll just hand you over to the Triple S council, poor little distraught Shield that you are. But whatever I have to do, I'm not going to let your thirst for heroics endanger Lord Shintaro."

Thirst for heroics? Son of a bitch. "Do you understand the bond works both ways?" I asked him. "If Karish dies, so do I. That's the fear that I'm living under right now."

This had no softening effect on Mulroney. "So I guess it's time for that stoicism you Shields are so famous for," he said. "And you'll appreciate why I want this job done right. There's no room for amateurs." He waved a dismissive hand at me. "Go home. We'll contact you when we find him."

Condescending, unimaginative, shortsighted bastard.

I left the office. Obviously I would get no help from him. I would have to manage something on my own.

I slipped through the chaos of the common area and headed for the exit. Aiden stepped in behind me. It was a fortunate thing that he had noticed my leaving because I wouldn't have called to him. I had, shamefully enough, forgotten he was there.

"What's happened?" he asked as soon as we were back on the street.

So I told him in a few short sentences. "The hell with him," I muttered, referring to Mulroney. "How dare he tell me where I can and cannot go? I'll go to Flown Raven whenever I damn well please, and it pleases me to go now."

"To investigate Lord Shintaro's disappearance."

"Of course."

"Because you can't trust the Runners to do the job properly."

The tone was mild, but the words jerked me to a stop. "What?"

He stopped, too. He faced me, farther away from me than he usually stood, his arms crossed. An uncharacteristic posture for him. "Do you really think you can do the Runners' job better than they can?"

Of course not. Not really. It was just . . . "I can help," I said through my teeth, "but they're treating me like a useless idiot."

"It has nothing to do with intelligence, Dunleavy," he said, his voice filled with an expression of patience that was just a little too obvious. "Every job requires training and experience. No matter how intelligent a person is, they can't step into someone else's job and do it as well as a professional. Except for you, of course. We all know the only reason you're not solving crimes and setting bones and writing wills is that you're too busy being a Shield."

Where had that come from? I had never said I could do everything, and I certainly didn't think it. On the other hand, my accompanying the Runners wouldn't do any harm. I wasn't a fool, and I would have done what I was told. "I am going to Flown Raven, and there's nothing yon noble captain can do about it." I started on down the street.

"Lord Shintaro's Shield isn't going to get anywhere poking her nose into everyone's business in Flown Raven."

He had a point. "So I'll take off the braid."

He looked stunned. "What?"

"I'll take off the braid," I said with a nonchalance I was far from feeling. Take off my braid? Every coat, cloak, shirt, blouse, and dress I owned had the white braid sewn into the left shoulder. I had waited years for the right to wear the braid. It meant something, and I had the ridiculous fear that I would feel naked without it.

Legally, it wasn't the best of ideas. It wasn't exactly illegal not to wear the braid, but should a Shield go about without her braid and then do something dangerous while under the influence of music, I imagined the authorities would be a lot less lenient. Which was only right.

Still, if it was necessary, I would do it. I'd been naked before.

"You'll need new clothes," said Aiden.

"So I'll get some."

"They'll wonder why a Shield is getting clothes without the braid."

"They can wonder away."

"All right, then, how much money have you got?"

What a stupid question. "None, of course."

"Then how are you going to pay for food, lodging, horses, tolls, and whatever else in your guise as a regular person?"

I opened my mouth to utter a cutting, witty response. I closed my mouth as I realized I was an idiot.

Aiden's expression was now one of annoyingly amused compassion. "It's not your fault, my dear," he assured me. "You were raised to be ignorant."

I could hit him for that, couldn't I?

"I suppose I should stop resenting Lord Shintaro for being an aristocrat and having such an easy life," Aiden said with a reluctant smile. "Yours has been much the same. You've never had to worry about how you're going to earn your food or shelter, or paying taxes, or what you're going to do if you're injured or ill and you can't work anymore."

What did that have to do with anything? "Is there a point to this little lecture?"

He shrugged. "No one knows everything, Dunleavy, not even you, and no one can do everything. Mulroney can't be a Shield, and you can't be a Runner. Let the Runners do their job. You concentrate on being a Shield."

"I can't be a Shield without a Source, can I?" I said sharply.

"That's not exactly what I meant."

"So what do you mean?"

"I'm not sure." He pulled at his lower lip. "It's all pretty weak, though, what they're doing. Four fellows rent a carriage that's going in the direction of Flown Raven, and they all flock off after them."

"And the Reanists in Shina Lake," I reminded him. "And as you are always saying, Karish is an aristocrat."

"If either the Reanists or the heir were interested in him, they would have killed him. Abducting him makes no sense. It takes too much effort, and the risk of getting caught is much higher."

"So what are you thinking?"

He grabbed my arm and pulled me close, lowering his voice as though he were revealing a secret. "It's that crazy Source from Middle Reach."

"What?"

"You said yourself he wrote to Lord Shintaro several times. He obviously really wants him."

I didn't want to hear this, because I'd thought it myself. "Karish refused."

"So maybe this fellow decided to convince him."

I shot him a derisive look. "By kidnapping him?"

"It makes more sense than the other two theories," Aiden declared. "Reanists or a rival heir would want him dead. This Creol character probably wants to use him for something."

"How would kidnapping Karish convince him to do anything?" I demanded.

"Maybe they've kidnapped him only to get him to Middle Reach, to talk to him. They might have him living in the lap of luxury once they've got him out there."

"But what would Creol want with Karish?" I asked, and the

answer came to me on its own. As a Source without a Shield, Creol was impotent, with no place anywhere. So maybe he wanted influence. A favored Source, a future duke, Karish would have a lot of influence over a lot of people. I wondered again about the nature of Creol's association. "I can't see Creol kidnapping Karish. It's too crazy."

"I thought he was supposed to be crazy."

"Not that crazy. And that's only rumor."

"You would know better than I. I've never met the man."

I had, but only for a moment. Did it really mean anything, that one shared glance? Probably not. The glance I'd exchanged with Karish had had a lot more weight to it, and I still hadn't known a thing about him.

"You can't go with the Runners," Aiden said. "The captain's threatened to toss you in jail if he thinks you're interfering. Everyone's going to Flown Raven. No one's going to Middle Reach. Don't you think it's a least worth looking into?"

I didn't know. It was all so confusing and insubstantial. The jealous heir seemed a more reasonable explanation, but the letters from Creol were unsettling.

I hated thinking. "It's just so farfetched," I complained.

"It's all farfetched," he retorted. "The very idea of Lord Shintaro being abducted is farfetched. But here we are. And there are threats from a few different sources, and no one's even considering the one in Middle Reach."

Because they thought it wasn't worth considering. If they were even aware of it. And what did they know, really? They were fixing on Flown Raven for very little reason. Weren't they?

"I mean, Middle Reach is at least a possibility, don't you think?" Aiden said. "Shouldn't all the possibilities be considered?"

The totally irrelevant thought that Aiden was really quite wonderful trickled into my slowly churning brain. He was no friend of Karish's, but there he was trying to figure out the best way to bring Karish back to safety. I'd have to do something amazing for him when this was all over.

"And Middle Reach is so much closer than Flown Raven. We could be there in a couple of days, look around, and be back before the Runners are even halfway to Flown Raven. We could probably catch up with them if we had to."

I cocked a brow at him. "We?" I asked. Not that I had a problem with him coming with me—I would like the company—but I hadn't thought of it. He had a life in High Scape, and it wasn't fair to ask him to risk it by getting involved in Karish's murky personal life.

"I will provide you with an excuse to be in Middle Reach, in case anyone asks," Aiden explained. "I have family there. And Ryan and his friends can help us look around. They probably even know something about that association of Creol's."

I didn't like the idea of leaving High Scape right then. I felt it was the only place where I could possibly learn anything from the Runners. But Aiden had been right to imply that I was redundant there. I could ask questions, sure, but of whom that the Runners hadn't already questioned? And what would I ask them? I couldn't think of anything more than "Did you kidnap Karish?" and, if the answer was in the affirmative, "Where did you put him?"

I'd be equally useless in Flown Raven, a remote city I'd never seen, filled with self-important aristocrats and slippery politicians. They would out-sophisticate me in two sentences and leave me standing there trying to remember my own name. And I didn't know anything about Shina Lake except that it grew religious fanatics. Plus there was that threat of Mulroney's, which I took seriously. I didn't think I would like jail.

But no one could accuse me of interfering with anything by taking a little holiday jaunt to Middle Reach. It was, as Aiden said, relatively close, and it would do no harm just to take a look. If nothing else came of it, at least I would learn something about Creol's little association. It was certainly better than sitting in High Scape doing nothing but going crazy with worry.

"Are you sure you're up to traveling?" I asked Aiden.

He didn't actually smile, but he seemed pleased. "I won't slow you down," he promised, responding to the spirit if not the letter of my question. "When will you be ready to go?"

"Tomorrow morning? Will that give me enough time to get everything I need?"

"I'll get everything."

"You will not," I objected. "That's my job."

"I'm not your Source, Dunleavy," he reminded me with

some sarcasm. "I know how to do things, and there are no roles each of us are expected to fill. And surely you have Triple S things to clear up before you leave."

Probably. And I had to admit Aiden was likely to have had more experience with planning trips than I. "I won't let you pay for everything."

"I won't. I'll say I'm going with you so at least your gear'll be free. If anyone gives me a hard time, then I'll bring you around. How about we meet at my place by sundown?"

"Sounds good."

I went back to the residence to pack. I had hoped no one else would be there at that time of day, and that I would be able to leave a note letting everyone know where I was going. Just my luck, LaMonte and Hammad were there, the Pair I least wanted to see. The feeling was mutual. LaMonte looked at me with some surprise and no pleasure. "Dunleavy," he greeted me with formal courtesy. "Is there something I can do for you?"

Of course there was nothing he could do for me, the supercilious old prat. "I'm going to Middle Reach," I told him.

The two men exchanged glances. "Why?" Hammad asked.

"Have you been reassigned there?" LaMonte added.

I searched his expression. Did he honestly think I could be assigned to Middle Reach? Or was he insulting me? I couldn't tell. "There's someone I have to see."

"This is personal business?"

"It's my business."

He didn't like that. Too damn bad. He had no authority over me.

Of course, I did work with the man. Or I had. I probably never would again. No sense in antagonizing him. Professional courtesy and all that. But I wasn't sure how to tell him that I was gallivanting off to Middle Reach to play amateur Runner. What would he think of that?

Who cared what he thought? "I think there's something strange happening in Middle Reach, and I think it might have something to do with Karish's disappearance." Perhaps I should have told him the vacation story, but if there was something strange happening in Middle Reach, I thought there should be someone who knew about it. In case I was gone too long.

He didn't laugh out loud. Neither did Hammad, but then, he wouldn't. "What sort of strange thing?"

"I'm not sure," I admitted. "Ever heard of Stevan Creol?" The look of distaste appearing on both men told me that they had. "He's been in Middle Reach recently, he might be there right now, and he's invited Karish to join him there."

That got a reaction. "To do what?" LaMonte asked.

"To join some kind of association that he's started. I don't know much about it. I've talked to the Runners about it—" Actually, that wasn't true. I hadn't gotten that far. "But for now they want to concentrate on some information concerning Flown Raven and Shina Lake."

A sardonic smile curved LaMonte's lips. "And they're all wrong, so you're going to go charging off in the right direction to save your Source and the day."

What was it with these people? I was in no way claiming to be a hero. That was Karish's department. "I don't know that they're wrong. It's just an option I want to look into."

"I don't think it's a good idea for you to go off on your own."

That wasn't genuine concern I was seeing, was it? "I'm useless here."

"I don't know that Val would agree with you."

Surprise increased tenfold. A compliment? "He's not a Shield."

"I believe all the Shields feel Miho overreacted."

Hammad nodded.

LaMonte smiled again, and this time there was real warmth in it. "But, of course, they would."

Absurd how good that felt, validation from someone I didn't even like. "All the Pairs on the roster are fit and ready to do their jobs. There's nothing for me to do here. I've got to do something."

"Aye, I imagine you do," LaMonte said with resignation. "But are you really going to just swan off without getting permission from the Triple S?"

"What, send off a message and wait for a response? That could take weeks." Or months. And chances were excellent permission would be denied.

"It's the proper thing to do."

"Aye, but is it the sensible thing to do?"

He rolled his eyes. "Must you have an answer to everything?"

"I'd hardly be the all-knowing omnipotent being that I am if I didn't."

I didn't know the act of holding onto one's patience could be a visual spectacle. It was kind of interesting to watch.

"I have to do something, LaMonte. I know it's abandoning my post, but I'm unfit for duty without my Source, aren't I? And I can't just sit here doing nothing. I mean, could you, if your Shield were taken?"

"Never flitting, still is sitting," said LaMonte, which of course meant nothing. "Kenton"—Hammad—"would never get himself abducted." Which was truly one of the stupidest things I'd ever heard anyone say. "But I suppose I see your point."

I nodded. "So please say bye to everyone, and I'll see them soon."

The third smile in a row. Get the almanac. "I take it you don't plan to be long," he said dryly. "That sure of yourself, are you?"

"Of course." Being unsure of oneself never got anyone anywhere.

"Good luck."

Aye, I'd need it.

I studied some maps of Middle Reach and the surrounding areas, just because I thought I should. I didn't know what I was looking for, but studying maps seemed like the thing to do before heading off on a journey. I packed a bag, mostly drab, comfortable clothes. Then I went to Aiden's house, long before we'd agreed to meet. Turned out I hadn't had much to do after all.

Aiden was a wonder and a treasure. In less than a day he managed to arrange for horses and gather all the supplies he claimed we would need. He had been to Middle Reach many times before; I had to trust he knew what he was doing.

I spent the night at Aiden's house, on the settee in the living room. I was too afraid to sleep. Because the truth was that I wasn't sure of myself at all, not in matters that had nothing to do with either Shielding or dancing the benches. Anything outside those two areas left me ignorant and helpless.

Don't think about it. Stay calm.

We left High Scape at the crack of dawn. Not my version of dawn, which was maybe a couple of hours before midday. Real dawn, before the birds had begun to sing. I felt oddly isolated as Aiden and I dressed and ate and rode out in preday silence. Isolated and afraid. For the first time in a great many years I was striking out without the protection of the Triple S, without the company of even a Source. It left me feeling weak and vulnerable. I hated that.

Karish had better appreciate it.

Chapter Eighteen

It was the worst week of my life.

Yes. Week. The trip that was supposed to take a couple of days ultimately ended up taking a week. For all his promises that he wouldn't slow me down, Aiden did. And I couldn't get angry at him. Because he was coming as a favor to me, and he would ride until he was white and trembling with pain, and all I could do was bite my tongue. Hard.

And during that unending week, I couldn't stop thinking about the fact that Karish, and then I, might die. At any time. In an instant. I couldn't stop thinking about that for a single moment of any day and much of the night. My brain spun with the knowledge, relentlessly.

When I could sleep, I had nightmares. Dreams of being swallowed up in the earth, screaming. Dreams of suffocating. Dreams of being lost. Dreams of being left behind. Dreams of blood showering from the sky.

There was something wrong with my training. Some lapse somewhere. I wasn't supposed to be so afraid. I'd have to do something about it when I got back to High Scape.

I controlled it as best I could. I kept my horse plodding onward into what I'd begun to think of as a great, fatal wasteland.

I forced myself to eat, though I could manage little. I kept a level voice at all times, and I smiled when Aiden tried to be funny.

But early one evening, when Aiden had given up for the day, I lay on my back and looked up at the darkening sky and realized I wanted to leave Aiden behind. That was horrible, and I was heartily ashamed of myself, but damn it, this was a nightmare. I should have been there by then.

I pulled in a deep breath and blew it out slowly, releasing my impatience with it. This was the time to stay calm.

"I know, Dunleavy," said Aiden. He had his leg stretched out on the ground, and he was massaging the knee. At least he'd regained some of his color. "And apologizing doesn't begin to cover it. I don't know what to do."

"It's not you."

"Of course it is."

"I mean it's not this"—I gestured vaguely, indicating the delay and being out in the middle of nowhere—"that has me a little . . . temperamental."

"Temperamental," he echoed with a faint smile. "Couldn't bring yourself to say 'upset,' could you?"

I ignored that. "It's just everything."

"What, life in general?"

I sat up and rubbed my feet into the ground, enjoying the prickly hardness of the grass against my bare soles, and I thought about that. "Aye," I admitted with some surprise. I hadn't really thought of it that way. "Ever since I was Chosen everything has been so chaotic, one thing after another. And I don't like it. I'm not suited to it." Life at the academy had been so peaceful. "I never wanted adventure, you know. I wanted a nice steady Source and a nice steady life. No excitement, no drama, nothing to sing about. But here I am, in the middle of this"—I searched for an appropriate word and had to settle for—"intrigue."

He smiled with a total lack of sympathy, which wasn't surprising. He did seek adventure. "You lie," he said, and that *was* surprising. "You could never be so staid. You just say that sort of thing because wanting adventure seems too immature to you."

"I think I know my own mind," I said coolly. I hated it

when people tried to tell me what I thought, as though they had some unique perception into me that I lacked.

"Huh." He sounded unconvinced. "Well, I always wanted adventure. I wanted to travel all over the world. I wanted to dance, to be the best dancer this world has ever seen. I wanted to dance for the Empress. I swore she would be so entranced by my skill that she would fall in love with me and offer me gold and jewels and everything I wanted. And the minstrels would sing about me, and apprentices would come from all over to beg me to be their master." As suddenly as the light in his eyes had appeared, it faded away, and he shrugged. "Plans change. Dreams change. Or they don't work out. Usually it's for the best."

Guilt was a waste of an emotion. "Isn't the Empress sixty something?"

"Aye, I believe so."

"And you want her to fall in love with you?"

He grinned. "A wealthy woman is forever beautiful."

I repressed a snicker, barely. "Amazing what money can do for a person."

"Aye, it is."

I saw movement, off in the direction from which we had been riding. I watched it, and it grew larger, and it turned into a rider. "Someone's coming."

He turned, and we both watched the rider approach. When it looked like the horse was heading straight for us, I rose to my feet and wondered what I was going to do if there was any trouble. Aiden was in no shape to fight, and I didn't know how. Something I'd have to remedy someday.

As the rider drew near I saw she was a woman, and I relaxed. I saw the white braid on her left shoulder, and I relaxed a little more. She was a Shield.

She was a pretty thing, maybe ten years older than I. Bright green eyes, long chestnut hair, good cheekbones. Karish would have approved.

She looked at us and reined in her horse. "Do you need help?" she asked in a light voice.

"No." The harsh tone drew my gaze to Aiden's face. He was scowling at the woman. "So you can move right along."

My eyebrows flew. What was that about?

She looked at him, irritated, then she returned her attention to me. "I've been traveling alone all day," she said. "I could use some company. May I join you?"

My first impulse was to hint her away—I was in no mood for additional company—but I was embarrassed by Aiden's rude behavior. "Please do," I said. "We could use a fresh source of conversation."

She nodded happily. "Thank you. You're very kind."

Aiden didn't look pleased, but he raised no objections, which was just as well, as they wouldn't have done him any good. I supposed he was in pain, but that was no reason to be so brusque with a stranger. The woman introduced herself as Alison Lynch. I helped her settle herself and her horse, and in return she shared with us some of the delicious little seed cakes she had picked up on her travels.

I'd tolerate anyone who gave me food.

"Where are you headed?" Lynch asked.

"Middle Reach," I answered, then added too quickly, "I'm not posted there. Just on vacation."

"I live in Middle Reach," she said, with that flat tone I was beginning to recognize, and I realized I'd put my foot in it. "I'm coming back from vacation. Middle Reach isn't exactly the place to relax in comfort."

I nodded at Aiden. "He has family there."

"Ah." She understood, and she didn't seem too offended by my instinctive denial of residency. A woman of honesty and sense, I thought.

I couldn't help but be curious about how she had ended up in Middle Reach, but it was none of my business, so I didn't ask.

Lynch stayed with us through the night. I was happy to have her with us. She was someone new to talk to, and she didn't remind me of what had happened in High Scape or why I was going to Middle Reach. She told me of her vacation, two months spent knocking around Under Range. According to her the scenery was lush, the food was divine, and the locals were sinfully alluring. I decided I'd have to go there sometime. We wandered into politics, of which I was pretty ignorant but which she made seem interesting, and fashion, which not even she could make a worthy topic of conversation. Aiden was sullen and silent the whole time, so we talked about how stupid most men were and didn't you often want to smack them and tell them to grow up?

But with all that chattering it wasn't until the next morning, after we had decided to go on to Middle Reach together and had eaten and mounted and were on our way, that Lynch asked me where my Source was.

"We're taking separate vacations," I told her.

"I see," she said, her words clipped with disapproval.

It surprised me. Few people felt partners should spend every moment of their lives together, and no one within the Triple S expected it, as far as I knew. "You've taken a holiday apart from your Source," I reminded her.

"Aye, I know that sort," she said sharply. "Unbearable is he? Or is it she?"

"He," I answered reflexively. "He's not unbearable."

Aiden snorted.

Lynch laughed bitterly. "You don't have to keep up appearances for me," she assured me. "I know exactly what you're going through. Why do you think I'm stuck in Middle Reach?"

I loosened my grip on my reins, then looped them back up a little more firmly. It was something to look at while I didn't answer. I didn't want to get into that kind of conversation, not with such a new acquaintance. I was disappointed in Lynch. She hadn't struck me as the type to complain about something so personal to a stranger.

"So let me guess," she went on, apparently not needing my participation to spur her on to what was clearly a favorite topic for discussion. "He mistakes you for a servant and expects you to be always fetching things for him. He expects you to make excuses for him when he offends someone. Takes all the credit for work you both do. Blames you when things go wrong. Speaks for you with others. Belittles your ideas and your opinions. And in other words acts like he's your master and you're his lackey."

Well. No resentment there. "I am fortunate enough not to have that kind of relationship with my Source," I said, and perhaps I sounded a little lofty.

"Huh," said Aiden.

"How long have you been bonded?" Lynch asked.

"About three months."

"That explains it. It'll come."

She sounded so sure of that, and I resented her certainty. She didn't know him, and she didn't know me. "I don't think so," I objected as civilly as I could. "He's not that way inclined." And neither was I.

"Really?" she challenged me. "So nothing I've said strikes any bells?"

I hesitated. I wasn't sure what to say. For certain, Karish never expected me to do things for him. Well, he'd expected me to keep him in chocolate while he was in the hospital, but that was the sort of thing one did for an invalid. I was expected to settle any feathers he ruffled, but that was one of the Shield's traditional duties, and I hadn't even had to do it yet. Karish often confused people but rarely offended them. And it wasn't that he claimed all the credit, but that regulars gave it to him without realizing my part in our work.

Karish's behavior could be made to look bad, taken out of context. But I was fully familiar with the context. "Not really," I said.

"Now there's a ringing refusal," Aiden commented dryly, the first full sentence he had spoken in hours. "What about when all those Pairs in High Scape died? You were the one who had to write all those letters to their families."

I glared at him. I knew how he felt about the relationship between partners, but did he have to talk about it in front of a stranger? "Actually, Karish helped me with them."

Lynch pounced on that. "Just the way you said that suggests it is your job," she said.

"It *is* my job."

"Aye, and why is it your job?" she demanded.

I shrugged, working to hide my growing irritation. Which I shouldn't have been feeling in the first place. When did I get so emotional? "You'll have to ask the Triple S council about that."

"No point. It's ruled by the Sources."

"It's an even split, plus a regular."

"The numbers are even, but the power isn't." She waved a hand dismissively. "Forget about the council. Last night you seemed to be a woman capable of thinking for herself." I cocked a brow but otherwise ignored the shot. "Tell me why it's always the Shield who has to write the condolence letters, and deal with the innkeepers and the shopkeepers and the Runners and the outraged parents and spouses, and make reports to the Triple S, and study all the research done on all the sites."

Again the list, stated so baldly, did sound bad, but again it was a matter of things being taken out of context. "Sources are by their nature distracted and possessed of a bizarre manner of expressing themselves." *Don't wince, girl, even though you sound like a textbook, but do try to tone it down a little.* "This can cause problems in their dealings with regulars, so it is better for everyone if—"

"That's tripe, Dunleavy," Aiden snapped. "Sources are allowed to be flighty and useless, so they are. I've met your Source, don't forget. He doesn't strike me as incapable, but he lets you do everything."

"You met him once," I reminded him. Again. "And I don't do everything."

"Aye, you do."

I could be tenacious when I was annoyed. "Sometimes Sources say things—"

"Sometimes everyone says things," Aiden claimed impatiently. "And we all know Sources are sometimes incomprehensible. No one's going to break heads over it. But Sources have been taking advantage of the fear that we will for generations."

"And while Shields are running around playing diplomat and nursemaid," Lynch chimed in, "Sources don't have to be anything but Sources. Channel a few forces once in a while and live like aristocrats. Is that fair?"

Who said life was fair? "Sources are expected to write reports, too."

"Aye, but no one cares if they don't."

That was true. "They have to guard us from the effects of music." And my, didn't that sound pitiful next to her list of complaints?

Lynch laughed again, an even harder sound than before. "Would you like to know how my Source 'guarded' me?" I didn't, but she told me anyway. "He bound me."

That was sometimes necessary. Some Shields were simply uncontrollable under the influence of music. "Are you particularly sensitive to music?"

"I'm particularly *in*sensitive. I'd be tone deaf if I were a regular. I was the joy of my professors. I have to be feverish or drunk for music to have any real impact on me. But Lang, my Source, didn't bother to learn whether I was sensitive or not, and certainly didn't risk having to go to any trouble for me. First time a festival was held at our site he had me bound, and no one objected because he was my Source and he had the right to do anything he wanted to me while there was music playing." Her eyes had that look that said tears wanted to come, but she wouldn't let them, her face settling into hard lines. "Believe me, none of the regulars had any trouble understanding him, then."

All right, I was shocked. Everyone had heard stories of Sources abusing their Shields, of course, a dangerous and stupid pattern of behavior considering the symbiotic nature of a Pair's relationship, but I had never before met a victim. Perhaps her bitterness was justified.

I had the feeling she was not the one responsible for their being posted in Middle Reach. "What did he do?"

"It's a very long story."

Having Aiden with us meant we couldn't move as quickly as I'd have liked. "We have all day." And she appeared to want to talk about it, else I wouldn't have asked.

She took a deep, calming breath. The tension around her eyes eased a little. Good girl, I thought. "Lang is addicted to drink," she said, and her voice was smooth and even, as it was supposed to be. "I'm not certain when it started, but the rumors said he started giving his morning tea its extra ingredient when he was twelve, and by the time he was sixteen he was living his life in a constant haze. Everyone knew about it, and they tried to break him of the habit in the academy. They kept him in the infirmary for months at a stretch, punished him every way they could think of, but nothing worked. As soon as he was free he went straight back to the liquor. But it never interfered with his performance, he was always reliable, so there was nothing else they could do. They couldn't even figure out how he was getting hold of it.

"So they sent him out on the field, and the drinking got worse because there was less direct supervision. He was often drunk, but again, he could channel well enough, so there was nothing anyone could do. He was allowed to participate in the Matches when he was old enough.

"None of us wanted to be Chosen by him, of course. We had all heard of him, and no one wanted to work with a drunkard. Even Shields who were desperate to be Chosen would have rather been unChosen than Chosen by him." She assumed an expression of disdain. "But I wasn't worried," she said harshly. The disdain had been directed at herself. "I was sure I wouldn't be Chosen by him. I was a nice person, and a good Shield, so I wouldn't be stuck with him." The sound she made in her throat might have been more laughter, or it might have been a sort of sob. "Stupid, eh? And strange, how we believe bad things can't happen to us simply because we don't deserve them." She sniffed and got herself under control. "Anyway, I was Chosen by him, obviously, and while everyone was giving me these horrible looks of pity, even the unChosen Shields, I tried to convince myself that the rumors were only rumors, and he couldn't be nearly as bad as everyone said. I learned better that night, though, when he tried to 'celebrate' our partnership by raping me."

I squirmed a little. I never knew how to behave in the face of such revelations. Did they want me to ask for details or let them skip over the news without interruption?

"He was drunk, so I could fight him off," Lynch said with a proud tilt to her head, "but you could say it set the tone for our relationship. He thought me something to be used at his will, and he resented it when I dared to fight back. And then he punished me."

"Punished you how?" Aiden asked. He, I noticed, had been won over. But then only a cad could remain cold upon hearing Lynch's story, and Aiden was not a cad.

She shrugged. "Nothing you would really point out as cruel behavior, not if you were an observer. But when he spoke to me he often used that sort of patronizing tone one would use on a small child, and he had a knack for putting things in the worst light when he was speaking in front of others. For example, say he'd ordered some new clothes and had sent me to fetch them for him."

I bit my tongue. *Just let Karish try sending me on such an errand and see how far he got.*

"Say they weren't ready yet and I'd tell him so. The next time we met in public he'd say something like, 'So you didn't manage to pick them up yet?' and the regulars didn't know enough to realize that's not one of my duties. Or he'd say things like 'Did you remember to write those reports this time?' The sort of thing that would make me look lazy or incompetent in front of other people."

I felt myself frowning, and I smoothed out my expression.

"And it wasn't just the way he talked to me," Lynch was saying. "He was always touching me. Not in a sexual way, he had learned better than that, but he was always pinching me or tickling me, even though he knew I hated it. Because he knew I hated it, I suppose. And when I complained, he claimed he was just being affectionate and I shouldn't be so unfriendly." She rubbed the back of her neck, a quick jerky movement, as though feeling her absent Source's touch right then. "He'd always go out of his way to scare me, jumping out from around corners or sneaking up behind me, slamming doors or dropping things with a bang. I was always a wreck around him. He'd claim it was my fault because I should always know where he was, and I wouldn't be startled if I were doing my job properly."

"This is outrageous!" was Aiden's quaint expostulation. "Wasn't there anything you could do? Couldn't you complain?"

"Who could I complain to?" she demanded. She sounded just a little melodramatic to my ears, but under the circumstances it was forgivable. "There are no laws that say Sources must treat their Shields well, no authorities who deal with this sort of thing. I wouldn't know where to go with a complaint. And what kind of complaint could I make? That I didn't like the way Lang talked to me, the way he touched me? No one's going to think that's anything serious. They'll think I'm an oversensitive prude and dismiss me."

Unfortunately, she was right. As far as I knew, there was no way to regulate relationships between partners. We were adults, and we were expected to take care of ourselves. That made things easier for the Triple S administration but ignored the fact that Sources had greater influence with the regulars than did Shields and that some personalities were stronger than others.

And she was right about the nature of her complaints, too. I thought most people could understand the damage constant cutting remarks could do over a lifetime, and the stress that could be created by such subtle physical abuse, but on paper it wouldn't look like much. Besides, what could anyone really do about it? Separating the partners would only render the Pair useless, which would be a counterproductive measure in the eyes of the Triple S council.

"That wasn't what landed me in Middle Reach, though," said Lynch. "As time passed, Lang's drinking grew increasingly worse. And he began slipping in his channeling. Because of the drink. Like he wouldn't notice the event until it had done some damage, because he was blind drunk. Or he wouldn't be able to channel all of the forces." She wrinkled her nose. "Part of that was my fault," she admitted. "It's hard to Shield someone when they're drunk. The alcohol does something to the way their mind works."

I'd never thought of that before, but it made sense. However, I felt part of Lynch's problem was that she wasn't too eager to be protecting her partner under any circumstances. That said a lot for the benefits of partners maintaining a certain emotional distance.

Oh lord. Lang and Lynch. I should have recognized those names immediately. But I'd never expected to meet them. They were posted in a place I, I had been arrogant enough to believe, would never be. I didn't know where to look.

"The Triple S became interested then, asking why Lang was getting so careless. As if they really had no idea. Everyone knew he had a problem with drink. But all he had to do was tell them it was all my fault, and because I wasn't the best of my year they believed him." She surprised me by giving me a hard, defiant look. "I was not the star of my class," she told me. "I admit that. But I worked hard and did my best, and my best was good."

I nodded. I believed her.

She lost her look of pride then and shifted with obvious discomfort. "You've heard of Over There."

Here it came. Everyone had heard of Over There. Once a

small but prosperous town, a sort of vacation resort for the
merchant class, it had been annihilated by a cyclone when the
visiting Pair had been too inebriated to function. "I know
about Over There," I said. "And I know who you are."

"I'll bet you do," she said angrily. "Aye, I was there. And
now I'm in Middle Reach. Indefinitely."

And her career was over. Once someone was sent to Middle Reach or any of the other punishment sites, no one wanted
them. In theory, a Pair could be sent to another site after
a suitable period in Middle Reach, but the site they were sent
to would be warned of their past. They would be sent to
sites that were the least likely to suffer calamities, and wherever they were sent, the regulars wouldn't be thrilled. The Pair
wouldn't be treated with any respect.

"I always knew I was only a moderate talent," Lynch was
saying. "I'd never envisioned a glorious future for myself, just
a mediocre Source and mediocre assignments. But I was all
right with that. We can't all be legends. All the same, I've
worked hard and I've been a good person. I don't deserve what
I've gotten."

"Obviously not," Aiden agreed. "And the worst thing is that
there is nothing you can do about it." He glanced at me, then.
See? the look seemed to say. "The Triple S did nothing to protect you from this man," he said to Lynch. "It wouldn't help
you with him when he was endangering you and all the regulars entrusted to your care. And now they've sent you off into
exile with him as though you were some kind of criminal. It's
irresponsible and cruel. I tell you, the Triple S shouldn't have
this kind of control over you." He fixed me with another glare.
"I've said this before."

Ad nauseam. "Armies and guilds have the same kind of
control over their people." But the protest sounded lame even
to my ears, for I could see their point. Lynch had been badly
used. The Triple S should have done something. I had always
known the Triple S had a few problems. I just hadn't realized
they were this bad.

"The difference there, my dear," said Aiden, "is that people
choose to join the army or guilds. No one chooses to join the
Triple S. You're taken from your families without any right to
refuse, and the Triple S controls you for the rest of your lives.

Because unlike members of the army or the guilds, members of the Triple S can't resign."

It was true. It had always been so, and having met a real victim of Triple S policy for the first time, I realized injustice could result. But there was nothing to be done.

I hated feeling helpless.

"They did the same thing to my brother," Aiden said to Lynch, and I thought I was finally beginning to understand the resentment he felt for the Triple S. "He was Paired to an unworthy man, and because of that man he was sent to Middle Reach. And it always seems to be the Sources, doesn't it, who commit the crimes and get both partners sent to Middle Reach?"

"Your brother is Ryan Kelly?" Lynch asked with a smile. "I should have recognized you. He speaks of you often. It's a very great pleasure to finally meet you."

And, strangely enough, they started rattling off stories about Ryan and seemed to forget the somber mood they had shared just moments before.

I couldn't join them. I was too busy thinking about how fortunate I had been, landing myself a Source who was, by all accounts, rather superior, only to despise him for it. I had ignored those who were less fortunate, feeling it was up to them to deal with whatever problems came their way. If they couldn't, there was something wrong with them. And if the Triple S was remote and indifferent, it was nothing to me, because I had done nothing to earn its displeasure.

Guilt was a waste of emotion.

Shut up.

I was an ungrateful wretch. I would do better. And there had to be something I could do for people like Lynch and, from the sounds of it, Ryan. I was an excellent Shield from a prominent merchant family. My Source was the Darling of the Triple S and a future duke. Surely the combination would give me some kind of voice, enough to make the council at least think about changing the way it dealt with erring Sources.

I didn't think I could change the whole system. I didn't even want to. But I had always thought it was wrong to punish both partners for the crimes of one. There had to be some alternative.

Later. Time enough to save the world after I'd found Karish. And figured out how I was going to deal with his being a duke. And, oh aye, what was going on with those strange Rushes.

The list just kept getting longer and longer.

Chapter Nineteen

Finally, we made it to Middle Reach. I was beginning to fear we'd never get there.

I'd never really studied Middle Reach, had never really thought about what it would be like to go there. Part of me had been expecting some kind of mud pit, with a few knocked-together houses and rough, downtrodden peasants. Another part realized this was ridiculous. Great things had once been expected of Middle Reach, and quite a few people lived there, so it had to be more than a swampy outpost.

Well, the mud was there, but there were also a lot of wooden sidewalks. There were enough buildings to satisfy the demands of a small town, and they were well built and in good repair. But they were ugly. I couldn't say why, exactly. There was nothing outlandish about the colors, and the architecture seemed normal enough. But there was no beauty about the place, either, and decades of nearly constant rain had given everything the feeling of being brown, even on a bright day.

One building, much larger than the rest but with the same air of ugliness, stood some distance from the town. "What is that?" I asked Lynch, pointing.

"Used to be the civic center. For town meetings."

Ah, a remnant from grander days. Back when Middle Reach had been on its way to becoming the mecca High Scape was. Now, the entire population could probably fit in that one building with plenty of room to spare, and I suspected the citizens weren't the most civic-minded group of people one could hope to meet. I wouldn't be. "What's it used for?"

Lynch shrugged. "Youngsters avoiding the disapproving looks of their elders, I imagine. It fell into disuse ages ago. It's probably a death trap."

Hm. Depressing.

As we moved through the streets I started feeling a little uncomfortable. It seemed to me that everyone was aware of our presence. Not actually watching us—no one stopped and stared—but giving us as much attention as peripheral senses allowed. I supposed that wasn't so strange, as Lynch was of the notorious Lynch and Lang, and possibly people remembered Aiden from his earlier visits, but I didn't like it. I didn't want anyone noticing me yet.

"How's your leg?" I asked Aiden, mostly to distract myself. He answered with a tight nod. I took that to mean there was some pain but it was bearable.

As in High Scape, all the Pairs in Middle Reach shared a residence. As we neared it, I expected to see some evidence of tension in Lynch, as she was no doubt dreading her reunion with her crazy Source, but she was calm. More than calm, she was cheerful. *Strong woman,* I thought.

The residence was not so large as the one in High Scape, but the building was in slightly better repair than its neighbors and had the air of being well tended. There were flowers in the front yard, the first evidence of an attempt of beauty that I had seen in Middle Reach. I had never before paid attention to things like flowers, but their otherwise total lack made me appreciate this small sample all the more.

I decided I liked flowers.

Ryan had been waiting for us. He came striding out of the residence before we reached the front door. He didn't look too happy to see us, though, unless he usually expressed pleasure with a scowl. He gripped Aiden by his shoulders. "I thought you said you were better," he said accusingly.

Ah. He was disturbed by his brother's limp. I couldn't blame him for that. It disturbed me, too.

"I am," Aiden answered mildly. "I can walk."

I didn't think Ryan was satisfied with that, but he didn't press. I wondered if he knew I was the one who'd crippled his brother.

They didn't look anything alike. Ryan lacked his younger brother's height and was of a broader build. Though hair and eyes were the same colors, they were of different shades. There was a grace to Aiden's movements that was absent from Ryan. To look at them, I would have never thought them siblings.

And then we were being introduced. "Dunleavy Mallorough, this is my brother, Ryan Kelly."

I hesitated in the act of greeting him. How did I address him? Shields were called by their family name as a matter of professional courtesy, until invited to do otherwise. Regulars often found it rude, and the siblings of a friend deserved a more intimate title. But what did one call the Shield brother of a regular friend?

He was perceptive for a man. His eyes twinkled in a smile, and he held out his hand. "Dunleavy."

If he could, I could. "Ryan." I shook his hand. "Very good to meet you." Sorry I haven't been taking better care of your brother.

He gave my hand a small tug before releasing me. "Come," he said, taking my bag from me before I could politely object. If anyone needed assistance, I thought, it was Aiden. "We'll get you settled, and then we'll see about tackling your problem."

So he already knew. I didn't know how I felt about that. I might have liked the option of discretion.

Like the outside, the inside of the residence was not so grand as that in High Scape. The rooms of the lower floor were smaller, the wood of the structure more worn. All the furnishings were new, though, and it looked well-kept and cozy.

Not what I would have expected from a collection of Pairs known for being incompetent or dilatory.

"We have plenty of free rooms," Ryan said, leading us up

the stairs. "I guess the Triple S anticipates a lot of us will end up here," he added in a bitter tone. "I hope you find it comfortable."

My box of a room at the academy was still a very recent memory. I had low expectations. And while the room Ryan lead me to was nothing like my suite in High Scape, being nothing more than a largish bedroom, it was perfectly adequate.

I decided not to comment on the need for additional rooms for future tenants.

Once Ryan had left me, I poked my head out the door to watch which room Aiden entered. When I was sure Ryan was back downstairs, I trotted down the corridor and knocked on Aiden's door.

I heard him sigh before he responded with an invitation to enter.

His room was virtually identical to mine. I sat in the chair beside the door. "I like your brother," I told him.

"Of course you do," he said, slowly sinking onto the bed.

"How's your leg, really?"

He eased closer to the wall so he could lean his back against it. "I really don't want to have to go anywhere tonight." He massaged his knee and sighed. "I'm so sorry it took us so long to get here, Dunleavy. I know you would have gotten here much faster on your own."

That was true, but there was no point in hanging on to the irritation. I'd been overreacting, anyway. It wasn't as though Karish could have been lingering on the edge of death for the past week. It would have happened already. He was all right, and it would be better to undertake looking for him in a rational and thorough matter, rather than rushing around and possibly scaring his captor into doing something fatal. "We're here now, and I'm glad to have your company. I'm going to need your help."

He looked up at me then, and he smiled. A strangely pure, almost delighted smile that made me uncomfortable. I almost asked him what it was about but decided I didn't want to know.

I went back to my room, where I unpacked and freshened up. I joined Aiden and Ryan in the kitchen for a meal that was rather rough but tasted good enough. And I heard Ryan's story.

"You won't believe it," he warned me. "It's too fantastic. And it's been kept quiet. Most people would have expected to have heard about it."

And so saying, he practically guaranteed my belief.

"Paren is my Source," Ryan said. "A fairly talented one. And a nice fellow. A good one. Always helps you out, good with a story, fun at a party. Always has lots of friends wherever he goes. People always like him."

But.

"We were on a circuit, and we would visit a lot of sites in a year. We almost never made it back to Shidonee's Gap, because we were good. People often asked for us in particular. But after a while, we kind of settled into a routine. We were still a circuit Pair, but from one year to the next we were likely to be in the same place during the same season.

"I liked it. Liked going to different places. Saw some amazing sights, met some great people, did some good work.

"Anyway, things were fine for a while. Paren and I got on well. Did our jobs and had a beer afterwards. But we weren't best pals. Whenever we moved somewhere he'd go his way and I'd go mine. Not that we didn't get along. Just had different interests and different friends. So it took me a while to really notice what kind of friends he was making."

"Undesirables, were they?" I asked.

"Not hardly. When I did take the trouble to notice, I was amazed at how many dukes, earls, councilors, and wealthy merchants he called friend. Every site, it seemed, he called on someone. Long dinners, sometimes spending the night." I tried not to look at him as though I was wondering why he was so intimately aware of his Source's every move. Because I was wondering. He blushed anyway. "Started thinking something was up," he said gruffly. "Started following him around. Got chased from some mighty fine houses. Asked him about it. He claimed they were all family acquaintances. Only his file never mentioned such lofty connections, eh?"

"What did you think was going on?" Because obviously something was.

He shook his head and shrugged. "Didn't really think anything. Didn't have any real suspicions. As I said, he's a nice fellow. Thought maybe he was some kind of pet to the aristocrats. Some of them get a kick out of having a Source wait on them. Giving them advice. Giving them other things. Maybe it started with one of them and they spread the word. That sort's all related, eh? And if that was what was going on, and Paren was willing—he never seemed reluctant to go—it was no real harm and none of my business. Course, the trial really opened my eyes."

That last, being tacked on so nonchalantly, took a moment to sink in. Then my breathing suffered a little hitch. "Trial? For what?"

"Crimes against the Crown." I frowned. He was right. I should have heard about something like that. Shouldn't I? "I told you they kept it quiet. Can't have the regulars knowing what Pairs might get up to, can we? And it was six years ago." Six years earlier I probably would have had little interest in that sort of thing. "So I'm in a tavern in White Horse with some friends, playing cards and having a good time, and these Runners come in. They ask to speak to me, real polite. I'm not worried, I haven't done anything. And anyway, I'm a Shield. So I go outside with them. Once we're outside they ask me to go to their Headquarters, because they've been having some trouble with the Pairs, and they want to ask me some questions. I think they must mean White Horse's permanent Pairs and they want to know what Pairs can do, from an outside, objective source, so I say sure." Suddenly he exhaled, looking very tired, and rubbed his eyes with one hand. "I lived in a tiny room, a cell really, for nine days. That's what I was told, after. Don't quite remember it, myself. Lost track of the time. They sat me in a chair and wouldn't let me out of it. And they asked me questions." He smiled at me wearily. "They didn't do anything else to me, you know. Just asked me questions. Have I ever met the Head Trader of Red Deer? The Countess of Sea Scape? The Minister of Roads and Canals? Did I know about the Shidonee's Gap property pool? The proposed wheat tax?" He laughed. "What the hell do I know about any kind of tax? I don't pay taxes. I don't know any aristocrats or ministers, either. But those were the kinds of questions they kept asking, over and over and over again." He picked up his wineglass but didn't take a sip, just stared into the contents. "Exhausting it is, listening to questions you can't answer. At least, not to their satisfaction. You get so thirsty. You get a headache. You get nauseous. Each bone in your body gets to weighing a hundred pounds, and your head fills with sand, and then with stone, and it gets that you can't even understand the questions anymore. Hell, once they asked me my name and I couldn't answer them. But still, they kept asking." He shook himself, shaking away the memories. "They never touched me, but I felt like I'd been through some kind of nightmare."

Aiden put a reassuring hand on Ryan's arm. Ryan smiled at him. I suddenly felt intrusive, and I wondered why Ryan was telling me all this. I remembered Aiden once saying he wanted me to talk to Ryan, to describe to him what was good about being a Shield. How could I do that? Whatever was coming next in the story, it was big, and it was serious. Crimes against the Crown. And then I was supposed to give him my fairy tale? Look, Ryan Kelly. Look at my life. See how much better it is than yours?

Karish and I had been bonded for only a few months. It sounded like Paren had fooled Ryan for years. Maybe Karish was fooling me, too, or would be once he was on his feet for more than two moments in a row.

"They didn't tell me anything, though," said Ryan. "I hadn't a notion until we were in court, me and my good-fellow Source, who I hadn't seen in all this time. Calm he was. Not a care. Told me not to worry. It would all be fine. And then it all came out." Another long, deep breath. "Paren had been carrying information from site to site."

"As in information he wasn't supposed to have?" I guessed.

"Aye. You know the sort of thing that goes on in those circles. The government wants to build a highway and a noble wants to sell some land and a merchant wants to sell some stone and steel. So certain information gets passed around before it should be, and money goes where it's not supposed to, and the highway gets built to certain people's advantage. I don't know why it's so illegal, really, but I guess I don't know much about that sort of thing. Though I heard more about it than I wanted during that damned trial.

"Anyway, it seems Paren was happy enough to play messenger, and so when the 'ristos came up with a new scheme his was the first name to come to mind." Bored with swirling the wine in his glass, Ryan tossed it back with one swallow. "Do you know about the tax concessions made to the merchant class a while back?"

He was surprised when I nodded, but I belonged to a merchant family, after all. Tradition granted tax concessions to the aristocrats because they created their own policing forces, raised their own armies, ran their own courts, and often built their own roads and waterways. Merchants had been granted the same concessions decades after assuming similar responsibilities.

"And then they granted that trader a seat in the Imperial court. Did you hear about that?"

I nodded again.

"The aristocrats were getting hysterical, and apparently a few of them decided the Empress was giving away too much of their authority and privilege. They decided she'd gotten too weak, and we'd outgrown the monarchy. So they decided to get rid of her, or at least turn her into a figurehead. Rhetoric was being shipped around, and councilors were being bribed, but it really hadn't gotten off the ground when it was discovered, which is why we're not dead." He grinned humorlessly. "And why no one else heard about it. Didn't want to be giving people ideas. It was a very small and secret trial. Some ministers and bureaucrats were fired, some titles were relieved of their responsibilities, and we got sent here."

And there was the end of the traveling life Ryan loved. "Why did he do it?" That was the thing I couldn't understand. The only motive for such behavior that I could think of was money, but a Source had no use for money.

"He said he did it for fun," Ryan said with disgust. "Apparently they treated him real well, especially after he'd carried a few messages and could blackmail his masters."

"Blackmail, too?"

"Oh, he had everything going, he did. So they'd treat him real nice. Had servants jumping at his every word. Served him the best food and wine and 'entertainments.' Offered up their sons and daughters. He bragged about it after the trial."

Idiot. "Is he bragging about it now?"

A grim smile of satisfaction. "No." There was a certain

finality about that blunt answer that was just a little chilling, but I supposed Ryan had a right to it. He pulled in a deep breath, his expression clearing to something more calm, and began stacking dishes. "You know, though, I wouldn't want to leave now, even if I could. I guess I've grown to like it."

I maintained a blank expression. Like it? Middle Reach? I felt some amazement at hearing those two concepts linked together.

He laughed a little sheepishly. "I know," he said, and I realized my face wasn't so blank after all. "But no one looks down on me here. If I tried to work at another site, people would believe I was incompetent or criminal because I had once been stationed in Middle Reach. Other Pairs would have nothing to do with me. I know it. But everyone in Middle Reach has been marked in some way, so it's forgotten. We're all judged by our true merits here. I like that."

I could understand that. He and Lynch had to hide in Middle Reach for the rest of their lives. Anywhere else, they would be treated with disgust and disdain. And it was so unfair, damn it. These people had done nothing wrong. Because of the actions of other adults over whom they had no control, their careers were as good as finished, and their freedom was sharply curtailed. It was wrong.

And it could happen to me. It could. How well did I know Karish? Not well at all. If he did something illegal, and it was all too easy to imagine Karish doing something illegal, I'd be punished with him. Just thinking about it started a slow burn in the pit of my stomach.

Lynch suddenly rattled down the stairs, and I wondered why she hadn't joined us for the meal. Moments later, I heard people at the front entrance. "Ho, there!" a man called, and then a young woman and a middle-aged man strode into the kitchen. They both wore white braids.

"Mallorough," Lynch said. "This is Sandy Wyman." She indicated the young woman, a petite blond creature. "And this is Jerrod Dakota." He was the serious-looking middle-aged man.

Ryan took over the introductions. "You two remember my brother, Aiden, and this is his friend, Dunleavy Mallorough. They're here looking for her Source."

Lynch didn't appear surprised, though I had told her earlier that Karish was merely on vacation. I envied her her control. Maybe when I was her age I would be able to appear so serene.

"What, has he done a runner?" asked Dakota, taking a seat at the table.

"A runner?" I said.

"Taken off because he happens to feel like it," Dakota explained. "Fielding had a habit of doing that."

"Fielding's your Source?"

"Aye. She sometimes felt her duties were too much of a burden"—heavy sarcasm there—"and she'd take off. That the site might get into trouble in her absence either didn't occur to her or didn't concern her. So disaster struck and dozens of people died and we got sent here."

She took off? Abandoned her post? Well, aye, one could say I'd done the same, but my Source had already been abducted.

The others were waiting for an answer. I wasn't comfortable with the idea of telling these strangers everything, but we'd planned to ask them for help. They were the only people in Middle Reach I could talk to with any hope of being understood. "We think he's been abducted," I said, and I explained about Karish's brother's death and our theories about a possible battle over succession.

Dakota whistled. "A duke, eh?"

"But why would his relatives bring him here?" Lynch asked. "Do some of them live here?"

It sounded so weak, I was reluctant to ask, "Do you know a Source by the name of Stevan Creol?" If he had ever been in Middle Reach the others would have known about it, it was such a small place.

Recognition on all their faces. "Ah, that one," said Wyman. "He's got flair."

"For what?" I asked.

"Everything. Art, drama, music, rhetoric."

Really? I'd never heard he was a dilettante. Of course, I thought he was a crazed barbarian, and crazy people weren't interested in the finer arts, were they? Idiot. "Is he here now?"

"I've run into him in town, several times, but he never stays at the residence," Wyman told me. "Do you think Creol has something to do with your missing Source? What's that got to do with his title?"

"Are Creol and Karish related?" Lynch asked.

What a horrible idea. Was that possible? They didn't look anything alike, but that didn't mean anything.

Think down one path at a time, girl, or you'll get yourself in a tizzy, and what would that accomplish?

Wyman's question made me feel foolish, so I tried to avoid answering it directly. "Karish had been receiving some correspondence from Creol over the past couple of months," I said, doing my best to sound like I was competent and rational. "Apparently Creol is trying to establish some kind of independent Source group, to prove to the world what Sources can really do and earn the respect they deserve."

Ryan snorted. "The Sources here have all the respect they deserve," he said dryly. "And more."

"So you haven't heard about this association?"

"Oh, aye," said Wyman. "He's talked to us about it."

"Really?"

"Of course. Sources can't function without Shields. Creol recognizes that, even if none of the others do," Wyman commented acerbically.

"So what did he say to you?"

There was an exchange of glances that immediately roused my curiosity and my suspicions. A short pause—was I trustworthy or not? I caught Lynch nodding at the others. What, was she considered the authority on me, possessed of expert knowledge about my character?

Don't be ridiculous.

I was getting paranoid.

"It's true Creol is trying to found a new association," said Dakota. "Maybe a new kind of Triple S. Because he doesn't like the way the current Triple S is run. He's been abused by it."

That, to me, seemed a drastic change of tune. "This is a Source we're talking about, right?"

Irritation flashed across Ryan's face. "We don't believe all Sources are evil or shiftless," he said coolly. "Just because we've been Paired with bastards doesn't mean we don't recognize that most Sources are decent enough people. We just think they're poorly educated about Shields and how to treat us, and that they're given too much autonomy. Creol is trying to change that."

I couldn't help cocking a brow at that. "I never heard of Creol being accused of any generosity of spirit." But then, it seemed I had never heard a lot of things.

Lynch flipped her hair off her shoulders. "Oh, we know all about what you've heard," she said dismissively. "Tales of rape and torture and possible murder. Creol told us all about it. It's all lies. The Triple S wants to discredit Creol because he's trying to change things. They don't want anyone to be influenced by him, so they spread rumors about him being violent and even crazy. But that's all they did, start rumors. They've never brought him to trial. There's no evidence of anything."

I couldn't believe the Triple S would bother to destroy a man's character in such a fashion. What did one dissident matter? And I just couldn't picture Creol as the messiah of the downtrodden. "He's a Source. What does he care how Shields are treated?"

"His father was a Shield, and his Source was everything Creol is reputed to be. As soon as Creol was discovered as a Source, his father made him swear to treat everyone, especially his Shield, with respect. It's an oath he takes very seriously."

"Only Creol has no Shield," I mused.

"And he's pretty much lost hope of finding one. So has the Triple S, which is why he's allowed to wander around without being Paired. So he's decided to watch out for all Shields."

But it all sounded too altruistic for a person I'd always heard described as a maniac. "I've met him." *And he'd looked like a maniac.* "At my Match."

"And what was your impression of him?"

That he looked like a maniac.

But not really. Thinking back, I remembered being terrified that I'd be Chosen by him. I remembered steeling myself to meet his gaze and swearing I wouldn't be trampled by him should I be so unfortunate as to be Chosen by him. But if I swept that aside and pictured him . . . "He looked rather bored, to tell the truth." And normal enough. Regular features. A rather penetrating gaze that could be disturbing, but nothing to be locked up over.

"He hasn't had much hope the last few Matches," Ryan

told me. "So not much interest. But did he seem like a slavering
lunatic to you?"

"No." I hated honesty.

"Because he isn't. He's just trying to make change."

"From Middle Reach?"

Lee, dear, would you like some sauce to go with your foot?

But no one seemed offended. Dakota grinned. "I know it
seems an unlikely choice at first glance," he admitted, "but it
really does make sense if you think about it. This is one of the
few places where erring Pairs are sent. This is where a lot of
us who have something to complain about end up. We talk to
each other here, share sympathy and support, and gather evidence to put before others."

"Are you all the Shields in Middle Reach?" I heard a few
notes of muted music. Aiden had pulled out his lyre and was
playing a gentle, melancholic air. Perhaps not the best choice
for an audience of disgruntled Shields, but the music was
softly played, and no one was objecting.

"No," Wyman said in answer to my question. "There are
two more Pairs. Williams and Masters and Smith and Fellows."

That was an awful lot of Pairs for a site that really wasn't
all that active. "Why are they here?"

"Williams is a decent enough person, I suppose, but she's
totally incompetent and won't admit it. According to Masters,
she let the first three disasters whip right by her. Couldn't do a
damn thing."

I'd never heard of anything like that before. "Are they sure
she's a Source?"

"Aye. She can access the forces, she just can't channel
enough to be effective. She was offered a teaching position,
but she felt she had too much self-respect to teach." Wyman
rolled her eyes. "I'm sure saying she's been posted here does
wonderful things for her self-respect."

"We don't know why Smith and Fellows are out here,"
Dakota added. "They won't talk about it. I can only tell you
that Fellows is the sweetest fellow you could ever hope to
meet, and Smith is a total bastard."

That was blunt enough. I looked at Wyman. "Why are you
out here?"

She snorted. "O'Sullivan got drunk one day, forced the driver of a public carriage to turn the reins over to her, and ran over the thirteen-year-old son of a member of the Triple S council. This was about a week after our bonding. We were sent straight here. That was about eight years ago."

Good lord. "All the Shields are here because of their Sources?" That was unbelievable.

They all looked at each other again. "Aye," said Ryan.

One sudden, discordant note from Aiden. It seemed to strike right into my heart, but I managed to keep from jumping in my seat. "I see." I loosened my iron grip on the arm of my chair. *Must stay calm.*

"How are you going to go about looking for your Source?" Wyman asked me.

"I really have no idea," I admitted. "Just . . . look, I guess." Excellent plan. I was a genius.

"I'll take you about," Ryan offered quickly.

I hesitated. "You're very kind," I said. "But for the first time I want to check things out on my own." Without anyone looking over my shoulder. "I want to feel things out myself, so I'll know what questions to ask. And it's not like I can get lost here."

Ryan nodded. Aiden segued into a more cheerful tune.

"And it's not like you can do anything tonight, either," said Lynch. "We'll have enough work to do soon enough. Come on, Mallorough, tell us about you."

I was supposed to spill my life story? Was that the deal? I never agreed to that. "Karish and I were bonded—"

"We don't want to hear about Karish," Dakota interrupted me. "I'm sure everyone gets to hear about Karish to the point of wanting to scream with it." That was a little harsh. "We want to know about you."

What was I supposed to tell them? They were the ones with the interesting, tragic lives. But to be polite I told them a little about my family and about High Scape, and when their questions started to irritate me, Aiden, blessed boy, distracted them with music. And then *they* started talking, about the lighter side of Middle Reach, the jokes they had played on each other and some of the good times they'd had. The atmosphere in the residence changed in time to one of cheer and goodwill. The gathering began to feel like a party.

I relaxed for what seemed like the first time in weeks. I had made it to Middle Reach, and my Source was still alive. I had a half-dozen intelligent people willing to help me find him. It was going to be all right. I could feel it.

Chapter Twenty

Karish invaded my dreams that night. I didn't appreciate it. He didn't do anything useful. He didn't speak to me, giving me directions to his exact location or beseeching me for help. All I recalled about the dream was that he had cut his hair quite short, and he was ignoring me. If there was any significance to that, it eluded me.

I woke while it was still dark and couldn't get back to sleep. I slipped out of bed. I dressed as quietly as I could and left the bedroom for the living room, where there were plates and goblets left over from the night before. Now that the party was over I was heartily ashamed of drinking and eating and laughing while my Source was being held in who knew what kind of environment.

Don't think about it. Plenty of time to punish yourself after Karish has been found and everything's back to normal.

Aiden would wake long before I returned, probably, but he would know where I'd gone and he would just have to understand. I couldn't wait until he woke.

It was time to get to work.

I knew where I wanted to start. The abandoned civic center. Perhaps it was too obvious, but then Karish's abductors probably weren't expecting anyone to be looking in Middle Reach. And it was an easy place to start, something to look into. I had to look everywhere.

I started off at a smart pace.

He's not going to be there, I said to myself. It would be too easy. Only an idiot would keep him in a place that practically screamed "Criminal activity here!" *He's* not *going to be there.*

Yet no matter how often I repeated that most sensible sentiment to myself, excitement insisted on thrumming through my veins.

Because what if he was?

Once I passed the last line of buildings I began to jog. It wasn't a conscious decision. I felt driven to it. The sun peeked over the eastern horizon. I scarcely noticed. Warmth wafted through the early dawn air.

He's not going to be there.

Stay calm.

When I found him, I was going to kill him. How dare he do this to me? What did he mean by getting himself kidnapped? He was a man, for gods' sake. He was supposed to be able to fight off kidnappers. He was a bloody hero, talented and beautiful and an aristocrat to boot. Heroes didn't get kidnapped. Heroes rescued kidnap victims.

Leave it to a man, and a Source, to screw up something so simple.

He was not *going* to be there.

When I found him I would probably kiss him. Yes, I had to be honest. It would be my only chance to find out just what was so entrancing about one Lord Shintaro Karish. I could say it was because of the stress I'd been under. He would believe that. Or I could claim I was drunk. Or that I'd been listening to music. Sure.

Of course, I'd be honestly relieved when I found him. If for no reason other than it would be the first step to putting my life back in order. But one must have one's priorities.

Lee Mallorough, you are such an idiot. Who do you think you're fooling?

"I am not in love with him," I swore. "And I will stop talking to myself."

He was not going to be *there.*

But what if he was? What was I going to do? Charge in there like the cavalry? The only meat I'd ever used a knife on had been lying on a plate. If Karish was being held captive in the civic center, and there were a few good stout guards about, I had no hope of accomplishing anything on my own. I would only get myself captured, too. And I remembered all too easily Captain Mulroney's warning about slicing off body parts. After all, I was no one's prize. For Karish's sake they had to keep me alive, but they didn't have to keep me whole. There wasn't much I could do to defend myself from the violently inclined.

I swallowed. I would be careful. I would be quiet. I would watch, remember, sneak back out and get help. I was not seeking glory, I was not playing amateur Runner. As soon as I saw anything worth seeing, I would be out of there. I would leave the heroics to people suited to such games.

But he would not be there.

I couldn't sneak up on the place. There were no trees, no hills or buildings to hide behind. If there were anyone lurking around, they would easily see me coming. Perhaps it would have been wiser to come back at night, but I thought that would make me look suspicious. During the day, I could claim I was a visitor with an urge to explore. No harm there. Even if someone stopped me and made me turn back, it would sort of answer a question or two. I'd know someone didn't want me there.

It was a big building, five stories high with the circumference of a small arena. A sturdy-looking thing that wouldn't fall apart in an earthquake. It had survived the last one fairly well, apparently. It had been painted in places, but much of the paint had worn off. I counted three unbroken windows in the dozens that faced me.

I approached the building as stealthily as I could, feeling like a fool the whole time. I listened, I looked, I felt. No faces appeared in any of the windows, no lethal projectiles came flying out at me. So far so good.

The doors of the principal entrance were two big solid slabs of wood. Fortunately, they hung open. I pulled one just a little wider, grimacing in anticipation of a loud, rusty creak. But the door moved easily and silently. I stepped over the threshold.

The sun had risen high enough to send light oozing through the eastern windows, enough to see that the civic center was a wreck. There had once been at least three upper stories, but all the walls and much of the flooring had been ripped away. By fire, I thought. I could see straight up to the bare rafters. There were a couple of stairways that began or ended in midair.

It hadn't been deserted, though. There was a kind of new-looking multilevel wooden structure, I would have called it a stage of some kind, off to one side. And some of the flooring had been ripped up, revealing the earth beneath. The dirt had deep holes driven into it. In one corner was a pile of steel rods. I had no idea what its significance was. The only thing I could think of was that someone was using the place to practice theatricals. It was being used for something, though, because it was clean. Which made it unlikely that Karish was being held there.

The place felt empty of life. Of the human kind, at least. Still, I spent the next two hours crawling over the ground floor and as many staircases as I could climb. There was nothing in the place big enough to hide a person. I even knocked on walls and tapped the floor in search of hidden rooms and passages. Nothing.

So Karish wasn't there.

Disappointment was a waste of emotional strength, especially when it weighed one down so. And I'd known he wouldn't be there. I'd told myself over and over and over again.

Hell.

I dragged myself back to town.

It hadn't been a waste of time, though. I'd had to get that place out of the way. If I hadn't searched, just because it was too obvious, its presence would have nagged at me, distracted me. I would have been forced to search it at some point. Having gotten that necessary though fruitless task out of the way, I was free to concentrate on the town. A tiny little town. Surely he would be easy enough to find.

Somehow I couldn't see anyone keeping Karish under wraps for long. He was too dashing, too full of flair, too Karish. I had a bizarre image of his sly cheer and exuberance and sheer beauty oozing out from under doors and through window sashes, leaving a glowing little path for me to follow.

I rolled my eyes. *Get something to eat, girl. You're thinking like an idiot.*

Aye, I'd get something to eat, and then I'd start banging on doors. Well, I paused, happening to glance down at myself, I'd go back to the residence first and take a bath. The main floor of the center had been clean. Many of the staircases had not. I looked like I'd been trying to climb through a chimney. Anyone who opened their door to me would be quickly slamming it in my face.

I headed for the well in the town square to wash off some of the more obvious grime. I didn't want to nauseate any of the patrons of whatever unfortunate restaurant I decided to inflict myself on. No soap, but painful determination returned my skin to its natural pallor. I was wiping my face on my sleeve—so elegant—when *he* walked up.

I'd only met him the once. After I'd been Chosen I'd somehow never expected to see him again. I supposed that somewhere in the back of my mind I'd pictured him haunting the Source academy, rejected at every Match, dwindling into a useless old man. Or perhaps not managing even that, cut down in middle age by the avenging relative of one of his victims.

He smiled a little, bent in a slight bow, and I tried to swallow past the heart that was frantically beating in my throat. *Scared? Me?* "Dunleavy," he said.

He didn't sound crazy. I didn't like the use of my personal name, though. "Creol."

"You're looking well."

I looked like a drowned rat, but I supposed if one looked beyond that they could see I was healthy enough. I was surprised to find the man almost handsome. His eyes were still rather disturbing, that piecing yellow brown that I imagined would suit some bird of prey, but he had strong, regular features and nice thick, dark hair. I wondered why I hadn't noticed it at the Match. Too terrified of being Chosen by him, I supposed.

But I wasn't going to exchange useless pleasantries with the man. I doubted he really expected it, and if he did have Karish, it would be in my best interests not to tip him off with any odd behavior. "Is there something I can do for you?"

He made a sound of disapproval at my lack of manners. "There's something I might be able to do for you."

He sounded like a salesman. "Oh?"

"I hear our Taro has gotten himself lost, and you're currently engaged in seeking him out." How the hell had he learned that? Who had told him? He chuckled at my expression, which was apparently as transparent as glass. "It's a small town, dear." Hackles rose then. I was no one's dear. "Everyone's noticed your appearance. And the news that the future Lord Westsea is missing has reached us even here. It was easy enough to figure out the reason for your coming here. The only thing left for me to decipher," he said, putting a finger to his lips in a staged gesture, "is why you've chosen Middle Reach as a place to look."

I wasn't answering that. "I congratulate you on your excellent logic," I said coolly.

He tsked with annoying good humor. "I'm sorry. Am I spoiling your fun?" He leaned in much closer than I liked. "Were you looking forward to playing spy? Cloak and dagger can be so diverting."

Oh, shut up. "I appreciate your offer of assistance, but right now all I'm interested in is getting something to eat. So if you'll —"

"Accompany you to a good tavern?" he finished smoothly. He easily lifted my hand to the crook of his arm, and I just as easily slipped it away. He smirked but didn't persist. "I would be happy to."

"Please don't trouble yourself," I said. *Please.*

"It's my pleasure. On the way I can answer your questions."

"I have no questions."

"Of course you do. This way." He ambled down the street, so certain I would follow him that he didn't once glance back.

Taking off in another direction offered some entertainment, but I followed him instead. I was curious. I wanted to know if it was possible those rumors were all fabrications, if he were really some kind of revolutionary victimized by the system. Of course, proving one didn't necessarily prove the other, but it would be an interesting study. Aside from that, it was an opportunity to learn about that association of his. If it were shady, I would have to inform the Triple S as soon as possible. If it were legitimate, well, then I'd have to see.

"So why did you decide to come here?" he asked.

I wasn't sure how to handle this. I'd already told all the Shields I thought Creol's association might have something to do with Karish's disappearance. Possibly that had been really stupid, because if they talked to him, he might already know all about my theories. In which case telling some version of the truth might be the best way to go.

Or it could be the worst. All I could do was trust my instincts, which had not proven to be all that accurate so far. "I read his mail," I said, my tone much more polite than it had been before. He was being decent. I'd better be, too. "I found some letters from you."

He frowned, looking a little puzzled, then his expression cleared. "Ah, yes, I invited him to join me here."

"To join your association."

"Is that the expression I used? How melodramatic."

Tread carefully, now. "I've heard rumors that you might be starting some kind of anti–Triple S movement."

He seemed to think about that. "I don't know that I like that choice of words," he said. "I don't want to destroy the Triple S or anything like that. I just want to change it."

"Seeking independence and power for the talented?"

His eyes widened. "Good gods, is that what the letter really said? Ah," he pointed at a low door. "This is a fair place, as long as you don't order anything too complicated." He ducked into the tiny dark hovel of a place that I wasn't too sure I wanted to trust my innards to.

What the hell. I followed him. "Don't you remember what you wrote? Or did you write so many letters?" Maybe he'd been trying to recruit everyone.

We settled at a small table in the corner. "To be honest," he admitted with a grimace of embarrassment, "I don't write very well. I can read easily enough, but when I try to write, the letters seem to jump off the pen and land on the paper in a mess. I had an acquaintance write the letters. It appears her style was a little . . . excessive."

"I see." The waiter, I noticed, was in no hurry to serve us. "Maybe if the tone had been a little different, he would have been willing to come here." *But probably not.*

Creol shrugged. "It's just as well things turned out as they did," he said. "I've come to think he may not be an asset to our cause after all."

"What's made him undesirable?" *Too smart, too normal, too disinterested?*

"The title," he said with an expression of distaste. "The useless younger brother of a duke is a good figurehead to fight the oppression imposed by the powers that be. But as a duke, he *is* one of the powers that be, and the struggles within the Triple S no longer concern him. Please!" he called out to one of the servers. "Two breakfast specials and coffee." The waiter nodded and disappeared to the back. If I'd known it was that easy I would have done it myself. "I apologize for ordering for you," said Creol. "But that really is the best food to be had at this time."

Whatever. As long as it was edible. "I've been told it's the Shields who are oppressed. Why would Sources be interested in fighting for them?" I expected to hear the sob story about his father. I was surprised.

"I'll admit I'm not doing this from the goodness of my heart," he said. "I expect to benefit from the changes I hope to make. In this case it just happens that helping the Shields is the first step to helping me. And the other Sources. Everyone, really."

As an answer that kind of meant nothing. It certainly didn't tell me what his final goal was. "What kind of changes do you hope to make?"

He studied me for a moment, as if trying to figure out whether he could trust me. Rich. Apparently I passed the test. "First thing I want to do is eliminate the bonding."

That caught my attention. "You want to what?"

"The bond between one Source and one Shield. I'm going to get rid of it."

He might as well have said he was going to learn to fly. It couldn't have shocked me any more. "That's impossible."

"How do you know?"

Because Shields and Sources have always bonded, which was no answer at all. "Bonding is involuntary. We don't choose to do it, it just happens."

"Aye, but we've all been prepared for it. The Triple S has

complete control over our minds from the time we're very young. For most of our lives we're told we will bond, we must bond if we want to go on to the greater glory of active service. Wouldn't that message, pounded into our heads from the time we're very young, make us highly susceptible to this bonding?"

Reminiscent of something Aiden had said, which I didn't like at all.

"And then comes that special occasion, when we're Chosen," said Creol. "It is at night, when the light of torches can offer the most dramatic contrast. We're all given special clothing, and taken to a place we're never allowed to visit on our own. Most of the participants have never met their opposites, unbonded Shields or Sources, before. Most of the participants are still very young. They're all desperate to be Chosen, they're all eager and scared and nervous. A highly emotional state." He smiled, then, and it was only slightly condescending. "Even the Shields." That was true. "If you take any group of people, even regulars, and put them through all that, you're going to find at least a handful who will end up bonding. And so some do."

"The first Pairs bonded with no prompting from anyone," I reminded him. "And there are spontaneous bonds between people who don't even know they're Sources and Shields."

He nodded as though he'd been expecting me to say that. I hated being predictable. "Let's address your second point first," he said, sounding like one of my professors. "When was the last spontaneous bond?"

I thought about that and realized I had no idea. I'd heard no stories about it when I was at the academy. "I don't know."

"There have been no spontaneous bonds in the last quarter century," said Creol. "I've checked."

I didn't think that was so very odd. Once the Triple S was up and running, the number of spontaneous bonds had dropped dramatically. The more efficient the Triple S became, and the better informed the regulars became, the fewer spontaneous bonds there would be. "What do you think that means?"

Creol accepted a cup of coffee from the waiter. "That perhaps bonding isn't necessary anymore," he said. "Maybe it was essential in the beginning, when there was no Triple S and no knowledge of Sources and Shields. Maybe back then people needed help finding each other and figuring out what their roles were, what they could do. It's impossible to really know. But maybe we've outgrown all that by now." He sipped at his coffee, winced, added some sweetener. "And I believe we're changing all the time, in our abilities and our needs, but the Triple S won't let us grow. It's more convenient to put us in a certain category, wrap us in rules, and leave us there."

He was making a certain amount of sense. That couldn't be good. "I have bonded with Karish." I really had. I'd felt the difference immediately upon meeting him, and I'd continued to feel it ever since. No one would be able to convince me that was all in my head. And Creol had never bonded with anyone. Perhaps he couldn't understand what it really meant. "And believe me, no one pushed me into it. He was not one of my preferred choices."

He smiled again, and this time its component of condescension wasn't so slight. "Are you sure?"

"Yes," I told him sharply.

He conceded the point with a tilt of his head. "You've Shielded Sources you weren't bonded to. I've been Shielded by people I wasn't bonded to. It's part of our training."

"But it's easier to Shield my own Source."

"Because you've been taught to fixate on him to the exclusion of all others. If you were given the time and encouragement to study others with the same intensity you're expected to use on your own Source, you could Shield them just as well."

I didn't know about that. I was sure it was the bond that allowed me to observe Karish so closely in the first place. Without the bond, I wouldn't have been able to Shield him through the cyclone in Over Leap so soon after meeting him.

"You have trouble imagining it because it opposes everything you've been trained to believe," said Creol, "but I swear the bond can be eliminated. And it should be."

The food arrived then, and I attacked my plate with something less than finesse. I wasn't at all worried about impressing Creol. And it gave me an excuse not to talk while I was trying to think.

"The way the system works now is wasteful," Creol was saying. "So the ratio of Shields to Sources is what, two to one? So half of all Shields are redundant. They're forced to work at the academies, or look for young Sources and Shields, if they want to do anything. Some are left to wander around as I do, and they're considered useless. Have you any idea how many of them kill themselves?"

No. I'd never heard of anything like that. All of a sudden I wasn't at all hungry.

"It's the Shields that do the hard work. Sources just open themselves up to the forces. It's practically an animal instinct. Shields are the ones who have to exhaust themselves to focus on both the Source and the forces at the same time. There is no reason why two or more Shields couldn't care for one Source, to lessen the load. Why else would the ratio be so uneven? At the very least, those Shields could be used as backup should bonded Shields become exhausted or injured during an event."

I broke a slice of bread apart and thought about that. He had a point. If a Shield became incapacitated during an event, the Source could still channel if he had another Shield to guard him. And unbonded Shields would not experience the same difficulties with Sources who were not their partners that Paired Shields had. Definitely something worth thinking about.

"And look at me," Creol continued, his fingers brushing his chest. "For some reason the training didn't take, and I haven't bonded. I can't work. The Triple S feels I will never work, and believe me, they've made it clear what a sorry waste of resources they consider me." And suddenly, out of nowhere, he was all intense. He leaned across the table to stare into my eyes. I almost leaned back in my chair to get some space. "I'm good, Dunleavy. Very good. In my not-so-humble opinion I am more than a match for your Taro. But that's been thrown away because I haven't bonded. And it's not like there are so many Sources about that one should be so casually dismissed."

He was right. There was no reason why he couldn't work, no reason why an unbonded Shield couldn't protect him.

"Think how it would be, Dunleavy, if there were no more

Pairs. Think of all the problems it would solve. No one would be considered redundant. People who hated each other wouldn't have to work together, which makes everyone miserable and endangers everyone. And one person wouldn't have to die just because his partner did." I had to admit that I was all for avoiding that aspect of the bond. I'd never understood the necessity of it, myself. "Death is always unfortunate, but without the bond, the surviving partner would at least be able to live and work with others."

Aye, and she wouldn't have to walk around wondering when her aristocratic, apparently always-embroiled-in-something Source was going to get himself killed and take her with him. I certainly could have done without those weeks following Karish's attack, and the fear I continued to feel while he was missing. Of course, even if avoiding the bonding was possible, it was too late for me. The bond was there. I knew it.

"And then, there's the situation that's happening in Middle Reach," said Creol, waving his coffee cup. "One partner does something wrong, both get punished. If Sources and Shields weren't bonded, when one committed a crime or was proved incompetent, that one would be properly dealt with and the other would be able to move on and work with someone else. As it stands now—Well, have you met the Shields here, Dunleavy? Every single one of them has been exiled to Middle Reach because of something their Source did. It's almost enough to make one embarrassed to be a Source."

I pushed a sausage around my plate with my fork. I would have never expected to encounter a reasonable, sensible Stevan Creol. I didn't know what to think. Except that it was highly unlikely he had anything to do with Karish's disappearance, so now what was I going to do? "What's your plan?"

He shrugged. "I'm not sure. I'm feeling my way around right now. Talking to people. Seeing what kind of support I can get. I'm starting with the Shields here, and they will talk to their colleagues, those who are Paired with more reasonable Sources who will listen to them. All of these people have families, some of them highly placed. They can put pressure on the Triple S. Which, you may recall, is completely dependent on the public purse for funding. If it should reach the

Empress's ears that the Triple S is failing to meet the needs of its members and, by extension, all citizens, she just might have someone take a look into it."

It sounded a little sketchy to me, which made me feel he wasn't telling me everything. He'd already been planning these changes for years, hadn't he? Then again, maybe he just didn't have much of a plan. I wouldn't know how to go about making changes to the Triple S, either. "Is that all you're going to do, then? Talk?"

He smiled. "Well, no," he admitted. "I do have some . . . demonstrations in mind."

That didn't sound good. "What kind of demonstrations?"

"I told you I believe we are changing," he said. "I think one of the ways we're changing concerns our talent, what we can actually do. Our powers are increasing."

So that wasn't restricted to Karish. How . . . alarming. "Our powers?"

"Well, powers among Sources, anyway. I don't know about Shields." He paused in invitation. I said nothing. "But I've learned some Sources are developing new skills."

Gods, drag it out a little longer, man. "What kind of skills?" *Healing, maybe?*

The tension that suddenly appeared on his face surprised me. "You're asking a lot of questions," he said, an edge to his voice.

I thought I was just following the script. "You offered to answer them. Besides, I'm interested."

"This is not the sort of thing I want to have misinterpreted by the wrong people. If rumors start about wild Sources with mysterious powers, it'll kill my plan before it's even had a chance to start."

"I can be the soul of discretion," I promised.

He winked at me. "I like you, Dunleavy." *Oh, goody.* "But it's not yet time, I think."

Hook was baited, but was I caught? I didn't think so, but then I didn't know the game. Or if there even was a game. I needed to think things through, and talk to someone. Only I didn't know who. No one who came to mind struck me as being objective and impartial.

Don't try to think too much, dear. You'll only confuse yourself.

The meal was over. So, I gathered, was the conversation. Creol settled his cutlery on his plate in the manner of a man who was ready to leave. "Thank you for your company," I said politely.

"Oh, no, thank you," he responded with too much enthusiasm. Was he mocking me? He grabbed my hand and bowed over it. "I'll see you again soon."

I hoped not. So he wasn't crazy. He still made me uncomfortable. I watched him leave and felt my shoulders relax.

Alone again, I lingered a little and savored the last of my coffee. I thought over the past hour and dissected the conversation. What could he have learned from it? Not much, I thought. He had done almost all the talking. I had confirmed that I was looking for Karish and that I knew of Creol's association. Would that have been of any use to him?

If he had gained anything from the conversation, it was more than I'd gotten. I still had no idea what was going on, and had gotten no hints as to whether Karish was in Middle Reach at all.

I went back to Ryan's house. He was the only one up, picking up some of the mess scattered about the living room. He smiled when he saw me. "Are you an insanely early riser?" he asked.

"Not usually." *Not ever, until recently.* I joined him in picking up some mugs and plates, though he tried to shoo me away. "I went to the civic center to see if there was any sign of Karish."

"Obviously you had no luck."

"Aye." *Obviously.* "I'm just back for a bath, and then I'll crawl over the rest of town."

"I'll fix you something to eat while you're washing up."

"Thanks, but no. I've already eaten." With Creol, though I didn't mention that. I wasn't sure why I kept that bit of information to myself. Habit, I supposed.

The others were in the kitchen by the time I had bathed and changed my clothes. They greeted me cheerfully, their hangovers not too debilitating, and they expressed their wonder at my being up and active so early in the morning. They were relaxed, they were enjoying themselves, and they were too tempting. I marveled at how quickly they accepted strangers, and I envied them that they apparently had nothing to do that day but bask in each other's company. I, however, did have a chore or two to perform, and I couldn't afford to let myself be distracted by them. Making my way to the front door, I called out my farewells.

"When will you be back?" Aiden asked.

"I have no idea." I wanted to look around carefully, and I wanted to follow up any opportunity that presented itself.

"Be careful, Dunleavy," he said. "It's not exactly high-class society out there."

"Not exactly high-class society in here, either," Wyman retorted.

"Don't worry, Mother. I'm a big strong girl. I can tie my own shoes and everything." I bounded out the door before anyone else could offer any unsolicited advice or, worse yet, company.

Perhaps I'd find Karish that day. I really hoped so. Then I could be out of Middle Reach and back in High Scape doing the job I'd been trained my whole life to do. I'd been useless for far too long.

Chapter Twenty-one

Twilight found me tired, frustrated, and unsuccessful after a day of knocking on doors and asking stupid questions. Hunting down the Runner Headquarters had been useless because, it appeared, Middle Reach had no Runners. I didn't know what the citizens did about any criminal issues they might have. Maybe nothing. Or maybe they didn't suffer any crimes. All I knew was that without that basic service, I had nowhere to start.

I went to the mayor's office, hoping someone would have some suggestions. They had heard of Stevan Creol, but it appeared everyone knew everyone in Middle Reach. They hadn't heard of his association. Certainly, I was informed with a stern glare, he hadn't asked for any permits. Only one secretary had heard of Karish, and she thought he was a prince from a collateral line, exiled to Middle Reach by the Empress for impregnating her daughter.

The Empress didn't have any female children.

I wandered around and looked. I visited all the public buildings and asked about Creol's association, and about any recent visitors. The answers, civilly delivered or not, were all negative.

So then I went to private homes. I was invited in for tea. I was sworn at. I was in danger of losing my nose, or my toes, in all the slamming doors.

I was unsuccessful. I was discouraged and scared. I didn't know what to do next. I was probably wasting my time. Karish probably wasn't anywhere in the area. I returned to Ryan's home, wishing I could give up, as I was clearly incompetent at this, but knowing there was no one else to assume the task.

I found Ryan alone in his kitchen, sitting at the table and working on something involving wood. He seemed relieved to see me. "There you are," he said, a mild rebuke. "Aiden's gone looking for you."

That irritated me. "I told him I'd be a while."

"He's bored, I expect."

I pulled up a chair. "He knew we weren't coming here for a vacation." On closer inspection, the thing he was working on proved to be a beautifully carved bird. I was impressed. "You made that?" I asked. I so envied people who could do things with their hands.

"Aye, for my niece."

I frowned. "Whose daughter?"

He smiled. "Not Aiden. He has no children. That we know of."

Of course he didn't. And if he did, it would be no business of mine. Not at all. Really.

"For our sister's daughter."

"Oh. I didn't know you had a sister."

"Aye. She's a Source."

"A Source and a Shield in one family? That's unusual." I wondered why Aiden had never spoken of her. It seemed odd that he hadn't, and that he had such sympathy for Shields but none at all for Sources.

More unusual was that she had a daughter. It wasn't impossible for working Sources and Shields to have children, especially if they didn't work on particularly active sites. Still, channeling and Shielding was hard on the body, and it made siring and conceiving children difficult.

"It's rare, I guess," Ryan said. "She's the oldest. Mother realized what she was when she was still quite young and sent her to the academy. I remember her well. I don't think Piers and Aiden do, though."

I asked, "What does she think of Creol's cause, here?"

His expression tightened, and he suddenly became engrossed in carving one more small detail into the bird's wing. "She doesn't," he said in a flat tone. "Sympathetic to my case, and to the others', but doesn't feel it warrants changing the whole system. Do more harm than good, she says, for the sake of what are really just exceptions to the rule."

I gestured at the carving. "But you don't resent her for thinking that way."

"Course not. Family. She can't help how she thinks. All those ideas pounded into her head from the time she was a wee thing." He blew some wood dust off the carving. "But she'll learn."

There was something about that last statement which I found just a bit chilling.

"'Sides, she has the good side of things, being a Source. Hard to see the evil of a system that's treated you well all your life. Harder still to stand up to it, once you have seen it."

"Unlike Creol?" That kind of slipped out. I hadn't planned on mentioning Creol in any context. But I wanted to hear of him from others who had met him.

Ryan grunted. "Man's no saint. System hasn't been so good to him, has it? He's a Source but he's got no Shield to master. And whether the Triple S started all those rumors or not, they've made it clear they've got no use for him. No reason why he can't be assigned to a site, as a backup if nothing else, but he's not bonded so they think he's useless." He looked me right in the eye. "It's the bonding, I figure, that's the real problem."

Creol figured the same, but I wasn't supposed to know that. I just cocked my head and my eyebrow and hoped I looked interested. "I have no cause for complaint."

"Hope you won't have any in the future."

"Can't convict a man before he's even committed a crime."

"But you can protect yourself in the face of certain tendencies."

"Of which Karish has so far shown none."

He chuckled. "Stubborn."

When threatened with conversion, damned right. Too many people had tried to tell me how to feel about Karish. I wished they'd just leave me alone and let me make up my own mind.

The front door rattled, and a moment later Aiden was walking into the kitchen, Creol on his heels. I tried not to stare. When had those two met up?

Aiden smiled at me and snatched up the kettle. "Did you learn anything?" he asked, filling the kettle at the pump.

I wondered why Ryan hadn't asked me that. I wondered why Ryan wasn't reacting to Creol entering the residence like it was familiar to him. Hadn't I been told that Creol never stayed at the residence? "Afraid not."

"Where did you look?"

I didn't see any real reason to keep my efforts a secret from those in the room, not even Creol. He knew why I was there. I described my failures. Maybe someone would have some useful hints.

Ryan seemed particularly unimpressed. "I hope you didn't offend anyone," he said. "People here treat us well, but they don't have to. They know we're Triple S exiles. We can't be harassing them."

"I was perfectly polite," I said coolly. "It was necessary. I need to find out if Karish is even in the city. If he isn't"—as I was beginning to suspect, damn me for wasting so much time on nothing—"I need to learn that as soon as possible, so I can move on."

"Oh," said Ryan. "Then you're not looking to stay here long?"

"No." Ryan seemed, well, not quite annoyed by my answer, but it was clear he didn't like it. "Why?"

"Ah. I was just wondering what you thought about the other." He gestured at Creol, who hadn't taken a seat at the table but was leaning back against the counter, watching us. I guessed Ryan was referring to his cause.

"I'm not prepared to get involved with that right now," I said. Ryan nodded stoically. Had he protested or argued, I would have refused to defend my decision. As he did not, I felt compelled to explain myself. "I'm sorry, Ryan, but I've got to find Karish and patch up whatever needs patching. Then we have to go to Flown Raven and settle his title situation. Then we have to figure out what killed all the other Pairs in High Scape. I just can't handle another project right now."

Aiden glared at me. "How can you have heard all the Shields here and not want to do anything?" he demanded.

Annoyed by an attack from that corner, I snapped back, "Because I'm an apathetic, selfish bitch."

"Now, now," Ryan said. "He didn't mean to imply that."

"Aye, he did." I hoped I wasn't glowering at the idiot because that would be just too unprofessional. "Listen up, Kelly. When Karish is the Duke of Westsea he'll be able to take the Shields' concerns straight to the Empress's ear."

If anything, Aiden became even more incensed. "You're standing back to rely on Karish? When the hell did that start happening?"

"I've always been practical, Aiden. And the cold, hard truth is that the Triple S council will listen a whole lot faster to a peer of the realm than a band of disaffected Shields sent into exile. I find Karish, he gets his title, you have a strong ally in the Empress's court."

Aiden fumed. My words made perfect sense, but he wouldn't be able to understand until his blood cooled and his brain started working again. I left him to it.

Creol was looking thoughtful. "Do you really think Karish would support us?" he asked me.

"I'm not sure," I admitted, "but I think so."

"I don't," he said bluntly.

"Oh?"

"I've known Karish much longer than you have, Dunleavy. We didn't do a lot of training together, but I was at the academy the day he arrived, and I was there until he was sent out for field training. Everyone knew he was the second son of the Duke of Westsea, and everyone was aware of every move he made." That would have driven me crazy, everyone watching me all the time. "I don't claim to know him inside out, and I won't say he's a cruel person, but he's never struck me as being a selfless person, either. In fact, he appeared to me to be self-absorbed and thoughtless. I remember when he first came, he expected to be served his meals in his room." Creol shrugged. "He just seems the sort who doles out small kindnesses if they take no real effort but is otherwise a fairly selfish individual. Do you really think someone like that would go out of his way to help a group of strangers by changing a system that has always treated him well? I don't."

I wanted to grind my teeth. I wanted to get away from everyone and think for a week. Because I didn't know. A quick glance at the past revealed no instances of Karish ever helping anyone when it wasn't related to the job. He had received many kindnesses, and he hadn't always seemed to appreciate them, but I couldn't recall him doing anything for anyone else.

And then I could. I looked at Aiden. I saw him writhing in pain on the dancing ground. I saw Karish kneeling beside him and soothing away his pain. I saw Karish in the hospital, risking his mind to bring back Ogawa and Tenneson in a stunt that he didn't know would work and if discovered could subject him to the rigorous testing he seemed to fear.

I looked at Creol. "I do," I said.

He smiled. "Your loyalty does you credit."

Well, thank you very much, sir.

"And here you've come looking for him instead of sitting back and letting others do the work. Commendable. Not the sort of thing one expects to find in a Shield."

Was that just me or did everyone feel the sudden tension dancing about the air?

"Few Sources deserve such devotion," Ryan said in a cold voice.

Creol nodded. "Too true."

I picked up a discarded chunk of wood off the table. I didn't think that simple, mild answer satisfied Ryan. I thought he wanted an argument, felt Creol's first comment had earned one, but the Source's admission robbed him of the right. He worked on swallowing his anger.

The Kelly boys weren't having a good evening.

Creol seemed oblivious of causing any offense. "Tell me

about yourself, Dunleavy," he invited. "I know little beyond your reputation."

I didn't have a reputation. What was with all this intense interest in me? It was unnatural and irritating. And I wasn't going to put up with it, not after the grilling I'd gotten the day before. So I smiled at Ryan. "I'd rather hear about Middle Reach," I said. "I'm ashamed to admit that I know nothing about it, and I'm afraid I've never thought much about it. I'm sure it's more than an exile for Pairs who are out of favor."

"Shouldn't be," Ryan answered curtly. "Place is a hole." Which was in direct contradiction to what he had told me earlier, but I supposed he was in no mood to talk.

The comment seemed to kill any possibility of conversation. I was tired, Ryan was ticked, I could tell by the tightening around Aiden's mouth that he was in some pain, and Creol was being mysterious. I realized I was hungry.

I was relieved when Creol excused himself and left, but in a way I was glad he'd come. His visit had been aimless beyond a little probing in the interest of his cause, which was to be expected. I still didn't think he was entirely normal, but that in itself was no crime. Only made him interesting. And it was becoming clear that he'd had nothing to do with Karish's abduction. He was neither interested nor disinterested enough to be the culprit. That left me with no culprit at all, which was a problem.

I knew I was a fool. If Karish was in Middle Reach, his captor no doubt knew I was there, and why I was there. He was probably watching my efforts and laughing himself sick. Fair enough. As long as he felt I was harmless, he wouldn't hurt Karish or move him. I hoped. So I would continue to ask around and pray to stumble onto something significant and wonder why Karish hadn't managed to seduce his guards into releasing him.

I didn't know what the hell I was doing, or how to proceed. I was tired of thinking. I was not the loyal, faithful servant Creol had pegged me. I would have been delighted if someone had shown up to take it all out my hands.

I heard the door at the front entrance fling open. "Dunleavy!" Creol's voice called out urgently. "Please, come quick! I need you!"

Chairs crashed to the floor as all three of us jumped to our feet. We ran through the living room out to the door. I noticed a pool of water on the floor.

Creol stood just outside, his eyes wide. "Will you Shield me?"

Water was rising everywhere. A flood. I didn't wonder how it had progressed so far or why the assigned Pairs weren't doing anything about it. I didn't wonder why Creol hadn't asked Ryan, with whom he was more familiar, to Shield him. I only saw the makings of a disaster, and knew I could do something about it. I nodded. "Aye. When you're ready."

He grinned at me with relief. And then it began.

As with Tenneson, it was more difficult than it should have been. I couldn't quite reach into Creol as I could into Karish. The internal shifts felt a little muffled to me, like trying to handle cutlery while wearing heavy gloves. But I could feel them, and I could Shield him.

I felt the raw power flow though him. The directions of the power were strange. It felt like it was being pulled in, not that it was rushing through him. And the odd sense of familiarity I felt in shielding him puzzled me. But none of that mattered. What mattered was that I was doing what I was meant to be doing.

And if I weren't chained to a Source who was always getting himself attacked and kidnapped and promoted into the peerage, I could be doing it a lot more often.

It was over quickly. Not a lot of force involved, and the water sank easily into the ground. Not so easy to get rid of the water that had gotten inside Ryan's house. That would require ordinary mopping.

Creol held out a hand. "Excellent work." We shook. "Thank you." He walked off, whistling, and I breathed in the cool, fresh air. It was a beautiful evening.

I turned back into the house, closing the door behind me. Ryan had already begun to clean up the water. That's when I realized Creol should have asked him to Shield. Ryan would have done a better job, having known and observed Creol much longer. But perhaps it was a matter of some kind of protocol.

It wasn't until later that night, when we had all settled down to sleep, that a more interesting question came to me. I realized that other than Creol, I hadn't seen a single Source in Middle Reach. Where were they?

Chapter Twenty-two

"Karish."

Saying the name aloud woke me.

Hell.

I groaned and covered my face with a nice cool pillow. I was not going to take up the habit of dreaming about Karish. I was not. That way led to obsession and madness and other disagreeable mental states. It was not going to happen.

Worse than the mental chaos were the physical repercussions. Aching and restless in a familiar manner that I certainly didn't want to associate with Karish. I was sweating, and my breathing was something less than steady. Revolting.

I was not going to start lusting after my own Source. Not seriously lusting, with the intention of doing something about it. It would be stupid and careless and irresponsible. *Just put the idea right out of your mind, girl.*

Of course, the insidious voice inside my head whispered, lust wasn't nearly as inconvenient as love. It was much easier to satisfy. A few nights in bed and the whole problem would be laid to rest. So to speak.

I could rationalize with the best of them.

I threw back the light sheet with the intention of getting out of bed and pacing. I got as far as sitting up, then something niggled at my mind.

Something was wrong. The restlessness I was feeling, it did have some similarity to sexual tension, but it was different. I could feel something skittering under my skin. I couldn't explain it, and I didn't like it.

It was too quiet.

I left the room and stood in the corridor. Complete silence. Which was only natural, it was the middle of the night. But the silence felt too complete, too settled. Like I was the only person in the residence.

I quietly made my way downstairs, unsure why. I knew I wouldn't be able to get back to sleep. Maybe I'd warm up some milk, and in the meantime, take a look around.

Aiden's lyre wasn't where he'd left it the night before. Which, in itself, wasn't strange. He'd left it on a chair in the living room, in the way of anyone wanting to sit in said chair. Maybe he'd come back down to take it to his room.

Aiden, I had noticed, was not the most organized of people. But maybe someone else had moved it after Aiden had gone to bed.

But it wasn't anywhere else in the living room, either.

There wasn't a single pair of boots near the front entrance, where everyone had been leaving them the day before.

All right, I was going to make a fool of myself. I didn't care. I couldn't let these little signs slide, especially when there was still that feeling in the air making me so jumpy. I went back upstairs and knocked on the first door.

I got no response. So I opened the door. No one was sleeping in the room.

No one was sleeping in any of the rooms. The whole residence was empty, except for me.

What the hell was going on?

I went back to my room to dress, and then I left the residence, still taking pains to be quiet. I wasn't sure why, except that the feeling of the night seemed to demand it. Everywhere around me, it was dark and still. That just wasn't normal. In one of the domiciles about me, there should have been a light on for a late-night conversation or an aspiring writer scribbling away at a manuscript after the chores were done. A romantic tryst, an argument, an illness, there should have been something happening somewhere, but every house was dead quiet.

I wasted some time searching through the town, heading for the taverns first. The most obvious place, I thought, thinking of Aiden's missing lyre. But the taverns were closed, and pounding on the doors didn't rouse anyone. I looked through the windows of quite a few houses, much to my shame, and saw nothing. I even went by the brothels. They, too, were empty, which was almost unbelievable. That, more than anything else, convinced me something was seriously out of order.

The sense of restlessness, the need to do something, was still plaguing me, even after all that brisk walking. It wasn't natural for me. I didn't hold on to physical sensations for so long. I had to be reacting to something that was still active. The job was to find out what.

Where was everyone? Where could they all go?

Where could they all go?

Of course. How stupid of me. The civic center.

Perhaps the residents of Middle Reach were more community minded than I'd thought. Sure, it was the middle of the night, and the civic center was a tumbledown wreck, but that was the only place I could think of that could accommodate what seemed like the whole town. Unless they had all just decided to pack up and leave, and while I couldn't blame them if they did, doing it all at once in the dead of night without taking their gear would be a little weird.

Feeling a bit nervous, I turned on my heel and at a quick pace headed in the direction of the civic center. It wasn't long before I could see the dilapidated building, and the lighting and movement within.

Though I wondered why I bothered. What did I care if Middle Reach voted on community affairs in the middle of the night? It even made a certain amount of sense. It was a time when most people were free to participate in political debate. Businesses were closed, farming was impossible, children were asleep. I didn't know why more cities didn't do it.

I was wasting my time, that was the pathetic truth. I was out in the middle of nowhere playing hero while Karish was undergoing some horrible experience in Flown Raven. I should have gone to Flown Raven.

Calm down.

I couldn't calm down. It was getting worse. The restlessness was getting stronger. My heart was picking up its pace, and my feet were yearning to do something more interesting than walking. Dancing seemed like a good idea.

No. Fighting. That, to be honest, was what I really wanted to do. I wanted to find some two-dimensionally evil foe and beat the hell out of him. With a sword. With two swords. I'd be whirling them through the air with expert ease, wearing some form-fitting leather outfit that made me look lean and lethal. In my fantasy I'd slay him effortlessly.

In reality I'd be fish bait. I knew that. But that didn't stop the bizarre images rampaging through my head.

I wouldn't be fighting anyone that night. I would have to settle for jogging, which helped a little.

And then I knew what it was.

It was music.

I could hear it then, very faint, a barely perceptible sound, just tickling at my ears. And it was coming from the civic center, I was sure. I didn't know how it had affected me all the way in the residence, where I couldn't even hear it, but that wasn't important right then. I was just relieved there was nothing embarrassing causing my reactions.

So there was a late-night performance after all. I wondered why I wasn't told of it. It couldn't have been because I was an outsider, because so was Aiden.

Should I go on? The better I could hear the music, the more dangerous it became for me. This music, it was not just any music. It was pounding, jarring, glorious music, the kind that carried a person away and scared me to death. It was already making me feel aggressive, and I couldn't even properly hear it yet. What would it do to me when it was drilling into my ears at full volume? I'd never been exposed to such music except under controlled circumstances, at the academy. Out on my own, no one keeping an eye on me, I didn't know how I would react.

On the other hand, I couldn't believe everyone in town was gathering for a late concert. *Everyone* was there. There was something going on, I was sure of it, and as the only Shield in Middle Reach who wasn't suffering from a feeling of oppression, it was up to me to investigate.

All right. As rationalizations went, that was weak. But I liked the music, and I was curious.

And I could do it. I could control myself. I had at Karish's party, where the music, though different in nature, had been just as moving. Sure, I had gotten a little carried away in the beginning, but I had stopped myself before doing anything truly stupid. I would do so again. I just had to hang on to something and not let go. As I didn't have anything physical handy, I'd have to settle for something mental. Like an image of how Karish would crow if I lost control. Oh, aye, he would love that, to see me lose my balance. He'd never get the chance.

Hang on to that and don't let go.

I moved on.

But it was difficult, much more than I'd expected. The music got louder. It was beautiful, stirring, and yet there was something sinister about it, though I couldn't say what. Some of the notes, though all in tune, still felt a little off somehow, and it struck an eerie chord within me. And there were words to it. No stanzas or a chorus that I could hear, but some kind of chant. I couldn't decipher the words with any clarity, but the chanting added a chilling, urgent quality.

The closer I got to the civic center, the louder the music got, and the more difficult it became to hold on to my grounding thought. The images of running, of fighting, of danger, grew stronger. I bit hard on the side of my cheek and tasted blood. It helped a little. "Calm down!" I snapped at myself.

But I was running, a full sprint. I'd started running without being aware of it. When the civic center loomed large I wanted to run straight to the closest door and burst through it.

Calm down!

I ran to the closest window instead, the music and the light pouring over me. I rose to my toes and peered through the broken glass.

I stared. I hadn't actually believed that the entire town was there, but it seemed that they were, from the youngest toddler to the oldest crone. Hundreds of people sat or knelt on the floor, all of them dressed in black with thick red bands around their arms. Dozens more stood in some kind of formation, chanting to the accompaniment of an orchestra, of which Aiden appeared to be a member. And torches were scattered everywhere, painting bizarre, warped shadows on pale faces.

To one side was a huge cage, tall iron bars ground into the dirt where the flooring had been ripped up. All the Shields I had met the day before were in the cage, but they didn't appear to be unhappy prisoners. They were grinning like fools and dancing and pulling on the bars to the beat of the music, chanting with the others.

And at the center of attention was Creol, standing on a small platform, dressed in a black tunic and black leggings and a full cape of deep red. Very dramatically, he thrust his fist into the air as he and his followers chanted one word over and over. "Freedom! Freedom! Freedom!"

It was glorious.

It's ridiculous, girl.

He was standing so tall and strong, every hard line vibrating with passion.

He's wearing a cape.

And the music, it was so stirring, filling every heart with pride and determination.

If you like melodramatic drivel.

A double entrance in the background flew open, the doors crashing against the walls. Dressed in slim, trim fighting uniforms of red and silver, their swords held high, the cream of young Middle Reach society marched in, chanting the words, their faces glowing with visions of violence.

Got to love propaganda.

A sudden flare of light, something like a contained firecracker. It went off in time to a crescendo in the music and briefly illuminated one side of Creol's face before fading away to nothing.

Nice touch.

I dug my fingernails into the windowsill. I really wanted to run in there. They seemed to be having such a cathartic time. And I loved the colors.

I nearly swallowed my tongue when I was jerked from the window by the back of my shirt. Hands pushed me over the black grass. As I was stumbling over my own feet I managed to look back at two masculine faces just before being shoved at, and then through, the door.

No one noticed the intrusion at first. They were too wrapped up in the music and the sights and the flares of light. My captors dragged me through the crowd, indifferent to any body parts that might have been in our way. They threw me into the small space that had been left clear before Creol's platform. After a few more shouts of "Freedom!" he noticed my presence. He gave me one long, close look before raising both arms to signal an end to the theatrics. I had regained my feet and been shoved back to the floor by the time all the music and chanting had dribbled off.

And then there was silence. Not a single murmur, not the slightest rustling of cloth. Even the children were quiet as everyone in the building kept their eyes on the tiny circle around the platform.

It was hard, being forced to stay on my knees when I still wanted to run up and fight someone. My blood had slowed once the music had stopped, but the impulses were still there. I was emotionally unbalanced at a time when I really needed to be calm. Good thing Karish wasn't there to witness it.

Creol stepped down from the platform, came to me, surprised me by helping me to my feet. I let him guide me a few steps away from my captors, curious about what he was up to. "Do you like it?" he asked in a whisper.

That wasn't anything near what I might have expected, had I given the matter any thought. "Excuse me?"

He glanced back at the orchestra. "Everyone's susceptible to music, you know," he said. "Not to the extent that Shields are, of course, but it's a rare person who won't be moved by powerful music played under the right circumstances. Darkness, fire, strong colors, healthy young people marching in uniform, some stirring words. Administer a few doses of this, and you can convince a weak-minded person to do almost anything."

He was staring directly into my eyes, and I knew he was trying to communicate without using too many specific words. *Sorry, fellow. I don't read minds.*

It didn't seem to bother him. He smiled and backed away from me a pace. The two thugs immediately stepped forward to grab my arms. Creol leapt back onto the platform. "Friends!" he shouted in a voice that seemed to fill every nook of the immense hall. "Do you trust me?"

The resounding *"YES!"* almost made me jump.

"Do you believe in me?"

"Yes!"

"You know what I can do?"

"Yes!"

"I promised to bring to Middle Reach the prosperity it was destined to have, didn't I?"

"Yes!"

"I promised to do this by destroying High Scape, didn't I?"

Holy hell!

"Yes!"

"And you believe I can do this, don't you? I have proven I have the power to move earth and call floods, haven't I?"

The man was insane.

"Yes!" everyone screamed.

Move earth and call floods? No one could do that. It was impossible.

But then, so was healing people.

But this was different. Surely. This wasn't just redirecting forces, as all Sources did. This was creating them. And that had to be impossible, because the alternative didn't bear thinking of. But his audience believed him.

Creol dropped his arms to his sides, let his shoulders droop a little, and assumed an air of chagrin. "I did fail to destroy High Scape," he admitted. "But I think my failure can be forgiven under the circumstances." He swept a dramatic arm in my direction. "I beg to introduce Dunleavy Mallorough, most talented Shield of her generation, and the sole reason for my failure."

I tried to keep my expression blank as everyone in the building stared at me, but my poor mind was scrambling. What was he talking about? What failure? He was acting like there'd been some kind of attack on High Scape. And there hadn't been. Not to my knowledge, and I would have noticed something like that.

Well, there had been the Rushes, of course. But those had been natural phenomenon.

Holy hell.

He was claiming he had the power to move the earth. Was he telling these people he was responsible for those Rushes? That was absurd.

So was claiming I was the most powerful Shield in my generation. As though there were any way to determine such a thing. Nice piece of rhetoric there, Creol.

"Now, we must respect Dunleavy," Creol instructed the crowd. "She has, unfortunately, been in the power of the Triple S from the time she was a very young child, and as you can see she is still quite young. She has been trained to see the world through the perspective her academy has imposed on her, and she has not yet been out in the world long enough to throw off her childhood fantasies. Her Source, however . . ." He trailed off, shaking his head, and there were angry mutterings among the crowd.

"Damn them all to the seventh ring!" one man shouted, starting an avalanche of similar sentiments.

Creol put up both hands in a placatory gesture. "I know, I know," he said with artificial sympathy. "Sources don't have the excuses Shields have. They are let out into the world at a much earlier age. They have plenty of opportunity to see the danger, the evil, even, of the Triple S system. But do they admit it?"

"No!" the crowd shouted in unison.

"No," he echoed. "And why should they? They are given everything, are they not?" Grumbles of agreement from the crowd. "The best places to live, the best of clothing and food and luxuries. And the servile respect of their Shields and the regulars. Why would they want to change that?"

Someone said something I couldn't catch. There was laughter from a significant section of the crowd.

"Now, I'm a Source," Creol said in the tone of one revealing a shameful secret. "Some might say I'm a failed Source. I haven't bonded, as all Sources must. And I will admit that for many years it was difficult and painful to be continually rejected. To go to the Matches, year after year, and look in the eyes of so many Shields, who were becoming increasingly younger than I, and come away with nothing. To be standing with new ranks of Sources who wondered why I was still among them. Who would glance at me when they thought I wouldn't notice, and whisper about me." He smiled, and I doubted if many among the audience could see the weary-looking expression. Not that it mattered. His voice carried the feeling to every corner. "I remember my shock at first hearing my experience being used as a warning among Sources. 'Look at Creol,' they would say. 'He's crazy, and he'll never get a Shield.' " He paused, revealing a perfect silence that demonstrated the complete attention of his audience. "But now I know I am fortunate," he continued after a moment. "Though many would be appalled and terrorized by my fate, I know I am fortunate. Because I have freedom!"

"Freedom!" everyone screamed.

"Had I been bonded, no doubt I would still be under the heel of the Triple S. Living where they said I should, working with whom they said I should, thinking as they said I should. Instead, I have not bonded, and so I have been cast aside, as are many Shields, and that is good, I tell you. Good! Because it has given me the freedom to see, to learn, to speak. Without the enslaving shackles of the Triple S, I have been able to move among people freely, to learn of them, to see what they see. And I have witnessed the benefits Sources reap at the cost of Shields and regulars." Another pause. "I am a Source, but I was born of a Shield and a regular. My parents were worthy of respect. All people are worthy of respect. From my failures I have learned this."

He took a step back on the platform and looked down at his feet. It appeared that he was planning his next line of rhetoric. I thought he just needed to catch his breath.

"But before I could learn from them, my failures brought me very low," he admitted. "I was a Source with no Shield, and so I was nothing. I had no use, and so I had no respect. Not from others, and eventually not from myself, either.

Doing nothing is the worst thing in the world. People like you," he swept his hand before him, taking in the entire crowd with one long, elegant gesture, "who have had to work so hard all your life, you scoff at me when I say such things, and you have the right. For how dare someone who is given everything complain about anything? But," he put up one finger, "you cannot know how much better it is to work hard and receive little, than to do nothing and receive any amount. You work. You do something useful. You can feel pride in your skill, in your labor, and know you have contributed to your family and your community. You cannot know what it is like to do nothing, to know you can never do anything, to know you are nothing but a burden on your community, and always have been and always will be." He put a hand to his chest. "It eats away at the soul," he said.

Great. And that was the future I was staring in the face. Once Karish took his title, I would be just as useless as Creol.

Didn't think it would make me want to destroy cities, though.

"And then, there is the way people look at you," Creol continued. "The sneering, the contempt, the pity. Or the scrambling to find you something to do, some make-work project of no value, as a pathetic sop to your vanity. Such a transparent effort. Worse than the jeers." He shrugged. "And so I reached a point where I just wanted to be left alone. To get away from the looks and the tones of voice and the scraps of honor people tried to toss my way. I just wanted peace, and solitude, and to just not have to think about it anymore. So one night I went out to an empty field. I raised my arms." He raised his arms high. "I closed my eyes." He closed his eyes. "And I called the forces to me, to sweep me away so I would never have to see any of it again."

He'd wanted to kill himself? Was that what he was claiming? And he tried to do it by using the forces?

Well, at least it was a unique way to go.

"And you know what?" he asked, the tone somehow soft even though the volume was still sufficient to be heard by everyone. "The forces came." He chuckled, opening his eyes and lowering his arms. "Scared the hell out of me, I tell you."

Laughter sprinkled through the crowd.

"I stopped, of course. A Source can't channel without a Shield. And I realized I didn't want to die so badly, after all. But it was a revelation. For I discovered I have skills the Triple S didn't want me to know I had. For make no mistake, my friends, the Triple S controls Sources as thoroughly as they do everyone else. They robbed us of the knowledge that some of us could do more than merely channel forces when they are imposed upon us. Some of us can call them and have them do our bidding. The Triple S would deny us this power. But I was fortunate enough to throw off their yoke of ignorance, and now I am free!"

"Free!" the audience shouted back.

"I have power!"

"Power!"

"I can move the earth! I can call water! And with these powers I will lay waste the city that took the prosperity and prestige that should have been yours! I will destroy High Scape, I will bring back the waters to Middle Reach, and in doing so bring back the wealth, the people, the life!"

The crowd cheered uproariously. Creol's eyes were glittering with excitement. The shouting and the applause rang through the building. I could feel it on my skin. I suppressed a shudder.

It was hard to think through all that. He was honestly claiming he could cause disasters, not just subdue them. And everyone believed him. He, I thought, was suggesting he had caused the Rushes in High Scape, which had been admittedly bizarre and painful, unlike anything I'd ever heard of. But even if he could do these things, why would anyone want to destroy High Scape? What was his connection to Middle Reach that he would try to save it in this way? If it would even work. No one thought much of Middle Reach, and bringing the waterways back to it—was that his plan?—wouldn't be enough to restore it to the glory it had once promised.

And what the hell was Aiden doing there?

I looked at him. He wasn't caught up in the rhetoric as the others were. He was looking at me, and for the life of me I couldn't read his expression.

I was such a fool. I had believed every word he had ever said to me, not a doubt in my mind. Whatever was going on, he was a part of it, and I'd had no notion.

How could I have been so incredibly, naively, dangerously blind? He'd been lying to me from the day we'd met. I'd bought everything. When did I get so stupid?

I swallowed bitter bile. I had to calm down. There would be plenty of time to berate myself for my ineptitude later. I hoped.

"But I can't do it alone," Creol said once it was finally quiet again. "I need you." Another long sweep of the hand taking in the entire audience. "I need the Shields." He waved a hand at the cage, and the occupants cheered and shook the bars. "I need you to believe in me. I need you to trust me. And I need you to help me with this poor girl." He looked down at me.

Poor? Girl? Excuse me?

"Her Source," he began, and then he trailed off, shaking his head, as though what he had to say next was a terrible burden to him. "Her Source is the notorious Shintaro Karish. That's right, my friends," as the audience hissed and booed, "this poor girl is chained, for life, to a wastrel. A corrupter of innocence who abuses his Source privileges to their fullest extent, wallowing in wine and games of chance and whores, stealing from hardworking folk like yourselves, taking for granted the luxuries that most of us will never see in our lifetimes. Now I know what you're thinking." He put out both palms in an almost pleading gesture. "How, you are saying, could any self-respecting woman serve a man like Karish as our Dunleavy does?"

I shot him a look. *Our Dunleavy?*

"But please remember, this Karish, he is handsome, he is charming, he is aristocratic, he is talented, he is experienced. He has all the advantages. And our poor Dunleavy has never heard anything of him that the Triple S didn't want her to hear." He looked down at me again, right in the eye. "She knows nothing of his true character," he said, basically to me. "She was taken straight from her academy, young and innocent and naive and thoroughly trained, and given to this immoral, philandering parasite. She had no choice in the matter, no choice but to obey her Source in every instance. We can only imagine in what manner he has used her, all under the euphemism of Triple S duty."

Someone has a dirty mind.

"Believe me, friends, Dunleavy is as much a prisoner as any of us. Will you help me free her?"

"Yes!" everyone shouted.

Thanks. If only I could be sure their definition of freedom and mine belonged in the same dictionary.

"Dunleavy is the perfect candidate to test my little theory," Creol crowed. "She is the strongest Shield of her generation. If anyone can survive, she can."

What?

"Will you help me?"

"Yes!"

"Shall we do it now?"

"Yes!"

"Tonight, Dunleavy will be free. Tomorrow, High Scape will be gone. And soon, soon, the world will be ours!"

The following roar hurt my ears. It raged on as the Shields left their cage and followed Creol out of the civic center. Only Ryan wandered close enough to speak to me. He stared at me with eyes gone eerily dead and said, "It's been fun." He paused, trying to communicate some message I was failing to pick up. Then he grinned and walked out.

My two thugs picked me up by the arms—sometimes I hated being so small—and placed me in the cage. "What is going on?" I demanded. "Why are you doing this?"

I hadn't really expected an answer, but one of the thugs said, "We're working to get back what's ours." He slammed the door shut and locked it.

"What do you hope to get back?"

"All of it," he said. "The money, the respect. Everything High Scape took from us."

I didn't get it. If he envied what High Scape had, why didn't he just move there?

"We were supposed to be what High Scape is now," he said. "Everyone had big plans for Middle Reach. Libraries, theaters, universities. This was going to be the center of the world. But we lost it all when we lost the rivers in the earthquakes our Source was too incompetent to stop. And that was the end of it. No major trade routes, no money, no university, no business. No interest. No respect. The Triple S sends the worst of the Pairs here. No one thinks this place is worth having Runners. The healers and teachers and whatnot come here only because they're too incompetent to get work anywhere else. And anyone born here who has any real talent leaves as soon as their two feet can carry them, lying about where they came from. Because we're the hole of the world, something to be ashamed of. But that's going to change."

There was no way any of this was real. Creol was just as crazy as the rumors had said, and for some reason he had decided to stir up this tiny village and play god. And they were playing right along with him. Surely even a Shield was allowed to get hysterical under these circumstances? "What's going to happen now?"

The man smiled kindly. Kindly. "We're going to help you break your bond to Karish."

If he was hoping for any sign of excitement or joy from me, he was in for a disappointment. "And how is that to be accomplished?"

"You're going to kill him," he told me.

"Who? Creol?" I was all for that. If I tried hard enough I was sure I could dredge up some lingering reactions to the music I'd just heard. I could get crazy enough to kill someone if I really wanted to.

The thug, however, looked appalled. "No! Karish!"

"Really?" So Creol did have Karish. I was relieved, in a way, to finally know, but I was also furious. I had as good as crossed Creol off the list of enemies. I had practically believed that Creol was innocent. Odd, but innocent. I was useless at everything.

"Don't worry," the thug said. "You won't die with him. Stevan says if you're in enough of a rage when you kill Karish, the emotional turmoil will sever the bond."

"Interesting theory," I said dryly. "Only Karish isn't the one I'm mad at right now."

"Don't worry," he said again. "We'll fix that." He gave me another smile and then wandered away to join his uncommunicative partner.

I leaned my forehead against one of the cool bars. "Great."

Chapter Twenty-three

Karish was a mess. Filthy, his clothes stained and rumpled, his hair hanging in greasy strings, his fingernails caked with dirt. He was too pale, as though he had been ill, and he was looking a little thin. He was trembling, I could just see it. Exhausted.

I had some maternal instincts after all.

It was not the time.

The worst thing was how he looked at me. He was puzzled, uncertain. Not at all happy to see me. I could only guess that they'd told him what they planned.

And he believed them.

He was pushed into the cage with me, and as soon as he was free to do so he backed as far away from me as the bars allowed. I was astonished. He thought I was going to try to kill him.

Unbelievable. How could he think I was a willing part of this? And how could he think I was even physically capable of it? He was a man. Sure, he wasn't at his best, and I was strong and fast, but I knew nothing about fighting. And even if I did, how could he believe I would ever do anything to harm him?

It was one big, ludicrous scenario, and he believed it. What was wrong with him?

Of the Shields, only Lynch had returned with Creol. He said to her, "Forgive me, child, but we'll have to bind you now. I want you to see this, but the music will be extremely powerful. We can't expose you to it and leave you free."

Lynch, whom I had liked and pitied so much, nodded with no apparent resentment. The woman who had been rightfully furious at her legitimate Source for having her bound, if indeed he ever did, meekly submitted to it at the word of a Source who had clearly lost his mind. And the regulars who tied her did so with as much respect as was possible under the circumstances.

The others, all the spectators and the young pseudo-soldiers, sat around and waited. If they knew what was supposed to happen, that someone was supposed to die, they weren't about to raise any objections. No, they were prepared to watch. They didn't even send the children away.

I was confused. Really, what was going on? Creol had had Karish abducted. Why? Unless he really did believe he had the power to create earthquakes, and honestly thought Karish was the only obstacle. If so, why not just kill him? Why go through the trouble of kidnapping him?

Did Karish's future title have anything to do with anything?

I hated thinking. It made my head hurt. And none of that mattered right then. What was important was that Creol was planning to drive me to murdering Karish using carefully selected music. Did he really think he could do that? And what was the point?

I wasn't going to do it, of course. Nothing could drive me to murder. Except people who picked their teeth in taverns, that was so disgusting. So after I didn't kill Karish, then what?

Karish thought I was going to do it. Ignorant bastard. Like everyone else he thought I was a weak-minded fool with no control over myself. Once again I would have to prove everyone wrong. And then Creol would rage, and Karish and I would be killed together. My, how romantic.

One disaster at a time.

I put my back against the bars and slid to the floor. I linked my arms behind me, holding onto the bars. *Hold on to something, and don't let go.* "It's your duty to guard me through the music," I told Karish. "Now is not the time to live down to your reputation."

He blinked.

There were no more speeches. Creol was giving instructions to the orchestra and the choir. The audience was murmuring. I glowered at Aiden for a moment, and he had the gall to smile and nod at me. It was a look of reassurance. His insanity, I thought, had to be hereditary, as he hadn't been in Middle Reach long enough to be affected by the water. Then again, I didn't know how long he had lived in High Scape before I met him. Maybe he'd spent years in Middle Reach before then. All of his stories might have been lies. Maybe the reason I'd been able to beat him at bench dancing was because he wasn't a professional dancer after all. Which would explain why he had been so forgiving upon learning he would never be able to dance again. That hadn't been normal.

Maybe he'd always been a professional storyteller. And a minstrel. He was awfully effective with that lyre.

Enough. I had my own preparations to make. I leaned my head back against the bars and closed my eyes.

Hang on to something, and don't let go.

Stay calm.

Breathe in, breathe out.

Stay calm.

I waited.

I heard silence resettle in the center. I heard instruments being shifted in hands. I felt that pause as all the musicians looked at each other to make sure everyone was going to be starting in unison. I tensed, tightening my grip on the bars.

The first piece was not a martial air, which was what I had been expecting. A woman with a beautifully low voice sang of her innocence before a handsome, careless man bewitched her, promising her a bright future of simple joys and blessings. But he had tired of her and left her, and now her life had crumbled into ash. With a powerful voice filled with exquisite pain, she begged for an explanation of what crime she had committed, except to believe in love, and my throat squeezed shut and my eyes smarted.

Foolish woman, to trust in a man so completely. They always left. Look at Caspian. Or they betrayed you. Look at Aiden.

The next song was a duet, the first woman joined by a

second, a soprano. The song was warm, full of delight and reminiscence, as the two women sang of a strong childhood friendship. Two little girls who dressed as princesses together, and played house, and dreamed of marrying their perfect princes and living side by side for the rest of their lives, raising their daughters together. But then—and the music modulated to a minor key—one girl was revealed to be not so perfect. She had symptoms. She was a Shield. She was ripped from the arms of her friend and her family and sent to a far-off, mysterious, untouchable place. The girl left behind mourned for her friend, and when she was old enough she went looking for her. After years of searching she found her, but the woman who had been her childhood companion didn't know her. When reminded of their friendship the Shield sneered coldly, and went running off when her Source beckoned. And so the loyal young woman was left alone with her memories.

I couldn't believe I was crying over such mawkish garbage. I'd no doubt lost all my friends when I was sent to the academy, too, but I made a whole bunch of new ones. And if any of my childhood friends looked me up, I wouldn't turn them away. I'd be thrilled to see them. Even though I couldn't remember any of them. Because my academy friends were so very far away and I didn't have any in High Scape or Middle Reach.

Aiden, Aiden, how could you do this to me?

The tears were blinding me. I couldn't wipe them away. I tightened my grip on the bars behind me. *Hang on to something, and don't let go.* At least I wasn't actually sobbing. That was something.

A drum started pounding. A fiddle bow danced over strings. My blood picked up its pace. My feet wanted to tap.

"Will you join us?" cried the voices, the soprano and alto joined by a host of others. "Will you come? Will you take a stand and fight? There is glory on another day for those who would be free. It will be dangerous, and difficult, some won't make it through the night. But after we will drink a toast to the new life we will see."

I banged the back of my head against the bars. *Hold on to something, and don't let go.*

Pain exploded between my shoulder blades, and I was shoved forward. I got my hands in front of me just in time to avoid landing flat on my face. I looked up and saw one of the thugs just outside the cage bearing a staff and a menacing expression. I wouldn't be allowed to lurk about the bars. I would have nothing to hold on to.

All right. No reason to panic. I could handle it. I was a reasonable adult. No way was I going to let music drive me to irrational behavior. I paced, well away from Karish, who was still looking confused. The boy still hadn't figured it out. I'd thought he was brighter than that. The thug by the bars was jabbing his staff in as far as he could, trying to force me closer to Karish. I felt like sticking my tongue out at him.

"Will you join us? Will you come? Will you take a stand and fight?"

Shut up.

I could hear them, the voices. The sopranos pure and high, the altos rich and mournful, the tenors clear and stirring, and the basses—Oh, Zaire, the basses. Bass voices had always slain me, so deep and powerful they made the pit of my stomach vibrate.

Damn all basses.

And they were so beguiling. They sympathized with my state of isolation. They understood. They were just like me. But if I would fight with them, strike at the enemy, we would all be free. We would all be together, and no one would ever be able to hurt us again.

I shook my head to clear it and noticed I had wandered too close to Karish. He, too, had been shoved away from the bars. He was watching me, but without the hostility I'd noticed earlier.

When we got out of this I was going to brain him for ever thinking I could possibly be dangerous to him.

The tempo of the voices changed. Each word was forcefully enunciated and sung quickly, at a monotone for a few beats and then raised or lowered in jagged arpeggios. And visions formed in my head, visions of leading an army of good, loyal people, every single one of whom would gladly die for me. Cut and bruised but untiring, I leapt over walls with graceful agility, climbed mountains, traversed narrow bridges over raging rivers, and faced a shadowy enemy with nothing but bare hands and bravery.

The enemy lost its shadows, the face melting into Karish's. His eyes intent, he had crouched down a little, his hands raised, as I circled him. He was getting ready to attack me. I tensed.

No. I was getting ready to attack him. And I was no general of any army. And he was not the enemy. And even if he were, nothing could make me attack him with my bare hands.

The voices changed again, and I froze in panic. *Counterpoint.* In frantic rounds they went, challenging me, pleading with me, the drums and fiddles chasing them up and down the scales. Triumph in major, tragedy in minor, all of it ringing in my ears and careening through my brain.

I ran to escape from it. I ran smack into the bars and was forced back from them with a hard blow. I almost liked the pain, it pushed back the music for an instant, but then it came crashing back in again. I had to move. I couldn't stand still or I'd explode. With tears in my eyes and noise filling my head I ran, blind. Forces buffeted me about, and for a moment I thought I'd been caught in a disaster. I fell, countless times, and got up and kept running.

I was going mad.

Something caught at me. Unthinking I swung out and hit something. Sense returned for a moment and I crossed my arms tightly. Don't strike at anything. I tried to pull away, but the force that had me clung on. I struggled against it, pushing and squirming, but I couldn't see or think.

"Lee, it's me."

The words were heard but they weren't understood. They weren't set to music, after all. I pushed harder.

"Really, my dear," the voice said again, a soft deep voice, the *r*'s beautifully rolled. "You wouldn't want to confirm every bad thing Her Grace has said about slip collectors, would you?"

What?

"It's Taro, Lee. Shintaro. Karish. Whatever you like. But please calm down. You're hurting yourself."

The words, strengthened by a bond that was real and strong, penetrated my mind as they would not have, had they been spoken in another voice. It was Karish who held me, and he was not my enemy.

Though I thought it was probably the smell that really brought me back. The boy reeked.

The music still whipped around me, but suddenly there was a little breathing room, just enough to cast anchor and resist the pull. But my mind was tired, and the new, hastily built wall threatened to crumble even as I erected it.

Hold on to something, and don't let go. I pressed my face against Karish's chest and clutched at his arms. I breathed, in and out. Feel the air move through my nose and lungs, feel the flesh beneath my fingers and the heart beating against my cheek. Listen to the words whispered into my ear, in that calm and familiar voice, cutting through the hysterical lyrics whipping past a handsbreadth away.

But I still heard them. They still reached me, called to me. I'd never been forced to listen to that kind of music for so long. I trembled with the power of it. When would it stop?

Karish lowered us both to the ground. Kneeling, he gathered me close and held me reassuringly tight. "You're not alone, Lee," he said, his voice the most soothing sound I'd ever heard. "I'm here. I'll guard you through the music. Hold on to me, and I'll help you through it."

Only they could understand me, the choir warned me. Only among outcasts would I find where I belonged. Others only wanted to use me.

"So many people admire you, Lee," Karish was saying. "LaMonte thought you could do no wrong. You should have heard him lecturing me. A Source's sensibilities were no excuse for being such a sad trial to his Shield. Time to put aside my infantile habits and settle down to a proper job. He never knew the half of it, did he? And Val never blamed you for stepping in on Miho. Of course he was grateful to you, told me how lucky I was to have you. I know it. I swear I do. You can trust me, I promise you."

"We need you. If you desert us we shall fail. Our lives will be destroyed, and you will be alone in your slavery."

Hold on to something, and don't let go.

"Remember the bench dancing competition at Star Festival? You danced against the best in High Scape, and you beat them. Gods, you were magnificent to watch. You were so fast and sure. You were so much yourself. You were out to destroy every dancer you met, and you didn't care who knew it. You were beautiful. I didn't dare tell you what I thought. You'd rather hear your dog bark at a crow. But I didn't leave you that night, did I? I promised you I wouldn't, and I didn't. I always keep my promises."

Hold on, and don't let go.

I thought the music would go on forever. It felt like it had. And I longed to follow it. I wanted to jump up and run and fight, wipe out every bastard that had ever committed any wrong. I thought my muscles would tear themselves apart in the strain to keep still. My mind was spinning so hard. Tears were flooding my cheeks, and I didn't care. I clung to Karish, and he stroked my hair and rubbed my back, whispering soothing nonsense and countering the lies of the music with lies of his own.

And eventually the music stopped. I wasn't sure exactly when, for it continued to whirl around my head long after the last beat had been sounded. But I became aware of the silence, aware that I was curled up in a tight ball with Karish on the floor, my face wet with tears, my breath harsh in my throat, my whole body shaking so hard I doubted I could stand.

Karish was still whispering. "You're so strong," he said, the idiot. I was a total mess, an object of torment and ridicule, and we both knew it. "Thank you."

For what? Not killing him? That was more his doing than mine. If he hadn't caught me, there was no telling what damage I would have done to one of us. I should have been thanking him.

"Well," Creol said in a loud, flat voice. "That was disappointing." He approached the cage, waving away one of the thugs and leaning against the bars. He didn't look angry or frustrated. Bored, maybe. "Congratulations, Taro. You have her well trained. She's completely under your thumb. Tell me, do you throw her your table scraps when she sits up and begs?"

I was supposed to feel insulted. Perhaps it was a last-ditch effort to make me angry enough to attack. Instead, I laughed. A chuckle, really, and a weak one at that. I didn't know where the urge came from, because it wasn't funny. But I laughed, and it felt good, though I was so exhausted the movement through my stomach and chest was in danger of killing me.

Creol frowned. I guessed he didn't like being laughed at. Go figure.

"I've wasted a great deal of time on you two," he informed us. "Plans years in the making I have delayed because I was assured you would be of use to me."

So sorry to disappoint.

"I'll have to rush to make up the time. I hate rushing."

I started laughing again, and this time it was louder. Karish squeezed me. Either he agreed with me or he was trying to shut me up.

Creol sighed. It sounded like regret. "I'll have to kill you both," he said. "A public execution, I think. For my coronation."

I would have liked to have raised an eyebrow, but it was too much for me right then. A coronation? As in crown? As in an Emperor? "You can't be serious."

He cocked his head to one side. "Not completely, but then you never know how things might end up. I mean, you're both here now. So when I attack High Scape tomorrow, you won't be able to do a thing about it. After I destroy the world's richest city, I could take a look at doing the same to Erstwhile. Her Imperial Majesty is an elderly woman, after all. It's unlikely she would be able to survive a serious disaster. And even if her son does, well, we all know how resolute he is, don't we? How hard would it be to convince him to turn over the throne? Especially if I promise him his life and all the money to play with that he wants? Yes." He nodded, as though thinking this all out for the first time. "It definitely bears looking into. And so, my first public ceremony celebrating the first Source to be crowned Emperor would be an excellent platform for executing the traitors who'd so foolishly tried to stand against me." And he winked at me.

Holy hell.

"Hey!" Aiden called out. "You can't kill her!" He came striding over to the cage, lyre in hand.

Creol looked at him with genuine surprise. "Why not?"

"You told me you wouldn't kill her," Aiden accused him.

The tension in my chest eased just a little. Despite all that had happened, the knowledge that Aiden hadn't meant to kill me made me feel the tiniest bit better. I still despised him. He was still a total bastard for putting me through the most dangerous, humiliating, gut-wrenching experience of my life. And for lying to me all this time. And manipulating me with degrading ease. But at least he wasn't a murderer.

No, he'd been saving that honor for me.

I was beginning to get myself under control. My breathing was smoothing out, the sweat was drying, the shudders had shrunk into the odd tiny shock beneath my skin. Wanting to present a slightly less pathetic sight to my audience, I withdrew from Karish. I sat cross-legged on the dirt floor, elbow on one knee, my chin resting on my palm. Karish looked at me and smiled at my casual pose. He leaned back on his hands, his long legs stretched out before him and crossed at the ankles. We couldn't have looked more bored if we were stuck at a cricket match.

Creol seemed a little disappointed by Aiden's response, as if it were just too mundane for his taste. "Oh, that," he said. "You assured me she would make a decent Shield, but she'll just get in my way. I have to kill her."

Aiden drew himself up to his full considerable height. "I didn't bring her to Middle Reach so you could kill her."

Briefly, I closed my eyes. So he *had* been a part of it all along. And now I remembered. He was the one who had suggested I read Karish's letters, where I would have to see the correspondence from Creol. He was the one who had convinced me to come to Middle Reach when everyone else was thinking of Flown Raven.

I wondered when it had all started. When we had met for the very first time? He had been the one to approach us, after all, when Karish and I were bickering at the Star Festival. He'd had a shot to make at Karish for being a Source and then he'd tried to separate us. And he'd been so understanding about my crippling him—I bet he hadn't planned on that. What an excellent actor. And since then he'd been lecturing me about the abusiveness of Sources. I'd ignored it all as ignorant ranting.

I was such a fool.

"Well, aye, as a matter of fact, you did," said Creol.

Aiden's face assumed a most unattractive shade of red. "You said," he ground out between his teeth, "that the music would drive her to kill Karish, and then she would be free. You promised me that."

I felt a certain shallow sympathy for Aiden. It was hard to find in all the anger and pain and sense of betrayal, but there was a small sliver of it that I could catch and hold up. He had believed all the wrong people. So had I, but I hadn't willfully endangered anyone's life. And he hadn't gotten the results he'd hoped for. Well, that and an empty sack was worth an empty sack, but it had to hurt.

"And you promised to have her ready to kill Karish and to Shield me," Creol said to Aiden.

I couldn't believe that was really the plan. I was supposed to Shield Creol while he deconstructed High Scape? Why?

"I was supposed to have more time," Aiden protested. "She wasn't supposed to find out so soon. I would have had her ready if I'd had just a few more days."

The hell you would! Arrogant little prat.

"Then it's your fault that I have to kill her, because if you had kept her away from the center tonight, as you were supposed to, we wouldn't have had to rush things like this. It's your carelessness that's causing this. Really, one would almost think you wanted me to kill her."

Aiden's response to this was to try to smash Creol's face in with his lyre. He was obvious about his intention, and Creol had plenty of warning. He ducked. The lyre met the bars of the cage with almost explosive results. Keys and strings twanged and splinters flew.

Two new thugs came running to restrain Aiden.

"Bad form, Aiden," Creol chided him. "Obviously you can't be trusted to do your part for the cause. You're far too emotional, not to mention incompetent. But for all that, I'm going to give you a great reward. I'm going to let you die with your . . . friend. Terribly poetic, don't you think? Something someone like you can appreciate." Aiden struggled against his captors to no effect. "Who knows? You might even convince her to forgive you for trying to sell her to me. I hear starvation can addle the wits." A dismissive wave of the hand. "Take the fool away."

The two thugs grabbed Aiden by his hands and his feet, swinging him between them to carry him away. "Dunleavy!" he called as they carted him off. "I did it for you! You can see that, can't you? You were supposed to kill Karish. You would have been free!"

I grit my teeth. *Someone shut the man up, please.* He was carried out of the civic center; the door closed behind him. I could still hear him shouting, but the noise was easier to ignore.

Lynch had been freed during this little melodrama. She wandered over to the cage to stand beside Creol. She looked at me with a sad smile. "I'm sorry it had to happen this way, Dunleavy," she said, offering her hand for shaking. "I think we could have been good friends."

I, of course, didn't move from my comfortable seat on the dirt floor. I stared at her and wondered if she was insane. Not that it mattered. I looked at Creol. "What's going on?" I demanded.

He smirked. "Alison, dear," he said to Lynch. "You've heard all this before. People are starting to drift. Could you gather everyone back together and tell them the meeting will resume once we've dealt with our prisoners? Gary, Mark, why don't you give her a hand?"

Prisoners. Well, at least he was finally being honest about it. No more "our poor Dunleavy."

"Yes, Stevan," Lynch said dutifully, and she was echoed by the two thugs. The three of them wandered away.

Creol leaned against the bars of the cage and gave me a condescending grin. "A delay tactic, Dunleavy?" he asked. "Are you hoping to lure me into bragging about myself to give time to the Runners who are desperately searching for you?" He snickered. "I've probably seen all the same plays you have, Dunleavy. Only no one who knows you're in Middle Reach has had time to get worried. And there are no Runners here. So I can brag all I want, and no one will show up in time to rescue you."

I hadn't been thinking along the terms of rescue. I knew that if we were going to get out of this we'd have to do it ourselves. I was just curious. "Why is Middle Reach so important to you?"

"It's not. It's a mud hole. It's not important to anyone. But half the population is crazy and the other half certain the entire world is using them as a dumping ground. It's an excellent place to start. A bunch of malcontents stuck together, feeding off and feeding into each other's bitterness. Give them a target, and they can develop into the most useful army."

"To do what?" I asked. "You can't really hope to become Emperor."

He laughed. "No. Someone with brains will figure out who I am and have me killed long before that's a possibility."

And the getting killed part disturbed him not at all. "So why are you doing this?"

He shrugged. "What else am I going to do?"

Uh, how about not leveling High Scape? "What's this about, Creol?" I said, hardening my voice. Perhaps he would respond to the simulation of authority. "There has to be a reason for this."

"Aye, and the reason is that I can do it. And I'm bored. I have nothing to do, Dunleavy. Sometimes I'm so bored I think I'll go out of my head with it."

He was out of his head. Or maybe it was all just an act, and he didn't feel like telling me why he was doing all this stuff. So my curiosity would go unsatisfied. How terribly important.

"I can tell her the rest if you've got something else to do," Karish offered, sounding friendly and helpful. I wondered what was wrong with him.

"Ah, but that would be rude, would it not, to neglect to tell Dunleavy myself that it was I who arranged to have you killed."

That hardly came as a surprise. So Karish's title had had nothing to do with anything. "You didn't manage to pull that off, either," I sneered.

"Hey," Karish protested softly.

I looked at him. "Sorry," I said. "That didn't come out quite right."

"She has a point, though," Creol admitted. "Simon was dreadfully incompetent."

"Why am I here?" That was the thing that was really confusing me. What was the point of my being here?

"Well, you see," he gestured at the door through which Aiden had been exited, "I got this touching letter from the lovestruck Aiden, begging me not to have you killed. You're a talented Shield, he claimed, and I could use you. I had heard of you, of course, and I knew you were partially responsible for stopping my attack on High Scape. If I had you for my Shield, my plans for High Scape would be all that much easier to carry out. And using the Stallion's Shield offered me a sort of satisfaction. I thought it was at least worth looking into. So I told Aiden to bring you here so I could look you over. But to enable him to convince you to come here, because who volunteers to go to Middle Reach, I had to have Karish brought here." He shook his head with an expression of regret. "Unfortunately, you won't do at all. Far too stubborn and headstrong."

I was not a horse. "So sorry to disappoint," I muttered.

"No need to apologize," Creol assured me. "I've been enjoying myself. I've had messengers running between High Scape and Middle Reach almost daily. Aiden has kept me apprised of every move you've made. Watching your efforts has been most entertaining."

"So I guess I'm not sorry after all." *Zaire, girl, shut up. You sound like an idiot.*

He grinned. "But tomorrow the real fun begins." And he rubbed his hands together in anticipation. I didn't know people actually did that. "Stacius, Jacob, over here, please. We're going to have to put these two with the others."

"Others?" I said to Karish.

"The other Sources."

"I'd been wondering where they all were."

"You really don't want to know."

"Now, Taro," Creol chided him, wagging a finger at him. "Don't ruin the surprise for Dunleavy."

"She won't believe it until she sees it, anyway."

"No, that's true," Creol agreed.

He was so damn smug. He really thought he had everything under control. And hey, maybe he did, but did he have to be so blatant about it?

Creol called Lynch back over again. "I'm afraid I need your help again, Alison."

"It's my pleasure, Stevan," she said. He crooked his arm, and she took it.

"Shall we get started, then?" he said, and he escorted her out of the building, like a lord and his lady sweeping out of a ball.

I turned to Karish to ask where we were being taken. I was shocked to find his lips curved in a triumphant smile of his own. It surprised me into silence for a moment, as I worried whether the insanity was contagious. "What could you possibly have to smile about?"

"Shoes and ships and sealing wax, cabbages and kings," he said.

Mallorough, you missed your chance to smack him. You can't do it now.

I was once more picked right off my feet and carried out of the civic center. I thought again about how I wished I had more inches. And a different color of hair. And really chiseled cheekbones.

Chapter Twenty-four

Karish and I were taken past the crowds, who watched us but did nothing to stop the proceedings. We were taken out of the center to a small collection of people standing a short distance away. Aiden was among them, still struggling to free himself and still failing at it. "Dunleavy!" he shouted as soon as he saw me. "You have to believe me! It wasn't supposed to happen like this! It was supposed to ''

"Shut him up," Creol ordered, the first harsh words I'd heard from his mouth.

One of the thugs applied a fist to Aiden's jaw. Aiden was stunned into silence.

Thank you.

"Alison, are you ready?" Creol asked.

"Aye, Stevan."

"Then let's get to it." He released Lynch and stood a bit apart from her. And then, all of a sudden, his eyes went kind of blank, and his posture tensed.

I was a little confused. Had the program suddenly changed? Was Creol feeling something the rest of us were missing? No one seemed alarmed, but the thugs were watching Creol expectantly. They appeared calm, though. And Karish wasn't preparing to channel. So there was no disaster coming, right?

Then the earth started trembling beneath my feet. "Karish!" I hissed at my Source. Do something! Or had his incarceration affected his mind? He'd certainly been acting strangely.

His gaze met mine, and his eyes seemed sane enough. He shook his head once, just slightly. He was making an effort to mute the triumph he was obviously still feeling. Unbelievable. He was a physical wreck, I was an emotional one, something terrible was about to happen to us, there was a disaster coming that he was apparently unable to do anything about, but he was thrilled to bits. It had to be a nightmare.

The trembling grew stronger, and still no one seemed worried. My teeth were rattling, but that didn't stop me from wondering if it was all in my head. I would not scream, I promised myself. I would not screech and clutch at anyone else as if expecting them to save me. I would die like an adult.

The ground opened up. I bit my lip, hard. I would not make a sound.

And still, no one else looked nervous.

Only it looked odd. It wasn't a crack running from horizon to horizon, or a great jutting lip rising high while its fellow dropped to the center of the earth. It was more like a door sliding open right before us. A horrible smell curled out.

Back in the civic center the music started up again. Another martial air. Without thinking I strained against the hands that held me. The thugs weren't worried.

As the topsoil rolled away, there was revealed an underground room or cavern. The floor and walls had been constructed of stone brick. Not a natural formation. A handful of men and women, pale, emaciated, filthy, looking far worse than Karish, lounged on the floor. They looked up at us without surprise or even much interest.

Creol and Lynch relaxed, job done. I stared at the errant Source. He could do it. He could move earth. And call floods? Was he responsible for the flooding the day before? Why would he do that? A test of my abilities, perhaps.

He could really do what he'd claimed he could. We were all going to die.

"Dunleavy, my dear," said Creol. "Let me present to you

the Sources of Middle Reach." I looked down at them more carefully, trying to put the names I'd heard to the wretches I saw. "The incompetent, the criminal"—he paused, as though waiting for something, and in the interim the targets of his insults didn't even bother to toss any back—"and the lazy. Look at them, Dunleavy, just lying there. When I first put them in there a few months ago, every time I visited them they'd charge at the walls, scrambling to get out and screaming blue murder. Of course, I don't feed them much. And I don't know how much air gets in there. Do you think that has anything to do with it?"

"There is no way you've had them down there for months," I objected. "Someone would have missed them."

"Everyone in Middle Reach knows where they are."

This was unbelievable. "The Triple S, at least, would notice they weren't fulfilling their duties."

He laughed derisively. "What duties? I do all the channeling here. And Shields write the reports. Sources don't have to. And who knows if the Triple S actually reads any of them." He leaned a little over the hole and waved at the occupants. Some of them glared back, but that was all the reaction he got. "I'm bringing you two new playmates," he said cheerfully. "Aren't you grateful?" He looked at one of his henchmen and jerked his head toward the cavern.

With one hard shove Aiden was over the hole, then crashing into it. He, illustrating Creol's earlier description, started swearing and clawing at the nearest wall. He couldn't get a grip on anything. A couple of the thugs watched him, ready to push him back down should he show any sign of success.

"No need for pushing, dear fellow," I heard Karish say to one of his escorts in the ponciest tone I'd heard from him yet. "I know the way." Of his own accord he leapt lightly into the hole. Then he looked up at me, his eyes gleaming with unholy humor. "Care to join me, my love?"

Have you lost your mind*?*

Creol sighed. "It's too bad, Dunleavy," he said; and he almost sounded like he meant it. "You could have helped me destroy the world."

Never been one of my ambitions. Sorry.

Should I try to escape? Was there a chance in hell that

I could get away from all these men? No. And it would be cowardly for me to leave Karish and the others in there while I ran for freedom. But I couldn't just meekly jump into that pit.

The music was urging me to kill everyone. It was getting hard to think at all.

"Lee," said Karish. "Come join us."

That sense of triumph was still with him, and he was looking at me rather intently. He was trying to tell me something. The third man that night to think mind reading was a feasible method of communication.

I had trusted all the wrong people. Aiden. Ryan. Lynch. I'd even trusted Creol, after a fashion. But I'd never really trusted Karish. That didn't necessarily mean I should start, but what the hell. Might as well shoot the whole quiver. And it was always better to jump in than to be pushed.

So I jumped. It wasn't a long drop. The cavern wasn't that deep, just half again the height of an average man. But it felt cold and damp. Perhaps that was just the result of expectation. The reek was not.

I was expecting a bit of a speech from Creol, a poetic farewell, but he didn't seem prepared to give one. Perhaps he lacked inspiration. Or perhaps he didn't feel up to speaking over Aiden, who was screaming threats and demanding to be let out. I stood very still, fighting the urge to charge at the walls myself. The music was prodding me to do something brave and stupid.

Creol and Lynch backed out of sight. I knew they were preparing to move the earth back over us, to seal us in. We would be buried alive. Panic fluttered around the edges of my resolve.

Karish stood behind me. "It's frightening the first time," he said in a low voice. "But it'll be all right. I promise you."

Aye, he promised. He was going to be buried in the ground with the rest of us, and he looked like he wouldn't be able to keep his footing in a stiff breeze, but he was making promises. It was a nice thought.

The trembling started again. Aiden's scrambling and screams became more desperate. Any of the other Sources who might have raised their heads during our exchanges lowered them. This was an old show to them. Karish put his hands on my shoulders. A nice tight grip. And I felt my tension easing.

The earth moved over us, sliding like a plate. My throat tightened with the need to scream, to join Aiden in his futile struggles. *Stay calm.* "How is he able to do this?"

"He is able to control the forces to the point that he can hold the earth in place and move it around," Karish explained quietly. "He's incredibly strong."

"Stronger than you?" I asked, expecting a nice hearty denial.

"I think so."

That was just damn wonderful.

Earth met earth. It was black. But I could still hear the music.

"For Zaire's sake, man!" one of the Sources snapped at Aiden, "shut up!"

"He's going to kill us!" Aiden snarled.

"Lucky bastard. We're here for the duration."

What was said next was lost to me, for Karish let out a whoop and caught me in a rib-crushing embrace. "My girl, thank you!"

I tried to free myself. He definitely smelled. "For what, not killing you?" I asked tartly.

"Dunleavy," Aiden said to me, "I need to talk to you."

"I don't want to hear it, Kelly." There was nothing he could say to justify his actions.

"Don't think you can rule in hell," Karish commented to no purpose whatsoever.

"I need to tell you what happened," said Aiden.

"I don't care." It didn't matter. He had manipulated me and lied to me and tried to force me to kill another human being. His motives were irrelevant.

"Do I have no chance for explanation?" Aiden demanded.

Damn it. "Let me take a stab at it," I said sarcastically. "You'd been listening to Ryan's sob story for ages and believed it. You thought it would be an excellent idea to destroy High Scape and didn't seem to mind leaving Piers to it—"

"I didn't think he could destroy High Scape!" he protested. "I knew he was going to try to kill Karish, though."

Oh. That was all right, then.

"Ryan told me. And all that stuff started happening in High

Scape and I knew Creol was serious, about that part of it at least. So I wrote to him—"

"And told him he should use me as his Shield in his quest for his manifest destiny, I know, I know," I interrupted him impatiently. "None of it matters, Kelly. I don't care. I simply do not care." I'd believed every single word that had slithered from his mouth. I couldn't believe I'd been so gullible, so stupid.

"It's going to be all right, Lee," Karish said, sounding like he could see what was going on in my head. I hoped not. It was a mess in there. "I can get us out of here."

Someone started laughing derisively.

"The Darling of the Triple S, charging to the rescue," was added in a most sarcastic tone.

"You all could do it if you had just paid attention," Karish snapped. "He came down here every damn day. Didn't you notice what he was doing?"

"He opened and closed the ground above us. I kind of noticed that."

I focused my wandering thoughts and asked, "Creol came down here every day?"

"He got a kick out of tossing our food at us. His honor and privilege, he said, to serve such worthy bonded Sources. And he liked to brag. He never wanted to waste an opportunity to tell us how eagerly our Shields were serving him."

"Waxed poetic about it, he did," one of the other Sources commented. "Particularly about you. Said you were most keen to serve him in any manner he cared to suggest."

I sniffed, all the response such a comment deserved. Though I didn't like how often I had been portrayed as a devoted slave to whichever Source I happened to be working with at the time. "From his visits you figured out how to do what he does?" I asked Karish, my feelings a little too chaotic to allow this amazing discovery to cause any more mental commentary than *Zaire!*

"I think so," he answered with untimely modesty. He continued in a whisper, "It seems to me that all he does is lower his shields and invite the forces in. It's a little like what I did with Miho and Val."

"Eh, now, play nice," one of the others chided. "Share with your friends." Karish ignored her.

"That's it?" It sounded too easy to me. Especially considering all the damage it could do.

"I think so."

Not a rousing response in the affirmative, but he would know more about it than I, so I supposed I had to believe him. "Have you tried it?"

"Of course not. You weren't here."

I lowered my voice even further. "You can heal without me," I reminded him.

"I wasn't going to try it, Lee. I kind of like breathing."

I wondered that Creol had risked putting me in the pit with my Source. If shaking the ground apart were so simple as Karish implied, did Creol really believe none of the Sources would try it once a Shield was among them? Or did he honestly believe he was the only one who could do it? "Do you really think this'll work?" I asked Karish.

"I think so."

Gods, Karish, you're supposed to be arrogant. You're supposed to announce your expertise with annoying confidence. "Fine. Let's give it a shot."

"Not now. We have to wait until the meeting's broken up and everyone's gone home. If Creol's right on top of us when we do this, he might feel the earth moving and come to investigate."

The music had me itching to be active. But he was right. "And then what do we do? Once we get out?"

"I don't know." I felt him shrug. "I'm making this up as I go along."

So we waited. The music didn't last much longer, and while it did I curled up in a ball on the floor and thought about how much I hated Aiden. We waited a while longer, so we could be sure everyone was gone and at home before we made our attempt to break out. The other Sources, either believing the two of us were deluding ourselves or beyond the point of caring about anything, even their own survival, seemed to go to sleep. Aiden kept his mouth shut. I was happy about that. I didn't want to hear anything he had to say. Ever.

After a long period of beautiful silence I nudged Karish. He had fallen asleep, too, and he woke with a jolt. "What's wrong?" he asked sharply.

"Nothing. It's time to get going." I rose to my feet a little unsteadily, my legs numb with cold. "We don't want to give Creol a chance to get started."

He nodded, stretched a bit, and stood up with a discomfort I could feel through his movements. I wondered if he was up for experimentation but didn't ask. It was not the time to make him doubt his confidence. "Are you ready?" he asked me.

"Aye."

"Then let's get to it." He lowered his shields and I raised mine.

At first nothing happened. We just stood there, Karish's mind wide open, and I didn't like it at all. We had no real idea what would respond to Karish's mental invitation. Perhaps there were some weird forces out there that might rush in and warp his mind. Maybe that was what had happened to Creol. Maybe this was a really bad idea.

But then it started, and it was too late to stop.

It was different, but then wasn't it always? Instead of one great gush there was a quieter sensation of movement, almost like something was squirming. Like the power was a great slug writhing into Karish's mind. It was not a pleasant sensation. But it changed under Karish's touch, disintegrating, threading out, becoming lighter and moving more freely. And what swept through my Shields was more like what I was used to feeling.

The earth above us opened, and the weak sunlight of dawn streamed in. A welcome break from the unrelieved darkness. I watched the ground slide back and wondered again how that could work.

In no time at all it was done. Karish pulled the forces back from my Shields and sent the writhing beast back to wherever it had come from. I dropped my Shields as he raised his.

And something obvious sank in. Karish could make the earth move. Literally. He could heal—why hadn't I understood the true significance of that before? Who knew what else he could do? He did, probably, and he kept it under wraps and did his best to behave as if he were an ordinary person. What I'd always said in jest suddenly struck me as truth. Karish was something else, something other. I stared at him with wonder. "Holy hell," I muttered.

He was looking at me warily. "Don't you start, Lee," he said, almost pleading. "I mean it. Really."

All right. I could keep my mouth shut. Adoration wasn't my style, anyway.

I looked at the other Sources, who had been roused by Karish's stunt. Two women, four men, all of them staring at me blankly. I didn't know how long they had been down there, but they all looked awful. I wondered what lack of light could do to a person, combined with little freedom of movement, poor food, the stress of incarceration, hopelessness of rescue, and fear of death. Even if they were all guilty of the crimes of which the Shields had accused them, I didn't think rotting in a pit was a fitting punishment.

"How do we get out?" one of the men asked sourly.

"You're not getting out yet," Karish informed him bluntly. "Lee and I'll"—here he was interrupted by protests lodged in such weak voices that he easily rode over them—"get out and fix things and then come back for you."

"You go to hell, Lord Shintaro," one of them snapped. "You think you can leave us down here?"

Karish flicked his filthy hair back from his face with impatience. "We'll come back for you," he repeated.

"Excuse me if I have some trouble believing that."

"I don't care what you believe. You can't get out without help, and we're not helping you until we're ready."

"You're in no fine shape yourself, Stallion. You going to leap out of this hole all by yourself?"

The man did have a point. Karish was a mess, though by no means in as bad a shape as the others.

"I'll toss Dunleavy up," was Aiden's unexpected contribution. "Once she's up, she can pull while I push."

I looked at him. Who asked him? Awfully presumptuous of him to assume we weren't going to bury him down there. He didn't really think I'd trust him after all he had done, did he?

Karish put a hand on my shoulder. "We need a quick way out, Lee," he reminded me. "You two are the strongest people here, and he's the tallest. And it's in his best interest to help us."

We couldn't be sure of that. Perhaps Creol was only pretending to condemn Aiden, so we would sympathize with the poor, misguided, lovelorn fool and trust him again. He would listen in on our plans and go running off to Creol when it was convenient. He'd done it before.

Of course, he couldn't run anywhere if we left him in the pit. I could pull out Karish, and we would leave Aiden and the others down there until we were ready to come back for them. At this point the only way Aiden could betray me was to drop me, and I knew how to fall.

I nodded. Aiden cupped his hands and I stepped into them, climbing onto his shoulders as he straightened to his full stance. From there it was easy enough to scramble onto the ground.

I looked back down over the edge. "Karish next," I said.

"No goddamned way," one of the women snapped. She clutched at the wall and got herself to her feet with a disturbing lack of grace and surety. "Once you two are out, you'll take off and leave us here."

Yes, that was the plan, as we'd already said. "Aye, and we'll come back with an easier means of getting out, because there's no way you'll be able to do it the way I did," I pointed out. "You can prove me wrong by preventing Karish from coming out next."

She glared at me. Karish didn't look too thrilled with my suggestion either. I tried to prevent pity from rising in my chest. The Sources really were disgustingly thin. I wondered if any of the Shields had a real idea about how close to death the Sources were. Out of self-interest alone, I would have thought the Shields would have had more concern about how healthy their Sources were kept. But then, I was no healer. Maybe they only looked really bad. But that was enough to make me wish we could get them out of there and somewhere decent for a bath and some real food.

"What about me?" Aiden asked quietly.

"You'll be no use to us, and we can't trust you," I told him. "And there's no one here who can push you up, anyway."

He seemed to accept that. I'd never thought he was stupid.

"I'm not sure I can get out your way, either, Lee," Karish said. "I don't think I can keep my balance."

"Of course you can," I said briskly. "Use the wall. I'll help you from up here. Piece of cake." Because there was no way I was going to leave him down there.

Karish studied Aiden, who returned the look with glowing hostility. "I really don't think this is going to work," my Source muttered.

Aiden snorted. "Don't worry, Your Lordship. I won't dump you on your head."

"I have some difficulty believing that," Karish retorted.

"I'm not an idiot," Aiden claimed. "I know I've bungled things. It won't help my cause if I break your neck and keep her from saving the world, will it?"

Nothing would help his cause, but I saw no need to point that out at that exact moment.

"That's a motive I can appreciate," said Karish, and he stepped into Aiden's hands.

His ascent wasn't as quick or as graceful as mine, but we got him on the ground, where he stretched out on his back to catch his breath. His face was too pale.

"You need to get some exercise, Taro," I told him, and I grinned into the force of his lethal glare. "All that lazing about you've been doing lately. You've got to change that wastrel lifestyle."

"Now, Lee, you know if I showed the slightest trace of industry you would be left with nothing to do. Could I do that to you?" He gasped as he sat up.

I helped him to his feet, hoping he didn't need it. "Are you all right?"

"Are you kidding? I'm free. I feel great."

He didn't sound as though he were being sarcastic. Good enough. "We'll be back with a ladder," I called into the pit. Or we'd be dead. Still, if we failed, Creol would go back to see how we had escaped. They would be no worse off than they had been before.

"You can't leave us here!"

"Damn it, *come back!*"

Wordlessly, Karish and I left the hole, their shouts and protests following us.

I didn't like leaving them there. It had to be awful to have escape so close at hand, but impossible to reach. To be left behind with no control over what was going to happen next. It would have driven me frantic. But we couldn't take the time to get them all out. Karish had barely made it out, and he was the healthiest of the lot. It couldn't be helped.

Karish grabbed me again, and somewhere he found the strength for another bone-crushing embrace.

"Gods, man!" I gasped. "Stop doing that!"

He loosened his hold only long enough to kiss me. "You have no idea how it feels to be out and free," he swore fervently. "I thought I'd been tossed into hell."

I didn't want to talk about it. I couldn't stand to think of him stuck down there while I was eating and drinking and laughing with his captors. I managed to disengage from him. "We've got to get going." We started off to town at a pace that was slower than I liked but probably all that Karish could manage.

I would worry about the guilt later.

Chapter Twenty-five

Karish was in a bad way. He was walking as fast as he could—running or even jogging was beyond him—and it was draining him. I didn't know what we were doing, trying to dash back to Creol with no plan of action. I didn't know how we were going to find him. I didn't know where he lived, and anyone who saw us in the street would be able to stop us. And even if we did find Creol, what were we going to do with him? Tell him not to attack High Scape? That would be effective.

Karish stopped suddenly, his hand tightening around mine. His eyes got that faraway look. I caught my breath and readied for action, but his shields didn't drop. They only wavered a little. "It's started," he said.

"What? What's happening?"

"The attack on High Scape."

What, didn't Creol sleep?

Karish's tone was absentminded, most of his attention directed inward. "He's opened his mind. He's allowed in all the forces he can accommodate, many more than he uses to move the earth over the pit." A little line appeared between his eyebrows as he frowned in concentration. "He's directing the forces to High Scape. He's been there. I don't think he can attack a place he's never been. He needs to know exactly where it is in relation to him."

"What are you doing?" I asked him curiously.

One shoulder rose in a slight half shrug. "Following him."

"How can you do that?"

"I don't know."

All right. So now what?

"They're fighting him in High Scape," Karish told me. "They seem to be holding him off."

"So everything's fine?" Problem solved. We didn't have to face Creol at all. Just get ourselves to another city and tell them what was going on in Middle Reach and let the army deal with the whole mess.

But Karish's next words destroyed that little fantasy. "It's easier to attack than defend, I think. And Creol is incredibly strong. I think he'll wear them down."

"They stopped him before."

"We were there before."

"Aye, but we really can't make that much of a difference."

"Creol seemed to think so. That was why he tried to have me killed."

"Well, aye, but—" It seemed so arrogant to say we, just the two of us, were all that stood between High Scape and Creol.

"I'm going to see if I can stop him from here."

I didn't ask him how he was going to do that, or if he really could. He probably didn't know. I felt his internal protections lower.

And again, it was different. I was beginning to suspect I wouldn't recognize a normal channeling if I ever experienced one again. There were no forces moving through Karish. They were flowing around him, and I warded those off, but he wasn't channeling anything. It was more like he had become a window or a door through which I could sense more distant forces, like I was watching them. Beyond that, I could feel Creol's manipulative power. And beyond that, incredibly enough, I could feel the shields Lynch had erected to protect Creol.

A terrible idea blinked into my brain. I buried it. *No way.*

For a long time, I waited. I didn't know what Karish was doing. I could feel him "moving" every once in a while, and I accommodated him every time, but I could sense nothing of him beyond that. Usually I was one step away from the real action. This time I was three or four steps away. It was frustrating.

And I waited.

I watched Karish, and I didn't like what I saw. He was too, too pale, and sweat was running down his face. He was trembling. He was still holding my hand. I hadn't realized.

It was taking too long.

As if in answer to my thoughts, Karish's shields snapped almost painfully into place.

"Why'd you stop?"

He hesitated a moment, obviously reluctant to answer. "It's no good," he admitted. "I can't stop him or bring him back. I can only follow him and try to leech the power from him, and it's not enough to make a real difference. I'm not contributing much, and I'm wearing myself out."

"So now what?"

"I don't know," he said grimly. "I thought this would work. I was counting on it working. I don't know what else to do."

Damn.

The bad idea flashed back.

Gods, no. No way. I couldn't do it. It was monstrous. I was appalled that my mind had even imagined it. I really, really couldn't do it.

Creol could do what he'd claimed he could. He could cause disasters. If he destroyed High Scape, tens of thousands of people would die. And the Empress couldn't have him killed before he wiped out any number of cities, if she managed it at all. He could conceivably achieve his ambition, which seemed to be merely to do as much damage as possible before he himself was killed.

Karish and I were in no shape for a physical confrontation. We didn't have time to win any of Creol's people over, if that was even possible. There was no other option.

I really couldn't do it.

I didn't have time to dither. My peace of mind wasn't worth anyone's life.

I looked at Karish apprehensively. I was afraid, really afraid, that he would be disgusted with me when I told him what I was thinking.

He was watching me. "What?" he asked.

Deep breath. "When you were channeling," I said hesitantly, not sure how to introduce my suggestion. "I could feel Creol. And I've Shielded him before."

"I know. He bragged about it."

"Lynch is Shielding Creol now."

"All right," he said, no doubt wondering what that had to do with anything.

"But, of course, she's left a break in her Shields." To allow the forces flowing into Creol to flow out again. A very important part of Shielding, or the Source would explode like an overblown balloon.

Karish was a bright boy. His brain could move at least as quickly as mine. The uncertainty left his eyes, replaced by somber comprehension. "Of course," he said, and his hand tightened again.

Another deep breath. "I will cap the break."

He was not shocked. He had already figured it out. And he wasn't disgusted with me. He didn't think I was a monster. Relief flooded through me.

"You'll be Shielding two of us," he said. "Can you do that?"

"Yes," I answered. It wasn't bravado, not entirely. I was good. "I won't risk you. If I can't stretch to Creol, we'll try something else."

"I'm not worried about you dropping your Shields on me," he said. He rubbed the back of my hand with his other palm, treating my hand like some detached toy. "I've never killed a man before," he murmured.

"And you still won't have when this is all over," I pointed out. I would be the one who killed, perverting my skills to do something no one had ever anticipated. I would be the one who acted, while Karish would be the one to assist, an unnatural reversal of roles I had never wanted.

Enough stalling. I squared my shoulders. "Are you ready?" I asked him.

"Aye."

If Karish suffered any compunction about killing a fellow Source, he was hiding it well. I was relieved. If he had attacked my idea, or attacked me for having it, I wouldn't have known how to defend myself. And I would have had to, to force him to assist me. I couldn't do it alone. I was sure it was necessary, but I knew it was vicious and sinful. I hated having to do it.

And then Karish's internal shields dropped. That was it. I had his tacit permission to begin. To use him as a tool for taking another person's life.

Oh my gods, oh my gods. I was going to do this. I was going to do this, and it wasn't a nightmare.

Karish was like a tunnel, a link between me and Creol and Lynch. The river of forces was there again, just beyond my reach. I longed to dive right into it, to feel its power directly. But that was impossible for me, and I had something to do.

Keeping most of my attention on Karish, I followed the link to Creol and encountered Lynch's Shield. I crawled over the Shield and found the break. Then, very, very carefully— *Don't let go of Karish*—I capped the break.

I felt rather than heard the cry from Lynch. After a short moment of trying to fight me off, she dropped her Shields. The world tilted as I forced my Shields—*Don't let go of Karish*— all the way around Creol, with no break.

I had never done anything like it before. The forces pushed at my Shields, threatening to push them apart. I clamped down on my teeth as I clamped down on my Shields.

Don't let go of Karish.

Someone was screaming. I couldn't tell if it was Creol or Lynch or Karish or even me. Something seemed to be whipping around me, trying to carry me off or even kill me.

My feet were on the ground. Karish's hand was in mine. *Don't let go of Karish.*

How long was this supposed to take?

The forces were building within my Shields. They poured into Creol. I could feel him trying to disengage, trying to reestablish his own inner shields. He could not. Pressure was rising, blood was exploding through Creol's veins, lightning was dancing across his brain. And someone was screaming.

Pressure within, pressure without. Trying to crush my fragile shields. Trying to crush my Source. *Don't let go of Karish.*

The control was slipping. Not mine, my Shields were still strong. But the blood was rushing too fast, veins splitting under the strain. The heartbeat was beyond erratic, pumping almost at random in a desperate attempt to accommodate the gushing blood. The lungs expanded too far and shrank too quickly, out of rhythm with each other. The brain tore itself apart.

And then, Creol was gone. An image of flying flesh and blood was seared across the back of my eyes. I didn't actually see it, but I could feel it, in a way, a horrible sort of release that brought bile to my throat. My free hand whipped up to fend off splattering blood that wasn't there.

It all collapsed at once. I couldn't feel Creol, or Lynch. Karish's shields snapped me out almost rudely.

At least I managed to step away from him before I started throwing up.

When I was done, my stomach was twisted in agony, I was trembling uncontrollably, and tears clouded my eyes. It was very hard to breathe. I couldn't seem to think. I wiped my mouth.

Karish took my arm and pulled me a few paces away. Then he stepped close so my cheek rested against his shoulder. I closed my eyes and breathed, trying to banish the gruesome images spinning through my mind. I wished I could cry. Karish stroked my hair and kissed the top of my head. For some reason that just made everything worse.

Then he drew back. "Come," he said gently. "There's more to do." And we headed back to town.

At least the screaming had stopped.

Chapter Twenty-six

Karish was, as expected, the life of the party. Dressed in winter white trimmed in hunter green, his black hair tied back with a green ribbon and a green stone glinting in one ear, he was beautiful. As always. He smiled and laughed, never too loudly, and charmed everyone in the court. He was surrounded with people, and even those who refused to wait attendance on him couldn't help but be aware of his presence. I could see them shooting little glances at him.

So this, I thought, was what I had been missing, what Ogawa had told me about. At one point I'd thought I'd never get a chance to see it. I sipped at my wine and smiled.

After escaping from Creol's pit, we had learned the man had literally exploded in front of Lynch's very eyes. So she was a screaming wreck. Better her than me. I felt bad enough causing it, I didn't think I should have to see it as well. The threatening mob who'd relayed this information had been subdued by Karish's claim that he could do exactly what Creol had been able to do, the threat to bury the whole town if they put a single toe out of line, and a demonstration to prove he could do it.

Two days later, we'd left Middle Reach. Karish hadn't

been in shape for it, but we'd been afraid to stay any longer. Just before we'd left he'd caused a serious earthquake, serious enough to cause cracking in some walls, though no one was hurt. It was unnatural to be Shielding Karish while he called a disaster instead of channeled it, but he felt that was the best way to remind the residents of Middle Reach that they shouldn't do anything stupid. I agreed, but I didn't like it. It was wrong, a perversion of our skills.

We'd ridden as fast as we could to the closest village. From there we had sent a message to Shidonee's Gap. We had gone to the next village and sent another message, in case the first village was somehow caught up in Middle Reach's madness and our letter never even passed the gate. And we had sent a third from High Scape, just in case the others went astray.

Karish had insisted on writing the messages himself. At first I had thought it was just more of his insistence on not being useless, and I had objected to being prevented from doing my job. But I learned that when Karish insisted on something forcefully enough, I had a tendency to back down. Something I had to watch. And I let him write the letters. After reading them I understood the real reason he'd wanted to write them.

Very spare on details, they were. They said Karish had been held under the ground. Creol had been able to open and seal the earth. No mention that Karish could do it, too. Creol had died in the attempt to destroy High Scape, an accident, not murder. And the threats Karish had used to subdue the residents of Middle Reach into obedience had been empty, inspired by Creol's behavior. Very little mention of me at all.

Interesting.

The other Pairs of High Scape had been thrilled to see Karish back. They were full of questions and demands for the whole story. Not knowing how the Triple S would want to handle things, we both refused to tell anyone anything. No one liked that, but there was a grim air about Karish that they—and I—had never seen before. When he refused to elaborate on events, and I proved no more willing to talk, they let things drop. I was relieved. I wouldn't have been able to come up with a likely story to cover the bizarre events we'd experienced, and for some reason the truth felt dangerous.

We had waited anxiously for news from High Scape. We

were worried about the Sources in Middle Reach. The effect
of Karish's threats would last only so long. After a while the
residents of that backwater hell would regain their courage
and toss the Sources back into the pit. They didn't even need
to seal it back up to keep the Sources down there. The poor
creatures were so weak that they would be unable to scramble
out on their own.

Losing patience, we had almost come to the point of wondering if we could get away with taking ourselves off the roster yet again and riding to Shidonee's Gap and knocking some
heads together. Then we'd gotten a few knocks of our own. On
our doors, not our heads, but just as stunning. Senior members
of the Triple S council, sent to inquire into our activities in
Middle Reach.

From them, we learned all the Pairs in Middle Reach were
dead. Murdered, by the looks of it. The Empress, at the request of the Triple S, had sent members of her Imperial Guard
to investigate, and that was what they had found. All the Pairs
dead and the unapologetic residents full of stories of the exhi-
bitions Karish had put on.

Karish had looked sick upon hearing the news. His threats
hadn't worked, and we had left the Pairs alone. I couldn't believe the residents of Middle Reach had been stupid enough to
do something like that. They'd wiped out their protection
against natural disasters. And if they didn't think the Empress
was going to stomp on them with everything she had for wan-
tonly killing so many Pairs, even Pairs who were the dregs of
the Triple S, they were all nuts.

Well, I'd known that.

There was no word of Aiden at all.

We were questioned. Karish especially. For hours and days
I watched as he was grilled on the veracity of the letters he
had sent, and he never slipped or cracked. He kept his answers
short and simple, and easy to remember, and he was calm and
convincing as he delivered them. They had demanded to know
why I, as Shield, hadn't written them, as that was my duty, and
Karish had assumed an expression of mild astonishment. It
had all happened to him, after all, so of course he was the one
to write about it.

And what about the claims of the citizens, that Karish had

proved his ability to cause earthquakes with demonstrations? The answer was a languid shrug. Of course such a thing was impossible, he said. He had told the lie because apparently the residents of Middle Reach were ready to believe such things. That they thought he had really caused an earthquake, well, he couldn't explain that. Perhaps there was some kind of massive delusion involved. Creol had been skillful with his manipulation.

So that was the plan, I'd thought. Deny everything. In the beginning I had thought that was a bad idea. Lying was rarely wise. I learned better, for even with that innocuous story they had questioned us for weeks. Weeks. Testing us. Watching us. All with that air that said they expected us to lie to them, that we were on opposite sides. I was shocked.

This, then, was why Karish had always been so afraid of anyone finding out what he could do.

And then, with no explanation, they left. No final word as to whether that was the end of things, whether they found our explanations acceptable. They were just gone. And I couldn't help feeling that no, this was not the end of things. It would come back on us.

This was the Triple S council. Our people. They had raised us, taken care of us. They were supposed to guide us and watch out for our best interests. Why had we had to lie to them?

The day after they left, we received a summons from the Empress Herself. She had, apparently, had word of our brave and noble efforts in both High Scape and Middle Reach, and she was desirous of a meeting. There was nothing for it but to pack up again and head to Erstwhile, the Imperial City.

I thought that under the circumstances I could be forgiven for being frustrated, even though I was a Shield. I had counted the number of days I had actually been able to work as a Shield in High Scape, and it was a pitiful amount. But this was the Empress. When she called, you went.

So there we were. We had been in Erstwhile for nearly a week, and the Empress was throwing a party in Karish's honor. For exposing an evil plot in Middle Reach, enabling imperial forces to swamp in and kill Creol and save the world. That was the story being released to the public, anyway. I was happy enough to leave that version of the facts floating around. Karish said he thought it was best.

So we were in the ballroom of Zaire Manor in Erstwhile, surrounded by courtiers and ministers and other important people who were there only to tell Karish how wonderful he was.

While I liked a good party as much as the next person, formal affairs bored me blue. The dress I was wearing had been thrown together by the palace staff, and although I liked the color, hunter green, the style was far too—er, revealing?—for my taste. And as I'd underestimated how long it would take to squeeze into the gown, tie my hair just so, and paint my face, I'd been late.

That had allowed me to slip in unobserved. I watched Karish's impact on the denizens of Erstwhile. I grinned and shook my head. I didn't know how he stood the attention, never mind actually enjoyed it, as he seemed to. I eased my way to the side of the room, where there were hors d'oeuvres to be found. I had my priorities straight.

There was music, nice gentle music that didn't stir the blood. And it was interesting to watch the other guests, watch them play their little games, admire their clothes. And it would be a treat to see the Empress. But it really wasn't the crowd for a humble slip collector, and I knew they would look at me as a lower form of human if they knew what I was, so I didn't try to mingle.

One man who wasn't as entranced with Karish as the others noticed me and left the throng. I looked him over as he approached. A little too close to middle age and trying a little too hard to hide it, but he had a decent smile and his eyes didn't linger anywhere offensive. Not for too long, anyway.

"So," he said as soon as he reached me. "You're the Shield."

My, how polite. "So I am."

"You're his Shield?" he asked, gesturing toward Karish.

I looked at him steadily, face blank. "He's my Source."

I don't think he got the point. "I'm Lord Summit," he announced grandly. "I have a property on the southern coast. A huge, beautiful house, magnificent land, every convenience. I'm having a house party there in a couple of weeks. I'd be honored if you and Lord Shintaro would attend."

And would his real guests throw coins at our feet if we performed well?

I'd been mistaken. Lord Whatever was just as enamored as the rest of them. He was just going about achieving his aim differently. "I'm afraid I can't answer for Karish." And I wasn't interested.

"No? Thought you were the one to talk to. Thought the Shields made all the plans and appointments."

"Not concerning private matters. Karish's personal life isn't in my jurisdiction."

The lord winked at me. "Bet you wish it were," he snickered before sauntering back to the crowd.

I looked at the plate of food in my hand and set it on the closest table. Fresh air. I really needed fresh air. I marched the perimeter of the room until I reached the doors of the terrace. I slipped outside. It was a little chilly to be out without a cloak, even for me, but I was used to the colder winter of more northern climes, and I was too lazy, or something, to go back in for warmer wear.

I took a deep breath. It was stupid to be irritated by that lord's words. He was an ignorant mushroom, and I should have been able to laugh off his clumsy invitation and lurid suggestion. But I couldn't. It had been too long since I had worked. For months I had been nothing but Karish's adjutant, and I was sick of it. I was a person with skills of my own. I half wished for a disaster to strike just so I could prove I was more than a decoration.

Try not to be more of a fool than you can help, dear.

I found a small bench that was hidden from the door by the curve of the wall. I settled onto the cold stone. I would just think a bit and calm down before I went back in. I was overreacting, I knew. I had a tendency to do that.

But I didn't get my chance for quiet solitude. All of a sudden Karish was there, standing beside the bench and glaring at me. "What the hell are you doing?" he demanded.

Nothing criminal, I thought. "Excuse me?"

He was looking harried; all the sparkle evaporated. "You didn't even bother to show up on time," he complained. "You left me to deal with that," he gestured toward the door, "all by myself, for over an hour. You didn't even let me know you'd come when you finally did arrive. I was just lucky enough to look up when you were slithering out the door."

I turned it over in my head, looking for a problem in any of that. Nothing I could find. "So?"

He threw up his hands, and I thought he was going to tear at his hair. Sometimes he could be wonderfully excitable. "Why should I have to handle that horde by myself?"

It took me a moment to come up with an answer, I was that surprised. Was he honestly trying to convince me that he hadn't been enjoying himself in there? "It's your job," I said. "It's what you do. You've always done it. You're Karish, and everyone adores you." *Poor boy.*

"Doesn't mean I like it." I looked at him, and I was sure the skepticism beamed from my face. "I'm serious," he insisted. "Only an idiot would feel flattered by that sort of thing. They're fawning all over me and praising me to the sky, all the time thinking that I'm nothing more than a useless, empty-headed peacock who's somehow managed to capture the Empress's favor. And if I don't act like I'm absolutely delighted to speak to every single one of them, they'll sneer at me for being too proud." He sat down on the bench, pulled off the ribbon in his hair and made a fine mess of his mane. I wondered why he ever bothered tying it up in the first place. "They don't know me, and they don't care to. I'm just a novelty, and they'd drop me in a moment if something new came along."

I thought Karish was underestimating both himself and his fans. While some were probably ponces, I was sure others were able to appreciate Karish for the unique person he was.

And if he tried to tell me he didn't like having beautiful young people laying themselves at his feet, I'd call him a liar.

"Do you think I like dealing with all the impertinent, embarrassing, personal questions they think they have the right to ask?" He ran his hand through his hair again. Careful, love. Don't pull it out. "One woman actually had the nerve to ask me if my—" He stopped. And he blushed.

I couldn't help grinning. "If your what?" I demanded.

"Never mind," he snapped irritably. "You're coming back in with me, and you're going to do your fair share of performing."

"No one's that interested in me, Taro," I said. "You are

what you are, and everyone adores you. I'd think you'd be used to it by now."

"We're going to make them interested in you," he said. "We're going to tell them I couldn't have done anything that I did without a superior Shield. And that if you hadn't come to Middle Reach to find me, I'd still be holed up in that pit. Or dead."

"That doesn't jibe with the story we told everyone." And besides, it was Aiden who had convinced me to go to Middle Reach, the lying traitor. I hadn't thought of it on my own.

"So we'll think of something else."

"It's unnecessary. I don't care if they don't know I exist. And it's not my fault that they all love you. It's yours for smiling so much and being so famous." Oh, he didn't like that at all. "If they're bothering you in there, you can claim some kind of artistic fatigue and withdraw. You're out here now, aren't you?"

"But I'm expected to go back in. And you're coming back in with me," he declared, clutching my arm and pulling me to my feet. "And you will smile, and you will be charming, and you will behave as though you're perfectly delighted to be here."

I scowled at him but let him pull me along. "Don't tell me how to behave, Karish," I warned him.

"Did I tell you you're looking beautiful tonight?"

I rolled my eyes.

"Smile, Lee." And then we were back inside, and it seemed to me that the occupants of the room rushed back to Karish in one big wave. It was intimidating. Karish slid his hand down to mine and held on tight. So I couldn't leave, damn it.

My trial in the torchlight was fortunately shortened by the opening of a grand double entrance. A pompous-looking elderly woman walked into the room. "Her Imperial Majesty," rang out of her mouth, "the Empress Constia." She stepped to one side.

The woman who then sailed in, the ultimate ruler of us all, looked in no way extraordinary. I knew her to be in her sixties, but she looked older. Of average height, a little plump, and rather plain, there was nothing about her that I would think indicative of royal blood. Her attire was common, her graying brown hair tied up into a braid, her gown of simple cut and somber blue, with not a touch of jewelry anywhere. Her ladies-in-waiting were far more elegantly dressed than she. I would have never taken her for the Empress, but everyone else was offering her their obeisance.

As you should be doing, dear. So down you go, hold, then rise. There, that wasn't so hard, was it?

She walked up the center of the ballroom. She didn't glide, she didn't float, she simply walked, with the court dividing before her and keeping their heads down. Her journey was long and slow, and I didn't know where to look. If it were anyone else I would have watched them, looked them in the eye, but that kind of behavior might have seemed too bold before an Empress.

At one end of the room there was a dais with a thronelike chair and three lesser chairs. The royal train made its way to it, and the Empress was settled into the largest chair. The ladies-in-waiting sat in the smaller chairs. The Empress's husband, Prince Albert, didn't appear to be attending. I'd heard he was a useless fellow.

The Empress, wearing a slight smile, looked over the crowd. "Good evening, everyone," she said. Her voice was a light alto.

"Good evening, Your Majesty," we all echoed back.

"I hope everyone is enjoying themselves."

There were various comments made in the affirmative.

Her gaze settled on Karish and me. Well, on Karish. I tried to slip away. Karish, who hadn't released my hand through all this, tightened his grip until bones were threatened. "Let go!" I hissed through my fixed smile.

"Stand still!" he hissed back.

"Lord Shintaro," one of the ladies-in-waiting called. "Shield Mallorough. Please approach the Empress."

I had to step lively or it would look like Karish was dragging me by the hand like a child. We crossed the room with everyone watching us. Once we stood before the dais, we bowed again.

"Good evening," said the Empress. "It's a pleasure to meet you both." We murmured polite responses.

She settled back in her chair in a relaxed manner I wouldn't have thought appropriate for royalty. She linked her hands over her stomach. She looked at Karish, and her expression wasn't entirely friendly. "I have been advised that we have reason to be grateful to you," she said. Then she waited for a response.

Karish didn't have one, not immediately, because what was the smart thing to say to that? I prayed nothing incomprehensible came out of his mouth. The Empress didn't appear to be in a forgiving mood.

But I should have had more faith. "If I have been in any small way of service to Your Majesty," said Karish, "it can only be an honor and a privilege."

A little oily, but better than anything I could have come up with.

"Before this night, I wouldn't have accused you of modesty," said the Empress. "But I have been told that, of your activities in Middle Reach, you have been very modest indeed."

That didn't sound good. So, obviously, the Triple S still didn't believe our story, and they'd shared that opinion with the Empress. Why were we there?

"Middle Reach was the work of many individuals, Your Majesty," said Karish. He should get a prize, I thought, for the best giving of an answer that conveyed no information whatsoever.

"Quite," said Her Majesty.

She looked ready to smile. If I didn't know better, I would have thought Karish's evasiveness had begun to amuse her.

"So what boon would you ask of the Crown?" she asked.

That had come out of nowhere.

Karish seemed equally surprised. "Your Majesty?"

The Empress held out a hand to one of her ladies-in-waiting. A goblet was filled with wine and placed in her fingers. "A good ruler knows when to reward her subjects," she drawled, *r*'s a-rollin'. "And when to punish them." She took a long sip from her goblet, her eyes never leaving Karish. "This time, I choose to give a reward."

But watch yourself, because next time I might choose to cut your heart out with a spoon.

Karish looked to me, frowning, then looked back at the

Empress. "Forgive me, Your Majesty, but we never anticipated such generosity. We haven't discussed anything like this."

We didn't need to discuss anything. It was his boon. And he'd better hop to it and ask for what he wanted before the Empress changed her whim and decided to have him decapitated instead.

She was looking a little irritated. "You are the Source who saved Middle Reach and High Scape, are you not?"

Karish didn't know how to answer that, I could tell. To deny it wasn't to be done, insinuating as it would that the Empress was mistaken in her opinions. To agree would be to accept all responsibility and credit for what had happened, and I knew Karish wasn't comfortable with that. "I was there, Your Majesty."

A miserable compromise.

Nope, didn't want to be Karish. Ever.

"Ask your boon," she barked.

He looked at me again. He seemed rattled. Perhaps he couldn't think of anything he wanted, which would be an unfortunate embarrassment. And a real predicament. What could Lord Shintaro lack that any human being, even the Empress, could provide? I put my free hand on his bicep and squeezed, willing him to calm down and think.

He looked down at me for a moment longer, and he did seem to calm down. His shoulders lowered a little. He nodded, though I didn't know to what, and he looked back at the Empress. "Your Majesty may be aware that my brother, the Duke of Westsea, died about half a year ago."

I watched his face, hopefully keeping mine blank.

"I am," said the Empress.

"He died without children, without completing his marriage promise. That would have the title fall to me."

"It would," said Her Majesty.

"I don't want the title," he announced, and the audible signs of shock rippled through the ballroom.

I was no less shocked. He was going to do it. He was really going to do it. I couldn't believe it.

"So abjure the title," she suggested lightly, taking another sip from her goblet.

"Aye, Your Majesty, I will. But, you see, I find myself curiously reluctant to give up my family name." He smiled wryly. "If for no other reason than it would leave my Shield nothing to call me."

Prat.

"I'm sure you are aware, Lord Shintaro, why we require the severance from the family in such circumstances."

"Fully, Your Majesty. But I will never change my mind. I have never wanted the title, and never thought it possible that it would fall my way. When I received the news that he had died, realizing that I would have to assume the title brought me no pleasure at all. I am a Source, Your Majesty. That is what I was born for. I decided to refuse it soon after I received the news, only circumstances prevented me from doing it immediately. And I will decline it, as soon as possible. Whether this boon is granted or not."

I could breathe, that last nagging concern finally eased. Certainly, Karish had claimed over and over again that he wouldn't accept the title, but of course I couldn't believe him. What sane person would turn that sort of thing down?

Now I would have to feel grateful for his decision for the rest of my life. Ah, well. Nothing was perfect.

"You will not have to give up your name, Shintaro Karish," Her Imperial Majesty said. "I offered you a boon. You have named it, and I will grant it. But remember, Source Karish, there are a roomful of witnesses to your request. There will be no changing your mind. Keep in mind the repercussions should you choose to pursue the title at a later date."

Karish smiled, that unreserved, genuine smile that seemed to stun and capture anyone caught in its glare. "My most profound gratitude, Your Majesty."

I looked at the Empress. Oh, yes, she was indeed caught. "Come then," she said in a loud voice. "We have people. We have music. Let us dance." And she claimed Karish for her first partner.

Now I was in the mood for a party. The relief was crippling in its intensity.

Court dancing wasn't nearly as exciting as bench dancing, but it had its pleasures. Karish was an excellent dancer, of course. The other men ranged from very good to almost painfully bad. As the partner of the guest of honor, I never sat out a dance, and it felt wonderful to be doing something physical after so many months of inactivity.

After dancing was dinner, and the artistic array of food on the long table was beautiful enough to bring tears to my eyes. Soups, breads, cheeses, meats, fish, and vegetables, sauced when necessary and piled in mountains of plenty. All was accompanied by the appropriate wines, including a lightly sweet white from the south which I intended to abuse my Shield privileges to get a lot of. Dessert was a sinful display of cakes, pastries, puddings, and sugared fruits. Perhaps giving up access to the aristocratic world hadn't been the smartest thing Karish had ever done.

Karish and I had been seated at opposite ends of the table, so I hadn't realized he had left until the Empress rose to go. I knew no one was supposed to leave before she did, but I assumed Karish had charmed her. I was a tad miffed that, after that little lecture he'd treated me to, he'd decided to sneak out on me. I supposed he'd been blindsided by some gorgeous young thing.

Once the Empress left, the others began wrapping up their evening as well, as the two most interesting people of the party were gone. Once the crowd was considerably thinner, I snagged a bottle of that southern white and a goblet and headed back to the terrace. I hadn't had a chance to really appreciate it before. With the wine to keep me warm, I could contemplate the stars for a little while.

But again I was to be denied my solitude. Karish was there, sitting on the bench we had used earlier, and he was alone. He looked rather somber. I approached diffidently, and when he glanced up at me there was no telling if my presence was a pleasant surprise or an intrusion. "Are you all right?" I asked.

His spine assumed ramrod position. "Aye, certainly."

"You're shivering."

"You're not," he said with disgust.

I grinned. "Of course not. I'm me." And I hadn't been out very long. "Do you want me to go?" He shook his head. "Are you sure? I don't mind leaving you alone if you want." He shifted over to make room for me, so I sat down beside him and poured the wine into the goblet.

Immediately he took the goblet and drank. Then he made a face. "Too sweet."

"If I'd known you were out here I would have brought some of the full-bodied red."

He gave me back the goblet and pulled me to him, draping an arm around my shoulders. I leaned my head on his shoulder, and I could feel him shivering. I wondered why he was sitting out there all alone in the cold. I hoped he wasn't regretting giving up his title already.

So I would distract him. "I read your letters when you went missing, you know," I admitted.

"So you said. It's how you figured out to go to Middle Reach."

No, it was what made me susceptible to Kelly's suggestion that I go to Middle Reach, the prat. "Some of them were from a Professor Saint-Gerard."

That got his attention. I could feel his muscles stiffen up. "Were they?"

"He seemed to feel you created your reputation on purpose."

Karish relaxed. I supposed he had thought I was going to make some accusation about the other matter, about his asking for advice on how to deal with an unruly Shield. I saw no reason to do that. "Did he?"

"Would he perhaps be telling the truth?"

"Of course not," he answered too quickly.

"Really?"

"No one would go out of their way to create a reputation for being a wastrel."

"Only people who are jealous of you call you a wastrel," I assured him.

"And people who disapprove of me." He squeezed me. "It's exaggerated."

"Really?"

"Stop saying that. I couldn't breathe with as many people as they claim I've slept with. And when would I get the chance? I was always supervised."

"Hm."

"It was His Grace's fault. Apparently he slept with anything breathing. Everyone just assumed I'd be exactly like him. And once people start thinking that way, there's no point in denying it. No one'll believe you."

"So you did absolutely nothing to deserve any part of your reputation?" I asked skeptically.

I felt him draw in a breath to answer, only he didn't for several beats. Then he said, "Well . . ."

I laughed.

"Of course, it does drive Her Grace to distraction. So I've been told."

That was a motive I could appreciate.

I drank my wine. I looked at the stars, wondering which one we'd all come from. It was very odd to think that out there, there were other people, living whatever strange lives they lived, with no idea that we existed.

"I like you, Shintaro Karish," I admitted. I prided myself on being honest. Sometimes that meant saying what was pleasant, too.

"Of course you do," he answered. "How could you not?"

I smiled.

Karish was the Source that I had.

It was a good thing.

Continue reading for a special preview of
Moira J. Moore's next novel

The Hero Strikes Back

Available September 2006 from Ace Books

It had been snowing for three days. Big fat flakes that stayed on the ground, and accumulated, and built up, and soaked through boots and caused collisions in the streets and killed crops and generally infuriated everyone. Except the kids, who were having a grand time building snow forts and engaging in snowball fights. But it was winter, in the middle of summer. It was weird and frightening and really, really irritating.

I tapped my boot against the doorframe, dislodging the snow that had been caked to the sole. On the second day, when I realized that the snow was going to be around for a while, I had dug out my winter wardrobe, which only gave my mother fresh fodder for eye-rolling and pained expressions. My choice of winter clothing caused her some distress. She claimed it was possible to have clothes that were both practical and stylish. I had begged to differ. It seemed to me one always had to be sacrificed to the other, and I preferred to ditch the style and keep the comfort. Besides, there was a rush on materials that merchants had packed away or left to dwindle for the summer season. The tailors were in a panic and their services were scarce. As a Shield I could be put on the top of any list, my orders given priority over any, even the

High Landed, but I'd never felt right about pulling rank like that. Especially when I already had clothes I was perfectly happy with, my mother be damned.

"You're back quick," the bedamned woman called out as I pulled off my boots.

"The stalls weren't out." I'd been sent out by my mother to hunt down bay leaves. Being sent out on errands for my mother was a new experience for me. One I couldn't say I cared for.

"Oh well. I guess I can do without it."

I hung up my cloak on a peg by the door and wandered into the kitchen. "That smells really good."

My mother shrugged. "It's only stew," she said, stirring the pot. "Nothing special. I should teach you how to cook."

I pulled out some cutlery. "Ben usually cooks for us."

"Ben's not here, though, is he?"

There was something censorious about her tone that irked me. "No, Mother, he isn't."

"You shouldn't have to rely on others to cook for you."

I'd often thought so myself. Why did having her say the exact same thing irritate me so much?

We heard the entrance door open and close. A loud thud on the floor, followed by some lighter ones, as of someone stamping their feet.

"Ah, good, one of the others are here," Mother commented. "I've made enough for everyone. I can't believe, with six and a half Pairs living here, how empty this place always is."

I hated being called half a Pair.

I quietly stepped out of the kitchen, into the corridor to the foyer. I wanted to see who it was before calling out an invitation to join us. If it were LaMonte or, far worse, Wilberforce, I'd back into the kitchen unnoticed.

There was no chance of that once I saw who was standing at the door, reading a letter. He was shorter and slighter than most men, with golden brown skin and his black hair growing long in lazy curves, and he was most definitely a sight for sore eyes. I smiled. "Taro!"

Lord (former) Shintaro Karish looked up from his letter, the frown between his eyebrows melting away. "Evening, my love!" he said before grabbing me up in a bear hug and lifting me clear off my feet. I rolled my eyes and hugged him back and didn't dwell on the fact that I probably would have felt hurt had he done anything less.

It felt good to hold him. I'd missed him.

"You're back earlier than you'd said," I commented once he'd put me back on my feet. I brushed snow off his shoulder, the one with the black Source braid.

He grinned, the completely carefree grin, the one that made his black eyes crinkle at the corners. "Her Royal Imperial Majesty got bored with me, didn't she?" he announced gaily. "With what she most enjoyed contented least."

I was taking a good look at him, and I was shocked. Karish was a fine-boned, slender man. Right then he looked gaunt, his cheekbones jutting out harshly through his skin. He seemed a little pale, and he was obviously exhausted. "What the hell have you been doing to yourself?" I demanded. "You look awful."

He cocked an eyebrow. "Thank you so much, darling. You always know just what to say to make me feel good about myself."

"Were you reveling every night or what?"

"So I must have been."

"Zaire, Taro. You're not ill, are you?"

He was starting to look annoyed. "I've just gotten off the road, Lee. I pushed myself hard to get here. Give over."

All right. Fine. The solution was not to nag but to get him back into decent shape. "Of course. You're just in time for supper."

His eyes widened in panic he manfully attempted to hide. "Uh—"

I could practically see the wheels turning in his head as he desperately searched for a graceful way to back out. I thought about letting him hang in torment but decided to take pity on him. I hadn't seen him in months, after all. There would be plenty of opportunities to torture him later. "My mother's cooking, you snob."

"Oi, your mother! I forgot she was here. I'm sorry." He looked up the stairs and bent to pick up his bags, with the obvious intention of heading up to his suite.

I grabbed his arm. "Don't be ridiculous. She'll be thrilled to see you again. It's probably the real reason she came." She'd been disappointed, when she'd first arrived in High Scape, to learn he was still in Erstwhile. "Your cloak, sir. Mother!" He winced at the shout. "Taro's joining us for dinner."

"Good!" she shouted back. "There's plenty."

I raised my eyebrows at him. See? I took his cloak and hung it on a peg, then led him into the kitchen. "I don't know if you remember meeting my mother—"

"Holder Mallorough," he interrupted me smoothly. He just as smoothly took her hand and kissed the back of it. "My memory is indeed faulty. I'd forgotten you were so lovely."

"No flirting with my mother, Karish," I growled at him.

"Mind your own business, dear," my mother chided me in a preoccupied tone, her eyes never leaving Karish's face.

He laughed.

I went back to the cutlery drawer. Perhaps reintroducing my mother and my Source wasn't the best idea after all. They were both impossible.

**From the *New York Times*
bestselling author of the
Phule's Company series**

ROBERT ASPRIN

**Follow apprentice magician Skeeve, his scaly
mentor Aahz, and beautiful ex-assassin Tanda in
their high *myth*-adventures.**

Myth Directions	0-441-55529-2
MYTH-ion Improbable	0-441-00962-X
Something M.Y.T.H. Inc.	0-441-01083-0
MYTH Alliances	0-441-01182-9
Myth-Taken Identity	0-441-01311-0
Another Fine Myth	0-441-01346-5

Check out these 2-in-1 Omnibuses

Another Fine Myth/Myth Conceptions 2-in-1
0-441-00931-X

Myth Directions/Hit or Myth 2-in-1   0-441-00943-3

Myth-ing Persons/Little Myth Marker 2-in-1
0-441-00953-0

M.Y.T.H. Inc. Link/Myth-Nomers and Impervections 2-in-1
0-441-00969-7

M.Y.T.H. Inc. in Action/ Sweet Myth-tery of Life 2-in-1
0-441-00982-4

**Available wherever books are sold or at
penguin.com**

B519

New from Ace

Mystic and Rider
by Sharon Shinn
0-441-01303-1
Award-winning author Sharon Shinn weaves a new world wrought
with magic and mayhem, in which the fate of
a troubled land may rest in the hands of those few
who would remain loyal to their king—and each other.

Myth Directions
by Robert Asprin
0-441-01384-8
The beautiful Tanda wants the Trophy. The problem is, getting it
for her will take all Skeeve's unproven magical talents and a
charming demon not above a little interdimensional thievery.

Sharper Than a Serpent's Tooth
by Simon R. Green
0-441-01388-0
Private Eye John Taylor is the only thing standing between his
not-quite-human mother and the destruction of the
magical realm within London known as the Nightside.

Exit Strategy
by Pierce Askegren
0-441-01297-3
The terrific conclusion of *The Inconstant Moon* trilogy.

Wizard
by John Varley
0-441-90067-4
Second in the *Gaean Trilogy*.

Available wherever books are sold or at penguin.com

THE ULTIMATE IN
SCIENCE FICTION AND FANTASY!

From magical tales of distant worlds to stories of technological advances beyond the grasp of man, Penguin has everything you need to stretch your imagination to its limits. Sign up for a monthly in-box delivery of one of three newsletters at

penguin.com

ACE
Get the latest information on favorites like William Gibson, T.A. Barron, Brian Jacques, Ursula Le Guin, Sharon Shinn, and Charlaine Harris, as well as updates on the best new authors.

ROC
Escape with Harry Turtledove, Anne Bishop, S.M. Stirling, Simon Green, Chris Bunch, and many others—plus news on the latest and hottest in science fiction and fantasy.

DAW
Mercedes Lackey, Kristen Britain, Tanya Huff, Tad Williams, C.J. Cherryh, and many more— DAW has something to satisfy the cravings of any science fiction and fantasy lover. Also visit dawbooks.com.

Sign up, and have the best of science fiction and fantasy at your fingertips!